Twelve years ago, the disappearance of Sam's first son tore his marriage apart and left his life in a decade-long holding pattern. Now, raising Daniel, a second son who never knew his brother, Sam is at last on the brink of putting it all behind him when he is rocked to the core by the unthinkable:

It happens again.

With Daniel gone, Sam is flung into a desperate journey to rescue his son and uncover the truth behind a decade of pain. What he finds is a string of dark truths that span a generation and lead him across the world to an abandoned nuclear silo in the heart of a blighted jungle in Africa. There, what he learns will change his life forever.

Evan Kilgore writes and works in the Los Angeles entertainment industry. His prior publications include his debut novel, *Who Is Shayla Hacker.* He is currently at work on a variety of film and television projects. Visit www.evankilgore.com for more information.

The Children of Black Valley

EVAN KILGORE

The Children
of Black Valley

BLEAK HOUSE BOOKS

MADISON | WISCONSIN

Published by
BLEAK HOUSE BOOKS
a division of Big Earth Publishing
923 Williamson Street
Madison, WI 53703
www.bleakhousebooks.com

This is a work of fiction.
Any similarities to people or places, living or dead, is purely coincidental.

Printed in the United States of America

11   10   09   08   1 2 3 4 5 6 7 8 9 10

Library of Congress Cataloging-in-Publication Data has been applied for.

ISBN: 978-1-932557-88-6 (Trade Cloth)
ISBN: 978-1-932557-89-3 (Trade Paper)
ISBN: 978-1-932557-90-9 (Evidence Collection)

For my family.

Acknowledgments

As always, for a childhood defined by storytelling of all kinds, I owe my parents and my family the drive, the inspiration, and the love for creating worlds and populating them with characters that fuels my work every day of my life.

From the rawest stages of its inception, the excellent notes and guidance of Alison Janssen at Bleak House transformed this book from a hazy picture that only made sense in my head into something that can actually fit onto a stack of paper without oozing out of the pages in some kind of primordial slime.

All along, Benjamin LeRoy has been there in every way, running Bleak House Books as a family that comes together for its authors like no other publisher on the face of the planet. Dave Oskin and the good folks at Big Earth also deserve a standing ovation for making such lofty dreams and good intentions a reality.

Lastly, the close friends, the family, and the fantastic strangers I've met along this crazy journey have made everything worthwhile, and continue to do so from the moment I get up in the morning to the moment I set down the pen at night. Please stay out of my head while I'm sleeping, when possible, though.

The dog barked the entire time Daniel was in the shower. He was dressed and midway through wedging his spelling book into his backpack before he realized the noise had stopped. Perched on the edge of his desk, he paused and listened.

From his bedroom, the only sound he could hear was the central air. It made the papers under his bed rustle when it first came on.

His room was small. In the original plan, it had been twice its size, but developers had split it in half, and Dad wouldn't let anyone through the adjoining door. Thirteen years later, that side still belonged to Riley.

"Ralphie?" Daniel edged out into the hallway. His feet were still wet from the shower, clammy inside his shoes and socks. "Ralphie, c'mere boy."

The dog was trained to come running when Daniel called him. This time—nothing. Not a sound from the first floor.

It was Daniel's secret that he could see the front door in the reflections of the framed photographs, stair-stepped over the curling banister.

There was no motion downstairs.

He glanced to his father's bedroom, at the end of the hall. Already at work. Just like always.

Daniel shrugged into a basketball jersey as he descended, padding down the wall-to-wall carpet. He stopped short when he reached the bottom of the stairs.

Ralphie was sprawled on the polished hardwood floor, right next to the coat rack.

He was dead.

The man with the hammer standing over him was a stranger.

Their eyes locked.

"Daniel Mackie," the man said.

Daniel ran.

He made it to the kitchen before the man caught up with him. Daniel grabbed at the back door and fumbled with the latch. A streak of color barreled toward him in the reflection of the window.

Daniel dodged, and the man's arms upset the precarious pile of dishes Dad had been saving for Friday.

Pots, pans, breakfast bowls, forks—everything rained to the floor with a thundering *crash*.

The man pivoted. He lashed out with one hand and clamped around Daniel's wrist. Daniel yelped and kicked at somewhere in the vicinity of the man's stomach.

For a split-second, he was free.

Pounding back upstairs as fast as his legs would carry him, Daniel gasped for breath. He couldn't think.

Left, right—Dad's bedroom? His own?

The bathroom. Lockable.

He almost made it. Three more steps, a split-second earlier, and he would have been in the clear.

The man's arms close around his halfway-through-the-door shoulders. "Jesus Christ, kid!" His voice was like grinding machinery.

Daniel couldn't move. He heard a *pop*, something plastic, and then there was a sharp jab at the back of his neck. It stung, like the time he'd accidentally stepped on a bee in the grass out at baseball.

Daniel squirmed.

"Hold on," the man said. "Just hold on, kid."

The doorbell rang.

The man's hands tightened. He shoved Daniel to the floor and ducked behind the banisters that overlooked the entryway.

In the reflections of the framed photographs—Daniel and Dad, Mom and Daniel, Dad and Riley, nothing of them all together—Daniel could see the door opening. The man hadn't closed it all the way.

There was a muffled exclamation. Someone finding Ralphie's body. "Oh my—Hello? Anyone home?"

The man's fingers crept their way up Daniel's collarbone, searching for his mouth. Daniel had been too scared to remember to shout.

"Up here!"

Downstairs, a shape jerked—brown, a collar, shorts and black shoes. A deliveryman.

Ralphie's killer lunged and tried to get his knee onto Daniel's back. Daniel twisted around and rolled out from under him. He slammed into the open doorway around the stairwell and tumbled down a couple of steps before he found his footing.

Large brown eyes stared up at Daniel from below. "Oh... hi... sorry to walk in." A hesitant smile. The man read the label on the package he was holding. "You wouldn't be *Daniel the Birthday Boy*, would you?"

A squeal of brakes sounded from the street. Sunlight caught the curving yellow roof of the school bus.

Daniel glanced over his shoulder at the man plastered against the wall in the upstairs hallway. He had a big forehead, buzzed gray hair, tanned skin like leather, and eyes like drops of coal. Slowly, he shook his head at Daniel.

"Kid?" The UPS man's polished black shoe touched Ralphie's spine.

Daniel leapt down the stairs, three at a time, and bolted out the door. He made it to the bus without looking back.

All of the kids stared at him as he climbed aboard. He was panting, sweating, out of breath. There was a long, nasty rug burn on his right forearm. For a couple of seconds, he stood in the middle of the aisle, wavering.

The driver gave him a nudge. "Can't go 'till you siddown. C'mon."

Daniel sank into a seat. He couldn't make himself look out the smudged window at his house.

"Who's that man, Danny?" It was Megan. Once, she'd been an almost-girlfriend. They'd even kissed. Her head popped up over the seatback behind him. "Who's that man coming out of your house?"

Daniel only sank lower and squeezed his eyes shut.

During the three-minute passing period between classes, Daniel went to the office and asked to use the phone. He stood over it, receiver to his ear, listening to the dial tone. Dad wouldn't answer, anyway. He turned his cell phone off the minute he arrived at work, but he would be pissed if Daniel called Mom.

They weren't talking to each other again. Daniel never really understood it.

"Something wrong, hon?" The woman at the front desk was the kind of person who cooed at babies in grocery stores.

Daniel opened his mouth, but nothing came out.

"If it ain't an emergency, you shouldn't be playing with the phone. What room're you in, fourth period?"

Daniel hung up and went back to class.

He got in trouble from every one of his teachers for not having his books or his homework. A couple of his friends from the basketball team asked him what had happened. He couldn't figure out what to say.

In history, they had just gotten to the Cold War—the Cuban Missile Crisis, Kennedy, the Bay of Pigs. The teacher was lecturing about a weapons lobbyist named Ralph when Daniel burst into tears. *Ralphie.*

At lunch, on the playground, Kyle and Walt made fun of him. They were in eighth grade, but Daniel broke Kyle's nose without a thought. After he hit the ground, Daniel couldn't stop. He just kept kicking and swinging until there was blood everywhere.

He felt numb all over.

Two playground guards pulled him off. He was panting and his ears were ringing, and he couldn't really hear what they were saying to him.

A bead of something wet rolled down the back of his neck where the strange man had jabbed him. Daniel closed his eyes and wished that all of this would turn out to be a dream.

ONE

"MACKIE. MACKIE!"

Sam slipped into the men's room. Bob Frankel followed.

"What, you in the market for hearing aids?"

"Sorry, I was thinking about something ..."

"Yeah. 'Sorry.' It's not a good time, Mackie. I'm being honest. Recession economy, you've gotta make the effort." Bob sighed and fiddled with his wedding ring. He did that when he talked down to employees older than him. It served a dual-purpose, Sam thought: To remind everyone else that Bob was lucky enough to have tricked a bride into saying, *"I do,"* and to remind Bob that ending it was as simple as slipping off a piece of metal.

"Can I help you with something, Bob?"

"Where's the efficiency analysis?"

"Sorry?" Sam washed his hands and avoided Bob's eyes in the mirror. Talking shop in the can seemed like one step shy of assault and battery.

"The efficiency analysis? The *one*. We've got bids from freight at FedEx and DHL, and they both expire tomorrow morning. You don't think our guys deserve a chance to go over the fine print before we make a call?"

"That's Caleb's deal. He's got the report."

"God, you two. Maybe you should throw him a morning wakeup call, because apparently, he's sitting on 'em in his jammies."

Sam shrugged. "I haven't seen him yet today."

"No one has. Change that." Bob ran a paper towel over his bald head, squared his shoulders, and adjusted his tie in the mirror. "You know Malleson, Mackie?"

"The kid in marketing?" In his twenties. College hotshot.

"Let him go today. Not senior enough to make it through crunch time. It pisses me off to see good men walk out that door. I know you, Caleb, and Ramon have been here since the Reagan days, but this isn't a country club, okay? Clayton Wesley's not gonna be running this show forever, and there are those of us who actually value *results*. You hearing me?"

Sam said that he was hearing him. Bob nodded, clicked his heels together like a drill sergeant, and strutted out the door.

After he was gone, Sam drew in a deep breath and let it out very, very slowly. He stared at himself in the mirror. Bob was right. He looked—*old*. Forty-six, and all those wrinkles, all those gray hairs. He'd been with the company for twenty-eight years, nabbed at eighteen, even after dropping out of high school, and he still had to take shit from people like Bob. Maybe he should have been reading between the lines. He worked harder than anyone else on the floor, and his last major promotion had been before Daniel was born.

Caleb's cubicle was deserted. His computer sat lifeless, monitor dark. It was the first thing Caleb touched when he came in every morning. That, and the army of digital pets he kept beside the keyboard.

Sam grimaced. He didn't have time for this.

He stepped to the next door over, identical to Caleb's.

The office hadn't always been a labyrinth of fluorescent and pastel. Back in the 1980s, when C.W. Medical was still young, they'd had desks out in the open, like a newsroom floor. There had been the constant chatter of voices, telephones, typewriters. Even through all the transformation, Sam could still see traces of the way it once was.

The wall clock was an IBM original, built into the plaster. The pneumatic tubes still hung from the ceiling, though now they sat ensconced between security cameras and snarls of high-speed internet wiring. The last message ever sent was jammed in one right over Sam's desk. Sometimes, when he closed his eyes, he could imagine it—being back there, back when everything was still good.

"Ramon." Sam knocked on the padded cubicle wall.

Ramon looked up and winced. "Don't tell me. They fucked you with the doughnuts. You asked for chocolate and they gave you that cherry bullshit."

"They haven't brought doughnuts in since 1996."

"Really? Whose have I been eatin', then?"

"Probably Bob's."

"No fuckin' way! No wonder I've started going bald and my dick's shrinking."

One of the new juniors across the hall fixed them with a disapproving stare. Probably a friend of Malleson's.

When Bob had rearranged things upon taking the reins five years ago, he'd put Sam, Ramon, Caleb, and a few of the other older guys in a quad together. Sam had heard their corner referred to as "The Pasture." As in, *put out to …*

Sam had been a loner, even growing up. With different parents every few years, it was hard not to be. The growth spurt he'd endured in middle school hadn't helped. It wasn't until he had come to CW that he realized what everyone else had liked about being a teenager. This was his family. In the last decade, he'd seen most of the other familiar faces move on. Lately, he'd felt like he was grasping at sand.

"So, this your new job, then?" Ramon put down his pencil—an old-fashioned Number Two. "They promote you to 'Ramon Hemorrhoid,' stand there and harass me all day? 'Cause if that's on the docket, I need to raid our prototype cabinet for a new ass cream."

"Couldn't pay me enough for a job like that. But I can delegate if the position's open."

The junior across the hall cleared his throat and put on some headphones.

Sam sighed. "Bob's looking for Caleb."

"That dick. Been a total hermit. Whole last week, I can't get him to do nothin', y'know? Not even beer, and you know him."

"Maybe he's sick. Or he met someone."

"Yeah, right—who lives in Singapore and charges by the hour to show you her tits on webcam. Knock down his door, I bet you find some kinky shit."

"Huh." Sam shifted. The wall clock counted off another minute. He had half an hour to catalog one hundred client response cards, or he'd be facing Bob Frankel again. "So—seriously, no ideas?"

"Try the roof?"

"This early?"

"It's Monday, man. If there's ever a time to smoke out at nine in the morning ..."

Sam headed for the stairwell. When he had joined the company two decades ago, Caleb had brought a wave of subtle change. He was the son of bona-fide hippies, and he was so talented that he could get away with virtually anything. Including joints on the roof. Just when CW had been veering toward the stiflingly corporate, Caleb had reminded them all that even mass-marketing antibiotics could be fun.

Caleb played guitar in his Volkswagen minibus and talked about the Grateful Dead like he knew them. He was the sort of guy who wouldn't have given Sam the time of day when he was a kid.

It wasn't until much later that Sam got to know Caleb's inner nerd. Then, they'd clicked like lifelong brothers.

It had been Caleb who, thirteen years ago, drove Sam door-to-door with pictures of Riley when Ann wouldn't get out of bed.

But that was a long time ago.

The stairwell smelled of smoke, paint, and piss. Water rattled the pipes up and down the giant concrete shaft.

The door at the top was supposed to be for emergencies only, but Caleb had foiled the fire alarm with a well-placed chunk of wood. Outside, it was chilly. Winter was starting early this year, and the sky was the kind of gray that would harbor snow in another month.

Sam made a quick circuit of the roof. He found a half-dozen hand-rolled butts among the gravel. They were concentrated between the skylights over the top-floor atrium and the executive conference room. Sam squinted down through the glass. Condensation clung to the inside. Foggy silhouettes sat before a PowerPoint slide projected on the wall.

Sam could still remember sitting in those same chairs for his orientation. He'd been eighteen, just a kid with a newborn, happy for a paycheck.

He shivered in the cold. There was no sign of Caleb. He was wasting his time up here.

Sam paused with his hand on the stairwell doorknob. For a solitary instant, he stared out at the city. In the distance, groups of teenagers thronged around a coffee shop. Stay-at-home mothers and fathers hustled toddlers into minivans with bags of early Christmas shopping. They seemed impossibly young and carefree.

For a decade, all of that had been his. Now, looking back on it, it seemed as remote and foreign as the strangers twelve floors down.

Sam closed his eyes. Better not to think about it.

5

Bob was furious.

"Look, this is—it's unacceptable. You're telling me ... the three-'a you are like a sewing circle, and you're telling me you don't have a clue where he is? If this is some kind of labor protest or something, Mackie, I swear to god, not even your friends are gonna be able to save you."

Sam tried calling Caleb's home, but no one picked up. Not even an answering machine. Caleb didn't believe in them. *"If I'm not there, I'm not there,"* he'd say. *"There's no point in pretending. Just try again later."*

"Guess he's sick," Sam told Bob Frankel. "Ramon said he's been a bit out of it the last week or so. Look, I know this is important, but I've got my own stack of—"

"This is more than important. Do you even—this is everything, Mackie. We come back an hour late on this, they'll be working the competitors already. You and Juarez, you grab his research and recompile the report yourselves."

Sam clenched his jaw. Dinner at eight-thirty was becoming frozen leftovers at ten. Daniel would already have put himself to bed.

Bob looked up from his computer screen. "Something else, Mackie?"

Caleb's cubicle smelled like incense and butterscotch. Poised at the doorway, Ramon shook his head. "I'm not goin' in there. Dude probably leaves, like, mustard gas everywhere, mousetraps and those nanny cam things, just to make sure no one touches his shit."

Sam made a halfhearted attempt to find the original reports Caleb had been using. The file cabinets were double-locked. His computer had a twenty-four letter password. Even his trash can was sealed with a locking paper shredder.

After twenty minutes of searching, Sam went back to Bob's office.

Bob was watching football recaps on his computer.

"We can't find the reports," Sam said.

"Can you show me where in that answer is anything productive?"

"It's the truth."

Bob scowled. "Sam. Mackie. Have you been listening to a word I've said to you this afternoon? Change is in the wind for this department, and I swear to God, I'm not going up there to bat for you if the shit hits the fan."

Sam said he understood that, and went back to his cubicle to finish five hours of work he'd been too busy to even look at.

At eight-fifteen, Sam and Ramon walked down to the parking garage. Sam liked taking the stairs. The juniors always looked at him like he was some kind of septuagenarian freak who didn't know how to work electronic machinery, but this building was like his home, and Sam had no desire to accelerate his departure.

They ran into Elroy, the custodian, sweeping up the remnants of a Slurpee by the elevators. Sam and Elroy locked eyes. "Kids." They had the unison thing down.

Sam liked Elroy. He was sixty-seven, and he had been with the company since the start. Everyone else in the building pretended he didn't exist, but each Christmas, Sam invited him out drinking with Ramon, Caleb, and a few of the other old timers. Elroy had stories from Vietnam that gave Sam nightmares. The twinkle in his eye when he talked about the "good old days" before the war was worth the trauma.

"What you need," Ramon said as they got to their cars, "is a woman."

"You're a fine one to talk." He searched for the keys to the Silverado.

"Eh, I got my sister to worry about. When she's better ..."

"Right, right."

"I'm not kidding. Don't tell me you're still hanging on some prayer that someday Ann's gonna shape up and come back. Do not tell me that, man."

"No prayers." He'd stopped praying eleven years ago. Fourth of July. Ann had left Daniel alone in a stroller at a downtown fair when she thought she saw a boy who looked like Riley. The kid had looked nothing like him, but then, Ann had been operating on a bottle-and-a-half of Seagram's Seven.

"Good." Ramon patted him on the back. "'Cause that woman is the last thing in the world you need in your life right now."

That night, when Sam got home, he almost burst out laughing. Ann's car was parked in the driveway.

TWO

THE FIRST THINGS TO HIT SAM when he walked in the door were the smell of rotting meat and the sound of the vacuum. He wanted to cover his ears and his mouth at the same time.

The rug in the entryway had been dragged over a lump of something wet roughly the size of a coffee table. Sam stopped. He gave himself a moment to take it all in. Then he set down his briefcase and advanced.

Ann was in the kitchen. He glimpsed her through the archway from the dining room, and it was enough to make his breath catch in his throat. For just an instant, it was her again. It was *them*. How many times had he come home to find her just like this? Riley would be upstairs drawing or reading, never with friends. Ann would be getting dinner together or going over real estate forms. He still remembered the autumn when she'd taken all the tests—so excited to be getting back into the working world again.

The grandfather clock by the stairs chimed. Ann looked up and saw him.

In an instant, the moment was gone.

She shut off the vacuum and came out into the dining room. They stood at opposite ends of the table. Ann put her hands on her hips, just the way she used to. "You look … good."

"I look like shit. What are you doing here?"

"Well. It's a relief to see the old charm never grew back."

Sam followed her into the kitchen. There was still some broken glass on the floor. Dust hung in thick clouds that made his throat itch. Bills and papers were stacked in neat lines along the countertop.

Sam forced himself to take a breath and try to swallow down the old, familiar anger. "What's...all this? What are you doing here?"

"This place is filthy. It's filthy, it's not even a home."

"Ann." Sam gripped the back of the barstool. He tried not to watch her face because it scared him. The slash of blond hair across eyes green as a jungle. The lips—tight, pursed, matching the line in her forehead, like there was something seething and clawing to get out. "Ann, stop." He reached across and shut off the water as she started to scrub a dessert plate.

She looked up at him. Sam willed himself not to blink. "You know the rules. Every other weekend. You have to call to make arrangements if there's going to be a deviation from the schedule. You have to—Ann..."

She was stalking back into the hallway. Sam kicked a dented skillet out of the way.

"Ann, damn it, you can't just show up without—" He broke off.

Ann was holding up the hallway rug, just high enough for Ralphie's head to poke out. The eyes were wide, glassed over in a milky, dead stare. His tongue dangled onto the hardwood floor like a little pink ribbon.

"What the fuck happened?"

"Oh, really? Really, Sam? *Now* you give a shit?"

"Did you—how could you..." He swallowed, throat parched. "Did you do this? Have you been drinking?"

Ann dropped the rug and clutched the hems of her jeans until her knuckles went white. "I can't believe," she said in a voice so measured that it scared Sam, "that you would say that."

"What are you doing here? Did he call you? I told him not to call you."

"I am on—I am in the last *week*. The last *week,* Sam, of two *years*, and you have the balls to—to...You think I did that? I *gave* him that dog!"

Sam went to the bottom of the stairs and squinted up toward Daniel's door. It was closed. The crack beneath it was dark. "Did he call you?"

"The school called me."

"The school? Why did the school call *you?*"

"Because they couldn't get you. Voicemail. They got your voicemail. Your emergency contact number is supposed to be one you *answer*, Sam."

"What's wrong? What—what happened? What's *wrong?*"

He was halfway up the stairs before she caught him by the shoulder and pulled him back. "He's sleeping," she hissed. "Come downstairs, God damn it."

Sam's shoes crunched on broken glass in the kitchen. He stopped by the sink and spun around. There was soap splattered on the stove, wadded paper towels all over the counters—mess, everywhere.

"He got into a fight. They sent him home for the day. He broke some little boy's nose." Ann picked up a dishrag. Sam snatched it out of her hands.

"Danny doesn't fight."

"He fought. He broke a boy's nose. Everyone saw it. Kids said he was crying in class."

"Crying? Why was he crying?"

Ann glanced at the entry hall. "He loved that dog, Sam."

"Jesus. What happened?"

"I don't know. A car?"

"On the—*in the house?* What, Danny dragged him up here?"

Ann shrugged.

"What did he say?"

"He didn't. He was sick. Feverish. That's why they didn't expel him for the fight. They think he was just—it was a bad day."

"Feverish?"

"Yeah, Sam. Maybe you would've noticed if you were ever here."

Sam opened his mouth and then forced it closed again. He hated this—how every time he saw Ann, all he wanted was to have her back, and yet every time, all they did was get to fighting so fast that he never had the chance to try.

Ann took his silence as a signal of defeat. "And the house, Sam? The dirty laundry and the dishes and the—"

"So I forgot to call a maid."

"And the yard and the bus driver who says you haven't seen Daniel out the door for as long as she can remember?"

Sam scowled. "He's twelve. He'd be embarrassed."

"Did he tell you that?"

Sam slammed his fist down on the counter. Ann jumped. He drew in another long breath and broke out coughing from all of the dust. "You have to go." He tugged her toward the front door.

"Sam, look, we need to talk—"

"No. That's what the lawyers were for."

"Sam—"

"Next time the school calls you, do me a favor. Tell them to try my office."

"They *did.*"

After she was gone, Sam came back into the kitchen. Ann had turned on all of the lights—even the bright hundred-watters over the breakfast nook. The ones that exposed all the dingy corners he never got to. There was something unutterably bleak about the harshness.

One by one, Sam extinguished them. He started putting dishes away, but it was too much to face at ten o'clock.

It took him fifteen minutes to scare up a shovel beneath all of the junk in the garage. Spider webs stretched from Daniel's tricycle to Sam's weight set. In the very back was the little old red wagon. The one they'd bought for Riley.

He found a place by the fence, near the property line, and dug a hole. It started to rain long before he was done. By the time the grave was deep enough for Ralphie's body, Sam was soaked to the bone and covered in mud. He was also exhausted.

Back inside, he changed into fresh clothes and then poured himself a glass of whiskey. After one sip, he washed it down the sink. Any other night, he wouldn't have thought twice about swallowing it in two gulps. Seeing Ann left it tasting sour in his mouth.

After checking all of the locks and windows, Sam crept upstairs and eased open the door to Daniel's bedroom.

It was dark. A thin sliver of moonlight made it through the blinds to slash across the bed. Sam squinted.

There was no lump beneath the covers.

"Danny?" he whispered. More light from the hallway spilled in over his shoulders as he eased the door wider.

The pillows were ruffled, sheets thrown back as Daniel must have left them that morning. Sam glanced down the hall, but the bathroom door stood ajar, mirrors over the sink reflecting nothing but blank white tile.

He was about to look back downstairs, check the basement, even call Ann, when he saw it:

The inside door. The adjoining door. The one to Riley's room. It was open.

5

Passing through the threshold brought tears to his eyes.

Sam hadn't been inside for thirteen years. Impossibly, the smell had remained—dust, mold, and the acrylic paint Riley used to love. He would fill notebook after notebook, tablet after tablet, with smears of color that seemed to mean something to him that none of the rest of the world could see.

The angle of the light through the window arrested Sam in his tracks. It was breathtaking—the bookshelves in the corner, the rocking chair, the shag carpets, the stuffed down comforter. All of it was just as he remembered.

He couldn't breathe, because every lungful he stole might still have a tiny piece of Riley in it, and once that was gone, it was gone forever.

Ann had never given up hope. That was what had destroyed her. In her heart, she still believed he was out there somewhere. She still believed that one day, she would walk into the grocery store for a bag of tomatoes, and there he would be, stocking a shelf or helping a stooped old woman with a box of bottled water.

Sam had wanted to believe that. He had wanted to believe with all of his heart, but in the end, it hurt too much—to be that powerless. To know his son was out there, and whatever happened, there was nothing he could do to find him.

It was for that reason that he couldn't give up this room. He kept it untouched not because, as Ann would accuse him, he was waiting to bring Riley back and pretend that nothing had ever happened, but because he knew this was all he would ever have of his first son, and it would have killed him to destroy it.

Riley had loved the room. He had raced to it the moment they moved into the house, back in 1985. Ann had thought it was the view of the back yard—expansive, captivating, the mountains rising in the distance.

Sam knew it was the security, because he knew Riley. The only way into this room was through another. It was a fortress.

Tonight, for the first time in over a decade, it had been violated.

Daniel was curled in a ball at the center of the bed. The blankets caved toward his slight little frame. His face was concealed between his pajama shirt and his mop of brown hair. For an instant, when Sam blinked, he saw Riley.

"Danny." Sam dropped to his knees. "Hey, Danny, buddy."

Daniel moaned when Sam shook him awake. His eyelids fluttered and then he rolled away and tried to shrug out of Sam's grasp.

"Daniel. You can't sleep in here. C'mon, buddy."

"I...don't wanna...go..." His voice sounded thick. Maybe Ann was right; maybe he was coming down with something.

"No. Come on. Let's get you back to bed." Sam hoisted him off of Riley's old blankets. God, he was getting heavy.

Daniel started to struggle as Sam got to his feet. "No, I wanna ... stay. I wanna sleep...in here."

"No, Danny."

"I don't want..." Daniel tried to pull himself free. His fingers caught a strip of loose wallpaper, and it tore.

Sam jerked him away as something fluttered to the floor behind them. It was as if it was Sam's own flesh. "No!" he snapped. "You can't be in here. Why do you want to be in here? What's the matter with you?"

Daniel lay back with a whimper as Sam eased him onto his own bed and pulled Riley's door shut behind them.

"The man with the hammer," Daniel mumbled. "I didn't want... the man with the hammer to...to get me..."

Sam frowned. When he'd been younger, Daniel had grappled with regular nightmares. Like father, like son. It had been years since he'd mentioned them, though. Stooping, Sam touched the back of his hand to the boy's forehead. It did feel warm. Maybe he was feverish.

"Go to sleep." Sam pulled a blanket up over him. "Go to sleep. And Daniel—please stay out of that room."

∽

Even though he was utterly beat, Sam lay awake in bed for almost half an hour, tossing, turning, and thinking. His mind kept kicking back and forth between Ann, their fight, Riley's room—and the day he had come home to find his first son gone.

He got up after forty-five minutes to make himself some hot cider and realized he was already dreaming. The stairs led not to the bare-wood entryway but to the carpeted split-level where he had lived for eight months in middle school. That house had always smelled like gingerbread.

The kitchen was not where it was supposed to be. Instead of modern appliances, the blocky putty-colored stove from the '70s, Sam found himself crammed between a big old porcelain sink and a washbasin that could have bathed a toddler.

It was the apartment—from third grade. One of his earliest coherent memories.

The TV was on. It was an old, wood-grain Zenith the size of a steamer trunk. There was something dark and grainy on the screen that made Sam look away. Only it was outside the window, too.

He felt his heart quicken in his chest. He knew this place. He knew that shape.

Tall, dark, a narrow spire reaching for the sky, it sent a shiver through his body.

He drew the curtains shut, but he could still see the silhouette through the thin white lace. The tower. The dark tower.

"No..." His voice sounded like it was coming from someone else.

He spun away and dashed back through the hall, only now, it wasn't the split-level or the apartment. It was a house he barely remembered. The most vivid images he had were of the carpet—the rough-edged industrial fibers where he had played with little metal cars and listened to shouting through the paper-thin walls.

The living room—a valley between the sofas, Sam's secret little nest—was full of branches. Gnarled, blackened, they looked like they had been through a raging forest fire. All at once, they were everywhere, reaching for Sam's hair and clothing. Plucking at him. Pulling him back.

Through the thickening jungle, he caught a glimpse of a place that was so distant it might have been fictional. A red-walled farmhouse he had probably seen in a storybook as a child. There was a ladder to a loft upstairs, hay, horses.

Sam dashed for it, but the bushes and brambles tripped him up and sent him sprawling.

A voice sounded through the woods. High, frightened, pleading. Riley.

Sam thrashed and swatted at the blighted foliage.

"Dad?"

He came up against a wall, tall, thick, impenetrable. Up above, through the treetops, he could see it again: the dark tower.

"Dad!"

Riley was on the other side. He knew Riley was on the other side as surely as he knew he would never get there. He'd never once seen the boy alive in a dream since the day he disappeared.

"*Dad!*"

Just like that, Sam snapped awake.

He blinked. This wasn't his bed. It wasn't a dream anymore, either.

It was Daniel's room.

Sam was standing at Riley's door. He turned.

Daniel had propped himself up on one elbow under his bedcovers, staring, bleary.

"Hey…hey, buddy." Sam wiped his forehead. It was drenched in sweat.

"Dad?"

"Sorry, Danny. Go back to sleep, okay?"

5

Sam gave up on trying to sleep. He cleaned until dawn, finishing everything Ann had started. He forced his mind into the repetition, into the absence of thought, because every time he let it stray again, he would close his eyes and see the dark tower.

He had no idea what it was. It had been appearing in his dreams since he was a child. He'd thought that was a fabrication at first—that his subconscious merely manufactured the sensation of familiarity. Then, years later, when they moved into the house, he had found a drawing he must have made when he was barely old enough to grasp a pencil, wadded up in a ball of old clothes and mementos. A drawing of the tower.

When he was in his early twenties, he'd gone back to the orphanage that had first taken him in as an infant. His file began when he was two years old. There was no record of where he had come from before that. The woman who ran the records department suggested that perhaps he had been born near a church, and the tower was a steeple he could see from his crib.

In his dreams, it didn't feel like a church. It felt—cold. Frightening.

"Dad?"

Sam glanced up from the sink. He had been scrubbing the same dented skillet for the last five minutes. His fingers were like prunes in the hot water. "Hey, buddy."

Daniel was still in his pajamas. His face was flushed. "I don't feel good."

He had a bit of a temperature, and he seemed groggy. Sam drove ten minutes to the twenty-four hour pharmacy and got a couple of things to make him feel better. He'd fallen asleep in the car by the time Sam got back. He hadn't wanted to drag the kid out of bed, but if Ann had circled back for one reason or another and found Daniel home alone, they would have been shouting at each other all night.

The faintest glow of dawn was just coloring the sky. There were only three other cars at the entire strip mall. Sam noticed the man at the wheel of the black Hummer beside the ice cream parlor because he didn't seem to be doing anything other than sitting. Sam squinted, but then Daniel woke up and tapped at the window from the inside.

The medicine helped a little. Sam made Daniel breakfast for the first time on a weekday in months. He checked his watch as he rinsed the dishes. "You should probably get dressed for school."

"I, uh … I don't think I feel good enough …"

"Oh."

Daniel never stayed home from school. He seldom got sick at all, but even when he did, he preferred to be with his friends.

"Uh …" Sam glanced at his watch again. This was already later than he'd gone into the office in more than a year. Sam was always early. If he pushed it past nine, Bob would probably throw him out a window. "If you're really … if it's that bad, I guess you could come to work with me."

Daniel screwed up his face. "And just … sit?"

"Well, I … this is a little last-minute. I just …" He thought of Caleb, the report, Bob's angry red face. Today was not the day to call in sick. "I don't know what else to tell you, Danny."

"We could call Mom."

Sam squeezed his eyes shut. "We can't do that."

"We could. She likes it when I come over."

"Danny—"

"*I* like it when I go over."

"*Danny.*"

Daniel blinked. Sam hadn't intended to shout.

"Sorry. But we can't. Okay, buddy? It's the—the whole court thing, okay?" That and the lockless liquor cabinet. "There's a schedule."

Daniel swallowed and looked away. "Fine."

Sam walked him out to the bus. Daniel didn't protest. He wasn't embarrassed. *Chalk one up for Ann,* Sam thought. He nodded to the driver as he helped Daniel up the stairs. The boy was moving with a sluggishness that bothered Sam.

"Good to see you, Mr. Mackie." The driver gave Sam a sarcastic nod.

Sam ignored her and patted Daniel on the back. "Have a good day, okay? Call me if you…if you need anything."

Daniel didn't answer. He didn't even glance over his shoulder.

As Sam watched the bus go, he was left with an uneasy feeling in the pit of his stomach. He turned back to the house as another car crawled away down the street. It was black.

THREE

RAMON LATCHED ONTO SAM as soon as he stepped out of the stairwell. "Shit is *going down*."

Bob Frankel was in the conference room. The college boys were all assembled in their cheap suits, legs crossed, nonchalant. Smug.

Bob looked over when Sam came in the door. His eyes flicked to the IBM wall clock. He shook his head. "Three minutes. Three minutes, Mackie, and you'd've been part of the speech I'm about to give you all."

Caleb hadn't come in that morning. His cubicle had already been cleaned out. Anyone else who wanted to test the system and rest on the strength of their employment history was welcome to do so. Bob hoped they knew the way to the garage.

Sam strutted straight to Bob's office after the meeting broke.

"Check your contract, Mackie. I think you'll find there's a clause that says if you don't do your job, you don't have one anymore."

The juniors circled around Caleb's cubicle like buzzards over a corpse. His leather office chair went to Malleson's friend across the hall. His twenty-two inch flat-screen got claimed by a girl from up front who liked watching movies on the Internet.

By the time Sam had a chance to stop by, it had been picked clean. There was no sign Caleb had ever worked for CW Medical, let alone spent two decades of his life there.

"Shit's fucked up." Ramon craned his neck to see over Sam's shoulder.

"Have you talked to him?"

"That dick's still not picking up. I know, what the hell, right? Maybe he finally started a hippie commune or a nudist colony or something. Bravo to him for getting out of the game."

Sam frowned. Something wasn't right.

"You two." Bob stood framed in the door to his corner office, arms crossed. "You want to charter a Caleb cruise for yourselves, you just keep right on doing what you're doing. I could paper this room with the résumés I'm already getting."

Several of the juniors snickered.

Sam shook his head and ducked back into his own cubicle.

"Oh, Elroy was lookin' for you," Ramon called after him.

Sam heard Malleson's buddy stifle a laugh. *"The janitor?"*

∽

With Caleb gone, there was so much work that Sam didn't have time for two consecutive thoughts until lunch. The FedEx/DHL report was passed to a team of hungry juniors who devoured it and spat it out within an hour. Overhearing them left Sam exhausted.

Just before noon, he tried calling Caleb at home again. He let it ring twenty times before he hung up.

"Dude." Ramon knocked on the cloth wall to his cubicle. "How about a soggy, overpriced sandwich from that shit hole across the street?"

They were on their way to the stairwell when they ran into Elroy. Bob had brought him up to scrub down Caleb's cubicle that morning. "I found something he left for you." Elroy patted himself down, checking each pocket of his blue jumpsuit.

Sam cocked an eyebrow. "Caleb left something?"

"Yeah, yeah... right... hold on, I know... oh. Yeah, here." Elroy fished an envelope out of an inside breast pocket. "That's right, didn't want it to get wet or anything."

"Thanks, Elroy."

"Caleb—good guy. Fuckin' Frankel, right?"

Sam shook his head. "Unbelievable."

"So open it." Ramon hustled to keep pace with Sam as they descended.

The envelope was wrinkled. A line of dust creased one end. Elroy said he had found it wedged behind the computer tower. As though it had been hidden on purpose.

Sam's name was scrawled on the front in Caleb's hasty chicken scratch. He hesitated, thumb under the flap.

"Oh, what, you afraid it's gonna be a private little love letter? Fuck's sake, open it already." Ramon made a grab for the paper.

When he tore the envelope and pulled out the slip inside, Sam stopped short. He was halfway between the eighth and ninth floors. Ramon staggered into him and almost sent him tumbling the rest of the way down.

"The hell, man? What?"

It was a scribbled sketch:

The dark tower.

The one Sam had dreamt about since he was a kid.

FOUR

THE SILVERADO'S TIRES SLIPPED on the pavement. Sam clicked the windshield wipers to the fastest setting. It was really starting to come down.

The trees grew taller, closer together, leaning across the winding road to block out the sunlight. The yellow line in the middle became spotty before disappearing altogether.

Sam didn't remember it being quite so remote or overgrown.

There used to be a 7-Eleven at the turnoff up the private road, but now the building was deserted. Most of the windows were smashed, and the sign lay on its side in what remained of the parking lot. There was a *For Lease* placard in the window. As though commercial entrepreneurs would be clamoring for a chance at a place like this.

When he climbed out to open the rotting wooden gate on the edge of Caleb's property, Sam got drenched. His suit was clinging to his body by the time he scrambled back into the Silverado's cab. Bob would probably find a clause in his contract about that, too—something about maintaining a positive face for the company at all times.

Branches scraped the sides of the truck. Caleb put little into the upkeep of the private dirt road that snaked through the forest. He preferred to let nature thrive, untamed. Vines dangled into the tunnel of foliage, sweeping leaves from the Silverado's windshield.

The pickup's tires bounced through large potholes, and several times, it felt as though it was about to slide off the road altogether.

Then Sam spotted the house. Perched on the crest of the gentle hill, it stood silhouetted against the sky. It looked dark—deserted.

Moss clung to the sagging eaves. The whole place was smaller than Sam remembered.

He parked in front of the garage. It was a separate outbuilding whose roof had caved in and subsequently been covered with a blue tarp. The rusted body of the old VW was just visible protruding through a hole in the plastic.

Sam checked his watch. He had twenty minutes before he'd need to head back. Bob would be watching the clock, hovering on every tick of the second hand.

Time had not been kind to Caleb's cabin. The wood-shingled walls were coming apart at the seams, and the porch felt on the verge of collapsing when Sam ascended to the front door.

It wasn't until he was at eye-level that he noticed the windows had all been blinded from the inside with plywood planks and taped-up cardboard flaps. Sam swallowed. He tapped on the door.

Nothing. Wind rustled through the trees. Some part of the cabin's roof groaned. Water drummed on the eaves, seeping through the cracks to dribble on Sam's shoes.

He knocked a couple more times and then he tried the knob.

The door was locked.

It took Sam a few minutes to find his copy of the key in the Silverado's glove box. Caleb had given him one right after Daniel was born. That was when Ann had been the worst. There were times when Sam had needed someplace to go, just to keep the baby away from her.

The door came open with a loud creak.

The overhead bulb in the living room popped and went dark when Sam hit the switch. For an instant, he got a flash of the room. What he saw scared him.

He jogged back down to the Silverado a second time and rooted around under the covered pickup bed until he found a flashlight. It was dim.

The flickering beam took in Caleb's sofa bed, an old TV, a card table and some chairs in the corner. They had played more poker hands than Sam could count on those dark days right after Riley had disappeared.

Back then, there hadn't been paper everywhere.

At first glance, it looked as though a Xerox machine had gone insane and started pumping reams everywhere. Sam bent and picked up a sheet. It was wet. Everywhere was wet from where the roof leaked, in the corner. Smeared writing covered the front and back, dribbled across blocks of type-written text.

He squinted and shook the flashlight. The beam flared brighter for a few seconds.

Sources report the project (Cde: BV – Cmd. Gen. D. Pryce) had been in development since the early-1960s, but repeated requests for official confirmation have been either denied or ignored. The International Radiation Commission (IRC) has refrained from comment on any of the cases mentioned here. Additional information has been difficult to come by...

Sam's eyes darted to a footer at the bottom of the page. An internet address, tacked on by whatever computer Caleb had used to print it out: *"thetheorist.org/query..."*

The Theorist. It was a favorite haunt of Caleb's, even at work. He picked up two more. They were all from the same web site.

Sam gulped and directed the beam toward the bedroom door. "Caleb?" His voice came out hoarse, his throat all at once parched.

Caleb had always had a thing for conspiracies. He'd been raised by parents who thought the moon landing had been faked and the CIA had killed Kennedy. This, though, seemed like more than idle water-cooler speculation.

The floorboards groaned as Sam crossed the room. He ran a hand along the back of the sofa bed. There was a still a stain where Daniel had burped up when he was maybe two months old.

Stopping at the threshold to the bedroom, Sam raised the flashlight.

His breath caught in his throat.

The bed had been turned on end and stood up against the wall to block out the windows. The floor was covered in butcher paper, and on it, Caleb had used large, blunt chunks of charcoal to scribble out a six-foot mural.

Photographs, torn-out book pages, and more scrawled notes lay in drifts like dirty snow around the edges. It took Sam several seconds to trace out the full image with the flashlight beam.

When he did, he felt dizzy.

The dark tower.

The smudged black lines and arching strokes were crude and feverish. They looked like the work of an infant. That, or a madman.

Sam moved around the edge of the poster. He didn't want to track mud anywhere near it.

A swarm of flies leapt into the air when Sam ducked his head through the bathroom doorway. The porcelain tub was full of clothes and furniture that had apparently been in the way of the bedroom studio. A stack of books sat opposite the toilet. A bedroll lay with its head near the sink.

When Sam opened the closet door, a messy tower of papers and photographs that rose to his shoulders overbalanced and spilled out onto the floor around his feet.

He couldn't believe it.

There was no way Caleb could have done all of this in the last two days that he had been missing. But how could he have been at work, plugging away at finance reports and efficiency evaluations with a secret like this waiting at home?

He turned back to face the room. It more closely resembled an animal nest than it did a place of human habitation.

A gust of wind swept over the house. Frigid air seeped through the cracks, and stray droplets spattered down from mildewed pockets in the ceiling.

All of this, and he had overlooked the most important detail of all: *Where the hell was Caleb?*

He got to his hands and knees to scour the poster for details, anything he might have missed. The flashlight beam caught a glint of something in the bathroom. It was small, square, metallic, set all the way back against the far wall, under the porcelain tub.

Sam winced as he flattened himself against the dirty tile. Ann accused *him* of letting the house go.

Wriggling under the tub, he reached through mounds of hair and dust. The tips of his fingers grazed the box. There was a path, he noticed, through the grime. As though someone else had been down here recently.

Sam strained and gulped in a breath of air to make himself as flat as possible. It was just enough to stretch the extra three inches.

Back out in the bedroom, he glanced at his reflection in the cracked mirror by Caleb's bed. He looked like a scarecrow.

The box was a cheap tin Caleb had probably picked up at a flea market somewhere.

Inside, Sam found two more curled pieces of paper. They were photocopies of photocopies, so smudged and dark that it would have been difficult to make out anything at all if the subjects hadn't been so familiar.

One was Sam's senior high school portrait, enlarged from a yearbook page. The corners of a few other kids' faces beamed out around the edges—tight clothes, turtlenecks, late-70s hairdos.

The other was a picture of Riley.

Sam choked the instant he saw it.

Over the past ten years, he hadn't let himself look at any old albums. Ann had taken most of them—or burned them, for all he knew—and the few Sam had kept were somewhere in the basement, safe from sunlight and dust.

It astonished him how much his first son looked like his second.

He was so taken by the face—slim, innocent, wide-eyed—that he didn't notice the clothes until the flashlight sputtered out. The white-collared jacket became the only part of the image he could see.

It had been a birthday present, when Riley turned thirteen.

He had worn it only once: the day he'd disappeared.

FIVE

SAM JUMPED as a jolt shot through his leg. It was his cell phone. He had been so worried about Daniel that morning and then distracted by Bob's meeting that he had forgotten to turn it off when he got back to his cubicle.

Fingers trembling, he slipped it out of his pocket. The Caller ID came up in a blue glow: *ANN*.

He clapped the phone shut, an involuntary reaction.

The light from the LCD made Riley's face melt out of the shadows on the page again. Sam swayed. It was impossible that he was seeing this—like a glimpse from the afterlife. The picture was a slice of Riley Mackie that nobody else in the world even knew existed.

Nobody except Caleb and whoever had taken the picture.

His phone shook again.

ANN.

"What."

Ann was sobbing and babbling something on the other end.

"What?" Sam said. "Damn it, Ann, slow—slow down, what are you saying?"

"The hospital," Ann choked out. "Come to the hospital, Sam. It's Daniel."

5

Sam had never driven so fast in his life. Barreling through the trees and then the crumbling warehouses and then beneath one amber light after another, he felt like he was in some kind of dream. It wasn't him at the wheel. It wasn't him squinting through the rain that drummed on the windshield, because days like this didn't happen to him. Not anymore. Not for the last thirteen years.

It was a stroke of luck that he didn't get pulled over.

When he reached the hospital, he left the Silverado parked across two spaces. A man with tattoos and a rag on his head rolled down the window of a Plymouth to yell at Sam.

"Mackie!" he blurted at the receptionist, inside the lobby.

She jumped and looked up from her computer screen. Disheveled hair, suit like an oil rag, hands covered in wet dust and splattered with mud—he must have looked crazy.

"My son...." He struggled to catch his breath. "My son. Daniel Mackie. He's here. Please—he's here. What room is he in?"

Ann leapt out of the padded chair the instant she saw Sam come in the door. It was visible in the stiffness, the way she moved—the strain it took to keep from hugging him out of instinct. Sam looked past her to the bed, and he swallowed a sob.

Daniel was okay. He was sleeping. His cheeks and forehead were a little pink, but there were no casts, no gashes, no blood.

"What is it?" Sam crossed to put a hand across the boy's forehead. It felt hot. "What's wrong?"

Ann came over beside him. "They're not sure yet. God, Sam, they...they're not sure..."

"But he's okay. He's okay."

"They're not sure."

"No, I'm telling you. Look at him. Shit, he's okay."

"He—" She swallowed. "He won't wake up."

"He won't..." Sam's mind was full of fluorescent and humming machinery and harsh, electronic *beeps*.

"Ah."

They both turned toward the voice at the doorway.

"You must be the father." It was a man in a white lab coat, salt-and-pepper hair, a face that was friendly even when it wasn't smiling. "Sam Mackie?"

Sam nodded.

"Doctor John Gideon." They shook hands. Gideon's were cold, smooth, antiseptic.

"What's wrong with my son, Dr. Gideon?"

Gideon drew in a long breath and furrowed his eyebrows. "Well. Let's talk about that."

It was infuriating how one question—the only question that mattered—couldn't find a straight answer with Gideon. Instead, he went through a litany of his own. Did Daniel have allergies? Had he fainted before? Had anything like this ever happened to anyone else in their families?

"No," Ann said.

"No." Sam shifted. "I mean, I don't think. I'm a...I don't know my family." After they started repeating questions, Sam bristled. "Doctor," he interrupted. "What the hell is wrong with him?"

Gideon drew in a deep breath. "We've run a CAT scan, and we've taken some blood. It'll be a few hours. Preliminaries aren't raising any red flags, but—"

"Great. So you know what's *not* wrong with him. I want to know what is. I want to know why he's not waking up."

"To be perfectly candid with you, Mr. Mackie, we don't have an answer to that yet. But his vitals are good and he seems healthy, and I give you my word we're going to get to the bottom of this. Listen...I've got three daughters, okay? I get it. We're doing our best."

They shook hands again and then Gideon was out the door.

Sam felt empty inside. His gut was a cavity. He drifted back to Daniel's bed and knelt, scooping his son's fingers into his palm. "Hey, buddy. Hey. Danny? Danny, you hear me? You want—you think you maybe wanna wake up now?"

"You don't think I've tried that?" Ann took Daniel's other wrist. "If it were that simple..."

Sam stared at Daniel's eyelids, the slow rise and fall of his chest. He was there. He was *there*. Eight inches away, and there wasn't a thing Sam could do to make him better.

It was just like Riley, all over again. For days afterward, every time he had blinked, he saw the empty chair.

It had been an award ceremony in the old Regal Hotel downtown. He still remembered the smell of the red velvet curtains, the champagne and the overcooked food. A dozen tables, a hundred people—the ballroom had been bustling.

Sam was the third to be honored. Dedication and continued

commitment to CW Medical. And a check for five thousand dollars. Solid gold.

It was the first night he'd ever seen Clayton Wesley in the flesh. They shook hands, and the flashbulbs strobed, and for a moment, Sam saw the rest of his life. No longer the kid who'd had to drop out of high school to raise a child. No longer the orphan who had married the girl from the trailer park with no options and no future. From that moment on, he was *someone*. He would have an office. A nice car, grandchildren, vacations to exotic places.

With his booming voice, Wesley had summoned Ann to the stage. She was already pregnant with Daniel, eight months. Wesley was making some point about how first and foremost, CW was a family company. As the applause died down, Sam and Ann wove their way back to their table.

And that was when he'd seen the empty chair.

At first, he'd thought, *bathroom. The catering buffet.* Something logical. Riley always did as he was told. He was quiet, introverted. He wouldn't wander off with other kids.

The party had broken down after Sam took the stage and it became apparent that something had happened.

Then the police came.

Just like that, in a single moment while Sam was smiling at a camera, his entire life had been lifted from his hands. Snatched away from him forever.

He looked across Daniel's hospital bed. Ann caught his glance. For a moment, they stared at each other. It was the first time—without blinking, without looking away, without shouting at each other—that Sam had faced her since everything had gone to hell.

"Oh, God, Sam," she whispered. "What are we going to do? If he doesn't…"

"He will."

"If—"

"He *will.*" Sam rose. He swayed as the blood drained from his head. He still hadn't eaten since breakfast. He wasn't actually hungry, but his head hurt, and his hands were trembling. "I'm going to grab something—from the cafeteria. If you wanted…"

"You're *eating?* How can you…Sam, how can you even…"

Downstairs, Sam found nothing appetizing. Wrapped sandwiches. Old fruit. He finally came back with some cereal and a bowl
of soft-serve chocolate ice cream. The latter was secretly for Daniel,
if he happened to have woken up.

When he fished out his wallet to pay with sodden bills, Sam
remembered the photograph—the one of Riley—and everything else
at Caleb's cabin. The folded Xerox suddenly felt like white-hot coal
in his breast pocket.

Upstairs, Ann was standing by the window. Rain streaked the
glass. Somewhere, across the street, far below, a man was singing and
panhandling for spare quarters.

Daniel lay unchanged.

Sam opened his mouth, tried to muster the courage to tell Ann
about the photograph, but he couldn't figure out how. There was too
much that he, himself, still didn't understand.

So they talked about nothing. Bullshit. Weather. Jobs. Like they
were strangers. It seemed to comfort Ann. To Sam, it was only
adding to the lump in his stomach.

"You should come out and take a look at the place." Ann paced
in front of the window. "Daniel loves it—the yard. There are these
bushes and they're so thick that he can make a little—it's like a
fortress. He loves it out there. Lord knows what he does. Reads, I
guess. I keep getting him books. That's my weakness.

"Sometimes, too—after dinner, it's funny, but he'll just sit there
and we'll talk. We'll talk, like two adults."

Sam grimaced. "Probably just misses his friends."

"He has all these thoughts, Sam. These thoughts and opinions
and I look at him, and I just think...I think, my God, you know...
He's become such a...a *person*. And somewhere out there...Riley'd
be...he's almost twenty-five now. You know? Did he go to college?"

"Ann—"

"Is he seeing anyone? Christ, I mean, we had him already when
we were his age."

"*Ann.*" Sam dropped the paper ice cream bowl in the trash and
walked over to her.

She turned back to the window, hiding her tears against
the glass. "To have one taken away is so terrible. But to lose one
altogether...forever...it's just too awful...too awful..."

Sam drew up beside her. He followed her gaze down to the street.

On the opposite sidewalk, the singing panhandler squatted under the eaves of a yellow liquor store. He'd tied a rain slicker around his shoulders. Ann's eyes were following the bottle to his lips between each verse.

Sam shivered. Ann noticed him looking and spun back—abrupt, guilty. "What?"

"Nothing. I didn't—I didn't say anything."

"You think I'm tempted. You're judging me because you think I'm tempted."

"Are you?"

The anger flushed across her cheeks like a cloud of smoke. "After … How can you say that after everything? After *everything*, Sam!"

"Old habits die hard. It's a coping mechanism. Isn't that one of the steps or something? Knowing yourself and– "

"I *do* know myself. I've been steady in this program for two years. Not a drop. Not a *drop*."

"Daniel said he's still seen bottles."

"I have a liquor cabinet. What's wrong with that?"

Sam sighed. "You don't see a recovering junkie with a box full of needles, Ann."

"I entertain guests! I have a party now and then."

"Fine—Ann. Fine."

"What else did he tell you? Since you talk so goddamn much. Did he tell you he hates it at school? Did he tell you he wants to drop basketball, and the only reason he hasn't is because he's afraid of what you'll do?"

"What?"

"Yeah. Sam, the Father of the Year over there. Did he tell you that half the time, he skips practice and comes home and just sits? And he wishes he wasn't so goddamn alone and that maybe one day a week you'd actually be there when he wakes up in the morning?"

"What are you—Daniel *loves* basketball."

Ann snorted.

"He loves it! And he's got tons of friends at school. And he's… he's not Riley, Ann!" The moment it escaped his lips, Sam wanted to suck it back in. The name rang in the air, in the metal of the bedposts, in the glass of the windows. It buzzed like a swarm of angry hornets that wouldn't go away.

Ann shook her head. "No. Because that would be a real tragedy, wouldn't it? If he were just another Riley. Or another you."

"Excuse me, Mr. Mackie?"

They both turned. Neither had noticed the man in the blue suit and beige overcoat arrive in the doorway. He was tall, broad-shouldered, a ruddy face and a no-nonsense mustache. He offered them a grimace that might have been a smile in better light. "Sorry if I'm interrupting something."

Sam and Ann exchanged a glance. *Thank God you're interrupting something,* Sam thought.

The man edged a couple of feet into the room. His eyes flicked to Daniel. "Your son?"

They nodded.

"Sorry. I know this might not be the greatest of times..." He produced a badge from an inside pocket of his jacket. The gold plating caught the light. "Gerry Crawford. Detective, actually. Still getting used to the title."

Sam blinked. Detective? "What can I do for you, Detective Crawford?"

"Well." He glanced to Daniel's bed again. "Again, about the timing, I'm sorry. But I was wondering if I could show you a—a picture of someone. And you could just tell me if you've seen him before, and then we'll go from there."

"Okay..."

"But maybe if there's a room with a... well, with a table and..." *Not an unconscious little boy and his hovering mother.* It made Sam nervous that Crawford was nervous.

Ann didn't want to leave Daniel alone, so Sam accompanied the detective down the hall to a sterile little lounge by the elevators. It smelled like bananas. The microwave door hung open, splattered with something explosive and red. There was a wad of napkins beside an overloaded trash bin. Sam found it a little disquieting to think that the men and women charged with saving lives were such slobs.

"Again, I'm sorry to bother you with this right now, but truth be told—"

"There's some soda or something, look out."

Crawford shifted to another part of the table. "Just a photocopy anyway."

A photocopy. Sam thought of the Xerox inside his jacket pocket. *Riley.*

"Truth be told," Crawford went on, "I kind of prefer just talking to you about this. Sometimes, cases like these, the mother can get a little—well, it's understandable, but she can get a little... emotional and all..."

"I'm sorry, cases like what?"

"Just look at the picture first, please."

Sam looked at the paper Crawford slid at him. By this point, he was ready for it to be anything.

It was just a man's face. The quality was terrible, blurry and black-and-white, but from what Sam could see, it was a perfect stranger staring out at him from the page. His hair was short, gray, buzzed, his forehead large, skin cracked and leathery. There was something about his eyes, too, that left Sam feeling cold.

Crawford was watching him for a reaction. "Anything?"

Sam shook his head. "What's this about?"

"Be sure. You don't know this man?"

"Listen, Detective, with all due respect, I'd like to get back to my—"

"He came to your son's school this afternoon."

"What?"

Crawford nodded. "The man in the picture. The lady in the office called us because she didn't recognize him. He claimed to be your brother, but she said he didn't look anything like you, and she thought she remembered you didn't have any family in the area."

Fingers of ice crept down the back of Sam's neck. "What did he want?"

"Well, Mr. Mackie—and this is the part where I'm kind of glad it's just you and me here—he told the school he'd been sent to pick Daniel up. Some kind of family emergency. He wanted to take your son away with him."

Sam dropped into the chair across from Crawford. If it hadn't been there, he wouldn't have stopped until he hit the floor.

"You can't tell her. Don't—whatever you do, don't tell her." Sam glanced to the hallway door. "Please, she'll...she's still recovering.

Thirteen years, and she's still recovering. She'll drink herself to death this time."

"Easy. Nobody's doing anything."

"Where is he? Did you get him? Where is this man?"

"It's okay. We have him in custody."

Sam stared at the picture—at the pure, frigid malice in the man's eyes. "I have to see him."

"Well, let's hold on a minute—"

"Detective, maybe you're not aware, but this isn't—we lost another son. Thirteen years ago. And if he... if this is the same man, who... if he might know what happened... I have to—you have to let me talk to him."

Crawford blinked. Evidently, he hadn't spent much time going through the old Missing Person reports they had filed, year after year.

"Please." The picture of Riley. The sketches in Caleb's cabin. Now this.

"Mr. Mackie..." Crawford shifted. "We've got policies—official channels, suspect procedures, paperwork, lawyers—"

"I'm the parent. What the hell kind of *policies* can you possibly have?"

"Well, the thing is, Mr. Mackie, we picked him up after the complaint at the school, but that's not what we're holding him for. You see, this picture is a capture from a security camera. On one'a those parcel delivery trucks."

"A... a what?"

"This man," Crawford nodded at the photograph, "is on video-tape."

"What's that got to do with anything?"

"The tape shows him killing the driver. They got concealed cameras in the trucks."

Sam blinked. "I... I don't understand..."

"The reason I came to talk to you, Mr. Mackie, is because that same driver made a delivery to your house. Yesterday morning."

SIX

SAM'S CELL PHONE RANG on the way to the police station. For the second time that day, he'd forgotten it was still on. He willed it to be Ann. Daniel was awake, he was okay, everything was—

OFFICE.

He wanted to throw the phone out the window. It would be Bob Frankel, smugly calling to tell him he was fired. It was two hours after the end of lunch. To Sam, work could not have seemed more distant and irrelevant.

When they pulled into the parking garage behind the police station, his chest tightened. It hadn't changed. The building was the same gray, concrete monolith he remembered from a decade ago. He and Ann had spent whole weeks of their lives here, waiting for news on Riley.

It was inconceivable that he was back here again.

Crawford made him wait in an office while he sorted out the paperwork and did what he could to get approval from his superiors. Dusty law books stared down at him from bowing shelves, untouched for years. Afternoon light fell through Venetian blinds, muted from the clouds and the rain.

Sam watched the hands of the clock edge forward.

By the time the door opened, he had almost given up hope altogether.

Crawford gave him a grim nod. "Okay," he said. "Okay. This way."

They moved down hallway after hallway, through door after door. Sam's head spun. Everything was becoming a concrete-and-fluorescent blur.

"Right through here." Crawford pushed open an orange door and led Sam into a broader room with a white tiled floor and cinderblock walls. A line of wood-grain cubicles cut across the middle, pairs of desks facing each other with privacy walls on both sides.

Sam didn't know what he had been expecting, but this wasn't it. No one-way mirrors, no suspect lineup. It could just as easily have been a study hall at the public library.

"Now, listen." Crawford grabbed Sam's shoulder. "You don't talk to him, you hear me? This is off the record. We don't have the lawyer shit worked out yet, and there are about fifteen people who'd try to have my badge if they even knew this was happening."

"I have to ask him—"

"No. That's a condition of this happening at all. You look him over, you make up your mind, you keep your mouth shut."

Sam swallowed and nodded. He'd come this far. It would be pointless to go back without anything.

Crawford glanced at a surveillance camera in one corner of the room and gave a single, curt nod. Three seconds later, a door opened on the other side. The man came out.

Sam dropped into a chair. It was happening too fast. After an hour in the car and then Crawford's office, he suddenly needed more time to prepare.

Before he knew it, guards were nudging the man into a seat on the other side of the cubicle.

One look at his face sent chills down Sam's spine.

The man's eyes appeared dead, cold, hollowed out from within. His forehead, his mouth, his cheeks—his whole face was slack. Emotionless. Bulging biceps and broad shoulders strained at the confines of his rumpled, wet shirt. He stared at Sam as he might have stared at a struggling turtle turned on its back in the sun. Without a care in the world.

The thought of this man anywhere near his son made Sam sick. His palms were wet. He glanced to the wastebasket by the door. Behind him, observing, Crawford arched an eyebrow at Sam.

The stranger gave the slightest of smiles.

In a flash, Sam was on his feet, helpless rage suddenly boiling over. "What did you do? What did you do to Riley? Why did you come back?"

"Damn it, Mr. Mackie, get away!" Crawford lunged.

Sam wriggled away from him. "Tell me! Tell me who you are! Tell me who the *fuck* you are!"

Two uniformed officers took Sam's arms.

The last view he got of the man was as both of them were dragged out opposite doors. In those cold, charcoal eyes, there was the faintest hint of amusement.

It was a couple of minutes before Sam regained control of himself. With another nod from Crawford, the uniforms withdrew, but they stayed at a measured distance. Crawford took Sam by the arm and led him back to the cramped little office. Then he disappeared for another twenty minutes.

When he came back, the detective looked tired and a little flushed.

"Sorry." Sam got up. "I'm—I just... when I saw him..."

Crawford waved him away. "My fault. Shoulda known better. There goes my Christmas bonus, but hey, I learned my lesson. C'mon, I'll take you back to the hospital."

∽

It had stopped raining, but the pavement was still slick. Everywhere, it smelled like wet concrete, and there was a certain fresh, crisp bite to the air. Riley had loved that, the moment's reprieve after a long, hard rain. He used to drag a kitchen chair out into the back yard and run his bare feet through the grass while he read or drew or just watched the clouds and thought about God knew what.

Sam made a conscious effort to concentrate on something else. It had been years since he'd thought this much about Riley. It shocked him how sharp the pain still was, even now.

"He has a tattoo." Crawford didn't look at Sam as they drove. "The guy. U.S. Army. We thought it might be a fake at first, but apparently, it's not. MPs aren't telling us anything more than that he's not an active officer." A flick of the eyes. "Military Police. Sorry. Played a lot of videogames with my nephew." He cut himself off.

Sam stared down at his lap. "The Army? He's got to be, what, fifty-five..."

"Closer to sixty-five, our guys are telling us. We don't have an exact DOB. He's in excellent shape. All that training, I guess. Self-discipline and structure."

"Detective Crawford…who is he?"

Finally, Crawford gave Sam a full-on glance as they drew up to a red light. "We don't know that, Mr. Mackie. But when we do, we'll give you a call, first thing."

Crawford said, *when*. His voice said, *if*.

ᔕ

Ann appeared to be sleeping when Sam got back. Her head rested atop the covers, on the mattress beside Daniel's arm. The moment he touched the doorknob, her eyes snapped open.

They didn't talk for several minutes. Neither of them wanted to keep arguing. Neither of them knew what else to do. Sam wished he could snap his fingers and make the last thirteen years disappear. He wished they could go back to the way it was.

They sat across the bed from each other. Sam looked at his sleeping son, and he realized with a pang of shame that every memory springing into his mind was one of Riley. In a lot of ways, the last decade *had* disappeared. Sam had just spent it tuned out.

"What did he want?" Ann asked at length. She nodded toward the door—Crawford.

Sam looked at her and considered for several long moments. Explaining it all, then managing her reaction… "Nothing. It was just—it was something to do with work. At the office."

That night, they both slept in Daniel's room.

It was the first time they had shared an enclosed space for more than eight hours in as long as Sam could remember.

There was a small sofa under the windows, and when Sam's neck started bugging him, he wedged himself into one corner and tried propping his head on the back. He actually drifted off for a few minutes here and there. At around two in the morning, Ann lowered herself onto the cushion beside him.

Sam went rigid.

After thirty minutes, she started breathing more deeply. Then, slowly, her head edged down the back of the sofa. She woke up before it touched his shoulder. He heard her grunt and pull back, and then, after that, she returned to the chair at Daniel's bedside.

It ached—to have her that close. To know what they had shared, in another lifetime, and not to be able to comfort her now.

He caught maybe an hour of sleep over the course of the entire night. If he dreamed again, Sam didn't remember it. In the morning, his throat itched from the dry hospital air, the fatigue, the clothes, still clinging wetly to his body.

Gideon came in at ten-fifteen, after the orderlies had been by to swap out Daniel's tubes. He went down a checklist and gave an approving nod.

"Wait." Ann stopped him at the door. "That's it? What's—what have you found? What do we do?"

"We're working on it, Mrs. Mackie."

"Don't tell me you're—you can't… We can't just sit here, Doctor. We can't just sit and do nothing. Tell us what to do. Tell us what we can *do*."

Sam rose beside her. The pleading vulnerability in her voice was enough to make his heart ache. He stared at Gideon over her shoulder, willing the doctor to say something hopeful.

Gideon sighed. He checked his watch and tried to conceal it by adjusting his clipboard in his folded arms. "Look, if you… If there are any personal items—you know, a teddy bear or something… anything that means a lot to him, you could bring it. For when he wakes up—you know? He'll be confused. Disoriented. It will help. When he wakes up."

Ann nodded. "Okay. Yes, that's—that's perfect, okay."

"Thank you," Sam told the doctor.

Gideon grunted and slipped back out into the hall.

5

It was decided that Ann would stay with Daniel while Sam went back to the house to get a few things. He had no idea what the hell he was going to pick up.

As soon as he stepped through the front door, his eyes fell on the cardboard box in the middle of the dining room table. *Daniel the Birthday Boy.* From UPS.

Sam shivered, but he picked it up anyway, because he didn't want to go back to the hospital empty-handed. It was a baseball glove. Daniel hadn't asked for it, but he hadn't really asked for anything, so Sam had taken his best guess.

Upstairs, Sam stopped in the doorway to his son's bedroom. He took it all in. The rumpled sheets. The dresser, drawers hanging open. The computer on the desk in the corner. A few sports posters and some old CDs Daniel hadn't finished copying onto his hard drive yet.

He picked out a jersey and found a dusty basketball in the closet. Sam could remember shooting a few hoops in the driveway, back when Daniel was five or six. Wiping it off on the carpet, Sam felt, all of a sudden, like a stranger in here. The memories he had of just the two of them, together, were spare. Where had he been the last thirteen years while this foreign little person grew up in his house?

He closed the closet door and froze. The mirror was framed to perfectly reflect the door on the other side of the room. Riley's door.

It stood ajar.

Anger swelled in Sam's veins. Daniel had gone back in there. After everything he'd said, after he'd made it clear that it was off-limits, the kid must have opened it again in the morning.

Sam crossed the room and reached for the knob. He stopped.

There was a piece of paper on the floor, just on the other side. He could see it. The slash of light through Riley's window made it glow as though it were electric.

Sam eased the door open a little wider and slipped through.

His shoulder brushed against a strip of torn wallpaper, where Daniel had caught it with his fingers, two nights before. This must be another strip of it, on the carpet.

Only, it wasn't.

It was square, yellowed, folded with the meticulous care that reeked of Riley. Each individual corner had been ironed out to a point. Sam recognized the feel of it the moment he squatted and picked it up. It was a page from Riley's old sketchbook. The boy had always liked the kind with thin, onionskin paper. He said it made his drawings seem important.

The shadow of an image bled through from the other side.

Sam hesitated. Opening it would be like cracking a tomb. Riley had been the last to touch the page. His fingerprints, the traces of the oil of his skin, still littered the surface. Sam would corrupt it.

But now, he couldn't let it go.

Walking to the bed, Sam unfolded the paper with as delicate a touch as he could manage.

His stomach leapt to the back of his throat as soon as he made it halfway.

It was the tower.

Sam staggered back from the bed. He was shaking all over. There was no way he could be seeing this. Caleb, he could perhaps explain away as something Sam might have mentioned over beers, a practical joke, something logical, rational.

But this? Riley? Where could Riley possibly have seen the same image that had been haunting Sam since he was a child?

The rendition was perfect. It was as if they had seen the exact same thing, yet to the best of Sam's knowledge, it didn't exist anywhere. It wasn't real.

He went back to the door and ran his fingers over the torn wallpaper. There was a slit. A carefully-concealed pouch that Riley must have made on purpose to hide these darker drawing from his parents.

Sam wriggled his fingers inside. The tear widened.

Two more folded pages fell out.

Skin crawling, Sam scooped them up and reached farther inside. There were seven, all told.

With each newly-unfolded shape, Sam felt colder, sicker, dizzier.

There were several versions of the tower itself, but it was the other sketches that left Sam even more uneasy. One depicted a black forest, crudely mapped out in leafless branches that held strange, blotchy shapes high above the ground. In others, doglike animals skulked behind mountains. Their bodies were little more than sticks, but Riley had been careful with their eyes. They looked like predators. Watching. Waiting. Yearning. They reminded Sam of the man behind the Plexiglas at the police station.

Something *snapped* from the other room. Sam jumped and spun around. His heart pounded in his chest, thumping in his ears, sending jolts of adrenaline to every corner of his body.

The world wasn't making sense right now.

The sound came again—a *tick* from the outer wall of Daniel's bedroom. From the window.

Sam crept back through the door. The curtains were drawn. He couldn't see anything from the other side, save a narrow slit of sunlight.

It came again, louder in here—something tapping against the glass.

Sam reached, threw back the sash, and flung open the window.

A pebble glanced off his chest and clattered to the floor. Two stories down, a young girl roughly Daniel's age clapped a hand to her mouth. "Mr. Mackie! I'm so sorry, I didn't—I threw it before you opened it."

Squinting at her, Sam thought he might have seen her before on the bus, or maybe at one of Daniel's basketball games. He leaned forward and planted his hands on the sill. His fingers were still trembling. "Can I help you?"

"Oh, I was just…my name's Megan. Daniel's gir—I'm a friend of Daniel's. He didn't come to school today, and I was just…some of us were just… I was hoping he was okay and everything. After that fight an' the way he—how he fell an' all…"

"He's sick. But he'll be okay."

"Oh. Oh no. What's he got?"

"He'll be okay. Okay?" Sam closed the window halfway. He halted to pick up the pebble hovering on the edge of the central air duct. His fingers found the corner of something else.

Sam got to his knees.

Hidden away under Daniel's bed was a small stack of loose-leaf notebooks. Sam recognized them; he'd bought them for Daniel only two weeks ago, for school.

Cover-to-cover, the style was different—Daniel's coarse, slanted strokes and scribbles distinctive and unique—but the content was identical. They were of the same dark tower, the same black forest, the same disturbing beasts that Riley had been drawing, thirteen years before.

Over and over again.

SEVEN

"TELL ME WHAT YOU SEE." Sam flattened the first page across the window outside Daniel's hospital room.

Ann didn't look at first. She was standing on tiptoe, craning to watch Daniel. When she finally allowed the page a glance, her impatience turned to anger. "Oh, Jesus Christ, Sam."

"You see it? You see the tower?"

"Really? Now? This is *really* when you're going to bring this back. After all these years, in the middle of all this bullshit and you're making this about *you?*"

"So you see it."

Ann tore the paper out of Sam's hands. He scrambled to get it back from her. Every crease in the surface was like a crack in his bones. "Don't—Ann, don't—"

She'd wadded it up into a ball before he could stop her. "I don't believe you. We send you home to get a few things *for Daniel* and you come back with this—"

"He drew it, Ann."

"—with this *bullshit*. And I don't know if you're maybe trying to...trying to..." She looked down at the crumpled sheet in her hands. "What did you say?"

"He drew it. They both did. Danny and Riley."

"Sam. Sam, this is you. This is your deal."

"No." Gently, Sam lifted it from her hands and began smoothing out all of the new creases. "I found this in Riley's room." He removed the stack of notebooks he'd brought from under Daniel's bed. "Recognize any of these?"

Ann blinked. "The—yes, the top one. Daniel brought it the last couple of times he came to visit. For homework."

"Open it."

Ann began pacing in a circuit around Daniel's bed. "Riley must have found an old book of yours. Drawings from when you were a kid. At school or something. And he copied you, and hid it because he didn't want you to know he was—"

"Ann..."

"He didn't want you to know he'd been through your stuff, and then Daniel found it, and he hid it because you always told him he couldn't go in that room."

"Ann, I burned all of those. I burned everything from when I was a kid." It wasn't a time of his life Sam had ever wanted to remember. The teasing at school—always the new kid, always the quiet freak who didn't know his way around the neighborhood, with parents whose names he could barely remember.

Ann kept pacing. "There must've been one you forgot. That's the only explanation."

"I'm just glad you see them, too."

"See them?" She snorted. "They're pictures. In books. On paper. What did you expect?"

Sam shrugged. At this point, strung-out, weary, the whole world becoming some kind of surreal nightmare, he'd wondered if he might have imagined the whole thing.

For the next half-hour, Ann pestered him about the image. He told her about going back to the orphanage, and the woman who had suggested it was the steeple of a church. He hadn't told her at the time because they were still young and unused to each other, and he was afraid she might think he was crazy.

He wouldn't have been able to bear that. Not from her.

Sam had been sixteen when they had met. He'd been fourteen the first time he saw her. Two years, two months, and eight days it had taken him to work up the courage to speak to her. From his first day as a freshman to the week before homecoming as a junior.

It wasn't that she'd been so unapproachably popular. Most of the other kids looked down on her the same way they looked down on him. Her family was poor. They lived in a trailer park. They drank, they hit each other, they yelled and when they came to parent nights, they smelled funny. But Ann—Sam was astonished because it seemed he was the only one in the world who had seen her for what she was:

She was perfect.

It wasn't just her looks. It was the way she hid it out of a tough, quiet modesty so inherent that she didn't even know she was doing anything. She had four brothers who yelled at the dinner table and who didn't give a God damn what she thought.

When they first started dating, Sam was sure she was mocking him. They went out three times—just to fast food joints, walks around town—and each time, Sam was waiting for her brothers to jump out of the bushes and beat the shit out of him. Or kids from school to run out and snap their picture and laugh at how he'd been duped.

He just couldn't believe that he could be so lucky.

After she got pregnant, Sam was sure it was over. It was the end of the world, and he was going to go back to being alone again. He proposed to her as an act of solemn desperation. A last-ditch effort to save his life. If she'd said no, he had made all kinds of plans, and most of them hadn't involved old age.

But she hadn't. And then CW had swept in with their job offer, and they'd bought a house and started a family and for thirteen years, everything had been perfect.

And now, here they were. In every word Ann spoke, there were unvoiced accusations. This was somehow all his fault.

"*I* didn't show it to them," Ann was saying. "I'd forgotten all about your damn dreams. Funny, I thought you had, too, but apparently—"

The door came open. Doctor Gideon knocked on the frame as an afterthought. "Sorry," he said with a stiff smile. "Seems like I'm always interrupting something."

As soon as he started talking, their anger evaporated—pooled together as a kind of shared grief and worry because there wasn't energy for both.

"We've come to a few conclusions. We're still running some more blood tests, and it's been a bit of a challenge finding the right specialists…"

"What?" Sam cut him off. "What did you find?"

"Well." Gideon went to Daniel's bedside. He knelt and squinted. "You didn't mention—I was wondering if either of you had any thoughts on the—the mark on the back of Daniel's neck."

Sam and Ann looked at each other. "What mark?" they asked together.

Gideon lifted Daniel's head off the pillow.

Right at the nape of his neck, just below the hairline, Sam could indeed see a pinprick of angry red. Neither he nor Ann had any idea where it had come from. Gideon nodded and absorbed the information as though he had expected it. He took a couple of notes on his clipboard.

Ann frowned at him. "Why are you asking us about this?"

"Listen—"

"Doctor, please." Sam grabbed his wrist as he started writing something else. "Just, for God's sake, tell us."

"The analysis we've done, we're turning up the preliminary symptoms of a—a variant of mild radiation poisoning."

Sam blinked. "Radiation. Like—as in, *radiation*...?"

"As in, we've found a reduction of red blood cells, his immune system isn't where we'd like it, and there's some trace material we shouldn't be seeing. Now, there are a variety of places where a person can come into contact with mild radiation, but what we're seeing in Daniel doesn't immediately suggest any of those solutions. The levels are a little on the high side, and there's some foreign material we're still trying to identify."

Sam jumped when Ann gripped his arm out of reflex. "What do you mean, 'foreign material?' What the hell are you talking about, Doctor?"

"We don't know. His body's reaction is particularly interesting, though. Ordinarily, exposure to this kind of radioactivity can be detrimental. It causes headaches, nausea, internal bleeding...we're not seeing that. It's almost like he's got a kind of—a kind of resistance to it, if you will."

Sam shifted. "Doctor, I'm...I'm sorry, but I just don't...I mean, what the hell do we make of all of this?"

Gideon nodded. "Exactly. Listen, I don't have anything more conclusive than that right now. I just thought you'd want to know what we'd found." Sam expected him to walk out the door.

Instead, he clicked his pen closed and made a great fuss of securing it back in his breast pocket. He tucked his clipboard under his arm, took off his glasses and looked at both of them. "Listen," he said. "This kind of thing is never easy, but I don't think there's much doubt that you should also get in touch with the police at this point."

"The police?" Ann said.

Sam stiffened. Crawford. The soldier in the cell. Everything he hadn't told Ann. "Why?"

"Because, that mark on the back of Daniel's neck... Look, more tests will help with this, but it looks—we're pretty sure that's a possible entry point for this foreign material. And unless you've got a nest of radioactive wasps in your back yard, it's looking an awful lot like someone did this to Daniel on purpose."

5

For a while after Gideon left, Sam and Ann sat together in silence. They didn't argue. She was still holding his hand, and neither of them let go as they sank into the sofa. They couldn't take their eyes off their son.

"Sam," Ann said at length. "That detective last night..."

So Sam told her.

She didn't interrupt. She didn't make a sound.

By the time he finished, she wasn't even looking at him. Her gaze, steady and cold, lay upon Daniel. "I need you to leave for a while."

"What?"

"I need you to leave this room. For a while. So that I can think about this."

"Ann, listen, the only reason I didn't tell you—"

"I need you to leave right now, Sam, or I don't know what I might do."

Sam stopped at the doorway. "I'll be right here in the hall."

Ann didn't reply.

Outside, Sam dialed Crawford's extension at the police station. He'd taken a card from Crawford's desk, the night before. The detective wasn't in, but a sergeant promised to pass along word that Sam had called.

After hanging up, he paced the length of the hall. Every time he passed Daniel's room, he stopped to look in the window. Ann never glanced up. She'd moved to the chair, so she could sit with her back to the corridor.

The nurses at the station up front gave him funny looks. Their conversation died down each time Sam passed by.

Christ, he thought, it was just like middle school again.

He paused again in front of the tempered glass to watch the rise and fall of Daniel's chest. He should've listened that morning when Daniel said he was feeling sick. He should have stayed home from work and taken him to the doctor himself. They might have been able to stop all of this before it had started, but instead, he'd had to run off to the office like a good little corporate drone and—

And.

Sam was wheeling away from the window. He halted. An orderly with a crash cart almost smashed into him from behind.

In his mind, he could see the ravaged nest of Caleb's cabin all over again. He could picture the papers strewn everywhere—and the printout he had picked up from the living room floor.

He could even picture the block-print lettering:

The International Radiation Commission (IRC) has refrained…

It was impossible that it was a coincidence.

ဟ

"Sam. Christ on a stick, man, we were starting to think that you and Caleb had run off on some kinda slut cruise with—"

"Ramon, I need you to shut up and listen to me. Okay—please?"

A pause. "Arright, man. You don't gotta be a dick. What the hell's happening? Where've you been?"

Sam glanced back down the sterile hospital corridor. One of the nurses from the station at the end had come out from behind the desk to point to a sign tacked up on a bulletin board: *Absolutely no cell phones.*

Sam grimaced and wheeled away, pretending not to see her. "I can't really—we can't talk, but I need you to do me a huge favor."

"I'm not doing all your reports. Bob's already got me doing Caleb's, and I swear to God, I miss one more dinner, Sofia's gonna be waiting with a shotgun this time—"

"Ramon. Please."

"Okay, okay. Christ. What?"

"You know where Caleb lives?"

The nurse tapped Sam on the back with a hard little finger. Out in the stairwell, the reception on Sam's phone began to break up. He told Ramon to go to Caleb's cabin and find out everything he could about what Caleb had been researching.

"This is bullshit, man. Why don't you just ask Caleb?"

"Have you been able to get in touch with him?"

"Well..."

"Something's wrong, Ramon."

"Look, Bob's already saying you're history the moment you come back here. Or not, by tomorrow. Just gonna junk your whole cubicle. And maybe you've got something in your savings account, but I—"

"Ramon. Please. Please do this for me. I can't leave here, okay? Daniel's sick, and I can't leave him. And I need this."

There was a long, crackling pause. Sam thought he might have lost the signal altogether. "Ramon?"

"Arright. Arright, man. Shit. This'd better be good."

ဟ

Sam paged through the sketches from Riley's room and tried to make sense of everything, but the more he thought, the muddier it all became. He was starting to feel like a captive in his own skull when, almost two hours later, his cell phone shook in his pocket.

He glanced at the Caller ID. It wasn't a number he recognized, but the area code matched Caleb's landline at home. Sam flipped it open. "Ramon?"

"We have to meet."

Sam gulped. "What did you find?"

"We're not talking about this over the phone. We have to meet."

"Ramon, what the—"

"Sam, I am not fucking around."

Sam swallowed. He glanced at Ann, who was listening, even though she still wouldn't look at him. "I'm at the hospital. Come to the lobby and I'll—"

"No fucking way. I'm not goin' anywhere. There's a diner just off the parkway, 'bout a mile from Caleb's place. The Silver Skillet."

"Ramon, what—"

"Just get over here."

When Sam hung up, he felt cold. There was something in Ramon's voice he'd never heard before—not in all the twenty years they had worked together:

Fear.

EIGHT

THE HIGHWAY OUT BY CALEB'S CABIN looked even lonelier and more secluded in the dark. For long stretches of the road, Sam's Silverado was the only car in sight. His headlights created a small pool of concrete before him, his taillights twin, winking specks of red in the mirrors. Beyond them—nothing but forest and stars.

The Silver Skillet was the only spot of civilization for miles. Sam saw the curl of smoke from the chimney, emerging through the treetops in a narrow column against the moon. Otherwise, he might have missed it entirely.

Set back from the road, it wasn't much more than a shack of cobbled-together plywood planks and strips of corrugated metal. The sign, unlit, was hand-painted over the bed of a dismantled wagon. The whole place looked like it could be dragged off by a pair of horses and a length of rope.

There were three cars in the little muddy clearing that sufficed for a parking lot. Sam left the Silverado on the shoulder of the highway and hiked in through the wet grass. He no longer made any effort to shield himself from the rain. The canopy of willows and pines provided something of an umbrella.

As he drew nearer, Sam caught a wisp of music and a hint of something fried from inside. It made his mouth water—sizzling onions, a juicy burger. God, when was the last time he'd eaten real food?

He was three paces from the door when a hiss from the darkness behind him stopped him in his tracks.

Sam turned. It was difficult to make out anything in the darkness. Just the faint glimmer of moonlight in the raindrops and chrome-cornered bumpers.

Something moved.

Sam tensed. He blinked and stared harder, backing toward the door. He thought he might have imagined it, but then the tip of a shoe sent a ripple through the puddle at the edge of the clearing.

"Sam."

Sam jumped. "Ramon?"

"Come here. Get away from there."

"Ramon, what the—"

"Get out of the light, damn it."

Sam crossed the parking lot, slowing as the shadows of the trees closed in around him. Ramon suddenly appeared out of the blackness. "This way."

"Ramon…"

"Shh." He led Sam to the door of his big old Cadillac. Sam still remembered the day he'd bought it, proud as a father, eager to show it off to Sam and Caleb.

He'd parked halfway under the trees, the trunk an inch from the muddy incline leading up into the blackness. "Get in."

"Ramon—"

"Get. In." Ramon eased the door open, careful to make as little noise as possible.

Sam had to duck to make it under the branches. Needles raked his forehead. Inside, Sam swept the hair from his eyes and found his palm covered in sap. He glowered through the windshield as Ramon's shape skulked around the hood and opened the driver's side door.

"Ramon, what the hell is this all about?"

Ramon didn't answer. He yanked the door shut, started the engine, and pulled out of the lot. He didn't turn on the headlights.

Sam sank back into the plush cushion, fumbling for his seatbelt. "Easy. Slow—Ramon, slow the hell down…"

"You bring your phone?"

"My…"

"Your cell phone. You bring it?"

Sam gulped and nodded.

"Give it to me."

"Maybe you should concentrate on driving."

Ramon reached over and made a grab at Sam's pocket.

"Whoa, Ramon, what—"

"Give it to me! You think I'm fucking around?"

They passed through a gap in the woods. For a moment, moonlight reflected off the Cadillac's hood and caught a glint in Ramon's eyes. His suit from the office was rumpled, tie loosened around his neck like an unraveled noose. His hair clung to his forehead. He looked—crazed.

Sam wrestled the cell phone out of his pants pocket and handed it to Ramon.

Without looking at it, Ramon rolled down his window and chucked it outside.

Sam jerked. He twisted around in his seat, staring through the rear windows as it skipped across the pavement and splintered into a dozen pieces along the shoulder. "What the *fuck*, Ramon?"

"Trust me."

"Pull over, god damn it! That was my phone. If Ann—"

"Trust me. You don't wanna use that."

"What are you talking about?"

"Look at your mirror."

"What?"

Ramon reached across the bench seat and grabbed Sam's jaw, forcing his eyes to the mirror on the passenger door of the Cadillac. Twin pinpoints of light had appeared on the road, about a half-mile back.

"Ramon. This is a highway. That's a car. Let's just slow down—turn on your headlights, slow down, let's—"

Ramon shook his head and slammed his foot on the brakes.

The Cadillac skidded into a long slide that turned to fishtailing as Ramon spun the wheel. Rocking on its bathwater suspension, the big old car bucked around and then shot over the shoulder of the road and onto a narrow dirt turnoff.

Sam clung to the armrests. He was breathing so fast that it was making him lightheaded. "Fuckin'—Ramon!"

Trees bowed in low from either side. Branches *thwapped* against the windshield and raked along the Cadillac's doors.

"You're going to get us killed!"

Ramon's eyes flicked to the rear-view mirror. He steered through another tunnel of foliage and veered off sharply to the left. The bushes suddenly parted in front of them. Out of nowhere, a vast, swampy lake sprang into view.

Sam yelped and braced himself against the dashboard. He felt the wheels lock. The car skidded, slipped and slid through the mud, and finally came to a halt less than a foot from the sharp drop-off to the edge of the water.

For a moment, there was silence. Ramon switched off the engine.

"What—"

"*Shh!*" Ramon rolled down his window.

Large, cold raindrops splattered across the sill and drummed on the roof, overhead. With the wipers off, the windshield became a slick, streaming waterfall.

After nearly a minute, Ramon let out a breath. It was cold enough to see. He twisted sideways and reached across the bench seat to nudge Sam's shoulder. "You okay?"

"Am I...? No! I'm not okay. You just went ape shit, destroyed my phone, and almost drowned us both. What the hell is the matter with you?"

"I'll show you." Ramon kicked his door open and climbed out into the rain.

He had the trunk open by the time Sam mustered enough steadiness in his legs to follow him. A dim bulb hanging from the inside of the car cast a yellow glow onto the leafy clearing in the woods where they'd stopped. Deep furrows led up through the mud to the Cadillac's tires. The surface of the lake danced beneath sheets and curtains of torrential downpour.

Ramon held the trunk open. Sam ducked, using it as a shelter.

It was big—big enough to hold a person, Riley had pointed out, just like in the movies.

Ramon hadn't filled it with a person. He'd filled it with the scribbles and printouts Sam had found scattered all over Caleb's cabin.

"I took what I could and got out of there after I'd read enough to be scared. I don't know how much is the good stuff and how much is shit. There was plenty of both."

"What...what good stuff?"

Ramon reached to the back of the trunk, where he'd pinned a sheaf of papers against the metal wall with a big old toolbox. "Lean in," he said with a nod at Sam. "So the ink won't run."

His back soaked to the bone, Sam bent to edge in farther. His head smacked against the trunk. Wincing, he peered down at the tiny type and tried to make sense of what he was seeing.

At first glance, it looked like a diary entry or maybe a love letter. Informal, chatty—sentences popping out here and there as Sam skimmed over the top of the page. Near the bottom, his eyes leapt to a word highlighted in bold. He choked.

Daniel.

Sam reread the preceding sentence.

> *...going to take* **Daniel** *this weekend, that's fine, whatever, your choice, but I'm not going to rearrange my whole schedule just because you've decided you need another session.* |SM
>   AM: *Decided? You think this is easy? Like choosing what to have for lunch? Damn it...*

Sam swallowed. "This is me."

"Yeah."

"Me and—and Ann. This is us on the phone, last—no, two weeks ago. Maybe. I dunno."

"Now you get why I threw your phone out the window? Here, there's more." Ramon leafed forward several pages in the stapled packet. He handed it back to Sam and nudged him toward the bulb on the underside of the trunk.

> *...for his birthday. I was thinking of maybe trying to do a whole party, you know? Get some of the others from the group.* | AM
>   SM: *The group? That's hardly the kind of... Look, what about his friends?* **Danny** *doesn't want to just sit around out there with a bunch of recovering drunks. It's his birthday, for Christ's sake. He should feel...*

Sam was feeling sick again. He thumbed through the packet. Twenty pages. No, forty—double-sided.

"That's not the only one. Hell, it's not even a fraction of all that's there."

"I don't…I'm not sure I…" Sam gave the wad of papers back to Ramon and stared down at the trunk. It was half the size of a Jacuzzi, and it was loaded all the way to the rim. "All of this is us talking?"

"Naw. Like I said, I was freakin' out, so I just grabbed everything I could fit and I got the hell outta there."

"What's the rest of it?"

Ramon shrugged, easing the trunk most of the way closed to keep out the rain. "From what I can tell—Caleb conspiracy shit. JFK. LBJ. Bay of Pigs, missiles in Turkey, some bullshit about Africa, a missing general…" He shook his head. "It's babble. And mixed in with it—this."

"But who…where'd this come from? Who was listening to us? And why?"

Ramon shook his head and let out a poof of breath that encircled his head in a steamy cloud. "You got me, man."

Sam stared at Ramon and shivered. The trunk light cast strange upward shadows on his face. All of a sudden, it seemed too surreal, too out-and-out bizarre to believe. This was his life. Things like this didn't happen to people like Sam.

Shifting his weight from foot to foot, Ramon wiped the condensation from the face of his Swiss Army windup and cringed. "Son of a bitch, Bob's gonna skin me alive. Skin us both. Fuck."

"Let me see the trunk again."

"Look, Sam, I think…look, I think we should just call the cops, okay? This—I've got my sister to think about, you know? Not like she can do shit for herself. I need this job."

"The cops? Who do you think has access to phone logs? Huh, Ramon? You think you can just buy this off the Internet?"

Ramon grimaced. "Man, she's got physical therapy at, like, five tomorrow morning. And that shit ain't free, either. What do you want from me?"

"Ramon. You've been gone from the office for three hours. What's another thirty minutes gonna do? Open the trunk. Please."

Ramon scowled and then let go. The Cadillac's springs creaked as it swung open again.

5

Sam carried the papers to the back seat in armfuls. He glanced at the dashboard clock. He'd been gone an hour. What if Daniel had woken up? Or, God forbid, endured some other—complication? Ann could be calling him over and over, and she'd only be getting through to a piece of scrap plastic alongside the highway.

Ten more minutes. Then he'd go back.

"Find anything that talks about radiation poisoning," Sam said, when Ramon asked how he could help.

Sam started flipping through the pages faster when he came to the Xeroxed copies of newspapers—smudged black-and-white images of Fidel Castro, Khrushchev, John F. Kennedy in the back of an open-topped limousine.

What the hell was the matter with Caleb?

Three pages later, he found another phone log and started skimming it from the top. He stopped halfway through and reread it again, this time hovering on each word.

> *...in a bit, okay?* | SM
> <u>AM</u>: *Just—can't we wait with the blood stuff until tomorrow, at least. It's almost his birthday, and I told him-* | AM
> <u>SM</u>: *You know how they are with policies like this. It's a safety thing. It's—look, it'll only take a second. Just a pinch and then it's over. Tell him we'll do something fun this weekend, make up for it.* | SM
> <u>AM</u>: *Sam.*| AM
> <u>SM</u>: *Daddy's gotta do it, too. Tell him that.* | SM
> <u>AM</u>: *He knows that. He knows where it's coming from. But damn it, Sam, he didn't choose where his father works.* | AM
> <u>SM</u>: *Look, just tell him -* | SM
> <u>AM</u>: *No, you tell him. Here, he's right here anyway.* **Riley!** | AM

Sam sat back against the seat. For a long moment, all he could hear was the blood pounding in his ears.

He'd forgotten about the tests.

In his early years at CW Medical, they'd insisted on regular vaccinations and testing for all employees and their families. It was a health code issue, something legal about working with pharmaceuticals. Somewhere along the line, after Riley, they'd stopped.

This was from an era he'd pushed away into the fog of his long-term subconscious.

Whoever it was that had been monitoring his phone calls over the last couple of years had been doing the exact same thing a decade ago. His sons' names had been flagged each time.

Caleb had figured it out. Or something about it anyway. And now he was missing.

"Ramon."

Ramon looked up from another Xerox. "Listen to this shit. From some web site called The Theorist-dot-org: '*General Donald Pryce was reported MIA in Cambodia, but four months later, radio logs seem to place him—*'"

"Ramon. We need to get to a phone."

"What?"

"You were right. We need a phone. It's time to call the police."

∽

There was a booth outside the Silver Skillet. It stood nestled among the ferns at the edge of the parking lot, branches bowing against the roof. Half of the glass was missing, and inside, it was cold. The floor was flooded, two feet deep in standing water.

Sam scraped together a few quarters and some dimes from the ashtray in the Silverado. Ramon added a couple of nickels. "Hate change," he said. "Always find someone to give it to if I possibly can. Sorry, man."

It took him a minute or two to scare up Crawford's card. Again, he got the desk sergeant at the police station. "Does he ever come in? Did you give him my last message?"

The sergeant cleared her throat and said, in a voice that suggested wireframe reading glasses: "He did want to speak with you. I see here he's tried the number you gave us, in fact. Several times in the last hour."

Sam flinched. "Yeah, that…the number's no good. Can you put him through here?"

"He's become unavailable again, sir. Would you like to speak with someone else?"

Sam glanced out the foggy door at Ramon and the Cadillac.

"Okay...sure. Fine." In truth, he didn't know Crawford that well, but the three hours they'd spent together gave him a certain sense of connection and trust. Ann always used to dog him about that—reaching out, latching onto people before they'd earned it. Either way, Sam wasn't sure how comfortable he would be, sharing all of this with a stranger, but by now, he didn't have much choice.

The sergeant put him on hold with an audible click of false nails. Sam drummed his fingers on the top of the telephone. He checked his watch, glanced over the graffiti stenciled into the steel surface. He'd been gone more than an hour now. Ann would almost certainly have called at least once.

"Look," Sam started to say when the phone clicked back in, "maybe—"

An automated voice told him to choose from a list of options. "For 'Emergency,' press one. For 'Legal,' press two. General inquiries..."

Halfway through the list, the phone beeped and asked him for more change.

Sam patted down his pockets. He'd put it all in the first time. It cut him off while it was still ringing for the operator.

He slipped back outside and jogged to the Cadillac.

"You could ask someone inside to borrow a cell..." Ramon nodded toward the diner. "If you'd trust it."

Through the glowing windows, fogged from warmth and condensation on the inside, Sam could just make out one or two hunched figures, a swath of silver-gray hair. Newspapers. Coke-bottle glasses. A waitress in a brown-and-white uniform slipped by with an armful of bacon and eggs.

Sam shook his head. "If someone's listening—if they've flagged my voice or Daniel's name or..."

Ramon shrugged. "I got a buck, I think, you wanna make change."

A car thundered by on the parkway in a sheet of kicked-up spray. Sam jumped at the sound. He turned to take in the rest of the parking lot—the leaning willows and the impenetrable shadows between them, curtained behind sheets of rain.

The place was making him paranoid. "Follow me back to my house," he told Ramon. "I'll try Crawford again from there."

"You think it's safe back there?"

Sam gulped. "I hope so. I'm not taking all of this stuff anywhere else until we know what we're dealing with."

The whole way back, he kept his eyes on the rear-view mirror. He was torn, wanting to drive as fast as he could to get home and wrap this all up, not wanting to risk an accident or anything else that would cast in danger the one meager morsel of a clue he now had.

Ramon tolerated thirty-five miles-per-hour for fifteen minutes before he roared around Sam and shot ahead into the night.

After that, every yellow light Ramon pushed, every lane change he made—even the slightest jerk of the wheel—made Sam's palms go sweaty. He'd always thought of the Cadillac as a lumbering old tank, Ramon's fortress on wheels, but now, its trunk seemed pitifully small and vulnerable.

When the house melted out of the night, Sam swallowed. It looked so peaceful. So quiet. So normal.

He parked on the street and leaned out the window to motion Ramon up onto the driveway. He had the garage door open by the time Ramon had turned the Cadillac around to angle the rear toward the house.

Bathed in the warm glow from the automatic overhead light, Sam hesitated. He held the trunk shut and peered up and down the winding little street. Here and there, candlelight from a romantic dinner or the blue-green flicker of a television set colored the windows on the opposite side. It was almost seven. Most of the other families on the block were home by now, brought together around a table or across the cushions of a sofa.

Sam couldn't remember the last time he'd been one of those people.

He waited a few more seconds for any sign that they had been followed, but not a single car turned down the road.

The Cadillac rocked on its springs when Ramon nudged the driver's side door shut. "So, you got a place for all this shit?" He nodded to the trunk. "C'mon, man, I gotta get going. Sofia's gonna go starving."

The house smelled stuffy and closed-up. There were muddy tracks all over the carpet from where Sam had gone up to Daniel's room that morning. Already, that seemed like two days ago, a week, maybe more.

He looked across the living room couches. Freshly vacuumed—Ann's work, the other day. The dining room table sat pristine, placemats ruffled only from the cardboard UPS box he'd grabbed six hours ago. Broad windows across the far wall looked out onto the neighbor's porch. Even with the curtains drawn, Sam felt naked and exposed.

"Let's keep it out here." He came back into the garage and pulled the door shut behind him.

Ramon sniffed as he took in the room. "Here?"

There was an old workbench buried in the back, beneath stacks of other things nobody wanted but couldn't bear to get rid of. There was history in this room. The sawdust on the floor from the rocking horse he'd built for Riley, back when the mortgage on the house was all they could afford to scrape together each month. The boxed-up old clothing from Ann's side of the closet. Unopened reams of *Missing* posters they'd printed up with Riley's face on them.

"Yeah. Here." Sam upturned two cartons of old jeans and dresses and planted them beside the Cadillac's trunk. "Come on. You in a hurry or not?"

By the time the compartment was a quarter of the way empty, Sam began to realize that there was much more here than he had thought. He emptied a couple more cartons, but like water from a broken main, it seemed to just keep on fountaining out.

"Here, we could use those…" Ramon pointed to some folded up, unmade boxes from back when they'd moved into the house in the first place. "You got some scissors and tape?"

Sam checked his watch again as he slipped back into the house. It was almost seven-thirty. Ann would be going crazy. He was at the kitchen drawer, rooting through stray twist-ties and napkins when he noticed the telephone. The *Message* light was blinking red.

"You have four unheard messages…"

Bob Frankel's voice squawked through the empty house as Sam searched for a roll of tape. "…kind of professionality, and I'm aware that what you're used to may be based upon standards of another generation, but…"

Ramon came in from the garage, holding an armful of paper. "Aw, shit, that's not Frankel, is it?"

Sam spun down the volume on the answering machine as Bob continued to opine on the nature of responsible employee behavior.

Ramon snorted. "Try the *Delete* button."

"Help me look for the scissors." Sam kneed shut another drawer and went for the cabinets by the fridge. Ann had been right; the place was a goddamn mess. There were straw papers in the knife drawer, a few shards of a broken plate scattered across the dish drainer.

Ramon shrugged and set down his current load on one of the barstools. It teetered and then overbalanced. Fifty pages of smudged notes and printouts went cascading to the floor. "Aw, shit." Ramon got to his knees.

Sam slammed the cabinet door and tried the cupboard over the microwave. Hands probing the bales of dust three shelves up, he accidentally knocked a plastic cup onto the counter at his waist. It was covered in faded cartoon bears, chipped at the rim, right by the handle. It had been Riley's.

"Man, you should...you ought'a take a look at this." Ramon got to his feet, holding a small strip of white plastic. It looked like a credit card.

Sam replaced the cup on the shelf. It looked so young, so innocent and small.

Ramon was waiting when Sam turned around.

The CW Medical logo was stamped on the back of the card, along with a name, a barcode, and a string of numbers. *Tillman, J.G.* On the reverse side was a small blue dot.

It was an ID badge, but not like Sam's—nor Ramon's, Caleb's, or even Bob's. Theirs had pictures, departmental clearance, and fine-print instructions for the return of the card if it was ever lost and picked up by someone else.

This one was featureless.

"It was wrapped in this." Ramon passed him another piece of paper. "It looks like some kind of library slip." More names, a couple of titles—mostly abbreviations. Call numbers. "Archives Department," Ramon said. "North Satellite branch building. You ever hear'a this shit?"

Sam had—once. Clayton Wesley had mentioned it thirteen years ago at the award ceremony, on the night Riley disappeared.

They'd been waiting to go onstage, and Wesley had approached him with a champagne-thickened smile and put an arm around his shoulders. He'd promised Sam an executive track. A corner office, two stories up from the cubicle floors. The company was going places, and Sam was going to go with it.

Later, through the filter of everything that had happened, Sam had imagined a hint of sympathy in Clayton's manner. Almost like everyone that night could feel the tragedy coming.

The North Satellite was part of Clayton's lofty new expansion. *"You're going to die when you see it,"* he'd said. *"You're going to die. It's amazing. The technology. It's amazing what this company's going to do. We're going to change the world, Mackie. We're going to change the goddamn world."*

What had proved to be even more amazing was what three weeks' absence had done to Sam's career. He'd been thankful, at the time, that Wesley had gone on signing his paychecks. He wasn't sure why the old man did it. He just humbly took them to the bank and didn't ask questions.

Sam turned the ID badge over in his hands. "J.G. Tillman."

He recognized the name from the placard on a corner office in the top floor of the CW Medical building. He'd run across it once, in search of a bathroom coming down from a break on the roof with Caleb. It had been shut and locked.

"I think I mighta seen his name in one of Caleb's files. Somewhere in there. God knows where, though ..." Ramon turned back toward the garage door. "No way I got time to look for it right now. Sorry, man."

Sam didn't have time, either. Every second that passed left him more and more conscious of how far away the hospital was. Everything around the house reminded him of Daniel, Riley, or Ann. The television in the living room was like the pulsing readout over Daniel's hospital bed, the white couch duvet like the starched sheet draped over his unconscious little body.

Sam tossed the badge and the library slip back to Ramon and yanked out another drawer. Old spindles of sewing thread were laced over can openers, wine corks, pencils and inkless pens. Ann was the only one who knew how to sew anything. What the hell was this junk still doing in here?

He spotted the yellow plastic of the scissor handles, three layers down, and went for them.

"Oh God, Sam."

Immersed in the drawer to the elbow, he froze.

Ramon was already crossing the other room, plucking at the roll of packing tape he'd unearthed in a cupboard.

The voice had come from the answering machine. It was Ann.

Sam wrenched free of the drawer. Whisks, measuring spoons, and spatulas clattered across the floor. He lunged for the machine, scrabbling at the volume knob. There was something about her voice—tense, urgent, desperate. Something was wrong. He knew it before she said another word.

"Sam. Where are you? Jesus, Sam, it all happened so—" *Click.*

"Six forty-five, P.M." The machine beeped. *"End of messages."*

Forty-five minutes ago.

Dread hit him in the stomach. Sam staggered back against the countertop.

"What?" Ramon had been tossing the tape to himself. He dropped it when Sam charged past him for the door. "Christ, Sam, what? What the hell?"

His hands shook. He had to redial Ann's cell number three times before he got it right. He was dizzy, sick. His life was flashing before his eyes.

Daniel must have—

No. That was unthinkable.

"Hi—"

"Ann!"

"You've reached the cell phone of Ann Mackie. I can't—"

Sam slammed the phone back into its cradle. It was all he could do to keep himself from smashing it to pieces in the sink.

Ramon stood stock-still in the doorway to the kitchen. The way he clutched the roll of tape to his chest, meek, silent, reminded Sam of Riley when he was little.

"Sam?"

"I'm going to the hospital."

"What happened? What's the matter?"

Ramon followed him through the living room to the entryway, feet treading over Ralphie's stain on the carpet.

"Sam...?"

"I don't know." Sam wrestled the keys to the Silverado out of his pocket. "I don't know."

NINE

WHEN HE SAW the flashing blue-and-red lights at the hospital, Sam forgot all about the ID badge, the sketches, Caleb's conspiracy theories, Bob Frankel, Ramon and his Cadillac. He forgot about Ann and their fights and the disaster the two of them had become.

All he thought was, *"Please, God, don't let it be that he's gone."*

Half of the parking lot was cordoned off by yellow police tape. Three squad cars sat diagonally, wheels jutting up onto the sidewalk, headlights piercing the glass lobby doors. There were broken shards all over the pavement, a gaping, man-sized hole in one of the automatic doors.

Sam threw the Silverado into *Park* and leapt out. He left the door hanging open. The truck was in the middle of an aisle, blocking two other cars from getting out. Finding a space was the last thing on his mind.

"Whoa, whoa, whoa." A uniformed cop grabbed Sam as he ducked under the yellow line and dashed for the lobby.

"My son!" Sam clawed at him. His chest felt tight, constricted.

The officer grabbed Sam's wrist as Sam tried to swat him free. "Sir, you need to calm down, or I'm gonna have to take steps here. Now, look—"

"Freemont!"

The cop swiveled.

Two sets of headlight beams arced across the shattered glass and the twisted metal of a broken stretcher. They made the spray of blood around the ragged hole in the lobby door glow like tiny streams of rubies. One belonged to a news van, blue and gold, covered in shiny logos and satellite dishes. The other was a black Hummer. It swerved and wove to get between the van and the police barricade.

The officer holding Sam—Fremont—cursed under his breath and let go. "You stay out here. I'm gonna send someone to talk to you."

"My son's in there."

"Stay out here, sir. You stay here 'till we get you checked off. I'm not—"

"Freemont—damn it!"

The news van's tires locked as a squad car pulled into its path. The driver got out and started shouting.

Freemont winced. "Stay," he told Sam, and then he took off running.

News techs swarmed out of the van in a bevy of more raised voices.

Sam watched a moment longer, and then, without a sound, he wheeled around, swatted away a tendril of yellow tape, and slipped inside.

The hospital lobby was chaos. A trio of swamped receptionists were struggling to fend off mobs of the sick, injured, and curious, while a couple of reporters who had snuck through the lines elbowed trauma victims out of their way to fling questions at the administrators. The people behind the desk must have been in their twenties. The dark rings under their eyes and the stress creasing their foreheads made them look even older than Sam.

Hospital Security was stationed all around the elevators—rent-a-cops in olive uniforms, tasers, rubber nightsticks.

Sam skirted past them. He slipped around the corner to an unattended metal door. *North Stairwell, L/1.*

Holding his breath, Sam tried the knob.

It was open.

Voices echoed down the concrete shaft. Footsteps from somewhere high overhead shook the metal frame under Sam's feet. He started off taking the stairs two at a time. Three flights up, he slowed. His lungs were burning. He was covered in sweat. Combined with the last couple of days, he hadn't been this active since Daniel was a toddler.

The thought of that gave him a second wind.

When he reached the door for the seventh floor, he was dizzy, panting, gasping for breath. The sharp crackle of radio static blared through from the other side.

Sam froze. It sounded close.

What if the cop downstairs—Freemont—had come back?

Turning the knob a fraction of an inch at a time, Sam eased the door open just a hair.

Light flooded in from beyond. There was the reception desk, the nursing station, the water fountain, the corridor—topography as familiar as his own living room at home after the last couple of days he'd spent here.

More yellow tape crisscrossed the entrance to Daniel's door.

Sam stifled a cry and slipped out of the stairway.

The nurses were assembled in a small circle, near the soda machine by the elevator. Three of them were crying and hugging each other. Two cops were talking to them, their backs to Sam.

Edging the door a little wider, Sam squeezed himself through the opening. He stayed flattened to the wall. Every few seconds, he checked on the policemen before his eyes flicked back to the harsh white corridor and Daniel's room at the far end.

If he could make it the twelve feet from the stairwell to the reception desk, he could hide behind the counter.

"...what you've been through, it's a traumatizing experience. We're here for you, we understand that," the officer on the left was saying. "But if any of you actually—if you saw the incident, okay, if you've got what you'd deem as *pertinent information*..."

The one on the right shifted his weight from foot to foot, antsy. Eager to be out there fixing whatever it was that had happened instead of talking to a gaggle of kids in scrubs.

Sam took one step. Then two, three. He glanced over, and he froze. A pair of eyes stared back at him.

It was the nurse—a skinny little woman who would have looked about sixteen in normal clothes. She was the one from earlier, the one who had yelled at him for talking to Ramon on his cell phone.

Their eyes locked. He saw the recognition flooding across her face.

Before she could react one way or another, the cop on the right noticed where she was looking and checked over his shoulder. "Hey!"

Sam bolted, crunching over broken glass that somehow seemed to be everywhere. He took off running down the corridor.

"Stop! Hey, stop!"

Daniel's door was fifteen feet away. Ten.

The window set into it had been smashed, embedded crisscrossing wire bowing inward as though blasted by the head of a sledgehammer.

Sam dashed around the corner and flung himself between the yellow tape as feet clattered down the tile behind him.

Inside, he stumbled to a halt, panting, absorbing the room. There was the bed—empty. The chairs—empty. Three giant tears in the sofa cushions. Bullet holes?

Stuffing lay strewn all over the floor.

And *blood*.

It looked like a war zone.

Sam swiveled around as the cop from the hall appeared in the doorway. His gun was drawn.

"Do not move. Don't even breathe. Just slow down and—"

"Where are they? The boy from this room—where'd he *go?*"

"Sir—"

"I'm his father, for fuck's sake! Where is he?"

"Sergeant, what's…?" Detective Crawford appeared in the doorway behind the uniformed cop. His face—tense, pale, grave—relaxed just a hair when he saw Sam. "Mackie. It's okay, Sarge."

"Sir, he—"

"Sergeant, it's okay. Put the gun down."

A cautious crowd of nurses and orderlies edged in behind them, craning their necks to see anything they could from the corridor.

Sam took a faltering step toward Crawford. When he looked back at the bed—the impression of Daniel's head in the pillow, starched white sheets now stained with blood and covered in glass—his knees buckled.

If it was…

If it was *that*…

He couldn't take it. He knew he couldn't take it. This would be the end of Sam Mackie.

A gasp rippled through the others in the hall when he hit the floor. Crawford grimaced. "Sergeant, get these people back to the front." He came inside and helped Sam to his feet. His usual gruff-ness was supplanted, if only for a moment, by genuine, honest concern. "Mr. Mackie. They're okay. Your family. They're safe."

ᘓ

Sam felt like he was walking on air all the way back down the passage. He didn't notice the stares. Doctors and police alike gaped at his appearance as whispered rumors spread behind his back.

They were okay. He felt like his head was about to float right off his shoulders.

The two-floor elevator ride felt interminable. How the hell did it take this long to lift two people twenty feet?

It was quiet on the ninth floor, no commotion, no reporters, no blood or glass. The only sign of anything at all out of the ordinary was the pair of uniformed policemen flanking the reception desk in the lobby.

Crawford gave them a nod and led Sam into the corridor at the right. Hallways, doorways, passages, stairs. Where in this labyrinth were his wife and son?

When he saw them, framed by another doorway, tears leapt to his eyes. He ran in, shoved an orderly out of the way, and dove to meet Ann with an embrace as she jumped from her chair at Daniel's bedside.

For one long moment, interlocked, absorbing her smell, her warmth, the feel of the heartbeat in her chest, Sam felt like they had never been apart. This was normal. This was how it should have been. Everything that had happened over the last thirteen years was some kind of nightmarish mistake.

It was only when Ann drew back that Sam saw the angry welt around her eye. Her shirt was torn at the shoulders and more blood leaked through the fabric from scratches underneath.

"Oh, Jesus, are you...are you—okay?"

Ann nodded. "I'm fine. Daniel's fine. We're...we're fine."

Sam dropped onto the foot of Daniel's bed. His body felt suddenly heavy beyond all reason. He reached for the boy but stopped himself, eyes tracing the IV lines, tubes, delicate feeds and needlework. The kid was twelve; it wasn't fair that he should be this fragile.

When Sam twisted around on the mattress, Crawford was still standing in the doorway. He fiddled with his badge and looked pointedly down the hall. Uncomfortable as an outside observer amid all of this intimacy.

"Detective."

Crawford blinked a few too many times and gave Sam a gruff nod. "Mr. Mackie."

"What happened here tonight?"

Crawford looked from him to Ann to the lump that was Daniel under the covers of the hospital bed. He bit his lip. "I'm sorry, Mr. Mackie."

"You're… you're sorry?" Sam didn't understand.

"He got out. He got out and he came for your son. Again. Killed two of my best back at the station, and we've got three of the security guys here in critical after what he did."

Sam's heart stopped. The soldier. The soldier who had stalked Daniel at home. The one with the eyes like death who had smiled at him from behind bars and never once opened his mouth.

He and Ann linked hands, a reflex—forming a protective barrier between their son and the rest of the world. "Where is he? Detective? Where—where is he?"

Crawford shifted in the doorway. "They're working on him. Right now."

"What do you mean? What do you mean, '*working on him?*' Interrogating?"

"Surgery. Door guard up front clipped him with a shot through the lung, halfway out the door. That's the only way they stopped him. Flesh wound on the head, too, but they didn't have details about that when they brought him back in. Got it all closed off, sterile operating environment. No press, no cops, nothing."

"He's…" Sam gulped back the bile suddenly bubbling up at the back of his throat. "He's… *here?* He's still *in the building?*"

Crawford opened his mouth and then he closed it. His answer was slight, subtle, barely-perceptible:

A nod.

5

Sam battered through the double-doors to the Intensive Care Ward.

"Mr. Mackie, you can't go in there." Crawford grunted as he dodged a nurse with a crash cart and squeezed between two stretchers.

"Sam! God damn it!"

Sam would have made it around the next corner if it were not for the pair of elderly ladies in wheelchairs barreling the other way. He had to flatten himself against the wall. Crawford caught up.

"Listen." Crawford barred his escape with an arm like a tree trunk. "Mackie. Listen to me. You think I don't want to grab that piece of shit and beat him into a pulp? Those guys—back at the station. One of 'em's my brother-in-law. I went to their weddings. We went to high school together. That asshole broke their necks like toothpicks. Like it was nothin', half a second each. We got it on tape and that piece of shit didn't even care. Smiled at the goddamn cameras."

"Sorry to hear that." Sam tried to duck away.

Crawford countered. "He's gonna pay for this, Mr. Mackie. But if you walk into that room…" He nodded to a heavy door at the end of the hall where a cluster of doctors and nurses were conferring. "You walk in there, screaming and shouting and hitting people, it's only gonna make things worse. Sam—Mr. Mackie. Listen to me. There's a way to do this. Follow the rules, we'll get this guy."

"Excuse me, sir…?" The youngest of the group from the end of the hall had peeled away. She looked back over her shoulder. "Are you a…you're a police officer, right?"

Crawford drew in a breath and nodded. *What now?*

"I think…I think we might need you."

Everyone was talking over each other. Sam trailed behind Crawford. He ignored the detective when he told him to go back upstairs, be with his family, mind his own business and let the police do theirs.

"Everyone—everyone calm down!" Crawford clapped his hands. "Hey!"

Three livid doctors rounded on him—in their sixties, white-haired and red-faced.

"What's going on here?"

Sam stepped to the plate-glass observation window. There were curtains, a buffer room to keep things clean and sterile. Both sets of doors inside stood open. Through a narrow labyrinth of gaps, he could just make out the operating theater, the corner of a stainless-steel table. A splatter of something scarlet. The ruffled shoulder of a white apron.

Sam clenched his hands into fists. The soldier. The man who had hunted his son. Lying right there twenty feet away, and all of these people around him with their decades of experience were trying to save his life, instead of Daniel's.

"Tell me," the eldest of the doctors was saying, "tell me, Detective, what part of the law says they can just storm in here, flash a few badges, sign a few papers and run off with my patient. *My patient.* Tell me that."

Sam spun around. "What are you talking about?"

The doctor thumbed his glasses back up toward his bushy gray eyebrows. "I'm sorry, and you are...?"

"Slow down." Crawford gave a piercing whistle when everyone started talking again. "Slow down and *be quiet!* And tell me—Wait a minute, tell me again...what do you mean they ran off with your patient?" He edged over beside Sam and leaned in close enough to the glass to leave it fogged from his breath.

When he looked back, the doctor crossed his arms. "Tell me what part of this you're not understanding."

Sam shoved his way to the door. Inside, shelves stared back at him—instruments, latex gloves, metal trays with sharp knives and plastic, bottled solutions. It could have been a storeroom at CW Medical.

Beyond it, through an inner arch, light made the white-washed walls and the floor tiles shimmer like sunrise on the surface of the ocean. A couple of masked surgeons were still standing beside the operating table, numbly scrubbing it down.

It was empty.

"Five minutes ago," the gray-haired doctor was saying. "Military medical team, said they had jurisdiction, some kind of national security bullshit. Waved a gun in my face when I told them to get the hell out."

"They had guns." The young nurse who had come and gotten Crawford nodded. "They brought *guns* in here. Into a *hospital!*"

Just like that, any shred of confidence that had rebuilt itself within Sam crumbled.

"The goddamn Army? You told me they said he wasn't an active officer."

"Shut up, Mackie." Crawford was already on his radio. The two of them wove between stretchers, heading toward the orange exit doors of the ICW. "Sergeant, can you get a visual?"

"They're just rolling away from the curb, Detective. They had all the right papers. This came down from somewhere pretty high up."

"Stop them."

"I, uh...I dunno, Detective."

"You having trouble taking orders, Freemont?"

"All due respect, sir, no; just yours. I ran all of this by Captain Malloy. You want to talk to him, I'll even dial you the—"

Crawford hit the elevator button and kicked the trash barrel beneath it. It was a hard enough blow to make a dent in the stainless steel.

Sam waved off the gathering nurses and drew up beside Crawford. "You can't let them do this. They can't do this. Crawford? You have to stop them."

"Mackie, go back upstairs. Go upstairs, be with your son. Butt the hell out of this. This is police business."

Sam shook his head. "Detective. You look me in the eye and tell me you don't know that guy's going to disappear without a trace if you let them get away with him."

"Mackie—"

"Look me in the eye, Crawford. You call up the nearest Army base, they're gonna tell you they don't know a damn thing about this."

"Now you're sounding paranoid."

"This is my son's life we're talking about."

"It's my wife's brother, too, okay? What the hell you want me to do?"

Sam looked at Crawford. Then he looked at the stairwell doorway, five paces away. "You know what? Do just what you're doing. Do nothing."

"Mackie—*Mackie!*"

But Sam was already yanking open the door.

ഗ

Crawford burst outside, three paces behind him. "Mackie, what are you doing? Sam!"

A shout arose from the swarm of reporters at the door. "Detective! Detective Crawford!" They surged past the streaming yellow police tape, ducking and dodging the uniformed officers.

Sam outpaced them, not an item of interest. They caught

Crawford at the curb. The Silverado still stood open, blocking three spaces. A tow truck was idling, a few aisles away. It was trapped by the blockade of ambulances and squad cars. A parking ticket already fluttered from beneath Sam's wiper.

"Mackie!" Crawford shoved his way around a couple of pushy anchors pressing microphones into his face. "Mackie, don't do this! Whatever it is you're thinking…"

Sam scanned the lot as he climbed in behind the Silverado's wheel. He spotted the car racing for the exit as he reached for his keys.

A large black Hummer. Sam had seen it twice before. Once, about twenty minutes ago, following the news vans up to the front doors of the hospital. The time before that had been several days ago. Late at night in the lot of a strip mall. Parked in front of an ice cream parlor when Sam came out with cold medicine for Daniel.

He shivered and grabbed the gearshift.

Crawford wrenched open the passenger door and shoved the muzzle of his gun in ahead of him. "Mackie, I'm ordering you to turn off the engine and step out of the car."

"Crawford—in three seconds, you're either going to shoot me, you're going climb in, or you're going to get real close with the asphalt down there."

"Sam."

"Not my choice, Detective. Yours." Sam dropped into *Drive* and hit the gas.

The lurch swung the door shut, smashing Crawford into the frame. His gun clattered to the ground and slipped under the pickup's rear wheel. "Mackie, are you fuckin' crazy?"

Sam hit the brakes and sent Crawford swinging back out over the curb. He spun the wheel and aimed the truck away from the hospital.

Back at the front of the lobby, a shocked cry rippled through the throng of reporters. Cameramen surged forward, anxious to get the scoop. They were loving this. Real human tragedy, evolving right before their eyes.

Fuck them, Sam thought. He glanced to Crawford, who'd just managed to hoist himself inside the truck's cab.

"You're insane. Damn it, Mackie, what's the matter with you?"

"Detective Crawford, I think you're going to want to fasten your seatbelt."

"Mackie—"

Sam floored it.

The truck sprang forward, away from a heroically-stupid hospital security guard who had been making for the rear bumper.

Crawford heaved his door shut. Sam reached over and caught his wrist as he was going for the can of pepper spray strapped to the back of his belt. Crawford swatted him back and flipped off the lid with his thumb.

He got off a solid spray before Sam veered the truck so hard to the left that Crawford was flung into the glove box. Sticky spray congealed onto the windshield.

Sam's eyes began to water. A flash of strobing blue-and-red melted out of the blur at the corner of his vision. Sam spun the wheel. The pickup bounced over a curb and flattened a strip of low shrubs before coming back down through the exit of the lot.

"Mackie! Jesus Christ, pull over!"

Sam grabbed up his sleeve in a wad and rubbed at the smear on the windshield, right in his line-of-sight. He dodged around a honking VW Beetle. As he swerved back, he cut in too closely, and he caught its nose with the Silverado's back bumper. A spray of sparks lit up the rear-view mirror. The Beetle skidded to a halt in the middle of the road, followed a moment later by a blaring chorus of horns.

"Listen, Sam…listen, I know what you're going through. I know your son—"

"Call the Army, Crawford. Ask them why the hell they won't let you question this asshole."

"Getting us—*Jesus, Sam!*—getting us killed isn't going to help a goddamn—"

"Hang on." Sam made a diagonal dive through a busy intersection and roared up onto the grassy median in the middle of a long parkway.

Lights sprang up out of the night on both sides—neon signs, the glow of restaurants. It was the East Ridge Mall. It had shot up in the last two or three years, sapping the life from the downtown district around CW Medical's offices. He couldn't tell any of it apart. Applebee's shared parking with TGI Friday's, Red Robin, Black Angus. Blink and they looked like kaleidoscope doubles of each other.

Sam wouldn't have ever known any of it existed if it weren't for Daniel. According to him and his friends, it housed the best theater in town.

Every evening, after school got out, it was flooded with throngs of teenagers with nothing to do. They mobbed the crosswalks, jammed the parking lots, and covered the concrete with skateboard tracks.

It was an automotive nightmare.

Sam fixed on the rear of the black Hummer. It was nine or ten cars ahead, but it was still stuck in traffic. Sam was gaining fast. He slalomed through a thicket of toothpick maple trees, planted when the mall broke ground, and barreled toward the gridlock at the next red light.

"Sam." Crawford had his knees braced against the dash. "Mackie, you hurt anyone, I can't stand up for you. This isn't pulling anyone into your side of the ring."

Sam scowled. "Trust me. I'm used to being alone."

"Mackie!"

Twenty feet away, and the black Hummer suddenly took a sharp left and crossed over the median. Sam slammed on the brakes and sent the Silverado into a long, sideways skid that landed him on the pavement at the wrong side of the parkway.

Headlights flashed through the pickup's cab, horns thundering into an atonal roar. Crawford slapped his open palms against the passenger window.

Sam glanced past him, out at the road and into the light. For the first time he could remember, he suddenly faced the possibility that he was about to die. In the blazing, blinding white, he glimpsed the faces of Ann, Daniel, Riley.

"Oh my *God, Sam!*"

Sam jammed his foot on the accelerator. The Silverado's engine roared. It darted across four lanes of traffic and made it to the shoulder on the other side. Free of the endless river of cars, he was just able to glimpse the hulking body of the Hummer as it zipped around the corner of the next intersection and vanished down another road.

From somewhere in Crawford's clothing, a radio crackled to life in a burst of static. The Detective ripped open buttons, fumbling to get it out.

"...*Crawford, what is your position? Please confirm—*"

"Eighth and Commerce, westbound, heading toward Interstate—"

Sam snatched it out of his hands and cracked it against the dash. Sparks spat from the speaker. It tumbled to the floor in a burst of electronic snow.

"Sam, you can't keep this up."

"Neither can they."

"You want me to call it in? Pull over. Pull into that gas station. Right there, I'll call the nearest base commander. We'll work this out, make everyone—" Crawford broke off into an involuntary yelp.

Sam saw them a split-second later: A herd of seven high school girls was just stepping off the crosswalk, followed by a couple of boys on skateboards.

The girl at the front of the pack wasn't looking. Headphones dangled from her ears. She was walking backward, talking to the other kids.

As Sam's headlights cut across them, a few of them turned. For an instant, one beam caught the face of the first skater, arm draped around a girl with long, black hair. He was wearing a jacket just like the one Riley had gotten as a present on the day he'd disappeared. In that fleeting fraction of a second, the boy *was* Riley.

All of the yelling, the squealing of the tires, the roar of the engine—all of it died away. It was *Riley*. Riley, older than Sam had ever seen him—living a life, out with friends. *Alive.*

Sam blinked. His son was gone when his eyes snapped open again, snatched away and replaced with a poor teenager scared shitless by some crazy asshole in a pickup truck.

Then Sam saw the bus careening toward the Silverado's hood, and he heard Crawford shouting at him.

He veered up into a gas station, wove around an island of pumps, and swerved back onto the road at the other side of the intersection. A street vendor with an ice cream cart let out a cry and threw up his arms. The pickup's front bumper slammed into the cart and punted it into the middle of the street. Vanilla-chocolate sandwiches scattered across the divide.

As Sam maneuvered back into the right-hand lane, he found the spare tire on the back of the Hummer, eight or nine cars up. He'd lost a half-block, saving ten teenagers' lives, but the other car was still clearly visible.

"Mackie!"

Sam ignored Crawford until he lunged across the bench seat. Sam thought he was trying to grab the wheel, and he started to fight him off until he saw where Crawford was pointing.

In the rear-view mirror, a second black Hummer was just skimming up alongside the Silverado. Had he been following the wrong one?

Sam's eyes flicked back to the windshield.

No. The one up ahead was still weaving wildly, careening onto the shoulder of the road as it angled toward the Interstate onramp.

A sharp *crack* resounded through the night. The Silverado's wheel jerked in his hands. The back of the pickup began to fishtail.

"Mackie, stop!"

Sam stared down at the gages, not understanding.

The Hummer eased up past the front bumper. This time, Sam saw the flash of light before the second *crack* came.

Then, he lost control altogether. As the left front tire collapsed, the Silverado swiveled sideways and drifted into a circular spin that thrust Sam against his seatbelt before yanking him back to press him into the cushion behind him, time after time after time.

The Silverado came to an abrupt halt as the rear bumper slammed up against the side of a bus station. Sam pitched forward and caught the steering wheel with his forehead.

Color flashed across his vision.

Dizzy, clutching his temples, Sam fought his way out of his seatbelt and kicked the door open. Crawford tried to stop him. Sam clawed free and staggered out onto the pavement.

A small crowd was already gathering around him, but they shrank back. Probably afraid he was drunk with a gun or something worse.

Sam took three faltering steps in the direction of the onramp and then caught himself on a support column at the corner of the green metal shelter. His shoulders sank. Even in the blur that everything had become, he could just make out the twin black silhouettes racing away onto the Interstate.

He'd let them get away. They were gone. And with them, the one man who might be able to solve a loss that had been draining him for thirteen years.

Just like that, it was over.

Sam went limp. Defeat overtook him.

"They got away," he rasped to Crawford after the Detective pulled himself from the Silverado. "They got…"

It wasn't until he'd said it the second time that he realized the full implication of it. *They* had gotten away. Not, *he.*

Whoever it was that was after his son—

It was more than one man.

5

Ann jumped to her feet and covered her mouth when she saw him. Sam had caught a glimpse of his reflection in the mirrored hospital elevator doors. It was distorted, brushed steel that warped and changed proportions, but he could make out enough to see that he looked like the living dead.

"What happened?" She kept her hand over her mouth, concealing anger or pain or most likely a combination of the two. It made her cheeks burn pink. She did that whenever she was furious or sad or even overjoyed. With her upbringing, Sam didn't blame her. Emotions usually led to blows in her family.

He fell into her arms, moaned into her hair. He didn't know what else to say, but he needed her. Right then, right there, he needed them not to hate each other. Even if it was just for ten minutes. Together, they sank onto the foot of Daniel's bed. Sam reached out and touched the boy's ankle with a trembling hand. A part of him needed to reassure himself that Danny was still there. That they were all still there—together. At least for now.

"He's ... he's not safe."

Ann's fingers, still laced with Sam's, squeezed tighter. "What do you mean? I thought they caught the ... the man who ... "

"They did. He's gone."

"You mean ... dead?"

Sam shook his head. "No. Maybe. I don't know. He got shot."

"I was there for that part."

He hadn't had the chance yet—to hear it from her, hear how it had unfolded. He wasn't sure he could take it. "There were these ... these people. They took him. He's still out there, Annie. God, he's still out there."

Ann shuddered. "What people? Who are they? Why do they want our boy?"

"I don't know." Sam pulled her closer. "I don't have any idea. All I know is that right now we ... we can't trust anyone." He hated how much he was sounding like Caleb, almost as much as he hated how true it was. He looked at Daniel's sleeping face, and he wanted to cry.

What in hell were they going to do?

Twenty minutes later, Crawford knocked on the door. Sam could hear arguing in the hall, the whole time. He looked up at the Detective's pale face, torn trousers, bruised shins, and he tried to prepare himself for the worst.

"I'm not pressing charges. The department—we're not pursuing this."

Sam wasn't sure he'd heard correctly. He blinked dumbly up at Crawford.

Crawford sighed, glanced over his shoulder, and shut the door on a huddle of uniformed cops and hospital orderlies waiting on the sidelines for the next display of fireworks.

"Look." He kicked a rolling chair toward the bed and dropped into it with a heavy, burdened sigh. "Sam—I'm dropping the 'Mackie.' We almost died together, it's fair. Sam, I get you, okay? You, your wife, your son. I can only imagine. Deb and I—we can't, but I've got this nephew… It was his dad, tonight, down at the station and I… This is my job and I don't have a goddamn clue how I'm gonna face the kid." Crawford set a plastic evidence bag atop Daniel's sheets and ran big, thick fingers through his brown hair. "I want you to listen very closely to me. Okay, Sam? You're a good dad. Your heart's in the right place. We're going to figure out what happened tonight. But if you ever do something like this again, they're going to put you in jail, and I'm going to turn the key in the lock. Are you getting me?"

Sam swallowed. "Yes, sir."

"You are officially on notice. You run a traffic light, I'm getting them to reopen Alcatraz for you."

"I understand, Detective."

Crawford nodded. He wasn't looking at Sam. He was looking at Daniel. For a couple of seconds, it was almost as though he drifted off and went somewhere else. "Poor kid." Sam wasn't sure if he was talking about Daniel or the nephew. At length, Crawford stood. "I'm going to have three guys circulating outside this room. One of 'em's going to stay there twenty-four-seven."

"It's not enough."

Crawford glanced at Ann as though seeing her for the first time. "I know. I know it's not. It's not going to be enough until we catch these guys. But right now, it's the best we can do." He swung the chair back to its position beside Daniel's bedside monitor and headed toward the door. "I'll check in. Every couple'a hours. I'll make sure you all are okay."

"Detective." When Crawford looked, Sam picked up the plastic evidence bag and shook it.

Crawford allowed him a fractional hint of a weary smile. "Next thing I know, I'll be forgetting my badge." He reached for it, took it by the Ziploc seal.

Sam didn't let go.

"Mackie. Sam. My department. You've been—"

"Where'd this come from?"

"What?"

"This."

"Oh." Crawford sighed. "Surgeons took it off the soldier when they were prepping to operate, and the 'men in black' were in too big a hurry to ask for his clothes."

Sam held it up inside the bag. It was a small white ID card. Just like the one he and Ramon had found among the things from Caleb's cabin.

TEN

CRAWFORD SEEMED TO SENSE there was something he wasn't saying. "Recognize it?"

Before Sam could consider whether telling the detective would be a good idea, Crawford added: "Because Freemont already called Captain Malloy, and he's fast-tracking this to forensics. Some kind of executive order."

Sam shook his head. "Nothing to recognize." It was all he could do to keep the shock off his face. He released the bag, but he followed it to the door with his eyes.

Crawford hesitated, hand on the knob. He looked at Sam long and hard, and then he sighed, shook his head, and pulled it open. "I want to introduce you guys to the first shift sergeant out here. This is BJ Cunningham. He and I go back to the academy. He's a good guy."

Cunningham stuck his head in the door and gave an obliging nod. He was a tall guy, probably a basketball player back in college. He looked friendly enough, but not at all excited to be posted by a hospital door for the next eight hours.

Sam and Ann shook his hand and thanked him for helping them out, and then Crawford took off for the night.

For the next hour, they sat and listened as the rain picked up outside.

Ann couldn't sleep, but Sam found it suddenly difficult to keep his eyes open. He sat back on the sofa, and tried to keep himself focused. God, when was the last, solid eight-hour night he'd had? He couldn't remember. Long before all of this had started.

The monitor over Daniel's head flashed.

Sam had caught it out of the corner of his eye—just a blink of color.

He glanced at Ann, but she was leaning over Daniel, gently brushing his hair with her fingers.

Sam watched for another couple of seconds.

Maybe he had imagined it. The monitor remained steady, three lines of vitals and a few columns of numbers and stats. No color, no sudden changes.

He drew in a breath and started to lie back on the sofa.

Another flash of light.

This time he sat up straight. He got to his feet, paced around the foot of the bed, and swung the screen toward him on its long, metal arm.

Ann frowned at him. "Don't touch that. What are you doing?"

"It was—I saw something on it."

"You're a doctor now? Know how to read all of that?"

"You didn't see a flash? Any kind of—"

Flash.

There it was. For an instant, a harsh black-and-white image flickered over the emotionless numbers and letters. Sam gripped the black plastic corners of the screen. He willed it not to be what he thought it was. This couldn't be happening.

"Sam?" Ann reached across the bed, fingers closing around his forearm. "Sam, you're sweating. And you're hot."

He was looking at her. He caught the next flash from the screen in the reflection of the window, rainwater streaming over it on the outside. But this time he saw it. Recognized it.

The Dark Tower.

Sam jolted awake with a start. Ann was still sitting over Daniel, but she glanced at him when he moved.

"Drifted off?"

Sam swallowed, throat parched, shaking all over. "Must have."

"You saw it again, didn't you? The—that thing in your dream. That the boys started drawing."

Sam didn't answer. He didn't have to.

"Sam, I'm wondering." She licked her lips and avoided looking at him. "I'm wondering if maybe we should consider—just for us, just to…I'm wondering if we should maybe consider looking into some kind of…of therapy."

Sam blinked at her, not even really hearing what she was saying. He could barely contain himself. There was too much floating around inside his head. The ID card Crawford had recovered, the Army, the papers back at the house—J.G. Tillman, the North Satellite library.

The idea of leaving Ann and Daniel alone here again was more than he could take. They needed to find somewhere safer.

Some part of the thought must have shown on Sam's face. Ann looked from him to the window, the door, the hallway outside. She drew in a deep breath. "There has to be a witness protection program or something, right? Some house they can take us to, somewhere that nobody knows about."

"We haven't witnessed anything. We can't—we're not testifying about anything. We can't help anyone."

"And no one can help us."

Sam instinctively put an arm around her shoulders and pulled her close. Ann didn't resist at first. It was only when his lips touched the side of her head—not a kiss, but an echo of something that once was—that she seemed to start and realize what they were doing.

She withdrew and paced to the window, brushing off her torn sweater as though he had somehow left a part of himself still clinging to her. "I could call my family…"

"No."

The abruptness of his reply stopped her in her tracks. "Still?"

"They still blame me."

"They don't blame you for anything."

"They still blame me. Taking their perfect little princess out of that redneck trailer park. Not letting them mold you into another one of them."

"That *redneck trailer park* is my home."

"Was."

Ann opened her mouth and closed it again. The instant she restrained herself, Sam felt ashamed. She had been attacked tonight. She'd been there when an armed stranger came after their son, and here he was, maligning her family, bickering with her about the same old nothings.

"Sorry." He stood up. He gave Daniel's foot another pat. "I'm going to run down the hall, grab a drink. A *soda*."

The amendment, more a natural reflex than a planned barb, made Ann bristle even more, but then, just as he was rising, she went stiff and clutched his arm. Sam followed her gaze to the window.

A shape flitted by outside, momentary, fleeting—just a doctor or a nurse. Ann's face had gone sickly gray and pale as the clouds in the sky. Sam understood in an instant. He sat back down, even as she was already pulling back, withdrawing, stifling herself.

"Do you want to talk about it?"

Ann shook her head. There were tears in her eyes. She flinched again, involuntarily, as another silhouette passed. "It was like that." Ann swallowed. "Just like that. A dozen other times right before it, all throughout the day. Except this time, it—the shadow stopped. I wasn't even looking. And then he…

"The door was locked. We were keeping it locked, when you were gone, just because… just out of habit. After he broke the window, it was all—it happened so fast. He went right for Daniel. I tried to stop him, and then he hit me, out of nowhere. I should have—I didn't have a chance to duck or anything, and then I was on the ground and there was this—a pole or something I must have landed on, and he hit me again, and all I could see was just these stars and colors. And the shadow of a man taking our son."

She covered her mouth, lower lip trembling.

As Sam looked from her to Daniel to the window, six feet away, he felt cold, angry determination taking over. He had been gone, and his family had needed him. He hadn't acted fast enough. This was happening to them, and he was doing *nothing*. He was letting them get torn apart. Again.

Sam hugged her long and hard, and stood up.

Ann blinked, flustered, half lost in the horrors still alive inside her head. "Where are you going? Sam?"

"I need to make a telephone call. Just outside. I lost my cell."

"Out…" Ann looked at the window again. "Outside?"

"Cunningham is here. I'll be back in five minutes."

"Sam…"

"Trust me."

For the first time, Sam was formulating a plan.

BJ Cunningham looked up from a hardcover. He was sitting on a small, uncomfortable gray chair on the opposite side of the hallway. Sam glanced at the spine. Edgar Allen Poe. Nice to know there were some literate cops on the street.

"You need anything, Mr. Mackie?"

Sam said that he did not. At the end of the corridor, he remembered he didn't have any change. There was a gift shop in the lobby full of teddy bears and picture books and a couple of cheesier odds and ends. Joke shot glasses for the outpatients. *Pushing liver disease at the hospital,* Sam thought. Someone wasn't thinking.

He got change from the girl with the braces and acne at the register, and he was heading back toward the soda machines when he noticed a little boy and his mother in the storybook aisle.

Sam gulped. He slowed. From the back, the straight brown hair, the tottering little gait—it looked so much like Riley that Sam couldn't look away.

Daniel had never been like that. He'd never been—*goofy.* Right from Day One, it was almost as though he was aware he was making up for a child that had gone and taken away with him a part of his parents' hearts he could never hope to replace. It had been Riley who pranced around the house as a toddler, singing or strewing things while Sam and Ann struggled to keep up.

Daniel had always been more interested in other kids.

The mother looked over and caught Sam staring. She glanced to the girl at the register with a meaningful glower.

Sam's cheeks flushed. "He reminds me of my son," he muttered to the woman. But as he slipped out of the gift shop, he glanced back and saw the boy again, reflected in the glass door. For a second, it *was* Riley again.

He started sweating. This happened to Ann, not him. It was Ann who saw Riley everywhere, Ann who insisted that he was still out there somewhere.

But—

But what if he was?

The main foyer was still closed off, doors shuttered with more yellow police tape. An auxiliary conference room had been transformed into a makeshift reception area. The entrance stood right beside the public payphones.

Sam made a beeline for them, reaching for the last receiver on the end.

It wasn't until he was shunted to CW Medical's general-purpose, office-wide voicemail system that Sam thought to check his watch. Eight-thirty. There were probably a few overachieving stragglers left in the grid-work of cubicles, burning the midnight oil. Certainly not Ramon—not with his sister waiting for him at home.

The mere thought of the place gave Sam pause. After the last couple of days, it seemed someone else, a stranger, must have sat in his shoes and whittled away the last twenty years in that building. How could he have spent so much of his life between those impersonal, padded gray walls, staring at a flickering computer screen while Daniel grew up alone and unprotected?

He stared at his warped reflection in the shiny metal of the telephone. He'd done it to Daniel. Without even realizing it, he'd spent so much of his life unavailable that he'd given Daniel the same childhood he'd had, himself. One of solitude and self-reliance. One without his family.

The gift shop door clicked shut. Sam glanced over his shoulder. The mother and her son. They made a hasty beeline for the elevators.

He picked up the phone again and pumped a few more quarters into the slot. It took him a moment to remember the number. Between the directory at work and the memory on his cell phone, he wasn't used to keeping anything in his head anymore.

Unease began to puddle in the pit of his stomach as the phone on the other end rang on. Where the hell was Ramon? Caring for his sister, struggling to stay on top of work, there weren't many options. Sam and Caleb were the only social life he had.

After fifteen rings, there was a *click* on the other end.

"Ramon?"

"We're sorry. We can't come to the phone right now." The voice was stilted, prerecorded, factory-installed on the machine Ramon had picked up for ten bucks at a closing K-Mart. *"Please leave your message after the beep."*

"Uh, hey…Ramon. It's Sam." He shifted his weight from foot to foot. "You gonna pick up? I need to—"

"If you are satisfied with your message, you may hang up now, or stay on the line for more options…"

Sam stared at the receiver. Then he had replaced it in the cradle. Something didn't feel right.

From the makeshift lobby next door, Sam caught the eye of a man checking in with the nurses. Paperwork was thrust into his hands. He didn't so much as glance at it. He was watching Sam.

Sam ducked back behind the door. He picked up the receiver of the pay phone, and with the last of his change, he dialed the office at CW Medical again. This time, he keyed in the code for the night-time operator.

"I'm an employee looking for another employee. I was wondering if you'd be able to page him or see if he was in the building."

The voice on the other end flowed out in a dull, beleaguered drawl. "You try their extension?"

"I did. Could you page him? His name—"

"You know for sure he's in the building?"

Sam clenched his free hand into a fist. He checked around the corner again. The man in the lobby was drifting slowly toward him through the crowd, clipboard and paperwork clutched under his arm.

"I don't know that, no." Sam shrank back behind the open door. "That's why I want you to page him." He told the operator Ramon's name and waited as the receiver went to fuzzy jazz.

Nearly a minute passed. Sam glanced out at the lobby again. His eyes darted from face to face, stranger to stranger. Children, elderly patients in wheelchairs, a couple of twenty-something daredevils supporting a buddy with a broken leg.

No sign of the man.

"Sir?"

Sam jerked at the sound of the tinny little voice in his ear. Not Ramon. Just the operator again. "Did you find him?"

"Sir, I don't think he's here."

"Can you tell me when he left this evening?" If Ramon had stayed late, he could still be on the road. There'd be no way to get in touch without his cell.

"What did you say your name was?"

"Please, just look up the time sheet, okay? Ramon's—he's got a file I need for the, uh…the follow-up with DHL tomorrow."

"I wouldn't know anything about that."

"Exactly. So unless you want me to tell Bob Frankel you're the reason we're bleeding ten million a year, you might want to find your keyboard and give me five more seconds of your time."

There was a pause. No jazz this time. "Ramon Juarez?"

"In distribution, that's right."

"Well, cap'n, looks like you're out of luck. 'Cordin' to the time sheet, Ramon Juarez never clocked back in after lunch. So you still gonna yell at me about your contract, 'cause I didn't catch—"

Sam hung up the phone. The twinge of unease was fast becoming something else:

Dread. Dread and panic.

He edged forward and peered into the lobby.

The automatic doors on the opposite side were just sliding shut. Sam thought the shape on the other side of the tinted glass might have been the man who had been watching him. Or it might have been someone else altogether.

5

Ann looked up when he walked back into the room. A flash of worry and subsequent relief dissolved into a mute, irritated stare. "You're back."

"Ann..."

"Find something at the soda machine? Or was that just a twenty-minute 'business' call?"

"Ann, I think something's wrong."

"You think..." She sat up and blinked at him like he'd just walked in off the surface of the moon. "You think something's *wrong*. Really? Because after tonight, I don't have the slightest clue what might've given you that—"

"I have to go."

Silence. Painful, awful, accusing silence. She drew in a long, slow, deep breath, and then let it out through her nose.

"Look, if I had any choice..."

Still not a word.

"Ann. Please...please say something. I wouldn't—you know I'd never do this unless I had to. I'm doing it for you. For *him*."

Ann glanced at Daniel. When she looked back to Sam, she wasn't crying. It would almost have been better if she were. Better than the cold, reluctant acceptance. It was almost as though she had been expecting this. Expecting him to run away.

"Okay," she said.

"Ann…"

"Go. Do what you have to do."

"I'll be back."

To that, she had no answer at all.

It was not until he got down to the parking lot, through the lingering news crews and security vans, that Sam remembered the Silverado had gone away strapped to the back of a tow truck.

Jogging now, he returned to Daniel's room. Ann handed over her keys without meeting his eye.

There were several more dents in her Volvo station wagon since the last time Sam had seen it. It was a classic, cream-colored, the original paint from 1963. Collectors used to make offers on it until she'd wrapped it around a tree stump. She'd been leaving the liquor store, two weeks after the night Riley disappeared. After that, the only people who ever expressed interest in the warped hood, the bent chrome grille, and the cracked windows were junkyard owners looking for a quick buck.

Sam fiddled with the lock for several minutes before it finally gave. He was sweating from the pressure, the impatience. Ramon could be anywhere. He could be racing away in the back of a black Hummer, for all Sam knew.

Inside, it smelled like her. Her perfume. The chocolate graham crackers, the shape of teddy bears, that she'd kept on buying because they'd been Riley's favorite. Her jacket was draped over the back seat.

Sam tried to focus, tried not to soak it in. He was jarred by the familiarity of it all. In high school, this had been their only car. A neighbor at the trailer park had informally given it to Ann when she turned sixteen on the condition that she never told her family. They would have sold it for whiskey or totaled it within a week if they'd ever known. She'd parked it two blocks away, on the street, just to keep it a secret.

It took three tries before the engine gurgled to life. Half the gages didn't work. The headlights were loose in their housings, skewed at rakish angles that made the pavement in front of the car look like the floor of a disco hall.

The Silverado was no Rolls-Royce, but even it had power steering. The first curve Sam took in the Volvo almost sent him careening into the cinderblock hospital wall.

Wrestling the station wagon back out onto the street, Sam eased onto the accelerator. He kept pushing until the pedal hit the bare metal floor. The speedometer edged up to forty-five.

As he came up to the corner of the East Ridge Mall, Sam was struck with a thought. What if Ramon had come to his house after work? They hadn't finished unloading the back of his Cadillac. What if he was there in Sam's own living room, watching TV and checking his watch and wondering where the hell his friend was?

Like Caleb, Ramon lived well outside the city. Sam hadn't been there in years. Somehow, when the three of them got together, it was always at a hotel bar or a decrepit nightclub, or a lonely hill overlooking the city. Their outings were escapes from the lives they carried on in private. Almost as though one might corrupt all the others.

Sam's house was on the way. He traced around the edges of the mall and took a couple of back roads to avoid thickening traffic on the freeway. Several teenagers in souped-up Hondas roared around him, music rattling their windows. He wished he could coerce the Volvo into keeping up with them.

He slowed at the mouth of his cul-de-sac. Orange sodium street lamps fell over pools of concrete and grass, oases between the darkness. It was dinnertime again. Lights shone down from living rooms on all sides.

There were no strange cars parked on the shoulders, nothing visibly amiss.

Not until he wrestled the Volvo halfway up the asphalt drive.

Sam slammed on the brakes. The Volvo wheezed to a halt. The motor shuddered and rattled beneath the loose hood. The lights shook from the rough idle, casting a tremulous whitewash over the lawn and the garage door.

There was a circular black hole where the lock was supposed to have been. The door itself had been raised just over a foot. Shadows tumbled out from beneath it. Almost consumed in the darkness, Sam could just make out the corner of a solitary sheet of paper.

A door clicked somewhere across the street.

Like lightning, Sam clamored for the gearshift. It was stuck. He grabbed it with both hands and forced it into *Reverse*. The Volvo coasted backward. Sam twisted the steering wheel with all his might. The arcing headlights caught a hint of a shape darting across the street toward him.

Sam yelped. He jerked so hard, searching for the accelerator pedal, that his elbow bumped the horn. The car gave an anemic *honk* that thundered out over the quiet neighborhood. Birds leapt into the air.

Sam didn't wait to see if the shape came back. He slammed the Volvo into gear and hit the gas. With a lurch, the station wagon rumbled forward. Then it choked and died. The wheel went limp in his hands.

"No!" Sam fought with the keys for a couple of seconds before he realized he was still in *Drive*.

Something rustled the grass somewhere in front of the house.

Sam whirled. With his left elbow, he slammed down the driver's side door lock and then twisted to reach across and hit the passenger one while he reset the car's gears and grappled with the ignition.

The engine coughed.

"Come on, come on."

A definite footstep landed on the pavement. It sounded close— ten feet from the Volvo's passenger door.

Sam pumped the accelerator and tried again.

With a snarl, the Volvo came to life. Sam floored it. Just as he was rolling forward, something smacked against the rear windshield.

Sam's heart leapt to the back of his throat. For an instant, the silhouette of a hand smeared across the glass before it disappeared into the dark.

Ten feet from the end of the block, Sam caught a glimpse of a man in jogging shorts and a tee shirt shaking his head to himself as he sprinted off in the other direction. Perhaps it had been he who'd made a grab at the Volvo—a frustrated runner almost run down by a paranoiac.

Or perhaps whoever had broken into Sam's garage and stolen the papers from Caleb's cabin had come back.

∽

The Volvo's radio didn't work. In certain patches of the Interstate, it picked up faint strains of right-wing talk radio, but the rest of the time, it broadcast only the soft hiss of blank, white static.

Sam found the noise oddly comforting. He left the knob almost all the way down, and he fixed his eyes on the road ahead. He tried not to think about anything at all. It was impossible.

Ramon lived ten minutes out of town. A hundred years ago, most of the surrounding area had been peach orchards and orange groves, but development had claimed all but one or two lots.

Ramon's house belonged to him and his sister. His parents had left it to them, and however bad things got, Ramon would never consider parting with it. A generation ago, his family had come from Mexico, covering the coast as migrant pickers. Slowly, they had worked their way up, toiling and saving for the future. When the Depression had undermined key investments for the company that had hired them, they made an offer on the land. It was theirs.

In the decades since, eighty percent of the original lot had been sold off to investors. Ramon had only two acres to himself, but it was more of a yard than Sam could ever dream of.

The house shared a private dirt road with three other home-steads, two of which had sprung up in the 1950s on land not previously subdivided.

There were no lights out here, and tonight, the rain clouds hid the moon in a swath of opaque blues and grays.

Sam almost veered off the road, searching for the Volvo's high beams. It didn't have any. To be safe, he should have slowed to a crawl, but the fuel gage didn't work, either, and with each passing mile, Sam became more certain that it was going to die with an hour's hike still to go. Stranded out here in the wilderness, anyone could get to him. And anyone could get to Ann and Daniel, back in the hospital.

The Volvo shuddered on its springs as it took a series of rough potholes at the mouth of the final stretch. Dust leapt into the air on all sides. It curled up to press in at the windows, forming a brown fog that reflected the headlights back onto the windshield.

At last, navigating by feel, Sam steered to a stop beside a decaying wooden fence. Most of the posts were listing at near-diagonal angles. Twists of barbed wire held it all together.

There was a gate ten feet up. It was lashed shut with a chain Sam did not remember from the last time he had been out here. He tried to untie it. Then he found the padlock, hanging down on the inside.

He glanced back at the Volvo. The engine had sputtered off as soon as he'd dropped it into *Park*, and the headlights were already dimming. The battery would fail in a matter of minutes.

Leaning in the window, Sam switched them off, and then waited for his eyes to adjust to the darkness.

Stars winked into view overhead through rare gaps in the cloud cover.

Eventually, when he could see enough to fumble his way forward, Sam hoisted himself over the gate and started up the sloping drive to the house. It was perched atop a gentle hill. Once, the kitchen had enjoyed a sprawling view of the orchards around it, but now, cookie-cutter suburban development was strung across the horizon. The glow from a dozen identical houses peeled over the edge of a stucco wall, half a mile away.

Sam used it to navigate and keep his bearings until he got to the top of the weeded hillock.

There were no lights on inside Ramon's house.

A chilly breeze picked up as Sam mounted the front stairs. The knot of dread in the pit of his stomach was getting tighter. Nothing about this felt right.

Sam stopped when he reached the porch. Here, from the elevated vantage point, he could see the garage around the side. The swinging double-doors hung open. Inside, even in the muted moonlight, Sam could just make out the distinctive, arching taillights of Ramon's Cadillac.

Run, he thought.

Sam didn't move.

Ramon had come home. He had come home, and for the last hour, he hadn't been answering his phone. Someone had broken into Sam's house, someone had come for Sam's son.

Every self-preserving fiber of his being was telling him to turn around, get to the Volvo as fast as his legs would carry him, and get the hell out of there.

Sam knocked on the front door.

He thought he heard the faintest *creak* from the floorboards. It could have been the wind.

Every muscle in his body tensed. He sidestepped to the front window beside the door, and there, he froze. He was staring at his own reflection, set against a dark brown matte.

The window had been blinded, boarded up with plywood and cardboard from the inside.

Just like Caleb's cabin.

"What the hell?" It came out in a whisper, but even hearing the faintest hint of his own voice was a comfort. As a kid, he used to talk to himself. It helped pass the long afternoons when no one else would.

He waited another couple of seconds and then he moved to the edge of the porch and dropped the four feet to the other side. Weeds rose in tangles around the drainage pipes. Tall stalks of grass brushed against his legs as he picked his way to the rear of the house.

In the back yard, the decaying remains of clotheslines still hung from rusted poles around the edges. It looked, in the dark, like a blighted forest, left on its own to rot into fossils.

An old Ford van rested on blocks at the far end. It had a camper top and reinforced shocks, sides bulging where it had been customized to support the hydraulics of a wheelchair platform. For Ramon's sister—back when she still left the house.

Sam had met her once. She hadn't spoken a word in his presence, but she had smiled a lot, and afterward, Ramon had said she had a crush on him.

Sam hiked up through the snarled dandelions to the screen door at the back of the house. The enclosed porch wasn't locked. The springs squealed when Sam pulled it open.

Sam squinted at the blackness inside.

"Ramon?"

Something sprang out of the darkness. Sam let out a yelp and stumbled back from the verge of the doorway. He clapped his hand over his mouth.

It was a cat. A stray, by the look of it. It streaked off into the grass while Sam was still trying to slow his pounding heart.

He knelt, scooped up a small pebble from the garden, and tossed it into the porch to scare away anything else that might be nesting inside. The rock bounced off the back wall and clattered to the floor.

Then—silence.

Sam waited, scarcely daring to breathe. After nearly a minute had passed, he stepped up through the doorway and onto the porch.

It smelled like dead birds and animal urine.

Ramon kept a spare key hidden atop the inner frame. Reaching for it in the dark, Sam plunged his hand through a taut network of spider webs. Skittering quarter-sized shapes with tiny legs darted in and out of the shadows.

Sam grabbed the key off the ledge and recoiled.

Inside, the odor intensified, joined, here, by that of sour milk, garbage, decaying food.

Towers of unwashed plates and glasses stood in the sink and on the counters around it. The refrigerator door hung open, unplugged, yanked away from the wall to expose the plug. There was a stereo boom box propped inside the oven.

Sam felt sick. Every time he blinked, he saw Caleb's cabin again. A trail of papers beckoned him farther inside.

All of the doors had been widened to make way for Ramon's sister's wheelchair. They left Sam feeling small and visible, a child in a household of giants.

More of Caleb's papers littered the dining room table. Overhead, the simple old ceiling lamp had been ripped from its chain and hacked into pieces, until three bare bulbs hung empty and limp from gnawed electrical wire.

The floor creaked beneath Sam's feet. As he passed into the living room, he thought he heard a rustle from somewhere behind him. He spun around and scanned the darkness.

He couldn't see anything.

There it was again—beneath the floor—the crackle of a heavy weight passing over something brittle. A basement?

Sam took a step back toward the kitchen doorway and then something a foot to his left *clicked*. A shape melted out of the shadows, silhouetted against the cracks around the blinded window.

A cold, hard muzzle jabbed against Sam's temple.

"Don't move."

Sam frowned.

He recognized that voice.

ELEVEN

"RAMON?"

"Don't move a goddamn muscle. Keep your hands where I can see them, turn toward me."

"Ramon, it's me." Sam was so relieved that Ramon was alive, that it was he and not some stranger with a gun to Sam's head, that he wanted to tug his old friend into an embrace.

Ramon didn't move. "You hear me?"

"Did I…" Sam blinked. "Ramon—Sam. Sam Mackie. Your friend. From work."

"I ain't got no friends. Not anymore."

"What are you—"

Ramon jerked, jabbed him hard with the barrel of the gun. It was a big old-fashioned shotgun, the size of a hunting rifle. Sam winced. "Hands."

He raised his hands over his head. Ramon lowered the gun just enough to pat him down.

"Now turn around."

"Ramon, this is—"

Another sharp *crack* to the side of his head. Dizzy, the world spinning, Sam obediently spun. He could feel the faintest hint of moistness seeping out into his hair. Blood. The son-of-a-bitch.

Ramon's hands traced down his back and around his chest. He wasn't looking for a gun, Sam realized; he was looking for a wire.

When Ramon was done, he drew back and gave Sam a shove toward the living room with the butt of the shotgun. Sam stumbled

over his own two feet. He was still reeling, still not sure he believed
or understood what was happening.

"Siddown."

"Ramon, why are you doing this?"

"Sit the fuck down, and don't say another word until I tell you."

Sam sat down. The couch cushions belched air that smelt of
sweat and other bodily fluids, of old marinara and spilled, sticky
beer. Sam tried to make out Ramon's face as the other man skirted
around the edge of the room. He was staying purposely in shadow.

"Okay." He'd come to a stop somewhere by the door.

Sam could make out only the faintest outline of his body and
the glint of the gun barrel, captured in a few stray glimmers of
moonlight.

"Okay. Start talking."

"Talking? About...about what?"

"Why are you here?"

"I called you. You didn't answer. They said you hadn't been to
work—"

"Who said?"

"The night operator. When I called. Looking for you." Sam
shifted, but when he leaned forward even a couple of inches, Ramon
visibly tensed and raised the gun to bear on his head. Sam raised his
hands again, placating.

There was a strained, desperate quality to Ramon's voice that
Sam had never heard before: "Why'd you come out here?"

"Are you listening to me, Ramon? I was worried about you.
Maybe the better question is, why the *hell* are you pointing a gun
at me?"

"Is it? Is that the better question? I don't think so." Ramon
edged forward. His blotchy, shadowed shape reached into his pocket and produced a piece of paper. He advanced just far enough for
the light to catch the side of his face for a fraction of a second. Fear
hung heavy around his eyes.

He flung the paper at Sam. It fluttered to the floor, three feet
away.

Sam didn't dare move.

"Pick it up."

He recognized it immediately as another of the pages they had
recovered from Caleb's cabin. It bore the signature repeating lines of

typewritten text, the random scribble of handwritten annotations. There was a black-and-white photo in the center. The page appeared to have been lifted from some kind of dossier. Sam couldn't make out the face very well, but he thought it looked a good deal like his own.

"I think the better question," Ramon growled, "is why the hell you never told me about *that.*"

"Ramon, I can't see. What is this?"

"Tellin' me you don't recognize it? That what you're tellin' me?"

"I can't *see* it, Ramon!"

"Tellin' me you don't know why they were lookin' for you your whole life? Tellin' me you didn't know they found you when you were eighteen? You telling me, Sam Mackie, that they never approached you in the hospital, brought you onboard, made you one'a them? Is that what you expect me to believe?"

"The... the hospital?" He angled the picture toward the cracks in the front door. A glint of light caught the surface. There was his face—thin, handsome, fit, a certain light in his eyes that he never realized had faded until just now.

He was holding a baby and beaming at the camera, the happiest man on Earth.

It had been two weeks since he or Ann had been to school. They'd been pushing it, trying to make it to the end of the term, but when she could no longer fit into the tiny classroom desks, and she couldn't get up without help anymore, they had realized it wasn't going to work out. Sam never told his foster parents. They were only dimly aware of his existence, anyway.

The days leading up had been defined by worry. They were kids. They had nothing. Sam would rather take their son on the road and pan for change than have him raised in the trailer park where Ann had grown up, but on their own, they didn't have a prayer of scraping together enough for a bag of diapers.

He hadn't slept for three days, and then it happened. It was early in the morning, and Sam woke up *knowing.* He drove to the trailer park. Ann was waiting for him.

Eight hours of pain and trauma later, Riley had been born.

In that first moment when he saw the baby—the tiny head, the curled little fingers, the eyes, like saucers, staring up at him in pure, infant adoration—all of it had melted away. Nothing else in the world had mattered anymore.

Some nurse at the hospital had snapped the picture with a Polaroid. Ann refused to be in it, pale, sweaty, dark bags under her eyes.

When he looked from the photograph to the dark, crazed silhouette with the gun that was supposed to be one of his best friends, Sam's mind was awash in confused memories. He wiped away the tears stinging at his eyes. "I don't understand." He heard the thickness in his voice—the grief, the remembered joy, everything he had been trying to force himself to forget for the last thirteen years. "I don't understand what you think this means."

"Oh, it ain't just that." Ramon snorted. "Turn it over."

Columns of text covered the back of the photocopied page. Sam had to squint to make out the tiny type.

Chemistry II: 9:05am – 9:59am | Rm. 13D | Babson
Algebra 5: 10:03am – 10:57am | Rm. 22 | Dale

The list went on. It was Sam's high school class schedule. There were also notes about his previous schools, addresses of foster parents, all the way back to when he was a young boy. At the bottom of the report was the date of its compilation: July 19th, 1980. Three days after Riley's birthday.

"Where did this come from, Ramon?"

"Where you think?"

"Who did this? Who—who put this together?"

"Them. *Them.* The same *them* who did all'a this. They've been following me. Everyone. Everywhere. Like they know. I've seen them watching. At work. Bob's the worst. He's got all the juniors in on it now. All of them watching, listening, trying to see what I know. They keep callin'—all these people keep callin', trying to test me, see if I'm still here, get me to give 'em *something.*"

"Ramon, you…listen to yourself. You sound…" Like Caleb. Like Caleb to the power of ten.

"I sound crazy, huh? Just another one'a them conspiracy nuts, huh?" He flipped something small and plastic across the living room table.

Sam grabbed it up and turned it over in his hands. Wires trailed out the back.

"What's that, then?"

"I don't know…"

"It's a bug! It's a *bug!* Found it behind the fridge in the kitchen. Found three more, other parts of the house. Just like the ones I found up at Caleb's place."

Sam swallowed. He was so nervous that his throat cracked, and it came out sounding like a snort.

In a flash, Ramon had the gun aimed at his forehead again. He shuffled a few steps closer, braced the butt against his shoulder. "You think this is funny?"

"I don't. I don't think it's funny, Ramon. I don't know what to think, but I'm not laughing."

"They've been following you, man. Your whole life. That's what the files say. The ones Caleb found. That's why he didn't tell you what the fuck he was doin'. 'Cause he knew you were part of this. Whatever it is. He *knew.* That envelope he left you—it had your name on it 'cause it was *about* you, not *for* you. They were looking for you all over when you were little, and when they finally found you, at the hospital, that's when they made their move."

Sam let a long moment pass before he spoke, gathering the energy to be as calm, collected, and reassuring as humanly possible. "Ramon. Whoever these people are, whatever it is they're doing, I'm not one of them. Okay?"

"Sure, you'd say that to me."

"You're telling me they searched for me for my whole childhood. They stalked me at the hospital, when I had my *son,* and twelve years later, they stole—" His voice cracked, but he forced himself to go on. "They stole him away from me. They wrote down every word I said to my wife. And you think *I did this?* You think I'm *part of this?*"

Ramon didn't answer. Sam couldn't see his eyes, but he sensed a crack in the armor.

"You watch the news at all tonight, Ramon?"

No answer.

"The news, the TV news, you watch it?"

"Took apart the TV. Thought they might have a camera hidden inside it somewhere."

"At the hospital tonight, some guy…he tried to come and he tried to take my son. Again. My son—Daniel. Ramon, he tried to— he tried to *take him away.* He hit Ann. And then these guys came and they let him go. And he's out there. Look at me, god damn it,

Ramon! Look at me! You think I came out here, you think I left them alone, helpless and vulnerable again—you think I did that just so I could fuck with you? You think I'm one of them?"

Ramon kept the shotgun level, but there was a tremor now. A tremor in the barrel.

"I came here," Sam said, "because I thought of a way to end this. Because I'm tired of running, and I need your help. Look around, Ramon. You want to live like this the rest of your life? Because I can't. I can't keep running. I can't keep worrying. For Daniel's sake. I can't."

Something rustled in the living room doorway. Ramon spun and cocked the shotgun in a single, fluid movement. As he turned, sweat glinted in beads on his forehead. He dropped the barrel as soon as he saw who it was. "Jesus Christ. Sofia."

She rolled forward into the middle of the room. She looked slighter, thinner, sicklier than the last time Sam had seen her, but there was still that glimmer of vitality in her eyes.

She couldn't move her head, neck muscles paralyzed by a progressive condition Ramon had never fully explained. She was propped against a padded cushion, and she had to spin the chair with its whirring motor to see Sam.

"Ramon." Her voice was just a whisper. "Ramon, *mi hermano*. I believe him."

ƻ

Sofia kept in the shadows as Ramon turned on a few lights and wheeled her into the bedroom. She was embarrassed. She didn't want Sam to see her like this.

Maybe Ramon had been right about the crush.

After five minutes had passed, Sam crept into the house and found his way to the lighted door. It stood ajar, and through it, reflected in a floor-to-ceiling mirror, he could just make out the bed. Sofia was nestled beneath the covers. She was so small and so frail that the stained teddy bears she clutched to her chest seemed to dwarf her. They made her look like wisp, a skeleton.

The other times he had visited, Sam had not been invited into this room. The wallpaper was a pattern of cartoon beanstalks. Towering shelves bowed beneath the weight of three dozen picture books and fairytale novellas. Battered old toys loomed down from above—porcelain dolls, wooden trains, handmade treasures that spoke to years of undying love.

Ramon was sitting over her, gently stroking her hair and whispering, softly.

It was then, for the first time, that Sam truly understood him.

Over the years, Ramon had used Sofia as an excuse to abstain from partying, a reason why he'd never found a wife, a constant force that drove his life—and often drove him away from ever changing. Caleb used to make fun of him for it. Ramon abided it as he abided everything Caleb said, but Sam had sensed he wasn't comfortable, and had never joined in.

Now, he was glad he hadn't.

This was all Ramon had left of his family. The two of them had been raised here, and for a few hours each night, as he helped Sofia through the most basic tasks even Daniel would take for granted, he got to be a father, a brother, and a little child again, all in one.

Suddenly self-conscious, Sam withdrew. He wasn't meant to see this.

This was private—sacred.

Ramon came out a few minutes later. His eyes were the slightest bit red around the rims. He pulled the hallway door shut behind him and rounded on Sam. For a heartbeat, there was an awkward silence between them.

"I'm…Sam, listen, if—"

"Don't worry about it. After tonight, I don't trust anyone either."

Ramon picked up the shotgun from where he had propped it by the door and started to open a cupboard.

Sam stopped him with a hand on his shoulder. "That," he said, "we might need."

TWELVE

SAM STAYED LOW in the back of the Cadillac as they glided up the ramp to the CW Medical parking garage and came to a halt at the security booth. The guard didn't look up from a small black-and-white TV set.

It was four-thirty in the morning. Everyone usually came in around eight, but there were always one or two of the new juniors there by six to get a jump on their colleagues. Even they weren't around yet. The garage was empty, and the guard was watching pay-per-view porn.

Ramon swiped his card through the reader. Bob had already deactivated Sam's. The automatic arm went up. Just like that, they were inside.

By the time Sam and Ramon had worked out a plan, there wasn't time to go back to the hospital. They stopped at a 7-Eleven along the way, and Sam called to check in with Ann from a payphone. She still didn't sound angry, but her answers were short and clipped. BJ Cunningham had gone home. His replacement was an older guy with a limp, but he seemed nice enough.

Sam hung up with a heavy heart. *Get through this*, he'd told himself, *and it can all be over.*

Now, sprawled on the carpet in the back of the Cadillac, Sam clutched the shotgun to his chest. His hands were sweating. His heart pounded in his chest. He wasn't used to doing this kind of thing.

All his life, he'd been the pacifist. He'd never been in a school-yard fight, even once. The more violent his foster parents had been, the more deeply he had retreated into his bedroom, the more removed he'd grown at school.

Ramon brought the car to a halt in his assigned parking space. He flipped the engine off. Sam heard rustling up front, and then the sheet he'd pulled over himself was lifted.

"This ain't gonna work." Ramon's eyes flitted around through the rear windows. "Cameras everywhere here. And people. You see the way that guard was pretending not to watch me?"

"He was watching the tits on TV."

"He was watching me. Out of the corner of his eye. You couldn't see from down there. He knows what we're up to."

Sam sat up and stopped Ramon from reaching for the keys. "Nobody knows what we're up to. Stick to the plan. We have the upper hand."

Ramon drew in a deep breath. His hands were shaking. Christ, they were both in their forties. They'd spent lives behind desks in cubicles that all looked the same. "You get us killed, I'm gonna have Sofia kick Ann's ass."

In spite of himself, Sam mustered a smile. "I'd like to see her try."

The familiar, musty smell of the stairwell fell in around Sam like a worn blanket. He squinted upward through the shaft in the center. Fluorescent lights flickered from every third floor. The others were left off during the night to save electricity.

There were only security cameras on the landings with lights. Skulking up through the shadows, Sam shrank back when he came to the first pool of pale white. He waited for Ramon to catch his breath, avoid suspicion. The two of them stood together, watching the automated arc of the lens.

It swung back and forth, regular, predictable.

"You got it?"

Ramon shrugged. "Not really. Best I can."

"You got it."

They edged forward, careful to move their legs together. They were roughly the same size, Ramon perhaps a little larger around the midriff. But Sam was wearing a jacket to conceal the gun. If some astute security officer was watching the feed closely enough, he would probably notice the extra girth in Ramon's shadow.

Halfway across, Sam felt the shotgun slipping down his chest. He tried to nudge it back with one wrist, but if he made a full grab for it, his elbow would show up to the cameras. Silently, he tried to urge Ramon to go faster.

It slid down past his stomach. The butt jutted out from the bottom of his jacket. Just as it was about to clatter to the floor, they made it to the shadows at the bottom of the next staircase, and Sam scooped it back.

Ramon had missed it all.

Two more floors, and they came to the final door before the roof. Both of them hesitated. They looked at each other. This was the point of no return. At this moment, they could still slip back downstairs, sneak past the cameras, and drive out of the garage as though nothing at all had happened.

"Sam, man, look, I dunno if—"

Sam grabbed the knob and tugged open the door. The electronic lock flashed red.

This was it. There was no turning back.

The twelfth floor was for the top executives in the company. Clayton Wesley had an office here, though no one had seen him in the building for at least half a decade. The corridors were wider, walls lined with wood paneling and framed, back-lit artwork.

Even the light bulbs had been replaced with natural daylight filaments that gave the impression of walking beneath the shimmering rays of the sun.

There was an atrium in the middle, a nest of plants, benches, fountains, and flagstones that flourished beneath a line of skylights. In the back corner, a coffee cart, not yet open for the morning, sported a tasteful menu of espressos, Italian sodas, sandwiches, salads, fresh fruit.

Ramon shook his head as they snuck past. "How many years you think we'd have to work in this place to get a spot up here?"

Sam glanced over and flattened himself against the wall as a security camera at the end of the passage shifted toward them. "I think it's already too late for us."

They halted before a mahogany door. A plaque of laser-engraved crystal hung just to the right. *J.G. Tillman, Executive Vice-President, Research & Development.*

Sam slipped the ID badge from Caleb's cabin out of his pocket. He turned it over in his hands, and then, with a deep breath, he pressed it against the magnetic card reader.

The small LED at the top of the terminal flashed red.

Sam's heart stopped.

Tillman must have canceled the badge the moment he realized it was missing. They were shut out and stranded in the middle of a floor where neither of them had any clearance.

A *clunk* from somewhere behind Sam and Ramon made both of them jump and whirl. Edging to the end of the hall, they craned their neck around the corner, through the white Roman columns to the atrium.

The rollaway shutters at the front of the coffee cart now stood open. A trim young woman with a bun of brown hair was tying a green apron around her back as she read over a printout of pre-orders for the day.

"Go," Ramon mouthed.

Sam shook his head. "One more try."

Ramon protested in whispers the whole way back to the door. Sam squeezed his eyes shut, hurried through a quick mental prayer, and then swiped the card again.

The reader flashed red.

And then it *beeped.*

With a *click*, the lock disengaged and the door popped open. They hadn't waited long enough, the first time.

Ramon stood and stared. Sam wasted no time. Edging the door wider, he slipped inside.

Early morning light illuminated the outer office in a delicate, pale blue. A desk sat positioned with its back to a broad window overlooking downtown. It was spotless—a lamp, a keyboard, a flat-panel monitor. A small stack of manila folders and newspaper articles. Tillman's secretary.

A large relief globe the size of a tractor tire stood in a polished wooden frame near the door to the inner office. It was closed. Venetian blinds covered all of the windows.

Nowhere was there any hint of who in the hell J.G. Tillman was. There wasn't a personal touch to be found.

Ramon eased the door shut as, out in the atrium, the young brunette barista dropped something, and swore. The echoes of her voice fell to near-silence as soon as the lock reengaged.

All of a sudden, it was stiflingly quiet. Sam slipped the shotgun from his jacket. The sound of the zipper against the scratched wooden butt was loud enough to make him cringe.

He'd never used a gun before, but as soon as Ramon had heard his plan, he'd insisted Sam be the one to carry it.

"Door." Sam's own voice almost made him jump.

Ramon stepped up to the inner door, and pulled it open after Sam ran the ID across the secondary reader.

Gun braced against his stomach, he thrust the muzzle in ahead of him. Most of the Vice-Presidents didn't get into the office until nine-thirty or ten, but Sam wasn't taking any chances.

A couple of paces into the room, he stopped short.

The office was empty.

Not just unoccupied—

Empty.

There was no furniture. Blank white walls stared out across a barren carpet covered in nothing but dust. A musty odor hung in the air, as though the room had not been occupied or even opened in months—if not years.

There was a single safe set into the innermost wall, door shut, held fast.

Sam glanced over his shoulder, mystified, as Ramon crept in behind him.

Together, they stared at the featureless vacuum.

Sam's spirits sank.

This had been his plan—his one hope of preemptively striking back and forcing some answers from one of the few with concrete connections he still had. This had to work, because there was nothing else.

Ramon cleared his throat. "So now what?"

Sam gulped. "Now… This changes nothing. Now we wait."

"For what? He ain't comin'. Whoever this J.G. Tillman is, we're not finding him here."

"There wasn't any dust on his secretary's desk."

"So?"

"So they still come in. Answer calls, handle the day-to-day stuff for him."

"Yeah, so?"

Sam lowered the shotgun and nudged the inner door shut. "So they're going to know where we can find him."

"Sam... It's just gonna be some innocent kid."

"If they're innocent, they'll probably talk with a shotgun in their face, won't they?"

"It's a—this is a crime, Sam. A *crime*. It's against the law, what we're doing."

Sam stiffened and clenched his jaw. "So's kidnapping, assault, and murder."

"So—what? You're going to fight fire with fire? An eye for an eye?"

"No. I'm going to protect my family. You want to go, Ramon, go. You can explain to Sofia why you'll never feel safe leaving her home alone again. Your call."

Ramon furrowed his brow, and stayed back as Sam took up a discrete position by the Venetian blinds. But he didn't leave.

Sam was more relieved than he would ever have let on.

2

At the edge of downtown, where the skyscrapers turned to warehouses and smut palaces, there was a tall, narrow smokestack that rose up into the clouds. As Sam sat, waiting for the morning to wear on, his eyes began to droop. The sooty chimney turned darker, grew wider, joined with his eyelashes and became, for an instant, The Tower.

A *thump* on the other side of the blinds brought Sam fully awake in a heartbeat. He was disoriented until he saw Ramon, the empty room, the shotgun in his arms. Ramon had drifted off, lying flat on the carpet.

Summoned by another sound on the other side of the inner wall, Sam gingerly got to his knees and edged himself around until he could see out between the bottom two Venetian blinds.

A person in a chocolate-colored business suit passed back and forth before the windows. He dropped into the chair behind the secretary's desk. He was a young man, closely-cropped hair, the picture of slick, corporate conformity. A wireless telephone earpiece clung to his ear. He was talking as he booted up his computer and logged in with a password.

Sam shrank back. The secretary's eyes flicked toward the inner office. Sam was afraid he might have been spotted, but then the young man laughed into the phone and spun in his chair to peer out the window.

Extending one leg, Sam nudged Ramon.

He grunted and jerked with a half-snore. Then his eyes fluttered open. "What—'"

"*Shh!*"

Realization hardened his groggy features. Ramon sat up and dusted himself off. As he crossed the room and joined Sam at the window, he accidentally brushed one of the blinds. It swayed and spat dust into the air.

Inwardly, Sam cursed. He held his breath, waiting.

Nothing from the other side.

When he worked up the courage to look again, the secretary was still sitting with his back to them, facing the window, looking over a couple of stapled packets of paper.

Ramon arched his eyebrows at Sam. "So…?"

Sam looked from Ramon to the gun and then to the window. *So.* It was one thing to lie in wait for J.G. Tillman, but to assault an assistant who only answered phones—that was something else altogether.

"Now he's logged on, we could check his computer when he goes for coffee." Even at a whisper, Sam barely breathed. The sound-proofed walls were so impregnable that it created the impression of talking to each other inside a sterile, steel drum.

"What, just sit another three hours? And what if he logs out when he goes, anyway?"

"Well, what you suggesting?"

"Suggesting? *I'm* not suggesting anything. I wasn't the one who—"

Without warning, the door swung open.

THIRTEEN

A HAND GRABBED RAMON by the shoulder and yanked him to his feet. He didn't struggle. Sam wondered why until the small, oblong, black-and-silver shape of a taser came into view.

"I'm going to count to three." The secretary's voice was as flat, measured, and restrained as his appearance. "If I don't know everything about who you are and what you're doing here, I'm going to press this button. Then, it will hurt. Then, we'll start over. One…"

Ramon flicked an involuntary glance toward Sam. Sam was hiding with his back plastered against the inner wall, just around the corner. The secretary noticed. A pristine, polished black shoe edged over the threshold.

"Two… Got someone stashed away in here? I can't hear you. Apparently this concept—"

The secretary's face appeared around the corner. Sam brandished the shotgun in front of him and lunged. The butt connected with the side of the young man's head. It made a sick, dull *crack*. His legs gave way and his body crumpled beneath him.

The taser bounced to the carpet at his side.

Ramon scooped it up and staggered back, one hand over his mouth.

Blood leaked from the secretary's lip. He moaned when Sam knelt at his side and nudged his ribs with the barrel of the shotgun. "Hey." Sam prodded a little harder. "Hey. Talk to me, damn it…"

"Sam." Ramon straightened, standing over him in the inner doorway.

"Where's J.G. Tillman? Where the hell is Tillman?"

"*Sam!*"

Sam looked up and then followed Ramon's gaze to the far side of the outer office—to the glinting lens of a security camera. It was propped atop the bookshelf beside the secretary's desk, out of view from the entrance, from where they had first scanned the room.

"Oh, shit," Sam breathed.

"Run!" Ramon dashed for the door.

Sam took a halting step after him. He tripped over the secretary's body, and the young man groaned and made a feeble attempt to roll over. Recovering his balance, Sam hesitated.

Ramon already had the door halfway open. "*Sam!*"

"Where is he? Where's Tillman?"

The secretary spat a dribble of blood onto the carpet. "Mackie. You're Sam Mackie." He twisted the grimace on his face into a grin.

Somewhere outside, footsteps—hasty and purposeful—sounded on the flagstones of the courtyard.

"Fuck it, I ain't waitin' any longer." Ramon yanked the door the rest of the way open and took off down the hallway.

Sam deliberated a half-second longer and then turned to sprint after him.

Barreling around the corner, he ran head-on into a slim woman with platinum blonde hair and a cardboard carrier of lattes. She yelped and staggered back as coffee splashed all over her dress and the carpet at her feet.

Sam shot past her.

Ramon, already to the end of the passage, wrestled the stairwell door open.

Shouts of surprise followed Sam down the hall, doors slamming at his wake as word spread that a madman with a gun was loose in the building.

Sam burst onto the twelfth-floor landing, and pounded down the metal steps. He caromed off the handrails at the next landing and plunged into another flight. Ramon was half a floor ahead of him. He cried out when the ninth-floor door banged open. It was the junior who worked the cubicle across from Sam's, the friend of Malleson's. He had a joint clutched between his fingers, and he'd been going for a lighter. His eyes went wide when he saw the two of them racing toward him.

"Mackie? Juarez—"

Two security guards with drawn nightsticks shoved him out of the way and made a grab for Ramon.

They didn't see Sam until he swatted one with the shotgun and butted the other in the stomach. Sam didn't wait for an encore. When he rounded on the spiky-haired junior, the kid threw up his hands and staggered back to grasp at the door.

Sam grabbed Ramon by a shirtsleeve and yanked him down around the next corner.

More footsteps thundered onto the stairs above them as they passed by the fifth floor, then the fourth, then the third. Shouting echoed up and down the shaft. Pulsing emergency lights flickered above every door.

"Sam!" Ramon stumbled to a halt, and Sam crashed into him from behind.

Two guards in heavy Kevlar vests were standing at the mouth of the garage door. They spun and glanced up at the sound of Ramon's voice.

Sam wheeled the gun around and fired off a load of buckshot into the plaster wall above their heads. The recoil forced the air from Sam's lungs, and the sound of the explosion left his ears deaf and ringing.

The guards dropped to their knees and covered their ears.

Seizing the opportunity, Sam bolted past them. Ramon was hot on his heels.

They pounded across the parking garage. "Keys!" Sam shouted over his shoulder. His own voice sounded distant beneath the buzzing in his ears.

Ramon struggled with the lock for several seconds before he got it open. Sam glanced back just in time to see the two guards sprinting out of the stairwell door.

"Ramon!"

With a *click*, the passenger lock popped open. Sam dove inside and slammed the door shut behind him. The Cadillac's engine roared to life. The giant car lurched backward, skidding around to smash a garbage can into a sideways roll.

"Hold on." Ramon floored it.

The Cadillac shot toward the security booth.

Sam noticed the spikes protruding from the ground beneath the automatic gate arm at the last moment. He shouted and pointed out the windshield.

Ramon jerked the wheel and veered into the oncoming lane just as a sleek, dark green BMW glided down around the sloping ramp. The Cadillac skidded and smashed through the gate. The BMW's tires locked. It ground to a halt six inches from the tail of the Cadillac as they raced past it and up the tunnel toward daylight.

Streaming rays of sun showered the windshield. Sam let out a long breath.

They'd made it.

Two seconds before Ramon steered onto Seventh Street, a CW security van screeched to a halt in their path.

Sam reached across, grabbed the wheel, and jerked it at the last possible moment. The Cadillac bucked around, hopped the curb, and slammed into the van's rear bumper. Ramon stomped on the accelerator, and with a shriek of metal on metal, they leapt across the left-turn lane and shot off through the intersection as the light turned red behind them.

Sam fell back against the seat. He was sweating, trembling, weak with spent adrenaline.

"What…what the fuck're we gonna do?" Ramon checked the rear-view mirror again. "Where're we gonna go?"

"The hospital," Sam said as he squeezed his eyes shut. "Please. Take me to the hospital."

He tried not to think of how things had gone wrong—of how little hope he had left for resolving any of this. All he could think of now were Ann and Daniel. That, and the way J.G. Tillman's secretary had said Sam's name: With recognition—as though Sam couldn't even begin to imagine what still lay ahead.

ა

Sam watched Ramon go and then spun around to make a bee-line for the temporary new entrance at the other side of the hospital. A couple of high school kids had been dropped into uniforms and conscripted as valets to accommodate the newly-limited parking situation. A line of empty cars stretched before the curb, waiting to be parked. As Sam passed them, a Rolls-Royce caught his eye.

Smooth, sleek, the ivory-colored Silver Shadow sported windows so darkly-tinted that the interior was utterly invisible from the sidewalk.

Shepherd, the replacement guard, stood when he saw Sam coming. He flashed Sam a friendly smile and gave a little wave with a rolled-up newspaper he'd torn apart for the crossword.

"Mr. Mackie. Nice to meet you."

Sam nodded.

"You got a visitor, just FYI."

"A what?" Sam shoved the door open.

Ann sat perched at the foot of Daniel's bed. Pulled up before her in one of the rolling chairs was a stooped old man with white hair. His clothing was immaculate, cashmere sweater draped like silk over his shoulders. A Rolex glinted from his wrist as he swiveled around.

The instant he saw the man's face, Sam recognized him.

It was Clayton Wesley.

FOURTEEN

WESLEY HAD HEARD. Somehow, he'd already heard what had happened at the office that morning, and he had come to personally place Sam under arrest. Trapped in jail, separated from his family, there would be no way to protect Ann and Daniel.

Sam's first instinct was to turn and bolt from the room, and if not for his wife and son, he might have done just that.

Clayton Wesley stood with ease and offered Sam a smile of sparkling, sharklike perfection. "I remember you." He spoke with the same booming, lulling majesty of a preacher at the head of a white marble cathedral. He glided across the room and took Sam's hand in his. "Clayton Wesley. And you are Mr. Sam Mackie. Though, as I was telling your wife, it's such a shame that we always meet under circumstances of such grave import."

"Mr. Wesley..." Sam could barely speak. His voice was hoarse, tongue a dead, dry weight in his mouth. He felt like a child in the principal's office. "Mr. Wesley, I want to—I want to tell you, whatever you've heard..."

"What I've heard is everything."

Sam flinched. "Then...then I can only say..."

"It saddens me, Sam. It saddens me, news like this."

"Mr. Wesley—sir. I have no excuse other than...I was only trying to... I was following what information I had, trying to do the best thing for my son. For my family..."

Wesley arched two large, bushy white caterpillar eyebrows. "Samuel Mackie, what ever are you talking about?"

Sam paused. He squinted at the old man.

Ann rose from the bed behind him. "Sam," she said. "I think you should listen to what he has to say."

"What he has to…" Sam gulped. "You're not here about the… the office…?"

"Ah." Clayton Wesley chuckled. Still holding Sam's hand, he closed his other palm atop it in a gesture of equal parts reassurance and captivity. "I can see the cause for your concern. But you should know that my sympathies lie only with you, Sam."

"They… do?"

"Mr. Tillman, I'm afraid, abused his position of power. It has come to my attention that his activities of late have left him associating with some distinctly—unsavory characters. He's been let go, Sam. I do not hold you responsible for anything you have done this morning."

Sam gaped. Of all possible responses he could have conjured up in his wildest dreams, this would have been beyond his imagination. Jail, he had expected. Instant termination, a shouting match, guilt and belittlement, over twenty years of service ending in a single, fell swoop.

But—nothing at all?

Wesley's grin broadened. There was something about him that left Sam wondering when the other shoe would drop. "My presence here, Sam, is not motivated by discipline. I came out of a personal concern for one of my oldest employees and his family." He rounded on Daniel, approaching the bed to take the boy's arm in his giant, bearish hands.

Sam had to swallow the protective instinct to leap on Wesley and wrestle him away.

"And to offer you an opportunity," Wesley went on.

"What kind of *opportunity?*"

"To save your son, Sam. To save your son."

ᔕ

There was a restaurant adjoining the hospital for the wealthier relatives of the sick and the wounded who would not tolerate the cafeteria. Ann didn't want to leave Daniel alone, but Wesley placated her by assigning his own driver to join Officer Shepherd at the door.

"He fought alongside me, over in Korea." Wesley told her. "I would trust him with my life. I have, in fact."

Ann left Shepherd her number, and ignored the signs at the front of the restaurant prohibiting cell phones from the dining hall. She turned the ringer all the way up and set it on the table beside her crystal water glass.

Sam had never eaten anywhere so dazzling. Even after things had gotten better for them—thanks, entirely, to his employment at CW—Sam and Ann had never been rich, by any means. On the rare occasions that they left Riley with a friend and snuck out for a night together, they usually wound up going somewhere with takeout so they could drive to a secluded spot in the forest. There, like teenagers, they would flop out on the hood of the car and watch stars through gaps in the trees.

Sam blinked over the ornate foliage of the centerpiece—lilies, roses, orchids. It was still Ann, across from him. Still the same little girl he'd fallen in love with back in high school.

Wesley ordered for them. Half of the menu was in French, and most of the dishes had names Sam would not have recognized in any language. It was surreal—sitting here across from the chairman and CEO of the very company whose offices he had broken into with a shotgun just a few short hours ago.

Sam glanced to Ann and caught her looking at the door, checking the time on her phone. Feeling the distance from Daniel. He drew in a shallow breath. He knew how she was feeling.

But Clayton Wesley was in no hurry. "The murals here." He nodded to the walls. "I've met the artist. I ate here almost every day while I was overseeing the construction of my wing. In the hospital."

"Oh." Ann folded her napkin into her lap and leaned forward. Doing her best to seem attentive—the prim, appreciative guest. Doing her best to avoid asking the question that was burning on both of their tongues. "I didn't see *Clayton Wesley* on the directory."

Wesley took a sip of chardonnay. "Vanity is not one of my interests. The more people want to look at you, I have found, the more you wish they would look somewhere else. I named it after my sister. The Agatha Pryce Center for Cancer Research & Treatment."

Sam frowned. Something about that name bothered him. Agatha Pryce. In a way, familiar.

"But I didn't invite you to lunch to boast about my achievements

or my predilections in interior design." Clayton Wesley squared his
shoulders. "I invited you here because I think I might be able to help
your son."

"Help him?"

Sam and Ann both sat forward.

"I understand he's suffering from some variety of radiation poisoning."

"How do you…" Ann blinked. "How do you know that?"

Wesley smiled. "Please. Do not be alarmed. Nobody's running
around telling the world about your son's…malady. I performed a
cursory examination myself. As we were talking. You see, I have seen
this before."

"You…have?"

"In the military."

Sam stiffened.

"In my time, there were a variety of developments in the chemical weapon field. Not all of them are fatal; not everything is the next
Agent Orange or Anthrax—what have you. As a veteran, myself, it
has been a mission of mine to dedicate a sizable portion of my business to helping victims in the armed services. I won't go into
details—"

"Go into details." Sam grimaced as the waiter ducked between
them. Wesley had ordered a calamari-and-marinara appetizer. It
smelled exquisite.

By the time he had gone, Wesley was spinning a baby squid onto
his fork. "We're not here to discuss problems, Sam. We're here to discuss solutions. I know we haven't talked much over the years, but
you should know that I have been aware of your progress in my company for some considerable time. Your hardships trouble me. Losing
a son like you did…"

Sam reached beneath the table and found Ann's hand. It was as
clammy as his own.

"I would hate to see that happen a second time. That is all. To
me, all of Clayton Wesley Medical is one big family." Wesley glanced
up from his plate and stopped chewing. "I am sorry. I'm being most
…indiscrete. I am not trying to deepen your emotional turmoil in
this…difficult time. As I mentioned up in your son's room, I wish
only to offer you an opportunity."

"With all due respect, Mr. Wesley, what are we talking about here? I still don't have any idea."

"I can cure him, Sam. I can cure him. But not here. I need him in my own facility. I need your permission to move him out of the hospital."

ග

"Absolutely not." Ann shook her head as they stepped into the hospital elevator. She interrupted before Sam could protest: "Sam, they tried it once with that... that *asshole* who came for him last night. Now you want to turn around and *sign him over?*"

"This isn't the same *they*." Sam could hear it in his own voice – the desperation, the need to believe what he was saying. The need for a hope of any kind, however small.

If there were any other way to save his son, he would have jumped at it in a heartbeat. Between Caleb, the reports, the tapped phone lines, the gunman, it was hard to trust anyone. But if there was a chance—the tinniest chance—that Wesley was promising the truth, that Daniel could be better, that there was a way to wake him up right now—they had to try.

It was their duty to try. As a parent, as his father, Sam's purpose for being was to save his son. So far, he had been failing.

"Look..." He swallowed. "Look, I don't like this, either. But Wesley—I've known him for twenty-five years, Ann. He paid our mortgage. He paid for Daniel's diapers. Hell, he paid for our groceries when you and I were spending every waking moment turning the city upside down for Riley."

Ann clenched her jaw. She fixed her eyes on the elevator readout. But Sam could feel her weakening. He took her hand, even when she tried to pull away.

"He has a billion dollars in the bank. He started with nothing, and he's built one of the largest companies in the world. If he thinks he can help Daniel—make him better..."

"Why, Sam? Why is he helping us? Did it even occur to you to ask yourself that? Why would he give a shit? And don't tell me—"

The elevator doors slid open. Fifth floor. Two brothers and a sister bustled aboard, in the midst of a loud argument. Sam and Ann were pushed to the back of the elevator car, pressed up against the mirrored glass.

"Don't tell me," Ann hissed beneath their shouting, "that you believe his little song and dance about the 'CW family.' You think the CEO really gives a shit about a midlevel distributing executive who hasn't been promoted in eight years? Nobody's that nice, Sam. Not even billionaires. *Especially* not billionaires."

Sam felt the blood rushing to his cheeks. "You know, just because your family wouldn't lift a finger doesn't mean everyone's the same."

The elevator *dinged* and Sam fought his way through the crowd to the doors before Ann could lash out at him and make things even worse.

She stalked after him into the hall. Shepherd stood up when he saw them coming and sat back down again as soon as Ann opened her mouth:

"You think I don't care about him, is that it? You think that just because you forced me out of his life once that I severed all ties? I'm not just sitting here through the nights for appearances, Sam!"

Sam yanked open the door to Daniel's room. He was conscious, all of a sudden, of the dozens of faces poking out from other rooms up and down the corridor. Sam and Ann—the problem family. Broken glass, cops, fights in the halls. They were getting a reputation.

Wesley's driver got to his feet as Ann followed Sam into the room.

"Mister and Missus—"

"Get the hell away from my son," Ann barked at him.

The driver blinked a couple of times and then stiffly turned to leave. Ann kicked the door shut behind him, but when she rounded on Sam, her eyes were on Daniel.

A charged silence fell between them.

"Look—"

"I'm scared, Sam. Okay? I'm scared. I don't know what the hell is going on, but I..."

"I'm sorry."

She nodded.

"I shouldn't have said that—back in the elevator. That was..."

Sam crossed the room and took her hands in his. She looked up into his eyes and he saw it again—that old beauty, that old intoxicating innocence and passion that he'd fallen head-over-hells in love with when he was just a kid. It was still there. "It was pointless. And cruel. If you want to keep him here, see what we can get out of Doctor Gideon—then fine. Let's keep him here."

Ann shook her head. "No, I ... I don't know. Do you really think Wesley can help him?"

Both of them turned toward the bed.

Daniel hadn't moved even a fraction of an inch. The covers were drawn up to his chin, pillows dwarfing his little head, moppish brown hair hanging over his eyes. He looked like he was sleeping. So close and yet still so far away.

"I don't know," Sam said. "I have no idea. But if there's even a— a glimmer of hope... Even the faintest chance... I think there's no way we can't try. We have to try." Sam's eyes were burning when he looked back at Ann. "Fuck, I love him so much. So damn much. I didn't—I haven't been... I don't think he knows it. I don't know if I knew it but God damn it, I can't... We can't lose him. We *can't*. I'll do anything. I'll do *anything* in the world. I don't care about anything else anymore."

"Oh, God." It was more of a sob as Ann stepped into his arms. They held each other for a long time, rocking back and forth in an awkward dance of mutual desperation. "If we do this, we don't let him out of our sight. Not once. Not even for a moment."

"Of course not."

Ann drew in a deep breath. At last, they drew apart. "Okay," she said. "Okay, Sam."

∽

Doctor Gideon didn't protest when Sam brought him the last of the paperwork. Perhaps he was simply weary, overtaxed with too many other patients, or perhaps he was tired of all of the trouble Sam and Daniel had already brought the hospital.

"I hope you know what you're doing," he said. Then he signed on the dotted line.

Sam was not surprised when Clayton Wesley steered them toward the Rolls-Royce he had seen on the way into the hospital. The driver ran around to open the back door for them, exposing an interior of leather smooth as silk, and the color of pearls.

Ducking, Sam squinted at the wood trim and polished accents. "There isn't enough room for all of us."

"I have another vehicle." Wesley motioned toward the lot, where a gunmetal-gray Range Rover was crawling toward them. "Better suited for your son and his medical needs. We'll stay a car-length away the whole—"

"We ride together."

"Sam. This will be more comfortable. I hope you appreciate, it is not just anyone I invite along to—"

"We ride," Sam said, "together."

The back of the Range Rover had been gutted to make room for runners that could accommodate a wheelchair and some oxygen tanks, a cabinet full of fluids and IV bags. The drivers of the two vehicles lifted Daniel, strapped to a chair, onto the tailgate and then rolled him inside.

There was a jump seat at the head of the stretcher catches. Ann took it. Sam climbed into the front, beside the driver.

Clayton Wesley was plainly displeased at being made to ride alone in his limousine. He made a show of tossing first his jacket and then his ivory-headed cane into the trunk while the Range Rover waited.

They cruised onto the road together, moving as a convoy. The city fell back as they sped onto the highway. Sam twisted around in his seat to watch his family—his life—in the back. A monitor was lashed to Daniel's wrist, sending a computerized pulse with each of his heartbeats.

The exit they took was not one Sam recognized. Nearer to town than Ramon's or Caleb's houses, it was still well outside the commercial districts where most of the population spent their time.

Sam could sense Ann's mounting unease as they rolled through neighborhoods with cyclone fences. Bars hung before the windows of nearly every house they passed, graffiti scrawled on walls and curbs. An entire public park was roped off altogether, the old play structure that stood in the middle reduced to a blackened char.

After they nosed into the parking lot of a large, abandoned mall, Sam asked the driver where they were going.

"Mr. Wesley likes his peace and quiet for his work." The driver nodded through the windshield. "The new facility is just on the other side of this property. You'd never know it was here. That is how it is supposed to be."

Sam frowned. Through the Range Rover's tinted windows, rusted signs drifted by—an old A&W burger joint, a crumbling Montgomery-Ward department store, missing half the letters from its rooftop sign. Many of the windows had been boarded-up. A lone shopping cart sat forlornly in the middle of the cracked sidewalk before the entrance to an old video arcade.

He met Ann's gaze. She was squeezing Daniel's limp hand. Not about to let go of him anywhere near here.

The driver chuckled under his breath. "Don't worry. I was scared the first day I came to work, too. Just wait till you get inside."

A small lake sprawled on the other side of the shopping center. Willows and dense vegetation bunched in on either side to overhang the murky shores. Across the water, a slightly newer-looking office building rose up from between the trees. It looked to be a restored power substation, windows replaced with tinted glass that reflected the green water back at itself.

There were no official signs.

Although it appeared the private road feeding off the back of the mall traced the bank of the lake straight to the opposite side, they had to stop halfway there for the Rolls-Royce's driver to get out an open a barbed-wire gate. That made Sam a little more comfortable. At least there was a nod toward security.

As they passed through, he swiveled around to read the sign that hung from the open gateway.

Private Property. Area monitored by video security and patrolled by armed response units.

"Armed response?"

The driver grinned. "I told you. Mr. Wesley takes his privacy quite seriously."

There were two women and a man of middle age—all dressed, head to toe, in white—waiting at the main entrance to the office building when they pulled up under the eaves. They moved to the Rolls-Royce before Wesley got out and redirected them.

"Mr. and Mrs. Mackie." The woman on the right moved forward and shook their hands. Her skin was warm and smooth, nails immaculate, smile right out of a magazine ad. "We've heard so much about you and your son. My name is Doctor Francie Ko, and I want to give you my personal assurance, that here, he is to be treated with the utmost care." She spoke with the slightest of British accents. Everything about her seemed perfect—and planned that way.

Ann still looked a little pale, but the woman's confident manner and frank reassurance seemed to ease her concern a little. She stayed close to Sam and kept a hand on the back of Daniel's head as the other doctors lifted his wheelchair out of the Range Rover.

"Sam." Clayton Wesley ambled over to them. "And Ann. Welcome to my newest facility, and please do excuse the surroundings. As we make this arrangement more official over the next several years, we plan on gentrifying the neighborhood and pouring resources back to the community. For now, though, it's nice to have a little peace and quiet."

Sam peered up at the building's ruddy façade. Old brick at the bottom gave way to larger faces of chipped stone, higher up. Concrete struts buttressed the first several floors, and the windows, narrow as slits, were each spaced at least ten feet apart. The place looked as though it had been built to withstand the apocalypse.

Sam licked his lips. "What is it, exactly, that you do here?"

Clayton Wesley smiled. "Research, development, and experimentation. Shaping the very future of the globe." He waved at the doctors with his ivory cane, and Ann followed them as they wheeled Daniel toward the entrance. "And now, Sam Mackie, I'm inviting you to take a glimpse at that future."

Potted plants filled the lobby, the floor done up in marble. A directory stood near a pair of bullet-shaped elevators—brushed steel and backlit lettering. Beyond partial walls that cut across beneath the high ceilings, Sam noticed what appeared to be stacked tables and dining chairs, even an old cash register.

"I do apologize for the décor." Wesley nudged Sam with his cane, drawing him back as Ann stepped ahead to keep pace with the doctors. "We're still transitioning into this site. It used to be a—I don't know what it was. Offices. Something. They had the most unrefined sense of style. This was a restaurant, if so it may be called."

They paused before an elevator whose doors parted after only a moment. Blankets and painter's tarps hung from the walls. The control panel protruded from a small section of cut-away fabric. The buttons were missing, exposing bare switches and wires.

"Ah. We would be saddled with this one." Wesley grimaced.

"The other car is finished already. The rare—and, to be frank, dare I say *deep-pocketed*—investor is allowed an occasional tour of this building. We have a whole path set up for them. Makes it look like we're a little farther along, but I trust you understand where all of this is going."

"Sure." Sam watched the doors shudder twice before finally closing.

Wesley smirked. "Sam. Your faith is evaporating before my eyes. Trust me, my boy. We moved in here only three months ago, and my first priority has always been the clockwork beneath the surface. Your son…" Ann tensed as he reached down to pat Daniel on the shoulder in his wheelchair. "Your son will be back on his feet in no time."

Without a working readout, Sam wasn't sure where the elevator stopped. As he stepped out, his misgivings diminished, slightly.

The corridor ahead of him—while, flanked on both sides by plywood structuring, unfinished sheetrock, and construction plastic—sparkled, spotless. The smell of fresh paint filled the air. A desk had been set up with a pair of brand new, top-of-the-line Silicon Graphics workstations that Sam recognized as newer models of the same systems they used at the CW office.

"This is our surgical wing." Doctor Francie Ko swiveled around to walk backward down the passage, like a tour guide. "You'll notice two state-of-the-art theaters up on the right. One is fully-operational. That's where we're going to try and help little Daniel here. The other's still in the plumbing and electrical stage. Subcontractors." She rolled her eyes.

Sam caught a glimpse of stacked tiles and exposed pipes through one of the two doors. The other was closed.

"What do you…" Ann gulped. "What kinds of… procedures did you have in mind?"

Ko looked to Wesley.

"Nothing dangerous, Ann. Believe me, Daniel is safer here than anywhere else in the world. I wanted you to see all of this, but next, we're heading up to where the three of you will be staying while we complete our work."

"We can—we can stay here?"

Wesley grinned at her. "This is not a county hospital. We recognize the needs of our patients and we do our best to cater to them." He winked at Sam. "They're our family."

"What kind of timeline are we looking at?" Sam asked.

"Ah, yes."

They came around full-circle and one of the other doctors pressed the elevator call button.

"I was retaining that as something of a surprise, but I suppose it is reasonable to be curious. I think you will be pleased." Wesley bowed and motioned for them to precede him into the elevator. "You see, while I can offer no promises about the scale, I can virtually guarantee you will witness results this very evening."

The rest of the ride up, all Sam could do was struggle to contain his excitement. He saw the same cautious glee on Ann's face—not quite believing, not quite allowing herself to buy into all of the smoke and mirrors, but wanting to so badly that it was impossible to remain completely at a distance. They would see results. Tonight.

For the first time since all of this began, Sam began to believe that Daniel was actually going to be okay.

Wesley led them around a corner and down another hall to a blank white door. "Not the Ritz, I'm afraid, but we've got grand plans for the residence area as well. Bringing in some top architects next month." He nodded to Ko, who leaned in to unlock the door.

The room could have been lifted from any hotel Sam had ever stayed in. There was a queen-sized bed, a small television, a floral-print couch beneath a window overlooking the lake. The walls were freshly-painted in bright white, and they seemed a little flimsy. They rose a few inches shy of the brick ceiling.

"Ghastly," Wesley said when he noticed Sam looking upward. "One of the first things I plan on having changed. But if this meets your needs…?"

"What about…?" Ann gulped and shifted her hand in Daniel's hair. "He can stay with us—can't he?" The question was directed at Dr. Ko, but again, she deferred to Wesley.

"Well…" He seemed reluctant.

"If it's a problem, we can go with him wherever is better. We've been—that's how we've been doing it at the hospital."

"Dr. Ko will need to check in on him every few hours. If you do not mind the disturbance, we can probably wheel a stretcher—"

"We don't mind." Ann looked to Sam.

"We don't," Sam said.

Wesley nodded. "Of course."

A momentary silence fell over the room. Ann shifted, brushed the hair from Daniel's forehead. "Mr. Wesley, you're being—I know you're so generous, and I hate to ask, but… Well, these results you keep talking about…"

"Yes. How about we let you see some of them?"

Ann blushed. "That'd be so wonderful."

Sam followed Wesley back out into the hallway while they waited for Ko and her colleagues to retrieve materials for an injection from a store room downstairs. "Mr. Wesley."

The old man was stooped over his cane, leaning against the wall and staring off into space. He arched his bushy white eyebrows. "Sam. Call me Clayton."

"I just wanted to … You've been—all of this is so overwhelming. You have to understand, back at the hospital, they didn't give us much hope. They told us they had no idea what they were dealing with and frankly…Ann and I were starting to—to have the kinds of thoughts parents shouldn't ever have to have."

Wesley nodded. "You have been through a lot, my boy. You deserve a little happiness."

"Is that all?"

"I beg your pardon?"

"Is that why you're—doing this? I mean, not to sound ungrateful or to imply that you would need a… It's just, my wife was wondering…"

The shark smile returned. "What's in it for me?"

Sam nodded vigorously, relieved.

"You get to a certain age, Sam, you make a certain amount of money, and some parts of the rat race cease to seem important."

"I didn't mean to imply that money—"

"It's about family, Sam. Mine…and others."

"Right. Of course."

"I don't want to proceed under false pretenses. You must be aware, from the paperwork at the hospital, that the…methods we are going to employ here are still somewhat in the experimental stages."

Sam swallowed. In truth, he hadn't taken the time to read the seventeen pages of small-print. Gideon had breezed over it, and he hadn't raised any red flags. "Okay…"

"Don't be worried, my boy. As I assured you, it is all perfectly safe. But as an answer to your question... Research. Data. That is what is in it for me. Your son is helping to provide Clayton Wesley Medical with the experience and confidence it needs to turn around and treat people with similar afflictions around the world."

"Oh. Do many people have...?"

"Ah." Wesley turned at the sound of footsteps. Dr. Ko and her sidekicks were coming back with a small, steel box. "Come, Sam. In fifteen minutes, all of your fears will be allayed."

Ann's eyes went wide when Ko removed the needle from the box. She had always hated them. When she was twelve, she had walked in on her uncle in his trailer, shooting up heroin. He had overdosed right in front of her.

"What's in that?" she asked.

Dr. Ko did not answer. She drew a milky solution from another bottle.

Clayton Wesley knelt beside Daniel's wheelchair, wincing and using his cane for support. "It's a vitamin complex. Along with a couple of other additives—one or two solutions CW has been working on." He gave a nod to Sam. "Patent pending."

To Sam's surprise, Dr. Ko handed the syringe to Clayton Wesley.

Before Sam or Ann could react, Wesley took Daniel's arm in his pudgy old hand and sank the needle into a vein.

Ann covered her mouth. Sam took her hand and squeezed.

Several seconds passed. Everyone in the room—Wesley included—seemed to be holding their breath.

Then Daniel moved.

FIFTEEN

DANIEL GAVE A LITTLE MOAN and his head lolled to one side in the wheelchair. Sam and Ann cried out together. They fell to their knees at Wesley's side.

"Danny!"

"Daniel, it's your mother. Can you hear me?"

"Danny, talk to us!"

Wesley waved them back, handing the syringe to Ko. "Sam, Ann, please..."

"Can he hear us?" Ann cupped the boy's chin in her hands. "Can he—is he listening? Is he awake?"

"*Ann.* Please. Calm down."

Calm down? It was all Sam could do to keep from jumping up and down. He'd *moved.* He'd made a noise. Daniel was okay. He was *okay.*

"As I attempted to make clear, what we have just administered is a booster. We're starting the process. We're still going to need a surgical operation. Daniel's bones are weak. The radiation has attacked his marrow. We have synthetic samples we've been working on, and they're going to help him. But this is just a first step."

"But can he hear us?"

Wesley looked from Ann to Daniel, sprawled in the chair. He sighed. "It's possible."

Sam stared at his son's face. The boy's eyes were still shut, but Sam could now imagine there was just a hint of color in his cheeks. "Danny. Hey, Danny. It's me, buddy. It's Dad."

"Daniel." Ann squeezed his shoulder. "Daniel, we're both here." "Together."

Clayton Wesley rose and backed away. Sam and Ann pressed in so close that their shoulders touched. *Just open your eyes,* Sam thought at Daniel. *Just do it. Do it.*

Daniel's eyes remained closed.

"Daniel, it's going to be okay. You're going to start getting healthier now. We've got..." Ann glanced up at Wesley, who retreated to the doorway with Ko and the others. The overhead lights caught the tears in Ann's eyes. "We've got the best people in the world, and they're all here just for you. Just to make you better."

Wesley edged outside and shut the door behind him.

Sam leaned forward. He took Daniel by the shoulders. He felt so—warm. So alive. So there, so present. "Danny. I..." Sam broke off, swallowed, tried again. "Danny, I know I haven't really—I haven't been there a lot lately. I should've. I should've been there, and none of this would have..." He drew in a ragged breath. Ann reached over and squeezed his knee. "Danny, I'm sorry. If you just— if you'll just...just wake up, buddy... If you'll just wake up, I prom-ise you... I'm promising you it's going to be different, okay? Everything's going to be different. I'm going to be there. I'm never going to leave you again." Sam sniffed. He felt a tear escape down his cheek. He didn't bother to wipe it away. "I love you so much, Danny. I love you so, so much, I just...I hope you can hear me, because— because you need to hear it. You deserve to hear it. I love you."

"We both do." Ann reached to Sam's face and gently blotted the tear with her shirtsleeve. It was the most intimate gesture she had made toward him in more than a decade. "We both do."

Something chirped. The sound was so foreign, so jarring that it took them several moments to realize it was Ann's phone. She wres-tled it out of her pocket and cut it off without checking the caller ID. She set it on the foot of the bed beside them and turned back to Daniel.

Sam watched her, and he watched his son, and he felt a glimmer of hope. That one day, it might be the three of them again. That they might be complete. That this could all work out, because they were here. Daniel had brought them together, and they weren't clawing at each other's throats. They could do this.

The phone rang again.

Sam pivoted around and grabbed it off the bedcovers.

"Throw it out the damn window," Ann told him.

Sam was reaching for the power button when he noticed the number on the tiny green LCD. He knew that number.

Detective Crawford.

Sam glanced at Ann and then rose and turned from Daniel to stroll to the window as he flipped the phone open. "Sam Mackie."

"Mr. Mackie. Detective Crawford here. I tried your number, but—"

"I broke it." He drew in a long breath, trying to reel his mind back in, to draw himself out of the emotional stew where Daniel had left him. "What's new? Have you turned up anything? Did you check with the nearest Army base?"

"Mr. Mackie, I need you to do me a favor."

Sam glanced over his shoulder. Ann was watching him, still crouched at Daniel's feet. She looked cold and distant again. She was furious that he had answered the phone. "What do you need, Detective?"

"Mrs. Mackie there, too?"

"Yes."

"What I need—I need both'a you to hop in a car and drive down here to the station."

"Why? What's happened?"

Ann arched an eyebrow at him. "What is it?"

"Just come down here, Mr. Mackie. Please. Both of you. Together."

"Detective, my son's still very sick. I can't—we're just making a little progress. This isn't a good time. Can't you tell me what this is about?"

There was a long pause on the other end of the line. Sam thought they must have lost the connection. He was about to ask if Crawford was still there, and then the detective finally spoke:

"Mr. Mackie, I need you and your wife down here right now because there are some very serious criminal charges against you that need to be discussed. If you do not transport yourself to the downtown police station within forty-five minutes, I'm not gonna have a choice, and I'm gonna have to have warrants drawn up and send officers to come get you."

"What?"

"Obstructing an investigation, on top of everything else. I'm not doing that yet, Mr. Mackie, as long as you come in. Let's talk this over, Sam. You don't have to go to jail."

As he flipped the phone shut, the weight of dread that had so briefly been lifted from his stomach returned like a boulder. It was the break-in at the CW office. It had to be.

But then, why would Crawford need to talk to Ann?

"What was that?"

Sam tried to explain. Ann started shaking her head halfway through. "I'm not leaving. I'm not. We're not leaving him alone."

"He said—"

"I don't care what he said! What if Daniel wakes up? What if he wakes up and there's no one around him but strangers? What if—"

The door came open with a soft *click*. Clayton Wesley's cane preceded him inside. "I apologize for the intrusion." He offered a sheepish half-bow. "Far be it for me to eavesdrop in the hallway, or intervene when my patients and friends are—"

"Mr. Wesley." Sam bit back a colder, crisper retort. "I'm sorry. We're in the middle of—did you need something?"

"Dr. Ko tells me it might be an opportune time to begin some of the pre-operation lab work on little Daniel here. There are certain portions of the procedure that I'm afraid you will not be able to spend with Daniel."

Ann leapt to her feet. "Not be able to—"

"For his safety." Wesley raised his hands, quieting, placating. "A sterile operating environment is absolutely crucial. An infection at this point, with Daniel's weakened immune system… I understand your hesitation as parents, but trust me when I tell you this is in his best interests."

Sam was getting an odd feeling from the old man. "So what you're telling us… You're telling us we're not needed right now. We could—if we happened to have some business, we could duck out. Take care of it. It wouldn't make a difference, because he's going to be in surgery anyway. That's what you're telling us."

Ann squinted at Sam, confused.

"Sam." Wesley dabbed at the corners of his lips with a delicate thumb, as though he were holding a napkin. "I'm afraid I've received a telephone call. Again, far be it for me to interfere with the… personal lives of my patients. But at this stage in our funding and research, a cavalcade of police officers would not be the most… beneficial component of our image."

Sam felt his cheeks coloring. "Why? Did he say why he wanted us?"

"I was not made privy to the details of your personal business."

Ann crossed her arms. "I'm not going. I'm not leaving Daniel."

"Ann. Daniel is safe here. His prospects with our treatments are very optimistic. But in the face of police involvement, such negative publicity and attention… Well, it may be significantly more difficult for me to rationalize helping you. I am a generous man. But even I have limits."

5

Ann squirmed in the back seat of the Range Rover. She twisted around and stared out the tinted rear window at the office building when they stopped to open the barbed-wire gate.

"I hate this." She shook her head. "This is wrong. This feels wrong. Something's… What did he tell you? What were the charges? Damn it, what's this about?"

"It's nothing. It will be nothing. We'll be back in no time." Sam couldn't reach her from the front seat, but he mustered for her benefit a false smile. In his heart, he felt the same way. This was about more than the break-in at the office. There was something *wrong*.

They had been given a different driver this time. She was slim, cool, and quiet. The whole distance to the freeway, she didn't say more than one or two words. She had the dashboard radio set to some kind of local channel that broadcast voices too soft for Sam to make out.

As she steered onto the Interstate, she reached for the center console. There was a GPS display mounted against polished wood grain, just above the gearshift. She flicked it on with a button along the side, and changed the channel a couple of times until the map gave way to an image.

"Your son," she said to the car at large.

Sam and Ann both locked onto the screen, drawn like magnets. The video was choppy, a low-res streaming input from the immaculate white operating theater on the floor beneath their guestroom.

Dr. Ko flitted past the camera, followed a moment later by a stretcher. Daniel.

Ann gulped. "Is he okay?"

The driver didn't answer.

For the next ten minutes, neither Sam nor Ann saw a single foot of the freeway. They were riveted to the ten square inches of the glowing LCD.

When Sam glanced up and saw the police station rising against the downtown cityscape, he flinched. He didn't want to leave the car, to break the one connection they had to their son.

"Can I stay here?" Ann sounded like a pleading child. "I'll stay in the car. Let me know when they need me."

On the screen, Ko and the other doctors formed a forest of white around the stretcher in the center. Daniel wasn't even visible for all of their hunched bodies and long, billowing medical gowns.

A uniformed officer tapped on the passenger window a moment after they had rolled up to the curb. Sam was so surprised that it took him a couple of seconds to find the controls to lower it.

"You can't wait here. This is a no-loading zone." He squinted at Sam, and then past him, into the back, at Ann. Recognition flashed across his face. "Sir. Ma'am. I, uh... I need you two to step out of the car."

Sam looked at the man. He'd never seen him before in his life.

"Step out of the car, please."

The officer escorted them up the crescent-shaped concrete steps to the front entrance of the police station. Sam had never come in this way before. Every other time, filing more paperwork on Riley, they had parked in the garage and gone in back.

He threw one last, longing glance over his shoulder at the Range Rover. The tinted windows reflected only his face and the looming police station façade, behind him. The car slipped away from the curb before Sam could tell the driver they would only be a couple of minutes.

This time, Sam and Ann were not taken to Crawford's office. Their escort led them straight to a blank white questioning room with a one-way mirror and a strip of fluorescent overhead bulbs. The ceiling stood high, fifteen feet overhead, supported by walls of bleak cinderblock.

Sam stared at his own reflection in the one-way glass. He looked like hell. It had been days since he last shaved. His clothes were filthy.

Dark shadows encircled his eyes, and worry lines crisscrossed his forehead. In the last week, he had aged a lifetime.

It was nearly ten minutes before Crawford came in. He had a manila envelope tucked under his arm. Sam was gratified to see that he looked every bit as worried and overburdened as Sam felt.

"Anyone offer you coffee?"

Sam declined. Ann didn't open her mouth.

The door shut with a metallic, echoing *boom*. For a few seconds, Crawford stood, sizing them up. He dropped into a chair across the table from the two of them and steepled his fingers in front of him.

"Better get started then."

"Detective Crawford. I'm getting the idea that this is pretty serious. But even if it is, you should know that Danny's going into the operating room as we speak and—"

"Caleb Pollock."

Sam broke off and blinked. "I'm sorry?"

"Know him?"

"Is this a joke?"

"Am I laughing? You're in a lot of trouble, Mr. Mackie. Both of you are."

"Yes. I know him. Caleb's a colleague. A friend."

"Anything you want to tell me about Mr. Pollock?"

Sam's mind raced. He started to shake his head before the obvious occurred to him.

"He's…he's been missing the last few days, I guess."

"Uh-huh."

"Almost a week now, actually. And he was acting a bit strange before that."

"Uh-huh. Any reason you didn't mention this in any of our previous conversations?"

Sam leveled a cold stare at Crawford. "Because I was too busy trying to figure out who the hell was coming after my son."

"So it just slipped your mind?"

Sam glanced at Ann. She was watching Crawford's face with a certain mute, intense concentration. Her parents had been in and out of the station on almost a weekly basis. Drunk and disorderly conduct. Neglect. Disturbing the peace.

The place was beginning to leave a sour taste in Sam's mouth, too. "Look, did Caleb do something, Detective?"

Crawford allowed him a humorless snort. "Yeah. Yeah, he did, Mr. Mackie. You know what Caleb did? He died. And he did it in your house."

SIXTEEN

SAM SAT BACK in the chair and stared across the interrogation table at Crawford.

"Caleb what?"

Crawford flipped open the manila envelope with a thumb and slid a large, glossy photograph across to him. "Maid's day off, I suppose."

It was the garage. Sam leaned forward and lifted the picture into the light, because at first, he couldn't make sense of what he was seeing. The rest of the cardboard cartons had been upended. There were a few of Caleb's papers left scattered around the middle of the room, where Sam and Ramon had carefully packed them. The vast majority were missing.

Sprawled across the lingering sheets was the shape of a man. Caleb.

His head was bashed in.

Sam covered his mouth, numb.

Crawford cocked a bushy eyebrow at him. "No idea how this happened?"

"Detective…" Sam's throat went dry. He couldn't take his eyes from the picture. The splattered blood, curled fingers, mouth half-open against the concrete floor. The *thing*—the wrecked, ravaged husk of a human being—that had been his best friend for the last twenty years. It wasn't Caleb. It couldn't be Caleb. It was too—grotesque.

"No idea at all?"

Sam felt sick. Still paralyzed by shock, it took him a moment to register what Crawford was saying. "Detective—Caleb and I...I don't... No, I don't know. How did this happen?"

"How does it *look* like it happened?"

"I don't know! Why would you think I'd know? Detective, we've been friends for half my life. He's my best—my best friend in the world. For Christ's sake..."

Crawford flipped another photograph onto the table.

Caleb's cabin. The mossy roof, the moldering VW bus, and the leaning vegetation.

"That's his—Caleb's house. What about it?"

The detective nudged it toward him. Sam looked closer. The windows had been smashed in, ragged sledgehammer holes in the walls.

"You want to walk me through this, Mr. Mackie?"

"I don't—I'm not...I don't understand..."

"Okay. How about I walk you through it, and you just nod. You get it into your head that your good ol' buddy Caleb Pollock has something you want. You break into his place, vandalize the shit out of it while he's at work. We've got your fingerprints all over to corroborate."

"He's my friend! Yeah, I've been over there..."

"Recent fingerprints. Lifting things, going through things. You usually go over to your friends' houses, pull treasure boxes out from under the bathtub and rifle through them, Mr. Mackie?"

"Detective—"

"So then you go home. Safe place to keep your loot till you figure out what to do next. Stash it in the garage, but your buddy, Caleb—he puts together what's happened and comes after you. You have a fight, you hit him—a little too hard—and then you freak, get out of there with the loot you stole, but you leave a few scraps." Crawford jabbed a finger at the first picture. "Exhibit A. Which, by the way—bullshit theories about the Cuban Missile Crisis? Castro, Khrushchev, stolen surveillance? Got a few hobbies you forgot to tell me about?"

"Those were—they were his. I was in them. My family...they weren't—"

"You have any idea how crazy this is sounding, Mr. Mackie?"

Sam swallowed. "Please..."

"Now, you're getting out of there, you're so panicked you almost run down your next door neighbor out on his evening jog. We got eyewitness testimony on that point."

Son-of-a-bitch, Sam thought. "Look, Detective—"

"Damn of it is, the jogger sees your wife's car, so now we got a complication. Me, I'd like to think maybe you just borrowed it, she's the innocent third party, but I guess we should leave that to the jury to decide, shouldn't we? No sense in making this a family matter unless we drag the whole clan in, right?"

"Detective. Listen to me. I can see that you've—you've put together this picture of what happened. Of a person who would do this kind of thing. But this isn't me. It's not me. Look at me, Crawford. I'm just a guy. I'm just an—"

"An ordinary, working average Joe, right?"

"Yes!"

"Who breaks into his office with a goddamn shotgun, violates private property, and assaults a secretary and two security guards." Crawford pulled the last sheet from the manila envelope.

It was a blurry screen-capture from a security camera. It was eerily similar in style to the shot from the UPS truck—the first glimpse Sam had ever received of the man trying to steal his son.

Sam recognized himself and Ramon, that very morning. They were a blur, pounding down the ninth-floor stairwell past the twenty-something junior, Malleson's friend.

"Detective." It was Ann who broke the silence. "My husband and I have not been on good terms for... it's been a number of years. We've had our share of bitter fights. But never in my life would I believe him capable of what you're describing."

"With all due respect, Mrs. Mackie—"

"Our son is sick, Detective!" Sam burst out. "Do you think we faked that, too? Do you think that's all just for show to win you over to our side? He's sick, and people are trying to get him, and you're sitting in here coming up with these *stupid theories,* claiming we're killers!"

"About that..." Crawford grunted. "I did call the Hogan Army Base. Forty miles out of town—nearest one. The base commander says he never sent any medical team to the hospital, and he doesn't know a thing about a rogue ex-soldier kidnapping little boys."

"You were there," Sam breathed. "That night. When we chased him. You're telling me that was some big show, too?"

"Didn't catch him, did we?"

"I tried! You saw me try! You were in the car, Crawford!"

"Yes. But how surprised were you, really, when that second truck showed up?"

Sam sucked in a deep breath and forced himself to hold it while he tried to work out what the hell was going on. "I thought you trusted me. I thought you believed me."

"That was before I found classified military files, wild-eyed conspiracy bullshit nonsense, and a dead body in your garage. Who the hell are you Sam? Just who the hell are you?"

"Why did you look in the garage?" Ann's voice was disarmingly soft and level.

She took Crawford off-guard. "I'm sorry?"

"Our garage. Why did you happen to look in our garage, where you say you found Caleb?"

Crawford bristled. "Ma'am, police work—"

"Did you have a warrant, Detective?"

"We had probable cause... from an anonymous tip."

Sam stared at Crawford. "An—an *anonymous tip?* Are you fuckin' kidding me?"

"Language like that, Mr. Mackie, is not going to improve the impression you make on a jury."

"It's a setup. This is a setup. It's..." He closed his eyes, thought back to the ID card, the surveillance papers from Caleb's cabin. "Tillman. Look up the name, J.G. Tillman, Detective. Please. I think you might find a military record. If we're lucky... you might find a whole lot more."

Crawford looked skeptical, but he took down the name with an old hotel ballpoint from his jacket pocket.

"Detective," Ann said. "I understand this is very serious, but can—are we under arrest? Because if not, our son... we need to be with our son right now."

"Ah." Crawford didn't look up from his writing. "The sick son."

"What the hell is that supposed to mean?" Sam reached across and snatched the ballpoint out of Crawford's fingers when he still didn't react. "You don't believe Danny's sick? You saw him at the hospital. Damn it, you talked to his doctor."

"Please give that back." Crawford stuck out his hand for the pen. When Sam bristled and returned it, he went on: "Dr. Gideon did not want to make any official comments, but we did get him to admit that your son's symptoms could have been artificially induced. He also said that frankly, your behavior at the hospital posed a danger to his other patients, and he has proof that you came to him with a request to sign your son out this very afternoon."

"That's right, because—"

"Convenient, don't you think? That just when someone might want to validate your son's condition—golly, he's disappeared."

Ann shoved her chair back from the table with a sharp scrape. "Don't you say that. Don't you ever say those words."

A flash of genuine surprise crossed Crawford's face. "I'm sorry. I forgot your—history. What I mean to say is that it seems convenient that your son is not available for medical examination by court order."

"He's available." Sam glanced at Ann. "You want to see him, Detective? You want to see where we've taken him? It's not a beach in Cabo, if that's what you've got in your head."

Crawford rolled his eyes.

"I'm serious, Detective. Seeing Danny—seeing he's still sick… Listen, you talked about a nephew, you've got to know…no parent would ever do that. We let you run some tests on him, will that convince you?"

"It'd be a start."

Sam stood. "There's a car circling out front. We can be there in fifteen minutes."

It took Crawford a half-hour to get all the paperwork settled and clear things with his boss. When they emerged from the station, he brought BJ Cunningham with him.

They waited on the steps for ten minutes.

The Range Rover never showed up.

"Must've gone back," Sam said. "I'll call Wesley and have him send another."

Crawford checked his watch. It was already getting dark, and as Sam came back up from the curb, the first light drops of another rainstorm began pattering on the sidewalk.

"You know where this place is, right?" Crawford said.

Sam looked at Ann. "More or less."

"You could get us there?"

"Yeah."

"C'mon."

Sam had never been in the back of a police car before. It felt like a jail cell. He watched the city streak by into the night. Should he be calling a lawyer? He felt lost, still reeling from everything that night. Hell, everything that *week*.

Crawford and Cunningham kept up a hushed conversation in front as they wove through the evening traffic. Sam peered out at the other drivers. Yelling into cell phones, thrashing along with music, staring straight ahead, lost in thought. All of them looked impossibly carefree. They were coming home from work, or perhaps going to a graveyard shift. Heading out for a meal. Linking up for a first date. Tending to their everyday lives.

Sam wondered if he would ever have one again.

They got off the highway. Crawford locked his doors as soon as he saw where they were.

A blighted post-industrial suburb during the day, at night, the neighborhood where Wesley had set up his newest facility looked more like a demilitarized zone. Hooded gangsters zipped back and forth across the road on undersized bikes. Backpacks slung over their shoulders, their eyes gravitated to the police car like jungle cats fleeing a hunter.

Light burned from behind boarded-up windows on all sides.

They passed another squad car, racing in the opposite direction with its sirens blaring.

The abandoned shopping mall was a looming, black hole in the night. None of the parking lot streetlamps worked, nor did any of the lights inside the deserted shops or commissaries. Here and there, through torn curtains or butcher paper, Sam glimpsed a flicker of something that might have been a flashlight or a fire. Every now and then, just outside of the police car's headlight beams, Sam glimpsed movement. Once, he thought he heard skateboards.

The place was crawling with the creatures of the urban night.

Crawford flipped on his high-beams and used the searchlight built into his window to find the road leading out the rear of the parking lot. Pale moonlight against the surface of the lake rendered every doubtful glance he cast at Cunningham in an eerie glow.

"Just up here." Sam leaned forward and tapped the Plexiglas

partition. "That—that tower." He faltered when he saw the office. It rose, monolithic, against the night sky. There were perhaps five lights on in the entire building.

"Sam." Ann gripped his arm.

She was thinking what Sam was thinking. *This was not happening. This could not be happening.* The tiny voice of reason in the back of his head was suddenly screaming at the top of its lungs.

Something was very, very wrong.

"You'll have to stop here to—" Sam broke off again, about to point out the barbed-wire gate.

It was hanging open.

Sam turned to Ann. "Give me your cell phone."

"Why?"

"I'm calling Wesley. Let him know we're coming."

Ann's hands shook when she handed it to him. She stayed glued to the window while Sam dialed. The trees, rustic, even somewhat pretty during the day, now arched over them with broad, leafy branches that muted out the stars to trap them in the mud.

"I'm sorry. Your call cannot be completed as dialed. Please check—"

Sam clapped the phone shut. He opened it again, redialed the same number, and listened to the same recorded message. *"The number you have dialed has been disconnected, or is no longer in service."*

His stomach lurched.

"Sam. Sam, what does it mean? Sam? Where are they?"

Calm. Stay calm. "They must have given us the wrong number, is all."

A pointed glance from Crawford in the rear-view mirror. Sam ignored him, averted his eyes, and returned to the window. The office building came into view, towering, crumbling—dark. How could they have left their son here alone with strangers? What had they been thinking?

A swell of anger bulged in Sam's chest. This was Crawford's fault. He could have interviewed them separately. They could have met somewhere nearby. They didn't have to go so far from Daniel. They didn't have to leave him alone again.

Crawford braked as they rounded the last bend and the covered turnaround came into view. "Where do I go?"

Sam stretched across the back seat to squint out Ann's window on the left side of the car. "Just park behind the..."

Range Rovers.

Gone. So was the Rolls-Royce.

"Up there," Sam said. He pointed, feeling weak.

They drew to a halt in front of the lobby doors—standing open.

"Sam...Oh God, Sam, what's...what have we...?" Ann scrabbled with the door latch.

"Maybe there was a fire. It was a fire. They had to evacuate."

Officer Cunningham removed a flashlight from his belt as they mounted the steps. Sam and Ann led by several paces. Sam's legs felt numb, rubbery struts dangling from the bottom of his torso.

Inside the lobby, everything looked more or less the same, but someone had turned off the carefully-positioned track lights overhead. Absent the glimmering spots of white, the marble floor looked scuffed-up and scratched. The half-built walls took on the appearance of mid-decay.

Crawford sniffed and squinted through the framework to the moldering remains of the restaurant off to the right. Dust hung in the air. Several of the stacks of chairs had fallen over, spilling chunks of splintered wood across the floor.

He glanced at Sam, face awash with disbelief. "You're telling me you left your son...*here?*"

"Upstairs," Sam croaked. "The elevator—up..."

The insulating blanket had been torn down. Underneath was not the fresh paint and exposed wiring Wesley had described. It was just an ordinary elevator. The second unit didn't work at all.

Sam crouched before the control panel. The buttons were still missing. He closed his eyes and tried to remember which floor Ko had pushed.

"Down there." Ann motioned toward the bottom. "Just press it, Sam!"

He had to use the tip of his fingernail. The elevator lurched, groaned, and began rising. Crawford and Cunningham stared up at the ceiling. Then at the floor. *How long*, their expressions said, *until it falls?*

The doors opened onto darkness. The policemen exchanged a glance. Cunningham stepped over the threshold and drew his flashlight again.

The beam traced the edges of a floor completely gutted. Only the load-bearing struts remained at the centers of the walls. Metal air vents dangled from the ceiling. Coils of wire looped this way and that. A plywood trail zigzagged across the floor, tiles missing from the planks around it.

Cunningham came back.

"Not it." Sam ducked back to the panel. "He said... Wesley *said* they were renovating the rest of the building." He could hear it in his voice—blind desperation. The need to believe what he was saying. The need to believe that this wasn't happening.

Because it couldn't be.

They tried the next floor up, then the next. They were near the top of the building when Sam stopped Cunningham from coming back in. "Oh, Christ, this is it."

"It is not." Ann shuffled to the elevator door. "You've still got the wrong floor. Come back in here and...and..."

Sam grabbed Cunningham's hand and directed the flashlight toward the ground. Ten feet from the elevator, two Silicon Graphics workstations stood stacked beside a pair of flat-screen monitors. Boxed up, ready to slide out. The receptionist must have been a few minutes too slow.

Too slow to get away before they got back.

Shuddering, Sam groped around on the wall in the darkness until he found a couple of light switches. Three fluorescent strips flickered to life. These carried no theatrical elegance. A harsh, sallow glow illuminated the half-built lobby and the mouth of the operating corridor.

"He's this way." Ann took off at a run. "Daniel's—they're working on him. Through here. Right through here!"

Sam, Crawford, and Cunningham jogged after her. Sam's skin crawled with the burning sensation of a thousand tiny needle pricks. He felt like he was walking on fire, on hot coals, only he couldn't feel anything. Slowly but surely, his nerves were checking out. Because all of this was too awful to absorb all at once.

Ann threw her weight against the door of the second operating room—the one that had been closed when they walked past on Wesley's tour. It didn't budge.

It was only with the combined work of all four of them that they managed to force back the grinding metal latch and heave the giant door open. Clearly, it hadn't been shut anytime recently.

The room on the other side was completely empty. Thick stone walls appeared, inch by inch, under Cunningham's flitting flashlight beam. Cracks ran the length of the room. The floor was concrete, too. In the building's previous life, it must have been some kind of safe or cold storage chamber.

There was no operating table. No high-tech medical equipment. No camera. Whatever feed they had received in the Range Rover, it hadn't come from here.

Had it even been Daniel in the video?

Had it even been shot today?

Sam needed to—

—to vomit. This couldn't be happening. This was every terrible nightmare he'd been having over the past thirteen years, come true.

Ann spun around, rage flickering in her eyes. "I told you. This isn't it. We're on the wrong floor."

"Ann—"

"This *isn't it!*"

They tried several other floors. At the second-to-last, one shy of the roof, they found what Wesley had presented as his visitor wing. The queen-sized bed was still there. The TV wasn't even connected to the wall. When Crawford reached out to fiddle with the controls, it fell over on him. It was plastic. Fake.

Ann fell to her knees. There were ruts in the carpet, carved by Daniel's wheelchair.

That was when she started crying.

Sam didn't. He wasn't sure why. Perhaps it was the shock, the emotional block—the impossibility of absorbing all of this.

"Stay with them." Crawford nodded to Cunningham as he flipped open his phone and stepped out into the hallway.

Sam helped Ann to the bed. He stared out the window at the lake and the hulking, crumbling wreck of the abandoned shopping mall. How could they have been so stupid? It was the desperation, the need for the one glimmer of hope that Wesley had dangled in front of them.

They'd taken the bait.

Just like that, just like Riley, Daniel was gone.

"We've got—we're going to search this whole building." Ann had gone rigid, and when Sam spun back to her, she was already wiping the tears away. "We're going to search the building and then the forest outside, and then that goddamn mall, and this whole miserable fucking neighborhood. Because he's out there. He's probably— he's hiding."

"Ann, sweetheart—"

"He's *hiding out there! He's out there!* Oh, what, don't tell me you're already giving up? Don't tell me, Sam, that you're running off, going to start over again. Guess he's gone, another one bites the dust. Is that it, Sam? Is that really who you are?"

"That's not who I am."

He stared into her eyes. Ann's lower lip trembled. She bit it back with such ferocity that a drop of blood sprang down onto her chin. In a flash, Sam could see it. Everything happening again—only Ann was right; this time there was no pregnancy, no starting over. She would go back to drinking and likely die in an accident or when her liver failed. And Sam?

Sam would be left in a quiet little house by himself. Ticking away the days that he passed in a miserable cubicle. Biding his free time watching TV, making frozen dinners, drifting from room to empty room, where the walls still echoed with the laughter of children that would never, ever, be coming home again.

Crawford stepped back inside, cell phone still in his hand. He looked grim. "Turns out your company doesn't own this building. It's being held by a real estate investment firm. Same one that owns that mall over there. They've been trying to offload the place for five years, but no one will buy or even lease because of the neighborhood."

Sam registered the lie.

"There's more. I checked in with Records, back at the station. They've checked our national database, and even tapped into the FBI. Mr. Mackie, they found two dozen people who could be your J.G. Tillman. But not one of them is employed by CW Medical. Not one of them even lives in this county."

J.G. Tillman was nobody. A fabrication. A name to take the fall while everyone else scuttled the ship and ran. The magnitude of it all was only then beginning to hit Sam.

His son.

Clayton Wesley had taken his son. His employer of twenty years—the man whom many saw as the promise of a brighter future. Magazines heralded him as the genius who would cure cancer, the forerunner in research that would change lives around the world.

He had changed lives. The lives of four innocent people no one would ever hear about: Sam, Ann, Riley, and Daniel.

"Wesley," Sam said. "Did you—did you check on Clayton Wesley?"

"Personal assistant says he's traveling." Crawford shook his head. "Says he's been traveling for the last week, off at some benefit in Africa."

"That's bullshit!" Ann got to her feet. "That's—we've got him! Don't we? That's bullshit. He was at the hospital. We saw him. Dr. Gideon saw him. Everyone saw him right there. He's lying. Tell him, Sam."

Sam looked from Ann to Crawford. *Tell him?* As if Sam's word meant a damn.

"Tell him, god damn it!" She rounded on Crawford. "You have to find him! You have to find him, because he has our son. He has both of our sons! You have to find him, Detective!"

Sam pulled her up against him and she went limp. Sobbing. Her head flopped back against his chin. Sam swayed. He squeezed his eyes shut. The tears burned as they trickled down his cheeks. Seeing her explode, seeing her lose that careful poise and control, pushed him over the edge.

Crawford sent Cunningham out into the hall to make a few more calls. The Detective stayed with his back turned, peering out the window, until Sam had gathered enough strength to say anything without breaking down altogether.

"You still think we're doing this, Detective? After everything, do you still believe this is—this is us?"

Crawford shook his head. "I don't. God knows, I should. You haven't—there's no evidence. Nothing concrete to support your story. But I believe you, Sam. So where does that leave us? What the hell do you want from me?"

"I want you to help us find Daniel." Sam rose, and because she was still clinging to him, Ann rose, too. Somehow, the weight of her body—the knowledge that she was there, hanging from him, relying on him as his son was—forced him to be stronger. "I want your word that you stand with us now."

Crawford looked at him long and hard. And then he nodded.

SEVENTEEN

ANN REFUSED TO LEAVE the derelict office. "He might come back." She resisted when Sam tried to pull her from the edge of the bed. "He'll come back. They've just gone out. They've gone out for a while. They'll come back, and someone has to be here for them."

It became clear that it would take some greater power than Sam's to pull her away.

"Maybe he's still here. In the building somewhere." In her voice, he heard the same forlorn conviction that had tempered every word she'd spoken of Riley in the last thirteen years.

And with each passing minute, the chances of stopping Daniel's abduction diminished.

Cunningham didn't seem happy when Crawford ordered him to stay with Ann. "Shouldn't we call this in? Get the Captain to confirm...?"

"BJ. Please. Just do it."

As they rolled back down the private road, through the barbed-wire gate, Sam swiveled around in his seat to watch the building disappear through the rear windshield. *Keep it together, Ann,* he thought. *Please keep it together.*

He should be up there at her side. She needed him. She shouldn't be alone right now. But Daniel needed him, too.

Right now, he could still stop this.

It wasn't over yet.

Clayton Wesley lived in a palatial estate on the west side of town. The houses sat far back from the tufted roads. Giant trees overhung wrought-iron gates and brick-walled gardens. Only the occasional lighted window emerged through the foliage, an aberration in a forest of private darkness.

There were few street signs and nearly no visible numbers. The message was clear: those with business in the neighborhood knew where they were going. Outsiders were not welcome.

Crawford circled three times before they picked out Wesley's house. From the street, it was visible only as a stone arch between two magnificent oaks that towered high into the sky.

He had to get out to ring the buzzer. It was seated in tasteful, polished steel, like the house itself, invisible from the road.

A woman answered. She hesitated when Crawford identified himself as a detective.

"Please, ma'am. It's urgent."

Another moment passed and then the heavy metal gate came open with a *clunk*.

The police car's headlights rose and fell over the winding private road on the other side. The forest thickened until it blotted out the sky. Sam felt as though they had traveled somewhere else altogether. It seemed impossible the city could be only fifteen minutes away.

At last, a break in the trees afforded a glimpse of the mansion. Large stones stood stacked to form the foundation of an edifice that resembled a cathedral. Flying buttresses and conical towers dotted a roofline of gargoyles and weathervanes, balconies and vaulted dormers. It was an ode to opulence. A loud proclamation of wealth and self-celebration, sequestered in the woods where no one would be troubled by the absence of modesty.

Crawford halted the squad car on the cobblestone drive, beneath the covered entrance. A butler was already waiting for them.

In another time, Sam might have laughed out loud. He was tall, stiff, dressed in a perfect tuxedo. Did people actually live like this?

The man dashed around the car to open each of their doors. "Welcome." He was younger than Sam would have expected—in his late-twenties, with sharp features and dark brown hair. How was it that someone like him came to work for Clayton Wesley?

Sam watched him as he climbed out of the car.

For just an instant, the thought crossed his mind: *Riley?* But no.

This man was too old, and anyway, Sam would have liked to think Riley would still recognize him.

The entrance hall just inside was a masterpiece of polished wood and vibrant stained glass. From the fold of the tablecloth atop the sideboard to the spotless frames of the paintings above it, every last detail was perfect.

With its air of magnificence, the house also contained a certain threatening edge—defying violation from without, as though Sam in all his provincial simplicity might somehow soil its spotlessness.

"This way." The butler strode past them, fast, practiced, blind to it all.

He brought them to a drawing room that made Sam feel small beneath its arched stone ceilings. Murals covered the walls. Misty greens and browns leaked into each other from the high peaks of distant mountains to the depths of a darker jungle nearer to the floor.

Near a grand piano, a reflective lake shimmered at the heart of the muraled valley. There was something about it that called to Sam—to a part of his mind buried in his subconscious.

The same part that came alive when he closed his eyes at night.

He stared at the walls until the butler cleared his throat and indicated a pair of large leather easy chairs by a hearth. The air was thick with ash.

"Someone will be with you momentarily, Detective. Can I bring you anything while you wait? Tea? Brandy?"

Sam and Crawford declined. It was in following his retreating progress to the arched doorway that Sam caught a glimpse of someone else lurking in the shadows.

She was tall, slender, regal in poise. Her silver hair captured the light from the drawing room for a mere second before she darted back into the darkness.

"Hello?" Sam started to get up.

A door opened on the other side of the room.

The man who stepped through was roughly Sam's age, but impeccable grooming made him more closely resemble a wax statue. His skin bore the glow of a day spent under the sun. His hair was drawn back from his forehead, each strand held precisely in place.

"Good evening." He bent to shake each of their hands. "My name is Denton. Jeffrey Denton, but everyone calls me…" He

offered Sam a grin that was coldly calculated in its friendliness. "…
just Denton will do. How are you?"

Sam didn't answer. He opened his mouth, but Crawford interrupted before he could leap up and squeeze some answers from
Denton's smug little smiling lips.

"Mr. Denton—I'm afraid we're here on business."

"Again, just 'Denton' is fine."

"Where's Clayton Wesley?" Sam snapped.

"Mr. Wesley. Ah. Unavailable, I am afraid. I am Mr. Wesley's
business manager, though, and if, as you say, that is the nature of
your visit—"

"We need to see him."

Denton pursed his lips and clasped his hands in front of him.
He directed at Sam a look usually reserved for very small children. "I
can sympathize with that, but I'm afraid Mr. Wesley is unavailable at
the moment. He is out of the country, at a benefit in Africa. Please
pardon my impropriety, but what did you say your name was?"

Sam stood. Crawford followed, more as a reactionary reflex.

Denton did not bat an eye. "Perhaps there is something *I* can
help you with…?"

"Denton." Sam balled his hand into a fist. "I'm going to tear this
place apart until I find him and my son. So if you want to save you
and the butler in there a whole lot of cleanup, I'd suggest—"

"Sam." Crawford put a hand on Sam's shoulder.

The corner of Denton's lip curled, ever so slightly. "I see that this
matter is perhaps more…personal than you may have indicated. My
sympathies. Unfortunately, though, when the truth is the truth, it
cannot be altered to fit your…"

"Mr. Denton—"

"Just Denton, Detective."

Crawford grimaced. "We're trying to establish Mr. Wesley's
whereabouts this evening as part of another…a matter of research. I
wonder if there is anything more concrete or—"

"I drove him to the airstrip myself, Detective. CW Medical leas-
es its own runway at the airport. I helped him file his flight plan."

Sam shook his head. "That's bullshit!"

Crawford's hand tightened on his shoulder. "Do you think we
could see that flight plan, Denton? Just to—to dot all the *i*s. You
understand."

Denton hesitated for a moment. "Of course. May I also, just by way of formality, perhaps see your identification, Detective?" Crawford handed over his badge. "I'd like to make a Xerox of this, if you don't mind, Detective Crawford. Just to, as you say—dot the *i's.*" Denton retreated through the same door by which he had entered.

A moment later, Sam glimpsed a flash of light through the crack beneath it. A copier machine whirred from the other side.

Sam crossed the room to the archway where he'd glimpsed the woman, just before Denton had arrived. Whoever she had been, she was gone now, but on the wall, in her place, he found a portrait of what might have been the same woman, many years earlier.

She was beautiful. Chestnut-haired, slender, skin like porcelain, she peered out from the tree-trunk arms of a dapper young man in a uniform. Judging by the medals and the rank insignia pinned to his chest, he'd had an impressive career. He looked all of about thirty-five. The date beside the artist's signature was 1960.

The inscription at the bottom, engraved into a gold plaque, named them both:

Agatha Wesley-Pryce & Lt. Col. Donald Pryce.

Sam stared. Donald Pryce. From Caleb's files. Married, by the looks of it, to Clayton Wesley's sister.

Sam skirted sideways, moving toward another door.

"Sam," Crawford hissed at him. "Stay away from there. We don't have a warrant."

Sam ignored him and reached for the knob. He twisted it and pushed the door a few inches open. It was dark on the other side, a small personal study. There was a countertop and an adjoining window that connected it to the office space where Denton had disappeared.

Sam froze in his tracks.

The whirring of computer equipment filled the air. As Denton's silhouette turned against another flash from the Xerox machine, Sam flattened himself against the wall. He dropped into a crouch beneath the countertop and held his breath.

For a few moments, all he could hear was his own breathing and the clicking of the machine.

His eyes began to adjust to the darkness, and it was only then that he noticed the large table in the center of the room. A glass case covered the top, allowing for a relief map several inches deep beneath the surface.

He straightened halfway, head touching the underside of the counter.

From there, the flickering from the adjoining room illuminated the rough, trace outlines of plaster-cast mountains and valleys. They were the same as those of the mural in the other room.

Sam jerked when Crawford reached the door and nudged it wider. Light spilled in from the drawing room.

The copier stopped. Footsteps sounded from the other side of the open window.

Sam waved for Crawford to get back. He flung himself at the door as, through the wall, he heard Denton heading for the drawing room.

Almost to the threshold, Sam stopped again. Something had caught his eye on the side of the glass case. It was a polished silver placard affixed to the flat end of the table.

Black Valley Project

Crawford grabbed Sam by the arm and yanked him through the door, swinging it shut just in time to stumble back into the drawing room at the same time as Denton emerged from the other door.

Denton's eyes flicked to the door behind them.

"Nice portrait." Sam nodded to the painting of the Pryces.

Denton smiled thinly. "Mr. Wesley and his sister are quite close."

"What about his brother-in-law?"

Denton handed back Crawford's ID, along with a computer printout. "Here is what you requested." He indicated a column at the end with a delicate finger. "See where the airport verifies Mr. Wesley's check-in and his flight plan to the Republic of Congo. They complete that portion of the plan on the runway, as he boards the plane. Not to mention that I witnessed the same with my own eyes."

Sam took the paper from Crawford. "He could have typed this up just now."

All traces of good humor dropped from Denton's demeanor. "Sir, I do not know who you are or what business you have with my employer, but I am afraid I cannot tolerate—"

"It's okay." Crawford stepped between them as Sam made a move toward the man. "I apologize for the insinuation, Mr. Denton. We were just leaving."

The butler watched Sam fight Crawford all the way down the steps and into the rain.

"You don't know what I saw in there! You don't know!" Sam swatted Crawford away. His hand caught the Detective across the cheek, and Crawford doubled over.

In an instant, Sam found himself pressed against one of the stone pillars at the front of the house, breathing in moss and wet concrete.

"Mr. Mackie." Crawford swallowed a gulp of air. "Sam, you are about four seconds away from a jail cell. I've got the cuffs, and by god, I've got the support of my Captain. You just struck a police detective, you idiot! And as far as the Police Department is concerned, you're a *murder suspect*. Not to mention a host of other—"

"You said you believed me."

Crawford yanked Sam back from the pillar. He spun him around and pulled him under the sheltered drive. "You listen to me..." He broke off, jaw tight. "Look, Sam. I don't think you're a killer. But this whole Clayton Wesley business... Frankly, I'm not seeing a lot of proof here."

"Proof? *Proof?* Walk back in there—"

"I don't have a warrant."

"*Walk* back in there and... For God's sake, you think I'd sign my son away to some—some random stranger?"

"I think, Mr. Mackie, that you were under a great deal of pressure, a good amount of emotional stress, and you acted in what you thought were your son's best interests. But do I think the leader of a major American corporation, a man saluted as one of the geniuses of our time, just waltzed in and walked away with your boy for no reason, when we have an eyewitness testimony to the fact that he was out of the country at the time? I'm sorry, Sam. I want to believe you. But I can't swallow that."

Sam stared at Crawford—and then past him to the heavily-curtained windows of the old brick house. One of them had just moved. For a second, Sam thought he glimpsed a lock of silver hair, and then a slender silhouette as it flitted away from the glass.

Agatha Pryce? The sister for whom Clayton Wesley had named a wing of the hospital?

Then it clicked in Sam's head. He spun back to Crawford and pulled open the passenger door of the squad car.

"What the—Sam, where are you going?"

"What if I can get you eyewitness testimony to the fact that Clayton Wesley *was* here tonight? What if I can do better? What if I can get you proof that he was the one who convinced us to sign Daniel out of the hospital?"

Crawford frowned at him and slipped in behind the wheel. "Okay, I'm listening."

EIGHTEEN

DOCTOR GIDEON was still wiping his hands with disinfectant gel when he came into his office. He slowed as soon as he saw Sam sitting in front of his desk, and when he spoke, it was to Detective Crawford. "I've got seven minutes. We've got one woman just starting labor, and I can't even tell you what kind of night it's already been."

Crawford nodded. "We appreciate your time, Doctor. I understand you've had a harrowing day, what with—everything."

Sam glanced at his watch. All of the delays were killing him. Another hour, and Wesley could be on a private jet, halfway across the country. With Daniel. "Tell him who you saw me with this afternoon."

Gideon raised an eyebrow. He pulled a bottle of vitamin water from a refrigerator behind his desk, and he took a long swig. "I'm sorry, Mr. Mackie—what are you talking about?"

"Wesley. Tell him about Clayton Wesley."

Gideon frowned. "Clayton Wesley. The research scientist?"

Sam waved his hand, impatient. "Tell him."

"Tell him what?"

"Tell him you saw us together."

"You and Clayton Wesley?"

"For God's sake—"

Crawford leaned forward, hands raised, placating. "Let's slow down and talk things through."

Gideon confessed that indeed he had seen Sam with an older man, but he couldn't identify him for certain. He'd been busy. There had been fifteen patients to attend to over the course of his shift that day, not to mention an interview from some of Crawford's subordinates about the incident the night before and a flock of reporters waiting when Gideon went on break for a quick lunch in the staff lounge.

As Gideon went on and on, Sam felt the frustration mounting. How was it possible that in spite of everything that had happened, no one was able to confirm something so simple?

Gideon got paged before he was finished talking and took off to deal with an unfolding emergency in the ER.

The nurses at the station on the ninth floor were all different from the ones on duty that afternoon, and the one or two residents and interns still finishing out thirty-six-hour shifts could remember nothing more specific than Gideon.

They tried the waiters in the restaurant next door, and even the valets in front of the hospital.

"Aw, yeah." The kid at the key cabinet was maybe seventeen, feet propped on a folding metal chair. A *Hustler* hung clamped between his knees. "Yeah, I remember that. Big old Rolls. Sweet car, I guess, but I mean, that kinda money, why not go for something sleeker, y'know?"

"Do you remember the passenger?" Sam pressed.

The kid shrugged. "I think it was some old guy. What, was he famous or something?"

Crawford said he would run the flight plan past some contacts at the airport, and while he checked in, Sam went back around to the entrance to the makeshift lobby and borrowed some change from an eight-year-old to call Ann.

"Hang up," she said, as soon as Sam uttered a word. "Damn it, Sam, what if he calls?" She sounded taut, thick-voiced, frenzied.

"Ann, where are you?"

"I'm hanging up. Don't call this number." A fractional pause. "You haven't found him, have you? He's not with you…?"

"I'm working on it. I wanted to know you were—"

Click.

Change rattled through the phone as Sam replaced the receiver. He leaned forward and rested his head against the wall.

It was all happening faster this time. Before, there had been a

few weeks of panic. There had been the new baby, the police, paperwork. There had been enough going on that it had taken almost six
months for his life to collapse completely.

This time, it would all be over in six days. Or less.

If Daniel disappeared—if the trail went cold—that would be it.
For him, for Ann, for everything.

Pulling back from the bank of payphones, he caught the eye of
a woman leaving the gift shop across the hall. With everything that
had been going on, it took him a moment to recognize her: the
mother from before, with the son who looked like Riley. Worry lines
etching her forehead, she hurried toward a pair of security guards
standing by the string of yellow police tape that still roped off the
main lobby crime scene.

They looked when she pointed to Sam.

His cheeks flushed. As he wheeled away, he heard their polished
shoes coming after him.

"Sir. Sir, can we talk to you for a moment? *Sir?*"

The police had issued an APB for Sam—*wanted for questioning*
in connection to the murder of Caleb Pollock. That earned him a
trip to the hospital security center. Cramped and dark, it reminded
Sam of a high school A/V lab. Flickering black-and-white monitors
surrounded three rolling office chairs and a picnic table covered in
candy, Cheetos, soft drinks, and doughnuts.

He was left in the charge of an overweight guard named Phil
while the other two officers ran outside to see if they could find
Crawford and confirm Sam's story. Sam glared at the back of Phil's
head. Then he looked past the man's mop of oily black hair to the
screen in front of him.

It was a feed from one of the cameras in the lobby.

Sam stood up.

"Whoa." Phil spun around in his chair, pudgy hands dropping
to the rubber club strapped at his beltline. "What do you think
you're doin'?"

"The cameras. He'll be on the cameras! Son-of-a-bitch, how
could I be so stupid? The *cameras!*"

He was three seconds away from a fistfight with Phil when the
other guards came back into the security room with Crawford.

"He'll be on their tapes," Sam struggled in the guards' arms. "Don't you get it? Clayton Wesley will be on their tapes. In the lobby. In Daniel's room. Hell, in the elevators. He'll be on their goddamn tapes."

After Crawford had smoothed things over, he convinced Phil to load up the security tapes from that afternoon. Sam was breathless as they slowly cycled backward. On the three monitors banked in front of the observation chair, black-and-white patients, doctors, and orderlies crawled backward from door to door.

The time code—large, white digital numbers at the bottom of the screen—ran backward in ten-minute chunks. "Okay…" Sam clutched the back of Phil's chair. "Here. Around here."

At 4:48 pm, he spotted himself and Clayton Wesley ambling down the hall on the ninth floor. "Right there!" He jabbed a finger at the screen.

Phil swatted him out of the way and scowled at the greasy print he left on the glass. "Get back, arright? Damn it."

"It's not enough." Crawford was squinting.

"Detective…"

"That's the back of an old geezer's head, Sam. That could be my grandpa, God rest his soul. We need a face shot."

Phil gave a put-upon sigh. "I'll try the room and the elevator. That make you happy?"

The room was a bust. Sam sat forward as soon as he saw Daniel, Ann, himself, but Wesley remained—purposely?—in the doorway. His shiny black shoes and tailored pants were visible in the corner of the screen, but there was nothing more. Not even a sliver of his face.

"Cut that out." Phil jerked his double-chin at Sam's fingers. He'd been drumming them on the back of Phil's chair.

"Sorry." Sam jammed his hands in his pockets. "The elevator. We've got to see him in the elevator. We've *got to.*" He glanced at Crawford, now every bit as intent and intrigued as Sam. "He has to be doing this on purpose. He has to know we'd come looking for him. And that means he knew he was doing something wrong."

"Maybe."

Phil made a show of switching discs and looking up the proper codes. "Elevator one?"

"I don't know which one it was."

The two screens on the left filled with a fish-eye view of the interior of an elevator. Sam scoured them both. A wheelchair carrying a man in his sixties, his family crowding around him. A pair of doctors conferring about a patient chart.

"Not either of those."

Phil huffed. "Well, there's just one left." He keyed in the log code. "Here it is."

The screen went black.

A single line of text flashed in the center:

Segment not found.

NINETEEN

"OKAY, SO IT'S WEIRD."

"It's—it's *weird?*" Sam rounded on Crawford.

Phil and the other guards were across the hall, in Archives, looking for the automatic backup the computer had made.

"It's beyond weird. It's *criminal.* You're going to tell me—you're going to tell me you don't think something fucked-up is going on? Now? After *this?*"

"It could be a glitch. They're looking for the backup..."

"They're not going to find it. You know they're not going to find it."

Crawford stared at his shoes. He sighed and met Sam's eye. "Yeah. Okay. I don't think they're gonna find it."

"So...?"

"The next step is to file the paperwork. Start an inquiry..."

Sam shook his head. "I went through all of that. With Riley. Inquiries and Missing Person reports, and on and on. By the time we got flyers on the phone poles, he could've been..." A breath. "He could've been across the world, okay? I'm not—I can't let that happen. Not again. We have to *do something.*"

Crawford plopped into a chair in front of the monitors. "Sam, look—"

"No, *you* look. You...Imagine, Detective, you and your wife and your nephew, happy, in your backyard. And you go inside for sixty seconds, and you come out and he's—he's gone. He's just gone.

You telling me you're going to sit down, drink your goddamn lemon-
ade and wait for the news to come in?"

Crawford looked away. He took a couple of deep breaths, shook
his head, and then rested his chin in his hands. "Okay. Okay, Sam. I
get it. And I want to help you. But what in God's name d'you want
me to do?"

"Get a full search of Wesley's estate. Haul that Denton prick in
for questioning."

"I can't just—"

"Detective."

Crawford bit his lip. "I can try."

Phil and the others came back in with a small stack of video discs.
They were labeled in red: *Division of Security, Archives Department.*

Archives.

Sam spun back to Crawford. "I think there's something else you
can help me with."

"What?"

"You can come with me."

Crawford glowered, face awash in flickering black-and-white.
"Where?"

ഗ

Brush at the entrance to Ramon's property concealed a couple of
cheap, battery-powered camcorders he must have picked up at a local
electronics store. Sam caught the glint of moonlight in a lens as he
was getting out to pull back the old wooden gate. He waved.

At the top of the hilly private road, Crawford pulled the police
car to a halt beside Ann's Volvo—right where Sam had left it, the last
time he'd come out here. The Detective leaned forward, all the way
to the dash, and frowned up at Ramon's darkened porch.

"What the hell is this place?"

"Stay in the car. I'll be back in a minute." Sam got out before
Crawford could stop him. He took the stairs two at a time. "Ramon!
Ramon, it's me. It's Sam. Damn it, where are you?"

He rapped on the front door.

A *click* from the boarded-up window at his left made Sam pivot.

The barrel of Ramon's shotgun protruded from beneath the plywood plank. "Ramon. I thought we'd been through this."

"That was before you brought a fuckin' cop." The voice came from the darkness, steady, but afraid.

"He's with me."

"Yeah, that's why you got a gun pointed at your face."

"I mean, he's with *us*."

Ramon's eyes appeared in the shadows, the tip of his nose in a shaft of pale light. "You know how long they questioned me? About Caleb. About the office. About all this shit I didn't do."

"Me, too, Ramon."

"Yeah? Well ain't that sweet. Sounds like you an' I are just two peas in a pod."

Sam glanced over his shoulder, down the steps to the squad car. Crawford had the driver's door open. He was pacing in the dirt.

"Look—Ramon, he's not here to arrest you. Just give me the card and we'll go away."

"The—the card?"

"The ID badge. Tillman's ID badge. To the North Satellite Library."

Ramon stepped out of the shadows. The muzzle of the shotgun jabbed into Sam's chest. "What the fuck you want that for?"

Sam didn't bat an eye. "Because we're going there."

"You're going there."

"I'm not running anymore. I told you that."

"Yeah, that turned out real well last time."

Sam shifted, clenching his jaw. "They got him, Ramon. They got Daniel."

The shotgun dropped away from his chest. "They what?"

"I don't give a shit if I get caught. I don't give a shit about anything except finding him."

Ramon stared at him for a couple of seconds. Then he lifted the shotgun again. For a terrifying moment, Sam waited for the blast. This was it. He was going to get his head blown off all over this wretched old porch in the middle of nowhere.

With a flick of his wrist, Ramon twirled the gun around and landed the butt in Sam's trembling hands. It was still warm, the wood like living flesh. Ramon produced the tiny white plastic card from his pants pocket. He turned it over in his hands and then replaced it.

"I got another gun. And I'm hangin' onto this 'til we get there."

"We?"

Ramon cocked his head toward the house. "Sofia's sick. Flu or something. Had it when I got back from the station, 'cause I wasn't there to make sure she was warm enough. Now, I can't even get out to the hospital. You wanna know why? 'Cause I got spooks followin' me wherever I go. Last time, riding in a cop car, they wouldn't dare do shit, but I saw 'em. I saw 'em, Sam." He reached through the window and fumbled around until he found what he was looking for. When he drew back outside, he was holding a second shotgun. "You're going somewhere we can teach these assholes a lesson, make 'em stop—get our lives back? I'm gonna be right beside you."

Sam couldn't help but smile. Over the last week, he had learned to stop expecting anything from anyone.

It felt good to know he still had one friend in the world.

∽

Ramon took another fifteen minutes getting Sofia ready. Sam waited in the hall outside, catching only snatches of what they muttered to each other.

"I'll be back," Ramon told her when he reached the door. "I'll be back before you know it, *hermana. Todo va a estar bien.*"

He looked grave when he came down to the squad car. "I need someone to stay with her. She shouldn't be alone."

Sam looked to Crawford, already reaching for the ignition. He clenched his teeth. "What am I, a genie? You think I can just snap my fingers and make—"

"Try, Detective. Please."

Crawford sighed. He spent the next five minutes on the phone.

Sam watched Ramon. He had always been a little more distant, on the fringe. It had been Sam and Caleb, with Ramon brought in to fill out the dynamic when he could pull himself away from Sofia. Sam had underestimated him. Behind the laid-back façade, the wisecracking and the sarcasm, was a man of more substance than most people Sam had ever met.

With a *clap*, Crawford hung up and paced to the foot of the porch. "I got someone coming out. Okay? Says it'll be fifteen, twenty minutes."

"Thank you, Detective."

Ramon nodded, grudging. "Thanks."

They traveled in silence.

It was after midnight. Places like the East Ridge Mall and other trendy suburban hotspots had thinned the downtown crowds during the day. At night, they became nonexistent. Where once, palatial movie houses, bars, speakeasies, and jazz clubs had kept the air alive with constant laughter and music, now, the sidewalks were lined with homeless people. Newspapers drifted across the street on a foul-smelling breeze.

Family-owned ground-floor businesses had long since given way to outlets—Office Max, Staples, Macy's—but even most of those had been forced to close out after their counterparts had outperformed them.

Now, at night, the city resembled a barren ghost town.

They passed by a burnt-out church, walls covered in graffiti, and wove through the streets for nearly half an hour. The nervous energy and adrenaline began turning to fatigue and despair in Sam's veins. This was hopeless. Why had he thought they could do this—just circle the block a couple of times until they found the right place?

"We're not going to find it."

Crawford signaled and made the same turn they had made three times already. "I bring you in, start making more of a stir—they realize I'm working with you, I'm gonna be sitting in the next cell over."

Ramon sat forward. A hint of a smile played on his lips. "I got an idea."

5

Bob Frankel lived in a stucco, ranch-style house in a neighborhood not unlike Sam's. The yards were divided by white, picket fences. Automated sprinkler systems filled the air with a moist, relaxing *hiss*. A gentle fog drifted across the road.

Every driveway sported two late-model imports.

Bob's hedges ran across the front of his yard, clipped into rigid, square perfection. Sprays of pink and violet erupted between them. Basketed geraniums and ferns lined the porch. Either Bob hired an expert gardener, or he had a secret green thumb that he'd concealed from the office for years.

At Ramon's urging, Crawford stopped directly in front of his house. There were no other cars at the curb—probably some gated community ordinance. Exactly one minute after he flipped on his flashing red-and-blue lights, shapes began to appear at windows all around them.

Lawn gnomes lined the sidewalk up to the porch.

Sam pounded on the front door and waited. A light came on, and footsteps sounded from somewhere in the house. Ramon was just reaching up to knock a second time, just for good measure, when the door swung open.

Bob Frankel was not a handsome man. Yanked out of sleep at one in the morning, he looked barely human. Thin strands of hair ran crookedly over the large bald crown of his head. His eyes were puffy, cheeks laced with pillow indentations. The tank top he'd shrugged on bulged around his belly.

"Mackie? Juarez?" His eyes flicked down to the shotguns in their hands. "Holy fucking *shit!*" Bob stumbled back from the door and tripped over his own feet.

He flailed on the floor and whimpered.

"Frankel." Sam edged forward and tapped Bob on the foot with his shoe. Frankel recoiled and raised shaking hands over his head.

"Christ, whatever it is…You want your job back? I'll get you— hell, I'll *promote* you. You and me, Mackie. Side-by-side. That what you want?"

Sam shook his head. "That is not what I want."

"Then what? Christ, what? What do you want?"

"Your computer. And your password. For about five minutes."

Bob Frankel gulped, gaze darting from Sam to Ramon and then to the flashing lights that framed them in the doorway. "You—you want what?"

∽

There was no map on Bob's computer, but with his login, they were able to access the CW mainframe. As a Senior Manager, Bob could tap most of the resources of the company, even if he couldn't walk in and use them directly. His ID wouldn't get them into the North Satellite Library, but it got them the address to which he could send requisition slips.

It was indeed downtown, though on the other side of Capitol Hill from where they had been looking. The warehouse district.

Purposely obscure. It would have taken them hours to find.

The North Satellite Library had been built into a nondescript brick manufacturing building perched on the side of a steep hill. A wrought iron fire escape crisscrossed one wall. It was flanked on either side by vacant lots and empty storage buildings. There were no signs, no labels, nothing to indicate it was anything more than just another sagging relic of the post-industrial era.

Nothing—save for the security cameras dangling from the eaves at each corner of the building, the coiled barbed-wire fencing, and the gated underground garage.

Crawford parked in front of a deserted hot dog stand across the street.

The night air was thick with dust, warm drafts from the subway tunnels below.

As they crossed the street, all three of them were careful to stay in the shadows of the fence. Transformer boxes dangling from wooden poles added a fierce *buzz* to the sound of faraway traffic.

Other than that, the library building was silent.

The ID card scanner blinked red—and then went green.

"I don't like this." Ramon glanced over his shoulder as they slipped through the opening chain-link gate. "They're gonna know. This guy's ID—they'd be idiots not to flag it or something. They're gonna fuckin' know we're in here."

"Then we'd better hurry."

No effort had been made to transform the dirt-and-concrete lot in front of the building into anything more presentable. Clearly, the North Satellite never made it onto Clayton Wesley's investor tours.

The front door was nondescript steel. A spray of scarlet graffiti arced across the handles. Broken beer bottles and cigarette butts lay in piles beneath the secondary ID scanner.

Walking through the door, Sam felt as though he had passed into another world altogether. In contrast with its exterior, the inside of the building was every bit as polished and refined as Clayton Wesley's estate. A striking arched corridor opened out into a large, circular lobby. Once upon a time, it had probably been a smelting furnace. Now, the ceiling had been hung with tasteful, shaded lights that cast down a warm glow.

A reception desk stood at the center. Hanging from the wall behind it, three large, flat-panel computer displays silhouetted the woman sitting before them with a grid of colored lines and dots.

She looked up at the sound of their footsteps—a little too stiffly. Horn-rimmed glasses perched on a nose curtained by curly hair. The quintessential librarian.

She popped out of her chair and skirted around the desk as they approached. "Welcome. Welcome, welcome—I thought you all were already...Well. I didn't know they'd be sending more of you. I thought you were just here for the..." She trailed off as she drew up in front of them, and squinted through her glasses. "Oh. I'm afraid we haven't met before."

Sam glanced at Ramon and Crawford. "Yeah. We're, uh—the company's been mobilizing all of us. You know—all hands in an emergency."

She clucked as she attached badges to each of their lapels. "Don't I know it. Haven't seen this much activity around here for ten years. Don't suppose you can talk about that, though, can you?"

Sam found his own eyes reflected back at him in her glasses. "No."

He turned and took in the room while she tended to Ramon and Crawford. Two elevators on opposite sides of the lobby. One door was bare brushed steel. The other had been painted a metallic blue.

Like the sticker on the back of Tillman's badge.

The left-hand screen over the reception desk blinked. A dot appeared near the bottom. A moment later, there was a second one, and then a third. Sam looked down at the badge hanging from his lapel. He took a couple of steps to the right, and the dot on the screen moved a fraction of an inch.

Tracking him.

The librarian cleared her throat. "Need a map, honey?"

Sam turned back. "Aren't there stairs?"

"Just the old fire escape outside. Something wrong with the elevator?"

Sam took the laminated map she was holding. "Guess not."

"It can't be this easy." Ramon shifted while Sam kept his eyes on the display. The elevator was small, built for only two people. The metal handrail dug into Sam's back. Their elbows all touched each other. It felt like there wasn't enough air to breathe.

They passed the second floor. Then the third. The blue elevator only went to the fifth floor. High-Security Archives.

"You listenin' to me? Ten to one, she's already called the armed friggin' cavalry."

"I hear you. You want to say it louder for the camera?"

Fourth floor.

Sam adjusted his jacket. There had been no way to keep the shotguns concealed, so he and Ramon had had to leave them in the car. All they had was a nightstick from Crawford's trunk and a tire iron that Sam had wedged into a spare holster under his arm.

It didn't feel like enough.

The elevator ground to a halt. For a second, nothing happened. Panicked thoughts shot through Sam's mind. They had already been discovered. Like fools, they'd walked right into a trap, and now, they'd be held here until Wesley's men could come and drag them away.

He broke out in a sweat.

Then the elevator chimed and the door slid open.

Sam tried to be ready for anything on the other side.

The traces of the original factory warehouse were still visible beneath the updated décor. Polished wooden rails and high-security door locks had been pasted atop brick, concrete, and exposed metal girders.

Sam edged out into the hall. He kept his hand in his jacket, clasped around the tire iron, as he looked both ways.

Nobody was visible. Reading nooks cut away from the central corridor between heavy metal doors that appeared to be locked and hermetically sealed. Padded benches sat ensconced around coffee tables. Above each, reflected in the polished surface, was another shimmering display of the facility and everyone in it.

Ramon stepped out of the elevator as Sam moved to the nearest of a series of laser-engraved plaques, one beside each door.

"You got the loan slip?"

"The what?"

"From Caleb's place. That we found with the ID?"

Ramon searched his pockets while Crawford approached one of the heavy metal doors. "This is some serious equipment." He ran an appraising hand over the reinforced bolts in the surface.

"Guess whatever's inside is pretty valuable." Sam spun the Tillman badge around and ran it through the magnetic reader.

The computer blinked red. He grimaced and tried it again. No luck. Not even the second, the third, or the fourth times.

"Here." Ramon unfolded the loan slip from his jacket pocket and squinted at a scrawl of tiny writing. "Last entry says DPCWBV-196-00-dash... You need me to read all of this?"

Sam squatted beside one of the coffee tables and spread out the map the receptionist had given him. He tried to ignore the shifting dots on the overhead display. Aside from the three of them, several yellow ones drifted here and there a few floors down, and there was a smattering of green ones at the bottom. They must have been the lowest-level access. Maintenance crews—dusting pages, updating computer databases.

"Here." Sam traced over the map with a finger. He looked up and tried to match it to what he could see from where they were standing. The hall curved to the right at the end of the current segment. The door just around the corner led, on the diagram, into a circular old tower at the back of the building.

Shaped like a grain silo, it was labeled, *DPCWVB-196*.

Sam pointed. "That way."

They rounded the bend in the passage and emerged upon another, identical to the first. Skimming along the walls with an outstretched finger, Sam stopped before last glass plaque on the left. It was room 196.

"Here goes nothing." He swiped the card.

The reader thought for almost ten seconds.

Then it flashed green.

Somewhere down the hall, around the corner, Sam heard a footstep.

He whirled. A shadow flitted away from the end of the passage, but when Sam spun to the nearest LCD, mounted over the nook at his left, nothing moved. They were the only three blue dots on the map. Behind him, a hiss of air escaped the edges of the door. One-by-one, equidistant latches clicked open, starting at the top and moving in parallel around both sides until they reached the floor.

"I think there's someone here," Sam hissed.

"You're imagining shit." Ramon pushed at the door.

The hinges groaned as it swung open.

The room on the other side was circular, carpeted, about the size of Sam's kitchen. A broad, mahogany table filled the center, surrounded by high-backed chairs. Behind them, rising toward the conical ceiling, were more books than Sam could count.

He stepped to the middle of the room and gazed upward, spinning in a circle as he tried to absorb it all. Visible only as a tiny point from out front, the top of the tower must have risen several stories above the roof of the primary warehouse, encompassing hundreds of volumes, most with nothing left on their old leather spines. Here and there, the books gave way to wooden cabinets or metal filing trunks—gaps in the patchwork of reds, greens, and browns.

"Jesus." Crawford holstered his nightstick and planted his hands on his hips. "What the hell is this place?"

Sam dropped to his knees beside a cardboard box that had been removed from one of the bottom shelves and brought over to the reading table. Black marker was scrawled across one of the open flaps: *00-LkK-Research-UK1827981.*

He pinned it the rest of the way open with his knee. Inside was a sheaf of plastic baggies. Sam lifted one out and held it up to the Tiffany desk lamp at the center of the table. It looked like dust. Ordinary rock dust.

A tag dangled from the top of the bag with a barcode and more strings of letters and numbers that seemed meaningless.

"Whatever Caleb was looking at, it's over this way, I think." Ramon stood on tiptoe beside a metal cabinet near the door. Two shelves had been removed to accommodate it. He showed Sam the slip. "Zero-zero-P63a. Whatever the hell that means. If it was even Caleb, and not someone else who checked it out before he found this shit."

There was a laminated sheet of paper tacked to the end of each shelf. Another diagram—a map of its contents. He traced the numbered quadrants along the curving wall until he came to a collection of leather-bound notebooks. They were held together by a rubber band. The paper labels taped to the bottoms of their spines all matched the final entry on the loan slip.

Sam scooped them into his arms and brought them to the table.

"Keep looking." Sam gestured to the rest of the room. "See if you can find anything with a—a dark tower in it. Or anything about a soldier named Donald Pryce, or Wesley Clayton, or a place called Black Valley."

Another sound echoed from the hallway. All of them stopped moving and looked at each other.

A blue glow leaked from another LCD screen framed over the

doorway. According to the monitor, they were still the only people on the floor.

Crawford grimaced and pulled out his nightstick again. "I'll check it out."

Sam flipped open the leather folder on the top of the stack.

Fastened to the inside flap was an old black-and-white picture of President Kennedy, Henry Kissinger, and several other diplomats huddled around the desk in the Oval Office.

Sam thumbed several pages in. It was all dense text, typewritten, official government seals heading each page. He tried to skim, but it was hard to make out what he was seeing.

The only common element was the faded, red-inked stamp, inserted as a watermark in the background: *Classified*.

It was Caleb Heaven. A conspiracy theorist could have had a field day in here.

Spinning away from the table, he peered up at the looming shelves as Ramon lifted out another box of files and began unpacking it.

Sam skimmed over the index a second time. Most of each entry was just code, but one part of every call number ascended alphabetically from one item to the next. The *B*'s were across the room behind him, the *M*'s a few feet to his left.

Sam edged around the curved shelves. He stopped before a stack of manila folders wedged between three massive leather volumes and a wooden cabinet. They were labeled with names. Most of them, Sam didn't recognize. He nudged one open and skimmed it over.

A military dossier—medals, combat history, time in Korea. The subject was a young man, pictured in an old black-and-white passport photo from the 1950s. Sam worked his way down the others. His fingers stopped on one file sticking a little farther out than all of the others.

The tip of a faded red paper protruded from inside, like a tongue. Sam stared.

He knew that paper. He knew it, because he had spent day after day pushing it into the hands of strangers on street corners near Riley's school.

It was one of the flyers he and Ann had printed up.

He yanked the folder from the pile.

MACKIE.

"Yo."

Sam jumped at the sound of Ramon's voice.

"Yo, man, were you even looking at this?"

Ramon had stopped going through the cardboard box he'd pulled and turned his full attention to the leather folder still open on the table. He turned a page.

Sam didn't answer. He dropped to his knees, positioning the manila file to catch some of the light from the rest of the room.

"Yo, Sam..."

"I don't care about the JFK bullshit."

The cover page he'd just come to took his breath away. It was from the hospital, the day Riley was born. Different from the picture he'd found earlier—a beaming young Sam, infant son in his arms, happy, leaning over Ann in her hospital bed. They were a moment away from a kiss.

"No, but—"

"*Ramon.*"

"Whatever, man. But you said to look for 'Black Valley.'"

Sam got to his feet and crossed to Ramon's side.

"Right here. And here—oh, here, too." Ramon leaned down and underlined the words with his index finger.

Sam skipped back a paragraph:

> *In keeping with principles and postscripts of said uprising [ref. 11-k; a.k.a. 'Bay of Pigs'], it has been deemed necessary by this institution to commence research and development of key assets in strategic locations with respect to existing hostile military assets held in the indicated region. Objective is military control of key political targets including...*

What followed was a list of names. Cities. Russian cities. Among them were Moscow, St. Petersburg, and several others Sam vaguely thought he remembered from junior high geography. He blinked and skimmed down a couple of lines.

> *Approval hereby issued for said project [codename: 'Black Valley'] at fifty-percent (50%) capacity, with subsequent full approval contingent upon verification of assets attrib-*

uted to said location [ref. 11-dd5 'Lake Kitoto, Dem. Rep.
Congo, Africa']. Additional verification and regular scien-
tific research reports required upon…

Sam flipped to the next page, growing impatient. It was the same—more long, unbroken chunks of executive orders, classified operations, and god knew what else. Each page bore two signatures at the bottom: one belonged to Donald Pryce, the other to Robert McNamara, United States Secretary of Defense under President John F. Kennedy.

Dates littered the margins. The first paragraph he'd read was labeled, *August, 1961*. The second, *October* of the same year.

"Ramon, what is all this?"

"I dunno, man. You tell me. What the fuck is this Black Valley?"

Sam scowled and slid the book toward him. "See if you can find anything else."

"*Anything*'s all there is. What part of 'anything' do you want?"

Sam didn't know, other than answers that still seemed as impossibly distant as ever. He turned and peeled back the second page from the manila folder. Cold sweat leapt to the palms of his hands.

The woman staring out of the photograph was instantly familiar—and yet not. He didn't remember ever seeing her before in his life, but there was something so elemental about the look in her eyes, the shape of her face.

She was family.

Not another foster parent, an adopted sister, a distant aunt of another stranger.

She was *family*. Sam's family.

And she was holding a baby.

He clawed at the photograph, flipping it over to scour the other side for anything that could identify it.

At the bottom left corner, there was a small inscription in pencil:

Grace – March 20, 1964, Ellis Ranch.

Beneath it was a torn envelope. The paper was soft, flimsy, lined around the edges with the red-and-blue checkered pattern of an international delivery. There were creases, the exact size of the photograph, where it had once made an impression from the inside.

The return address listed Grace Franklin and a house in Kearny Valley. It was a small town about an hour out of the city. It was also ten minutes from the orphanage and the oldest existing record of Sam's life.

The letter had evidently been intercepted. Grace had been trying to send it to someone named Monica, far, far away:

> *LK Research Ctr.*
> Lake Kitoto
> Democratic Republic of Congo
> Africa

Sam peeled open the envelope. Inside was a small note written in hasty script: *Mon – He's here. He made it. Love, G.*

Sam went back to the picture and focused on the infant in the woman's arms. The tiny, beady eyes stared not at the camera but at somewhere beyond it. Worry creased the child's young forehead, but there was something distant and thoughtful about its expression.

Something to which Sam felt a connection on a level he could not begin to explain.

"Whoa." Ramon had advanced a half-dozen pages through more dry blocks of typewritten text. He spun the folder around so Sam could see. "You're in here, man. Take a look."

> *Continued testing on the subject ['Sam Mackie'] has proven inconclusive. Results have yielded no productive analyses. In light of increasing demands from other military interests, and in combination with similarly disappointing results from all other quarters of BV facility, recommendation is a reduction in funding and possible closure on research project. Defensive measures can be maintained with minimal staff and limited additional expenditure.*

"They were...performing tests on me?" Sam rifled through three more pages. "What kind of tests?"

"I dunno, man. You got me." Ramon squinted past him to the picture and the envelope. "Holy shit. Who's that? She looks just like you."

Sam opened his mouth.

A *crash* echoed down the hallway from outside. It was somewhere close, somewhere just around the corner. Sam and Ramon both jumped. Before either of them could move, Crawford dashed inside and threw his weight against the giant metal door.

"Help me."

"Detective, what—"

"Seal this. *Now.*"

Sam and Ramon flung themselves against the heavy plank. It swung shut with a groan of rusting hinges and a loud, resounding *boom*.

"Press it—that one!" Crawford slapped his palm over a button just to the left of the door and nodded at an identical one on the other side.

Sam pushed it. The latches all around the door hissed and began clicking into place, one-by-one. Sam could feel the change of air pressure in his ears.

Something slammed into the door from the other side—bracing, clawing.

Sam staggered back and let go of the button. The latches stopped.

"No!" Crawford waved, frantic. "Get back there! Make it finish."

Sam dove at the button. Another *thump* rocked the door from the top right corner—the second-to-last latch. The metal shuddered and bowed inward before the seal drew it together and fastened it into place.

Crawford let out a breath, spent, and stumbled back. He was drenched in sweat and shaking. "They came so fast." He rounded on the room, eyes darting from shelf to shelf before turning upward. "We need to find a way out of here."

"Who came?" Sam rounded on the LCD hanging over the door. Still only three dots.

"They don't have IDs. They don't show up on the monitors."

Sam caught Crawford by the arm as he was reaching for the door to one of the metal cabinets. "Who are they, Detective?"

"Remember that armed response you were expecting?"

A loud metallic rattle echoed from a central air vent, squeezed between two bookcases by the floor. All three of them swiveled to stare at it.

"It's too small. Nobody could fit through that." Ramon took a cautious step back as a finger of black curled out from the grate.

It thickened and spread as it rose into the center of the room. Ramon sniffed. "What the fuck?"

"We have to get out of here." Sam caught a whiff of it, too. Acrid, stifling. It made his eyes burn and his throat close up.

He dashed back to the table and scooped everything he could into the manila folder. Tucking it under his arms, he grabbed the rolling wooden ladder and yanked it around until the tracks lined up with the small ledge overlooking the top of the highest bookshelf.

There was a spot, opposite the door, where a small halo of natural light came alive amid drifts of dust. A window. A window within reach of the ladder.

The smoke from the air vent thickened. Sam pulled his shirt collar up over his nose and mouth, but he could still smell it through the fabric. The cloud moved quickly, pooling at the floor to rise toward Sam's chest.

He climbed onto the first rung of the ladder.

Crawford pulled him off. "I'll go first. It's dangerous. You don't even know what's up there."

"Detective—"

"Damn it, let me by." Crawford scrambled past him and kicked his way up the ladder, two rungs at a time.

Sam tucked the file folder under his arm and mounted it. Ramon scrambled onboard behind him.

The room was even taller than it had appeared from the floor. Ten feet up, Sam checked his progress and saw he still had at least that far again to go before he got to the top. He stretched another several feet.

The lights winked out.

Ramon missed a rung and barked his shin on the next one down. "Fuck!"

Sam slowed and twisted around. "You okay?"

"Yeah, damn it, just a helluva bruise and—"

The first door latch—at the top of the frame—gave an anemic wheeze and then fell open. The second and third ones, on either side, followed suit. The power. They'd cut the power to manually override the latches.

"Ramon, hurry!" Sam lunged at the next rung up.

The manila folder, pinned under his arm, slipped onto its side. He tensed, stopped short, and tried to grab at it. His fingers closed around the card stock on the outside just as the contents dropped out the bottom and fluttered to the floor.

The photograph. The note. *The addresses.*

Sam's shoe came down hard on Ramon's hand.

"Son-of-a-bitch, Sam, what the—"

Sam swung out onto the side of the ladder and tried to shimmy past Ramon, but he missed a rung, himself, and suddenly, he lost his balance. Ramon caught him by one arm, but the weight was too much and at too awkward an angle.

With a grunt, Ramon lost his grip and then both of them fell.

They hit the floor hard, twelve feet below. Unpadded concrete. The drop was not huge, but it hurt like hell. Ramon winced and clutched his knee before he broke into furious hacking and coughing as the smoke pressed in around them.

Sam tried to call out to him, but the gas burned the air from his lungs. His eyes began to water.

"I'm... I'm fine..." Ramon limped to his feet. "C'mon!"

Two more latches clicked open at the door. There were only three more to go.

Sam started to rise, but then he saw the photograph, face-up, on the floor. The photograph of his—his sister? His mother? His *family.* He lunged for it, and managed to scoop it up along with the envelope that had held it before Ramon tore him back.

Sam struggled. This was why they'd come here. Evidence. Information. If they left it behind...

"We're gonna *die,*" Ramon rasped in his ear. He heaved Sam toward the ladder, wincing every time he put weight on his knee.

The second-to-last pair of latches shuddered open.

The smoke was so thick in the room that Sam couldn't even see the ceiling anymore. From somewhere far away, he was dimly aware of Crawford shouting something, but his head was now spinning. His ears buzzed, and blurry smears clouded his vision.

He tried to blink it away, but every time he closed his eyes, it seemed to get worse.

Ramon shoved him to the ladder. "Up! Get up!"

"You... you go first... I need to... to catch my... my breath..."

"Get the *fuck up!*" Ramon gave him a feeble boost onto the fourth rung before doubling over in another fit of coughing.

The last latch released.

With a *hiss*, the door came open.

Sam climbed. He climbed for his life, hand-over-hand, gulping in what air he could get and shutting down every other part of his mind until—

The gunshot.

He froze, hand reaching, midair, three rungs from the top. As he turned to squint back down through the haze, it felt as though everything was happening in slow-motion.

For one long moment, he locked eyes with Ramon, six feet down. Pain became fear on Ramon's ruddy face before it melted into a distant, lingering peace.

Then he let go.

The swirling blackness swallowed him. Some part of Sam heard his body hit the floor, but his mind refused to accept it.

"Ramon!"

Four more thundering gunshots left Sam's ears ringing. Bullets thudded into the bookcases on either side of him, spitting chips of wood and torn paper into the air. Another shot embedded into the rung he'd just grabbed, and it cracked and came apart in his hands.

"Mackie!" Crawford's head ducked out over the lip of the top bookcase, five feet away. "Mackie, climb!"

"But Ramon—"

"*Sam!*"

A shape appeared in the acrid black smoke below. For a fraction of a second, Sam thought it was Ramon. He had survived. He was on his feet—on his way to escape.

Then he caught the glint of a gun. The figure slowly tilted its head upward, face hidden behind a gas mask.

Panic. Before he knew what was happening, Sam was climbing again. One rung down from the top, something sharp nicked his calf. It stung, hot, cruel, unrelenting. Sam lifted his leg and found blood dribbling from his pant leg.

He'd been shot.

The world spun around him and he felt himself start to sway.

Crawford's hand closed around his shoulder. "Up here, Sam! Now!"

Grabbing him by the forearm, Crawford helped to heave Sam up over the edge as another volley of bullets pattered across the wood. The Detective smashed the window out with his elbow, glass spitting onto the wrought-iron platform of the fire escape in the open night air.

"Watch your head."

"My—"

Crawford pressed him through the ragged opening.

Wriggling through the dust, Sam glanced back and found himself face-to-face with the ID badge dangling from Crawford's lapel. He ripped it off, wadded it together with his own, and tossed them back into the smoke, below.

Then he was outside.

A cool evening breeze penetrated the grating. It sent a shiver over Sam's sweaty arms, forehead, and chest. He staggered to his feet and turned back to help Crawford out onto the platform.

"Ramon," Sam gasped. "Ramon—we have to go back. He's... he..."

"He's gone, Sam."

"No, he might've—"

"Sam." Crawford took him by the shoulders. "You can't help him. But you can still help your wife and your son."

Sam flinched. A fire bell went off somewhere inside the old library building. Sirens rose and fell in the distance.

Sam turned back to the window just as the masked figure appeared at the top of the ladder.

They pounded down the wrought-iron fire escape, taking the steps two at a time. The first shot came as they reached the landing on the third floor. It glanced off one of the weathered old railings, and sparks spat into the air.

Sam flattened himself against the brick wall, but Crawford shoved him forward. "We can't stop. We can't *stop!*"

Bullets spat down on them. Sam ducked, dodged, did everything he could to keep his movement fast and unpredictable. The toes on his right foot had gone numb where he'd been hit. He didn't dare look down.

A floor-and-a-half from the concrete parking lot, the iron struts supporting the stairs groaned and began to shudder free. Three shapes thundered from platform to platform above them. The bolts affixing the structure to the old factory building were starting to give.

At the next landing, Sam felt the whole construction shift beneath his feet. This time, it didn't stop moving when he did. "Jump!" Sam shouted. He heaved himself over the railing and hurled to the ground. Pain leapt through the wound in his foot as he landed on it with all of his weight. He couldn't afford to stop moving. Sliding across the ground, he dragged it after him as gunfire lit up the night and kicked dirt into the air.

The bending iron groaned. Suddenly, the gunmen broke off, and a shout arose from somewhere high up, near the roof.

Crawford hit the ground four feet away and leapt to his feet to pull Sam after him. They had just reached the outer barbed-wire gate when the front door to the North Satellite Library banged open.

"Stop!"

Sam didn't recognize the man in black fatigues who edged out. He leveled the muzzle of an assault rifle at them.

"Hands where I can see them." He was slow on the approach, cautious—professional. He moved, Sam thought, like a soldier.

Flattening himself against the cyclone fence, Sam felt something shift inside his jacket. The tire iron. The shoulder holster holding it had snapped in the last fall from the ladder. Now, it slid to the edge of his waistline, straining against the cloth.

"Drop the club."

Sam started to reach for his zipper before he realized the man was talking to Crawford. The police nightstick clattered to the ground.

The man was only five or six feet away now. His face was hidden behind another black gas mask, but his eyes were gray as gunmetal, weathered around the edges. Sam couldn't tell how old he was, but there was something world-weary about his voice: "Hello, Mr. Mackie." The gun barrel lowered a fraction of an inch. The man was three feet away. Sam could see his breath in the frigid night air. "You're lucky to be alive."

"Who are you? What do you want from me?"

"Just an instrument. So are you. And *you...*" He turned the gun on Crawford. "You're just in the way." His gloved finger stretched toward the trigger.

Sam's jacket shifted and fell open, and the tire iron dropped out the bottom. He spun and grabbed it out of the air, swinging around with the same momentum to strike it across the man's head.

It *cracked*, metal on bone. The man stumbled back and clamored to keep a hold of the rifle. Sam switched hands, wound up, and struck again.

The man's knees buckled. His gun fell to the pavement at Crawford's feet, and the detective swept it up before the man could get it back.

"Where's my son?" Sam swung again. The tire iron *thudded* into the man's chest.

He curled into a fetal position, clutching his stomach and coughing.

"Where?"

"Mackie!" Crawford caught his arm as he was about to break the soldier's jaw. "We have to go. Now!"

Sam glanced back over his shoulder. Smoke poured from the back of the building. The gunners on the fire escape had almost made it to the bottom, winding up for the last jump.

"Where's the ID?"

"The what?"

"The badge, Sam! Where's the badge?"

Sam fumbled with his jacket pockets. There was the photograph. There was the envelope. Where was Tillman's badge?

"It won't open. The gate won't open without it!"

The first of the gunners dropped to a crouch on the pavement beneath the wrought-iron stairs. Crawford spun, flicked off the assault rifle's safety catch, and sent a spray of gunfire ripping through the night. Chunks of brick and mortar rained to the ground. The gunner hit the deck and covered his head with his hands.

Sam kicked at the gate. It wouldn't give. He tried his pockets again, moved to his shirt, his jeans. *Where the hell was the badge?*

A hand closed around his ankle. Sam whirled. The masked soldier on the ground made a grab for the tire iron against the fence.

Crawford swung the butt of the gun and sent him crumpling back to the ground.

"Here!" Sam's fingers closed around the tiny piece of plastic where it had fallen inside the envelope. He swiped it through the magnetic reader.

The machine blinked red.

A second gunner leapt to the ground beneath the fire escape and drew his gun.

No green light. They had killed Tillman's card.

Crawford glanced over his shoulder as he braced the rifle against his chest. "Whatever you're doing, do it faster."

"It won't work. The card won't work!"

"Try his!" The detective jerked his head at the soldier on the ground.

The man's ID was pinned to the vest under his flak jacket. Sam yanked it free and swiped it through the reader.

The machine blinked green.

"Crawford!"

With an electronic hum, the gate ground open.

They were free.

Sam grabbed Crawford, and together, they wriggled through the widening opening and bolted across the street to the squad car.

The men from upstairs opened fire as they reached the edge of the vacant lot. Crawford twisted the keys in the ignition, dropped the car into gear, and floored it. The car leapt from the curb, windows shattering as bullets peppered the passenger side.

Sam ducked and threw his hands over his head. Glass shards pelted down over his neck and shoulders.

"Hang on!" Crawford twisted the wheel.

The rear of the car skidded around. Tires spinning, they roared through the billowing smoke of the North Satellite Library and then up Capitol Hill into the night.

TWENTY

IT WAS NOT UNTIL they were ten blocks away that Sam sat back and tried to brush the glass from his clothing. He was shaking all over, covered in dirt and blood and soot from whatever it was they had pumped into the archives room on the fifth floor. Lights rushed at him through the cracked windshield. The world seemed to be flying at a hundred miles an hour.

"You okay?" Crawford reached over and shook him. "Hey. Mackie. You there?"

"I'm... I'm here." Sam turned to peer through the Plexiglas partition at the back seat of the squad car. Ramon's two shotguns lay across the cushions. They slid over each other as Crawford took a turn.

Sam felt hollow inside. All parts of his body hurt. Dull, throbbing pain coursed up from his foot, now drenched in blood. His legs were bruised, cut in a dozen places, muscles spent. It seemed so— distant. Abstract. As though it wasn't even his body.

"...get you to a hospital," Crawford was saying.

"No."

"Sam, you've been shot."

"No, we have to—we've got to... here, I have..." He found the envelope wadded up in his jacket pocket and smoothed it out over the dash. "This address. In Kearny Valley... it's all I've—it's the only thing I've got. We have to get there now. *Now,* Crawford! Before they—if this is where they've got... it's the only—"

"Sam." Crawford slowed. "Sam, take a goddamn breath."

Sam inhaled. With it, he felt it all flooding back in—the sketches, the valley, his children, *Ramon*. "Oh, Jesus." He clutched his head in his hands. "Oh Jesus fucking Christ. Ramon..."

"Calm down. We're gonna fix this."

"Someone has to get to his—to his house. His sister, Crawford. His sister can't be alone. She's got—he gives her this...her medication and she's...she needs him. She *needs* him."

"I'm on it. Don't worry. I'll call it in. First, we need to get you to a hospital."

"No. I'm not going to the hospital. It just nicked me, see? I need..." Sam broke off, trying to put everything in perspective, force it all into focus. "Can I borrow your phone, Detective?"

"What for?"

"Please. Just let me borrow your phone."

5

He should have known she would go to her family.

Sam hadn't been out to the trailer park since Ann's mother had died. The last fourteen years had not been kind to it.

Crawford put the squad car in park and squinted out the windshield at the dangling wooden sign. "You sure this is the place?"

"Thanks for the ride, Detective."

"What about your leg?"

It still burned under the hasty field dressing Crawford had jerry-rigged with the First Aid kit in the trunk. It wasn't bad—compared with what had happened to Ramon.

"Later," Sam said.

The detective caught him in the midst of climbing out into the sprinkling rain. "Joe, my Captain—he's ordered me in for a chat. I'm gonna be out of touch for a little bit."

"Call me." Sam started to straighten again.

"It would help if..." Crawford bit his lip. "The envelope. What we got back there. A little evidence goes a long way with Joe."

"Detective—"

"Sam, I've put a lot of trust in you. A lot. I want to help you, but unless you want us doing this on our own, you're going to need to give me something."

Sam stared at him long and hard. When, at last, he handed over the envelope, it was like parting with a piece of himself. He tightened his grip when Crawford started to pull away. "Ramon died for this."

Crawford swallowed. "I know. I know that, Sam. I swear to you, I'm not gonna let this rest. I'm gonna get a team together. We're gonna do this. Find these people. Make them pay."

"Thank you, Crawford."

"Gerry. It's Gerry, actually."

Sam nodded. "Talk to you soon. Two hours, okay?"

"At the most."

He waited until the squad car had crawled away into the night and then, with a deep breath, Sam approached the front entrance. There was no gate. Once upon a time, the whole park had been surrounded by a wooden fence, but most of that had succumbed to time and weather. Plastic tarps and corrugated metal planks filled in some of the gaps, while others were left to gape into the night.

Most of the gravel had long since dispersed from the road, leaving twin muddy ruts down the center. Stickling trees protruded between the rusted carcasses of pickup trucks and muscle cars from the '70s.

Sam picked his way over standing water the color of chocolate milk. It smelled like piss and beer. Cigarette butts floated like dead fish in the puddles gathering between the ruts in the road. There was trash everywhere.

Even after all of these years, Sam remembered the way to Ann's corner. He'd jogged it with her father at his back, the first time he'd ever come to visit. The old man was three-quarters of the way through a handle of Jack Daniels at the time, and a pale young suitor with a nervous stutter was the last thing he'd been willing to tolerate.

Tramping through the rain, Sam almost imagined he could see his old footprints in the muck.

A third of the trailers stood derelict, windows boarded up, blackened from within by fire. Fences of empty bottles enclosed them like broken teeth.

Tents littered the children's play area at the center of the park. What remained of a jungle gym had been shrouded by a tarpaulin to form a hovel—home to the peons of a squalid kingdom.

Sam shivered.

It had been there, surrounded by the wasteland where she'd been born, that Sam had first fallen in love with Ann. It wasn't the bruises on her mother's neck. It wasn't the broken television with its scrolling snowy picture, the chunks of food splattered all over the kitchen walls. It wasn't the broken bottles or the tiny closet she called her bedroom. It was her.

The way she shone like a diamond, even in this rancid, hellish nightmare. The way she had endured for so long the kind of suffering Sam had never even imagined in his many afternoons alone. It was not pity that had drawn him to her. It was respect. That she could emerge from all of this and still be *her*.

Her family owned three trailers. Around here, that made them kings.

Her parents lived in one, uncle and aunt in another, a sister and her sometimes-husbands shacked up together in the third.

They were arranged in a crescent, backs to the road, circling their wagons to keep the prying world out.

Sam spotted them through the meager vegetation from several hitches away. Light glowed from the windows. Sam was drawn toward a candle near the ground in a gap between two of the trailers. He only picked out the umbrella when it moved. Ann's face appeared under the edge, awash in the warm, flickering firelight.

Sam jogged the rest of the way. She didn't bother to stand. He didn't have their son with him.

He drew up before her, panting, soaked. Ann didn't speak. A few seconds passed. Staring at her, into her eyes, all Sam could think was how much he still loved her. How much he wanted her back. She was his home. She was *him*.

"Hi." He dropped onto the severed tree branch that sufficed for a doorstep.

"There's chicken. Inside. If you want any. KFC, but it's still warm."

Sam nodded. "Thank you."

"I can get some for you. You know. If you're—if you don't want to talk to my dad still."

"Ann..." Sam squeezed his eyes shut. She sounded like a teenager, and, sitting next to her, shivering against the rain, Sam realized that was just how he felt. Confused, vulnerable, desperate, afraid. Twenty-five years, and they hadn't gone anywhere. They had come full-circle. And what did they have to show for it?

"I..." There was so much he wanted to say, but at that moment, he couldn't. "Aren't you cold? Sitting out here?"

"No."

"Here. Take my jacket."

"I'm fine."

He shrugged out of it and draped it over her shoulders.

Ann sniffed and looked away. "There's a trailer, a few stalls down. It's this family, five kids. I kept seeing them in the windows, earlier. Making dinner. Getting ready for bed. I kept thinking it was him. Them. Both of them."

Sam didn't know what to say.

"I was trying to get him back. I don't know if—I don't think you knew about it."

"What do you mean?"

"Daniel. I was going to get him back."

"Get him...?"

"As soon as I completed the program. I had two more weeks. And I got a lawyer. I got all the paperwork."

Sam stiffened. "What are you talking about?"

"I wanted him, Sam. I wanted him to have a mother."

"He did. He *does*."

"I wanted him to come home to someone who'd be there for him every day. Someone who would talk to him and listen to him and—"

"I *would* listen. We talked—"

"But he respected you so goddamn much."

"We would..." Sam broke off, digesting. "He what?"

Ann looked at him. "You didn't know that, did you? He was so desperate to be like you. To be what you wanted him to be."

"But I...I never tried to make him into anything. I never pressured him. I always let him do whatever he wanted."

"Maybe. But he wasn't going to be Riley. He's never going to be Riley. And that's all that mattered."

"I never tried to make him into Riley."

"Kids are perceptive, Sam. I'm not saying it was your fault. Lord knows, I blamed you, but I don't anymore. All those weekends he came to my house, all he'd talk about was you. The tiniest little nod from you—any time you noticed him, asked him a question, took him out to throw a ball around for fifteen minutes when you got home from work. All those hours we'd talk? That's all we talked about, Sam. We talked about you."

Sam stared out into the driving rain. There was a light on in the trailer Ann had pointed out—the one with the family, the five kids. It made Sam feel lonelier than he ever had in his life.

He caught a whiff of Ann's perfume, and then he found his arms around her. It had been a reflex. A deeper need than he could control. Sitting with her pressed against him, the two of them together—for a moment, he felt whole again. He felt *right*.

Slowly, they drew apart. The candle had blown out, but the reflected moonlight caught tears in Ann's eyes.

Sam kissed her.

"What are you doing?" Her voice was a whisper.

"What are *we* doing? What have we been doing? Why have we been wasting so much time?"

"What time?"

"Like this. Apart. Not—"

"Sam."

"Not *right*."

"Sam, it's too…we're not…we don't work."

"That's not true. We decided not to work. But we can."

"Sam, you're just upset."

"My life has been on hold for thirteen years. Breakfast, work, dinner, sleep, over and over… Waiting for it to mean something again. I think it's going to be on hold until I die unless I get you back."

"Sam—"

"Please. I need this. I need *you*."

"*Sam.*"

"*I need you.*"

She stared right back at him. Maybe it was the rain, or maybe both of them were crying. It didn't matter. When she kissed him, just for a moment, all of the sorrow melted away.

ഗ

That evening, when they were together, Sam kept slipping into the past. It was as though he was surrounded by ghosts of Ann and himself, younger, happier, whispering in the howling wind as they rolled about beneath the sheets.

They stayed in the same seedy motel, two blocks away from the trailer park, where they had gone the night after Ann's mother died.

He still remembered hearing her voice on the phone at work—thick with tears, quivering with uncertainty. Caleb had watched over Riley while they came out for the funeral. Even Ann had had to admit she didn't want Riley out there after she saw how much her father was drinking.

That afternoon, the old man had started shouting at Ann. Then her sisters had chimed in. They'd always blamed her for running away from them. Sam got involved, and it became ugly. After everything was over, they came back to the motel, and they just sat. Then, slowly, numbly, needing each other, they wound up together.

That was the night Daniel had been conceived.

Now, they made love with the same feverish desperation. The need to feel *something* other than what they were feeling.

Afterward, they lay together, and Sam was, for a few brief moments, at peace. With it came the guilt—the guilt of pleasure in the face of everything still hanging over them. The guilt of knowing that Daniel was still out there, and that time was ticking by.

He rolled over and looked at the bedside clock.

"What is it?" Ann asked. "Sam?"

After he told her about the address in Kearny Valley, she was out of bed in a heartbeat. "How could—how can we just…we can't just sit here." She wriggled into her rain-drenched shirt.

"Crawford has it. The envelope with the address. He said he'd be back in an hour or two and that he'd have a full team."

"It's been three hours, Sam."

"I know. Believe me, I know."

Ann flipped open her cell phone and tossed it onto the bed. "So call him."

Crawford sounded strained when he picked up. "I just got out, and I'm on my way."

Sam turned from the window to take in the dismal little room. The blankets were a twisted mess, water leaking in through the ceiling. The whole motel smelled like mildew and dust. "How about we meet somewhere?"

A moment of silence. "Other than the trailer park."

"Yeah."

"Corner of Creighton and Seventeenth?"

"Sure."

Ann planted her hands on her hips as Sam hung up. "So?"
"He's coming."

5

Sam huddled against the wall beneath the overhang of the
awning, and squinted out through the rain at a cluster of kids around
a pickup truck. A few of them wore hoods. A few were wet as dogs
and just didn't give a shit. They had skateboards tucked under their
arms, crisscrossing over the pavement at the fringes of the light.

He glanced at his watch. It was almost one in the morning.

Ann was sitting on the cinderblock windowsill. Beneath the
harsh fluorescent light, she looked like hell. She was watching the
kids, too, craning her neck. Straining for a glimpse at their faces.
Because anyone could be Riley. Anyone, anywhere. Or—now—
Daniel.

Sam grimaced. He caught the eye of the register girl through the
window over Ann's head. The store at Creighton and Seventeenth
purported to sell more than just liquor, but forests of colored bottles
were all Sam could make out. A few of the other windows had been
spray-painted over with graffiti and subsequent blotches of white.

A bundled sleeping bag in a snarl of blankets lay tucked at the
opposite end of the overhang. Even from here, the occasional waft of
beer and body odor escaped when the figure moved.

Sam shivered and squinted out into the night.

A skateboard kid zipped across the lot, arced around and came
swooping back. His eyes fixed on Sam from beneath the edge of his
hood—resentful, distrustful. What were these two middle-aged parents doing in the middle of this neighborhood in the early hours of
the morning?

Good question, Sam thought.

It had been twenty-five minutes since he hung up the phone
with Crawford. Both subsequent follow-up calls had met with only
voicemail.

When he lowered himself onto the sill beside Ann, she edged a
fraction of an inch closer to him. "What if he's not coming?" she said.

"He's coming." He had to be. He had the envelope.

The kids at the pickup truck drew together, huddled in some
kind of conference. Sam glimpsed an exchange—something plastic

that caught the light of the liquor store sign. Then they broke away. Three of them spun around and hopped onto their skateboards with a clatter. Slow, confident, self-assured, they rolled toward Sam and Ann.

Sam stood. He glanced over his shoulder, through the window. The proprietor was nowhere in sight. The counter was abandoned.

"Ann ... " He gulped. "Ann, get up."

A glint of something sharp flashed from two of the skaters' pockets. The third, in the middle, farthest forward, grinned beneath a patchwork of shadows from his hood. His face was cruel.

"Hey," he said. "Nice night, huh?"

Headlights cut across the lot. All three boys swiveled around on their boards.

A teal green Subaru wagon veered in from the street in a spray of kicked-up rainwater.

The boys shared one last glance and then they scattered as the car pulled to the curb. They had disappeared into the night by the time Crawford rolled down his window. "Sorry I'm late. Hop in."

The car was a mess. Fast food cups and napkins littered the seats. CDs lay strewn across the dashboard. There was a wire-frame cage in the very back, reinforced metal.

Sam froze halfway in and blinked at the empty car.

Ann twisted around in her seat to peer out at the parking lot. Rain streamed down the windows. Streetlamps cast pools of orange snaking off between the decrepit old shops and mobile homes.

She caught Crawford's eye in the mirror. "I thought you were bringing the cavalry."

He rolled up his window and locked the doors after Sam was the rest of the way inside.

"Detective? Where's the cavalry?"

Crawford grimaced. "You're looking at it."

"What?" Sam said.

"Things didn't turn out quite how I thought."

"What's that supposed to mean?"

"CW filed a complaint. They got me on a camera at the library. Said I didn't have a warrant, said it was breaking-and-entering and abuse of my position as a law enforcement officer."

"Did their camera also catch those—those people *shooting* Ramon?"

"There hasn't been an investigation yet. Obviously, this shit just went down in the last hour."

Sam slammed his fist against the dashboard. "Bet you CW gives them a nice, doctored little piece of footage."

"Wouldn't be surprised. But I'm on suspension, pending further inquiries. And you—" He eyed Ann in the mirror. "Both of you ... They've got APB's out. They've added our little party at the library to the list of things they want to talk to you about. Turns out it didn't look good for the three of us to take off together when, as far as the paperwork's concerned, you still haven't been cleared for Caleb's murder. Even talking to you right now, I could get thrown in jail."

"What are you saying?" Ann gripped the back of his seat. "What, this is you just cutting us loose? You're just walking away now?"

Crawford sighed. For a couple of seconds, the only sound in the car was the drumming of the rain on the roof. "That's not what I'm saying." He turned to Sam. "What we've been through, the last few days ... Look, they took my badge, they're sure as hell not giving me another gun anytime soon, and if we go anywhere public, I'd better hide my face. I can't bring any cavalry. I don't have any sway. But I look at you two ... I think about your son, all the shit you've been through ... I'm here. To the end. If you want me."

Sam looked from Crawford to Ann. He stuck out his hand. After a moment's hesitation Crawford shook it. "Then let's go."

TWENTY ONE

SAM PASSED the photograph and the envelope from the North
Satellite Library to Ann as they drove. She examined them in the
passing street lamps of the Interstate. "She looks so much like you."
She ran a finger over the penciled inscription and then turned it over
to stare at the image again.

"If Grace is a relative … I've never … I don't remember any of
this."

"Maybe you were too little."

Sam shrugged.

"What makes you think this has anything to do with … with
Daniel or Riley?"

"She's all over those files we found. She has to know something."

Ann pursed her lips. She passed the envelope back and slumped
to stare out the window.

"It's going to be okay," he heard himself say.

Ann didn't answer.

Kearney Valley was a rural community, nested between farms,
ranches, and large spreads of fertile land. At two in the morning, it
was difficult to see much of anything, but there was enough moonlight to pick out the occasional roof of a barn, a silo, a farmhouse
among the overhanging trees along the Interstate.

After they got off the freeway, the vegetation closed in from all
sides. Crawford switched on his high-beams and took each corner in

the winding road at a crawl. Just when Sam was beginning to wonder if they were going the wrong way, he caught sight of a gate rising up through the foliage ahead of them.

It was worn, rusty, overgrown. Arching over a tiny dirt offshoot from the road, the stone entryway looked abandoned. Crawford steered the Subaru to a stop in front of it, and all three of them got out.

It was still raining, but the thickness of the foliage over head provided something of a shelter.

Picking his way through the weeds, Sam slowed when he noticed the gate was open. That didn't seem like a good sign.

Ann tore away a mat of tangled leaves and vines from a weathered plaque bolted to the stone. She wiped dirt from the engraved lettering.

Ellis Ranch. Private Property. No trespassing.

Sam stepped to the middle of the arch and edged the gate the rest of the way open. The road curled away on the other side, rising over a grassy hill where the trees became sparser before dipping beneath the ridge and out of view. Grass and dandelions choked the path, but there were a couple of more recent tire ruts in the soft earth.

Back in the Subaru, Crawford flipped on the four-wheel-drive. Shuddering, slipping, and sliding, they rolled through the archway and into Ellis Ranch.

The first thing Sam saw as they crested the hill was the silo on the opposite side. A cluster of buildings filled the gentle valley in front of them, and the tower protruded like a thorn against the sky.

He held his breath.

As the Subaru descended toward the ranch, Sam leaned forward to press his face against the windshield. The angle wasn't right, the light too low to see enough.

Crawford braked as they crept past an abandoned pickup truck. It was at least ten years old, but while age had eaten away at the blue-and-white logo on the driver's side door, it was no less familiar:

CW Medical. Maintenance & Operations.

Sam gulped and peered ahead.

There were no lights visible at the ranch.

They rolled to a stop in front of the outermost building. There were three, all told. One looked original, a turn-of-the-century clapboard farmhouse with moss clinging to the roof tiles, grime coating the windows. The other two were newer, maybe fifty years old, built of concrete and metal struts. They looked like military bunkers.

"You want to split up?" Crawford nodded to the nearest bunker. "Each take a building?"

"I don't know if that's a good idea."

"I got walkies." He opened the Subaru's hatchback. "And flashlights. This way, one of us finds someone, the other two still have the element of surprise."

Sam took one and flipped it to the channel Crawford indicated. It came on with a burst of static. He handed another to Ann. "You okay with this?"

She took a breath, squared her shoulders, and nodded. Sam caught her as she started to turn away.

"Hey. Love you."

A hint of a smile. "Don't do anything stupid in there." Then she was off, tramping through the weeds toward the farmhouse.

Sam and Crawford broke away and headed to the pair of bunkers. The entrance to Sam's was on the opposite side from the car. He hiked up the gentle rise and around to the far wall. His feet landed in water as he came to a halt before the door.

It was pooled rain—in the tire ruts he had glimpsed from the service road. This was where they were deepest. Freshest.

Sam hopped to the concrete doorstep, clipped the walkie-talkie to his pants, and pressed both hands against the heavy metal door.

It was latched but not locked. The groan as it swung open echoed through the room on the other side. If anyone *was* here, Sam might as well have just rung a doorbell.

It was too dark to see anything until he flipped on Crawford's flashlight. The beam encountered exposed metal bolts, crisscrossing supports—not a place designed with an eye toward aesthetics.

The floor was covered in a cheap plastic sheet, printed to look like tile. To the right, a couple of padded, wire-frame chairs sat in a row beside a dusty table and a stack of magazines. Sam picked one up.

Time Magazine. New York Commissioner William Bratton squinted out at the camera, bathed in the lights of a police car beside the headline: *Finally, We're Winning the War Against Crime.* Dated January 15, 1996.

A small reception desk sat at the end of the entryway. Stenciled into the wood was an older version of the CW Medical logo. He craned his neck over the top and played the flashlight across a bulky, beige computer tower. The monitor consumed most of the space on the desktop. It was at least as old as the magazine.

Corridors cut away on both sides.

Sam picked one at random. As he advanced to the left, his footsteps echoed in the metal walls, against the constant patter of the rain on the roof. Around the corner, he drew to a halt.

Both sides joined in one single room that was divided by sheets of reinforced glass into a grid of smaller chambers. They looked like prison cells, lining the outer bunker walls. A large, steel surgical table filled the space at the center, and medical equipment and machinery stood arrayed around it—IV poles, EKGs, a couple of other blocky machines that looked like antiques. It was an operating theater.

Plastic tile had, here, given way to bare concrete. It was penetrated only by two holes. One was a drain, old, flaking, the edges stained darker by rust, and perhaps something else. A pipe stood roughly three feet out of the other, with a hole at the top.

The whole place gave Sam chills.

As he edged in from the doorway, he couldn't shake the feeling that he was being watched, even though the flashlight found nothing when he played it in a circle through the Plexiglas cells. Each housed a cot, a sink, a curtained toilet.

Whatever Ellis Ranch was, Sam was willing to bet it didn't appear in any official databases, expense reports, or documentation of CW's accounting.

Sam leaned over the jutting pipe and shone the light inside. It was a pneumatic tube. A sheet of paper, rumpled with water damage, clung to the base. Sam peeled it away. The type had worn off, ink bled into a puddle long since evaporated.

Straightening, he smacked his head into something sharp and heavy dangling from the ceiling. Sam staggered back, a hand to his temple, and directed the flashlight beam upward. It was a television set. There were three others, linked by a thick snarl of electrical wiring that traced along the wall to a metal box at the far end of the room.

He flicked on the power switch. There was a jolt of electricity, and then the monitor flickered to life.

Static.

The cold, uneven glow lent the room an even eerier look. Sam turned on each of the screens, but they were all the same.

He dropped to his knees beside the control box and nudged open the doors with the nose of the flashlight. Inside, a deck of hi-fi receivers stared blankly back at him. Dark. Dead.

He felt around behind them until his fingers found power switches. The TV screens flashed when he turned one on.

Red lights came to life all over the front panels.

Sam scanned the buttons and knobs. There was a tape flap at the bottom, older than most of the other equipment. The logo on the front had almost worn away: *Betamax*. A stack of small videocassettes stood to the right of the receivers. The one on top was labeled only with the number nine.

He tried to jam it into the tape player, only to find a cassette already loaded.

The screens changed again when he hit the *Play* button. Nothing. More static. He was about to eject the tape when the LCD readout stopped advancing. The time code remained frozen in place. The end of the tape.

After he rewound it and hit *Play* again, an image popped onto the four monitors. It was black-and-white, this very room, recorded from a camera that must have been hidden somewhere on the ceiling.

Sam got to his feet and crossed back to the middle of the room when he noticed something moving on the tape.

It was a person. Someone in the last glass cell on the end.

It looked like a child.

Sam strained to the tips of his toes. Even in the playback, there wasn't much light. The blur at the edge of the shadows swallowed the finer details of the prisoner's face.

Move, Sam willed him.

As though somehow hearing him, the child shifted. He had been sitting on the cot—the same cot now six feet away from Sam—but with what appeared a monumental effort, he dropped to his feet and ambled sluggishly to the glass door. With a tiny fist, he knocked on the wall. His mouth moved. The tape recorded no sound.

When the boy pressed his face against the glass, Sam choked.
It was Daniel.

A burst of static made Sam jump. It took him a moment to realize it had come from the radio clipped to his beltline.

"Sam. Ann. You guys there?" Crawford.

Sam fumbled with the buttons on the side of the radio. He couldn't tear his eyes from the monitor. Daniel. *Daniel.* Alive. Awake. A prisoner.

"Here," Ann said.

"Yeah." Sam couldn't muster more than a croak.

"You're … you guys are going to want to see this."

᠎   ᴐ

The lobby of the second bunker was almost identical to the first. On the other side of the reception partition, instead of an operating theater, Sam found himself surrounded by metal file cabinets and tables awash in paperwork.

Crawford stood in the middle, an open dossier in his hands. On the desk in front of him a pneumatic canister lay open—the receiving end of the same tube Sam had found.

Ann came in behind Sam while he was still absorbing it all. His mind hadn't quite caught up yet. He turned to her, swaying, dizzy. "Ann, you're not going to believe … I found a tape. A tape of Danny. Awake. Moving around."

"A—a tape? Where? Where is he? Is he here?"

Crawford cleared his throat. "Not anymore." He held up the open file folder.

Sam and Ann pressed in around him to peer over his shoulder. It was carbon paper, a duplicate copy of a list sent over from the operating room. Names were filled into a Xeroxed table in differing handwriting, supplemented in additional columns by dates, initials, and one final abbreviated two-letter code.

The last column was identical for each entry, save the final one.
Daniel Mackie, yesterday's date, a hastily-scrawled *CW,* and then the code: BV.

Black Valley.

All of the others were marked, *AL.*

"Angel's Landing." Crawford thumbed to a second page of

paperwork. "Maybe another facility like the ranch here. Maybe another building on the premises. I haven't been able to figure that out yet, but there are references to it in all the files here."

"They took him … " Sam's mind raced. "They took him to Black Valley?" Caleb's research. The smudged old newspaper print and military briefs Ramon had found in the North Satellite Library. The Black Valley Project. "But that's in … from what I've read, that's in Africa. Congo."

Crawford nodded. "Where Denton said Clayton Wesley was going."

"They've … " Ann gulped, looking suddenly weak. "They've taken our son to … to Africa? Why? What could they possibly … why would they possibly … ?"

"In the other bunker—it looked like some kind of medical research lab." Panic flitted up in Sam's chest. "And in the files back at the library—it said they had been running tests on … on me, when I was little. Somehow … for some reason, it seems like they think there's something—that I've got something. Me and—and Daniel … that we can help them somehow."

"There's more." Crawford flipped back to the first page. He ran his finger up the list of names and initials. "Here. This one—ten years ago. June Williams. Ring a bell?"

Sam and Ann looked at each other. Together, they shook their heads.

"It was all over the news. Little girl, about eleven years old. Just disappeared. No ransom, no nutjobs in the family. Bright kid, sensible—parents always said she wouldn't be the type to get into a stranger's car or anything."

Ann frowned. "Detective, you're losing me … "

"Her case was unsolved. Some of these names, I don't recognize. Some of them, I do. They're all children. Children who went missing. It looks like they were brought here. To this facility. Ellis Ranch. For some kind of … testing."

Sam's mouth suddenly felt like cotton. "Detective—Gerry … What did you say the date was?"

"About—about ten years ago, but they range a little farther back." Crawford skimmed up the list. He stopped, a few entries from the top.

Sam closed his eyes.

He knew what Crawford had seen without even looking.
"My God."
The third entry was *Riley Mackie*.

TWENTY TWO

ANN SNATCHED the file out of Crawford's hands. She was trembling so hard that she had to set it on the table. "Where? Where did—what's this ... this 'Angel's Landing?' Where is this? *Where is it?*"

Sam looked from the file to the other papers spread across the table, and then to Crawford. The Detective wasn't searching through the records. He wasn't looking at bookshelves or file cabinets. He was peering out one of the thin, slitted windows, across the rolling hills to something on the other side of the ranch.

Stepping beside him, Sam followed his gaze.

The tower on the hill stood perfectly framed behind the glass, protruding from the trees at the top of the opposite ridge. Angel's Landing.

A sick feeling began pooling in the bottom of Sam's stomach as they raced across the field, through the rain. Ann wouldn't wait for Crawford to get his car keys out. She broke into a run as soon as they'd gotten outside the bunker, and it was all Sam could do just to keep up with her.

Wet blades of grass lashed at his ankles and shins. As they climbed up into the forest, he had to duck low-hanging branches, jump knotted clusters of roots, avoid patches of deeper mud and puddled water. His shoes kept slipping on slick stones, catching on the tips of half-buried rocks.

"Ann ... " He was panting. "Ann, slow down."

The clearing around the tower was unnatural. The vegetation had been shorn in a circle around it sometime long in the past, but for whatever reason, it had never grown back. Leaves, ivy, and ferns gave way to light-colored mud and rock.

Sam caught a whiff of something in the air that made him want to turn and run in the other direction. It smelled—burnt. Not like logs on a hearth in the winter, not like match smoke or even a forest fire, but like something else. Something unconscionable.

That was when he saw that the silo wasn't a silo at all.

The sloping metal roof was edged with long, curving holes, blackened at the sides. Soot covered the brick walls, repelling the moss and mildew that lay in tufts beneath the trees.

Sam looked down at his feet—at the bleached earth. It wasn't sand or dirt.

It was ash.

"Ann." He swallowed back the jolt of bile that leapt to his throat. "Ann, wait."

She was already circling around to the other side, running her fingers over the walls, looking for a way in. Her shoes *clanked* on something metal, buried in the dead leaves. She dropped to her knees and started digging with her bare hands.

"Ann, stop."

"If you're not going to help, then get out of my way."

"Ann ... " It was a door. A trap door in the ground that clearly hadn't been opened in years. All of a sudden, Sam knew. He knew in his gut, beyond anything he could put into words. He knew what they were going to find.

Just as surely, he knew Ann needed to see it.

Sam stopped protesting. The mud and rainwater leaked through the knees of his slacks as he dropped to the ground beside her and helped her dig. When they had exposed enough to find the handle, he braced his feet against the ground on either side and heaved with all of his might.

Crawford, still standing at the fringe of the woods behind them, looked on without a word. He seemed to sense that this was personal. This was a place where he didn't belong.

They had to do this.

The door thumped to the ground. It must have weighed nearly

a hundred pounds. Spiderwebs stretched from the underside of the hinges to the flight of concrete stairs descending into the darkness below.

A string of bare light bulbs dangled by a wire from the ceiling. Sam tried the switch on the wall. Dead.

When Ann moved to the top step, he turned, reached out, and took her hand in his. Together, fingers laced, they descended into the pit.

The smell grew stronger. It was stifling, appalling—a combination of rot and smoke, and dank, wet earth. Water trickled through cracks in the walls to gather in puddles on the bare stone floor.

The tunnel below looked like a catacomb, a tomb. It stretched ahead fifteen feet before opening into a conical brick chamber that sloped into the chimney above. Beneath the bright white flashlight beam, the ceiling was shadowed black with soot.

Ann covered her mouth with one hand and slowly arced the beam across the passage ahead. She came to a halt as it crawled over the far wall. Beyond a towering metal furnace of battered panels and exposed bolts, a checkered pattern of boilerplate doors smattered the brick and weathered concrete.

"Oh, God. Sam." Her fingernails dug into his hand.

But Sam couldn't stop now. Not now—not in the same place where he had been the last thirteen years. Waiting, not daring to hope, not even daring to think. Only assuming. It was the assumption, the never knowing, that had killed Sam. And Ann. And their marriage. And their lives.

Their shoes left footprints in the grime.

Sam choked back a sob as he drew close enough to read the inscription on the first boilerplate door. *Anthony G. Carrey, 1994.* A name from the top of Crawford's list.

Four doors down, he found June Williams.

Sam's thumb hovered over the switch to his flashlight. Every part of him wanted to turn it off and stop looking. For the first time in thirteen years, Sam imagined Riley was still alive. He wanted it the way Ann had always wanted it. The difference was, lately—just in the last week, he had finally begun to believe—to hope—that it might be true.

"Oh, Sam."

No. It was in her voice. He knew without wanting to know.

"Sam." She fell to her knees.

Sam stumbled beside her, dragged by their joined hands. He didn't want to look, but then, he couldn't avoid it. The glow from her flashlight forced its way into his eyes, burning the raised lettering onto his retinas.

Riley Mackie, 1995.

"Oh, Jesus."

They fell into each other's arms. He wanted to be numb. The way he was when Ramon was shot. The way he'd been for the last decade— only now, for the first time, he couldn't. He couldn't swallow back the grief and the loss, however much he wanted to. Not anymore.

For the first time in thirteen years, Sam *felt—everything.*

"He's gone," Ann breathed. She was crying without a sound, tears streaming down her cheeks. "He's—he was always gone. He was gone in 1995."

"I didn't want—I don't want this. It can't … "

"But it is. It is. This is it. This is him." She set her flashlight on the floor and reached out to touch the door that held what was left of their son. "I think I knew. All along, I think—I think a part of me knew. But to not—to not *know* … I couldn't … if I'd given up, then it would have been my fault. If I'd let him go before he was gone … "

"I didn't give up. I just couldn't face the … the … "

"I know."

"I didn't give up, Riley. I didn't."

"He knew. He knows. But he was always gone. It wasn't you. And it wasn't me. It wasn't that we didn't look long enough. There wasn't a chance. We didn't have a chance."

"I … I can't … *Fuck.*" Sam tried to hide his face in his hands, but Ann wouldn't let him go, and so there, in front of her, he broke down. It felt—

It felt almost good.

Liberating.

To let go. To finally let go and just *be.* And as he felt it, he was ashamed, because to feel good at a time like this … to feel relief … It was unthinkable. It was unthinkable that it could be ending like this. That it could be *ending* at all.

"My God." Ann sniffed and wiped her cheeks. "My God, Sam. We've been ... we've made such a terrible—such an awful mistake ... "

"What could we do? What could I do? I didn't—there wasn't a day that went by I didn't think about him. There wasn't a day that went by I didn't secretly wish he could still ... still walk in that door ... and ... "

"No. There wasn't anything we could have done for Riley. That was the mistake." Her hand dropped from the door and landed, light, gentle, warm, on Sam's cheek. "I've been blaming myself for so long—needing him back for so long ... I haven't—I haven't even been here. I've missed everything that was important. Everything."

"What could be more important than losing our son?"

"Having one."

Sam finally met her eyes, saw in her face the blurred grief, the need, and also something else: freedom. Sad, devastated, uncorked after a decade of repression—but freedom, in all its ugly, miserable glory.

"He needs us, Sam. Daniel needs us. We can still be there for him. We still have the chance."

To be absolutely certain, they opened the door together. Sam had contemplated leaving it, but any lingering questions would grow and magnify over the years until it would become almost as if they had never found this place at all.

The urn inside was wrapped in the jacket. That was all Sam needed to see.

Ann looked a little longer. Because she had to. Because she had been farther from this moment.

Finally, when she was done, Sam put his hand on the door. He couldn't close it.

He couldn't leave Riley here.

Crawford had taken refuge under a rocky overhang not far outside. His eyes jumped immediately to the canister in Sam's hands. Momentary confusion. Then—understanding.

Sam was surprised by how it hit Crawford. He swiveled away, curt, abrupt. He was so drenched from the rain that it was impossible to tell if he shed any tears, but Sam thought he knew. There was something about the ache in his eyes, the way he stayed back from their heels as they tramped down through the forest and across the field toward the farmhouse.

Crawford may not have been a parent in truth, but he was a parent at heart.

5

They were almost to the Subaru when Sam's gaze fell upon the old farmhouse. The only building whose insides he hadn't had a chance to see.

He tugged at Ann's arm. "What was in there?"

"Where?"

"The house. What was in the house?"

Ann looked. "Nothing. Most of it was shut up. Blocked off. It didn't look like anyone had lived there for years." She still sounded distant, awash in everything they had just seen.

"Huh." Something about it troubled him—called to him.

Dark windows reflected the gentle glow of the moonlight, paint peeling around the frames. There were holes in the roof. Ann was right; it appeared abandoned. *But why here?* Sam wondered. Why had Wesley set up his lab all the way out here? What was the significance of this place?

A couple of paces ahead, Ann glanced over her shoulder at him. "It looked like the last person who lived in the part I could see was barely living there anyway. Letting newspapers pile up. Not opening her mail."

Sam slowed. "*Her?*"

Ann nodded. "It was an older name, not so common ... I think Wesley might have mentioned it, when we had lunch together that day ... "

"Agatha. Agatha Pryce."

Ann snapped her fingers. "That's it."

Crawford took Riley's ashes with him to the car. He cradled them as he might have held a newborn baby.

Ann followed Sam to the rear doorstep. "Sam. What is it you think you're going to find in there?"

"I don't know." He grabbed the knob and turned.

The house was a turn-of-the-century bungalow. Scratches covered the hardwood floors. Chips and gashes littered the plaster. The kitchen appliances all dated back to the 1960s—rounded edges, curving whites and pastels with chrome accents, like cars. The pantry door hung open, spilling ravaged boxes and dented cans. Most of the dishes still stood in cabinets.

Wallpaper still clung to the walls in peeling sheets around the dingy dining room.

A fold-out couch, not an original, had been pulled in and placed with its back to the windows. Agatha had shoved the table and chairs against the far wall. A few pictures adorned the wooden plate rail that encircled the room—envelopes, letters, a newspaper clipping here and there.

The narrow doorway to the back stairs wouldn't budge when Sam tried it. Nailed shut. He slipped around through the living room to the front of the house, but the staircase leading up from the entry hall had been swallowed by a sloppy plywood enclosure built up like a fortress around it.

He turned back, taking in the room. Dust lay in drifts around old furniture. A large wooden radio the size of a tabletop sat just to the left of a magnificent stone hearth. Wedged into another corner was a rocking horse. It was almost identical to the one Sam had built for Riley.

It was only in kneeling beside it that he noticed the crayon drawings on the running boards by the floor. Stick figures, bicycles, birds and mountains. The color had faded, but the crude, blocky outlines still remained.

This was a house of children. Once upon a time, a house of happiness.

"Sam." Ann stood in the living room doorway. "Don't you think we should go?"

Sam walked back to the rear stairs, leading out of the kitchen. He gripped the knob and pulled for all he was worth. The wood groaned. Somewhere around the hinges, something cracked, and then all of a sudden, it came loose.

Splinters of old pine exploded into the air along with rusted nails and screws. Sam staggered back, the door in his hands. He caught himself against the pea-green refrigerator.

Dust cascaded down through the gaping hole.

Propping the door against the wall, Sam wiped grime from his eyes and then aimed the beam of his flashlight up the steps.

There was something about the shape of the stairs, the curve of the banister, the architectural accents—something hovering just at the outer edge of his mind. It was like reopening an old storybook from his childhood, years later. It all looked different, nothing quite as he remembered it, but every now and then were bright, flickering glimpses of what it had once been.

It was the last house from his dreams; the one he'd thought was probably fictional. Here it was, in the flesh.

"Sam, what is it?"

"I know this place. I think I know this place."

He mounted the steps.

At the top, they split off. To the left, the house funneled toward a wide open hallway, ceiling sloped to a point where the roofline ran. On the right, the stairs dead-ended at a door. By design, a maid's quarters.

Sam advanced down the hall, eyes on his feet and the rugs beneath them. They were antiques, colorful Persian designs both elegant and unique. He had been too young to appreciate them the last time he was here, forty-odd years ago.

Five doors led off the hallway—two on each side, and one at the end that hung open to expose a mirror, a porcelain sink, a toilet.

Sam edged right and opened one of the others.

A stale, dusty smell breathed out when he released it. Heavy curtains masked the windows. He couldn't see much of anything until he crossed and tugged them open.

Bunk beds. Old toys. Kids' room.

So were the others. He lifted a monogrammed towel from the top of a dresser where it must have sat folded for the last several decades. *J.F.* Another, pink, lay beneath it. *M.F.* Franklin.

This house had belonged to Grace Franklin, before Agatha Wesley-Pryce had ever lived here.

And then Sam knew.

He drew up short before Ann, back in the hallway, but there must have been a certain urgent determination in his face, because rather than stand in his way, she peeled aside and let him pass.

He came to the door of the servant's quarters and stopped with his hand on the knob. Drawing in a deep breath, not sure he was ready for whatever lay on the other side, he steeled himself and twisted.

The room was small, the ceiling low and slanted on both sides. A weathered old crib sat beside an unused bed frame. Pens, pencils, and a few crayons lay in a pile on the floor nearby. A narrow, circular window looked out from the foot of the crib to the rolling hills, the forested ridgeline, the angry, dark spire of Angel's Landing.

Sam jumped when Ann rested a hand on his shoulder.

"Do you know what this is?" He couldn't look away.

"What is it, Sam?"

"It's my room. This was my room."

"You lived here? When you were—this was one of the foster homes?"

Sam shook his head. "Before all that. Before the orphanage. I don't even—I was too young to really remember ... anything more than—than impressions. Shapes. Just the faintest ... " He crouched before the crib and peered up at the room as he used to see it, four decades ago.

It was breathtaking. He slipped the photograph from his pocket and handed it to Ann. "Me. It's me. The baby."

"So that's your mother? Grace Franklin?"

"I ... maybe. I don't know."

Ann swiveled around in the doorway. "It doesn't make sense, Sam. Why would they make you sleep by yourself here? Were you sick?"

"I don't know." Maybe that was why he had been given away. Trimmed from the family to prevent the other children from catching whatever it was he had.

The *other children.* Could he have brothers and sisters?

Sam caught himself against the crib because his knees were shaking. This was all he had ever wanted. This. Having a family. Knowing who he was. He squeezed his eyes shut, and an echo of the room came alive in faded color all around him. The cries of the other kids—laughter, thumping feet, an angry shout from down below.

He wanted so badly to go back. To be there again—to feel what it was like to have been there and to not have been alone.

When he opened his eyes, Ann was standing at the window. "Is that it? The—that awful ... that place. Out there. Is that the thing you kept dreaming about? That tower?"

It was perfectly framed through the glass, but as he gazed at it, Sam felt nothing. No connection. No itching, tingling hint of a memory. Nothing but the shock and the horror of knowing, as an adult, the purpose it had served.

It wasn't the tower from his dreams. At least, he did not think so.

He blinked, and for a searing instant, sun bathed the grassy fields. Wind rustled the treetops. Dotting the hills in the distance horses galloped, cows milled, a tractor crawled through bowing wheat. "No. The—the bunkers, the lab ... Agatha. They came later."

He slipped the folded sheet of paper from the envelope. *He's here. He made it.* Addressed to a research center in Congo. The same place where Wesley was taking Daniel. The same place that showed up over and over again in the military memos Ramon had discovered at the North Satellite Library.

"I lived here, but I don't ... I don't think I was born here." He spun the envelope around and pressed it into her hands.

Ann caught up with him halfway down the stairs. "Who's left? Who's left who knows where this place is? Who's left that can tell us how to get there?"

Sam emerged into the kitchen. He glanced through the dining room door to the plate rail, the photographs, the newspapers, the fold-out sofa bed. "I know someone."

ᴒ

"We can't just walk up to the desk and buy a ticket." Crawford steered the Subaru onto the Interstate. "You need a visa. Inoculations. It's not like a vacation to San Diego."

Sam shook his head. "We won't need a visa."

"Sam, I know a few people at TSA. I know how they run. They're not just gonna wave you through airport security."

"We're not going to the airport."

Ann and Crawford both looked at him.

TWENTY THREE

THE RAIN HAD EBBED, and the first light of dawn was beginning to color the sky when the Subaru's headlights caught the glint from the wrought-iron gate at the front of Clayton Wesley's property.

Crawford unbuckled his seatbelt and reached for the door. Sam stopped him. "I'll handle this."

He climbed out and walked around the hood to the callbox.

"Can I help you?" It was Denton.

"Sam. Sam Mackie."

A sigh crackled through the speaker. "Mr. Mackie. As I explained before—"

"I know Clayton Wesley's gone. I want to talk to Agatha Pryce."

"Regarding what?"

"None of your business."

"I'm afraid it is my job to make it my business."

"Tell her my name. And tell her I know about Grace Franklin and Ellis Ranch. Tell her I'm looking for my son."

A couple of seconds passed. Crawford's Subaru purred, exhaust pooling around Sam's ankles in the brutal morning air. Sam glanced back through the windshield at Ann. He shivered against the cold. This wasn't working. Agatha wouldn't talk to him. Why would she talk to him? He could only bring her trouble.

Then, with a buzz, the gate came to life and began rolling open.

Ann was speechless as they drew up beneath the covered driveway of the mansion and Denton came out to open her door. He looked her up and down. "Ann Mackie."

"Do I know you?"

"Doubtful."

Denton made them wait in the drawing room. The glass-topped map through the adjoining door was gone, and the computer, the Xerox machine—the whole home office—had been packed away into stacked-up cardboard cartons. Moving tape covered the exposed edges.

Sam swallowed. The house gave the impression of transition.

Another day—perhaps less—and any trace of what had been here would be gone forever. No evidence. Nothing left. They'd gotten what they wanted. That thought made him cold inside.

Denton cleared his throat from the drawing room doorway. "Mrs. Pryce will see you now."

The staircase at the center of the house was like a thundering waterfall of stone and marble. Long, flowing tapestries adorned the walls. Plush carpet, royal blue, padded the steps. By Sam's estimation, none of it had seen sunlight in decades.

Opposite the drawing room was a sweeping lounge with curving windows that bowed out into a circular tower. On Christmas morning, a tree at the center, ice-white light streaming in from all sides—the place could have been magical.

Blackout curtains kept it shrouded in dusty gloom.

It felt like a life arrested, frozen, mummified before its time and left to crumble in death for longer than it had ever breathed.

Upstairs was even worse. Empty picture frames stared out like blinded eyes from wood-paneled walls. Here and there, stacks of books stood in towers. They were suspended in mid-transit, a moving job begun a half-century ago and left in motionless oblivion.

Through doors left ajar, Sam glimpsed whole rooms standing empty. Occasional slits of light managed to make it through the shades and sashes, glimmering on bare floors and abandoned walls. The second floor smelled of old wood and hearth smoke, with occasional hints of meals burnt and consumed years before.

Denton took a left into a partial hallway that dead-ended at a pair of lavish double-doors. Carved wooden figures anointed the framework overhead, and the paneling was covered in more fine stencil work.

He tapped with a single finger.

"Enter."

Several steps into the room on the other side, all Sam could see was fabric. A looming four-poster bed was planted in the center of the room, mattress hidden from view by dangling silk and gauze that looked like mosquito netting. Draperies adorned the walls, so thick and so heavy that the chamber may have been several feet larger on either side without them.

Rugs overlapped each other on the floor—colors, shapes, enchanting designs.

A fire crackled in the small stone fireplace, not far from the foot of the bed. Only one of the two high-backed chairs facing it was occupied.

It was not until Denton gave a dry cough that Sam finally edged toward the other. He had not been sure how to proceed. It felt as though he had just stepped into a time warp.

As he approached the hearth, his eyes continued to wander. Two slatted closet doors flanked the bed on either side. One was draped with dazzling dresses, hats, pearl necklaces—the fineries of another generation. From the other hung only a single garment. Olive green, starched into crisp corners and sharp angles. An Army uniform.

A portrait much like the one in the drawing room hung over the mantelpiece. Agatha and Donald Pryce. Here, she stood behind him, Donald in full military dress, peering fearlessly—distantly—off to the right of the canvas, Agatha behind him, half-hidden in shadow.

"Samuel Mackie."

He slowed. Her voice sounded like the ocean washing over a sandy shoreline.

"Mrs. Agatha Pryce."

The fire lent her skin a certain glow. Without it, she would have looked like a corpse. Gaunt, almost skeletal, she was so small and so light in the massive chair that her clothing all but swallowed her.

But her eyes—

They weren't alive so much as they *reflected* life. There was a milky age to them, but in her regal stare, Sam saw the echoes of a woman who once had been as beautiful as she was rich and powerful.

"Sit. I'll have Denton bring … " She broke off when she saw Ann. Crawford lingered behind her, out of view. "This is your wife?"

Sam nodded. "Daniel's mother."

"Daniel ... " Agatha squinted into the fire. "Ah. I had lost track ... "

Ann stiffened. Sam slipped an arm around her shoulders and moved her toward the other chair.

"Not that one." With a nod from Agatha, Denton brought two wooden stools from the closet. Agatha's gaze remained on the cushion of the armchair. "It belongs to my husband," she said at length, after Sam had assumed the matter was concluded. "I reserve it for him. For his return."

Sam blinked. "Oh. I assumed ... "

" ... that he was dead. He's not."

"My mistake."

"No. Mine." Agatha drew in a weary breath. "Do you know what it is like, Samuel, to sit in wait of something that will never happen? Do you know what it is like to hope when there is no longer a point to hoping?"

"I know," Ann said.

"You ... " Agatha frowned and studied Ann. "Ah. The other son. Of course."

"Why did you take him?"

Sam tightened his grip around her waist, but Ann pulled away from him, sitting forward, suddenly tense.

"Why did you do it? You owe it to us to tell us. Was it just for the test? Something you could do faster if you had a little boy instead of a lab rat?"

Agatha arched her eyebrows. "What kind of monster do you take me for?"

"You stole both of our sons. You killed one of them."

The old woman swallowed and looked away, back to the fire. It danced in her eyes, and it was then Sam noticed that her hand was shaking. There was a sadness hanging about her neck that dragged her down beyond her many years. She must have been seventy-five, maybe eighty. She looked one-hundred-and-ten.

"I am sorry about that."

"Why? Just—tell me. Tell me why."

"I never meant for it to happen that way. It was not what Clay told me. I never knew, not until very recently ... what he had done. You see, he did it for my husband."

"Your husband?" Sam exchanged a glance with Ann.

"My husband. Donald." When Agatha tipped her head back to gaze at the portrait over the fire, the shadows under her eyes darkened. "He is sick. Clay has been trying to heal him for … almost as long as I can remember. We were so young when he left. On assignment."

"To a place called Black Valley. In Africa."

Agatha seemed surprised. "You know about that? Did Clay tell you?"

Sam grimaced. "Never mind. So your husband is … where?"

"Still over there."

"What?"

"They told me I could not visit him until he was better, or I would get sick, too. He cannot leave, either. Fear of an outbreak, or some such … " She broke into a long, languorous cough, and fumbled with a handkerchief. At length, she regained her composure. "They told me—when it first began—that they would have him cured within a month. They had a lead. An answer. A child who was immune to the sickness. He was the key, and before I knew it, they would have him right as rain and home again.

"When that—after they lost him, the boy … that was when Clay invited me to move in here. It was supposed to be temporary. He was finding new investors for his pharmaceutical company. To help Donald. It was not as though we could not spare the money and they went back many years. They were deployed together in Korea, before poor Clay was shot in the leg."

"The boy. The child … What happened to him?"

Agatha gave an anemic shrug, but when her eyes fell on Sam, they carried all the answer he needed. "He slipped through their fingers. His guardian did not approve of the reasons we needed him."

"You killed her. Grace. Her family—Christ, all those kids."

"I do not know what you are talking about."

"You lived in her house, after she was gone." Sam scooted to the edge of his stool. "Ellis Ranch."

"Clay bought that property. Wanted to get me out of his hair, I suppose, but it was too lonely for me. Nobody was living there when I moved in. It felt … sad."

"Clay murdered the woman who lived there. Because she refused to give me to him. Because she gave me away to an orphanage and buried the trail before he got there."

"I have never asked anything of my brother. He does as he pleases.

He always has."

"What did you do to him?"

"Who, my dear boy?"

Sam glanced at Ann, her arms planted on the stool, shoulders like a brick wall, beside him. "Our son." He strained to control his voice. "Our son. Riley. What did you do to him and those other children?"

"That was Clay's business. In the beginning, he would bring me reports on his progress every week, but after we lost the first child … well. I concentrated on keeping my hope alive. He rebuilt his company around finding a cure, but without the natural key … I understand this illness is not easily treated. Even if we found someone—one person with an immunity—Clay said it would be a … a donation. There would be no miracle cure, no hope for any of the others, but in a way, that was liberating, wasn't it? They could give up. Go on with their lives. But me …

"I had such hope—such incredible hope—when we found you again."

Sam swallowed. "The hospital. When Riley was born. All those tests … "

When he closed his eyes, he could see it again. The tumult of the Emergency Room. Rushing Ann to the doctor. Everything snowballing, the hours of labor, screaming—the two of them just kids, themselves … and then the first cry. And the relief. The weakness, the fatigue, the joy.

Sam hadn't thought twice when the phone call came. *Just a few more tests—to make sure the baby is healthy. The father is traditionally screened, as well, in order to spot any hereditary issues early enough to deal with them.*

"And when the results came back." Agatha shook her head. "You were useless. Whatever immunity lives in your blood, it does so on its own. Clay and his best scientists could not separate it from your body. Can you imagine? Searching for eighteen years, only to find … nothing. A broken machine. A puzzle with too many pieces missing.

"But then there was your son. There was hope again. His tests took longer. It was more difficult to find, but Clay said it was there, in his genetic code, latent. When he matured, we would be able to observe how his body handled its release, how it was naturally introduced into his system. Clay told me we could mimic it, once we saw.

We could recreate that process, and we could give it to Donald." She drew in a ragged breath. "And he would be home. He would be back. Back here. Do you see? He could come home. He could be sitting in this chair." Her hand left a dust print on the cushion.

"It didn't work. Something went wrong."

The excitement that had flushed Agatha's cheeks and brought a glimmer to her eye for a fleeting moment began to fade. She sat back into the pillowed grasp of her chair and drifted into a faraway gaze. "Clay never went into the details with me. They were unimportant. The fewer who knew, the better. But his process was rushed. It was my fault. I wanted Donald back for his—it was my birthday. It had been so long, and I wouldn't ... we so wanted children. And I was getting older. I wanted him back.

"Clay was unsure of what he was doing. It was uncharted territory, he said, but he was confident enough to try. For my sake. For Donald's."

Sam could barely form the words with his lips. The roaring fire in the hearth might as well have been a lump of ice. "What did you do?"

Agatha gave a dismissive wave. "You would have to ask Clay. To my understanding, they gave him the ... the illness. To trigger his immune system. Only—it was too fast. He wasn't ready."

Ann covered her mouth.

"And we lost our only chance. After that ... Clay and his scientists tried fabricating it a couple of times. They even tested it once or twice, but I understand the results were similarly ... disappointing."

"Disappointing?" Ann was hoarse. "They died. Nine other kids died just for you and your husband and your goddamn cure. And Riley ... " She choked, clenched her teeth, forced herself to go on. "Riley died. For you. Riley, our son. Our *son.*"

For the first time, a glint of a tear appeared in Agatha's eyes. "I know. I know. I'm sorry that it had to ... Clay never—he never told me what happened to the kids. I never thought to ask."

"You never cared."

Agatha nodded. "That is true."

At the back of the room, a silent, stewing phantom in the shadows, Crawford shifted. Sam halted him with a glance. The Detective's hands were clenched into fists at his sides. Blood made the veins stand out on his neck.

Agatha inhaled. "Did you ever ... want something for so long that you forgot why? You forgot even how not to ... to want it?" Her fingers slowly caressed the leather seat cushion beside her. "I have not laid eyes on Donald since July 2nd, 1961. The day he shipped out. He took me to dinner. I cried that whole night, while he packed, but I was young back then. Young*er*, anyway. We hadn't known each other for long. Only five years, but I loved him so much." She looked from the chair to the fire, and then to Sam and Ann, sitting together, arms around each other because both knew that they could not swallow another word on their own. "I haven't really lived a day since then. And now I'm old. I'm so ... so dreadfully old. I cannot get out of bed in the morning without Denton's help. Do you know how that feels? It feels like I shouldn't be getting out of bed at all. I don't even know Donald anymore. I haven't the faintest idea what I would say to him if I saw him again. What would we talk about? What would we do? We've lived separate lives for longer than we ever lived them together.

"If he appeared on this doorstep tomorrow ... We couldn't travel. We used to play tennis together, before he went away. We couldn't do that. We couldn't even go for a walk. My liver cannot even tolerate a glass of champagne anymore.

"And yet I sit here. Hoping, because I do not know what to do without that. Hoping that he will come back."

She looked Sam in the eye, and at that moment, he no longer saw her as evil. Not a butcher, not a criminal mastermind, not a kidnapper or a thief or a villain. She was a little girl who had been sentenced to a life of tortured hesitation by the events of a world beyond her control. All she needed was to be told that it was going to be okay. She needed to be told that her life had meant something.

Another tear rolled down her cheek. She didn't bother to mop it up. "The only thing that scares me more than the thought of him never returning," she breathed, "is the thought of him walking through that door. Because, what then? What then? What will it all have meant?"

For nearly a minute, no one spoke a word. The fire crackled and popped at their backs. Sam and Ann held each other. Crawford stared at Agatha's head with venom leaking from his eyes.

Finally, Sam broke the silence. "Mrs. Pryce—Agatha ... you have to help us."

"Help you?"

Sam nodded. "Yes. Help us. Help us find our son. Help us get him back."

"Your ... your son."

"Daniel. Our son. The one your brother has taken away with him."

She blinked, as though surprised by the request. "If I do that, it is almost certain I will never see Donald again."

"That's possible, Mrs. Pryce. But you have to do it anyway."

"Why?"

"Because. Because he's twelve. Thirteen. He turned thirteen ... " Sam looked at his watch. "Two days ago. Forty-nine hours. You know how I know that so exactly? I remember the moment he entered the world. We didn't make it to the hospital. We were staying with friends—different friends, because we couldn't stop arguing. Because we couldn't be—we weren't ourselves anymore. He was born in the back of an ambulance. I barely got there in time. And even though the first time we heard his little voice, it should have been the happiest day of our lives, we couldn't—we never celebrated. Because we felt like our lives were over. Because you took Riley away from us.

"And for the next thirteen years, we lived as you've been. And that's all Danny's ever known. A world where the two people who are supposed to love him most have been grieving over something that happened before he was born.

"And now we have a chance. We have a chance to give him back what we've taken from him. We have a chance to fix it. To be there. To make his life—to make our lives ... worthwhile. Bearable. We even have a chance to be happy—really *happy*— again.

"You took my life, Agatha. You took my life, and Riley's, and Ann's. Danny has a chance. Do this for him. Do it because he's the most innocent, most goodhearted, most wonderful child in the world. Do it because he doesn't deserve this. Do it because if you do, the last forty-five years you have spent alone can still mean something to someone."

Agatha put a hand to her mouth. She was weeping openly now. "Oh, God," she breathed. "Oh my God. What have I done?"

Crawford's eyes were red when they left the study. Denton escorted them back downstairs and made them wait in the drawing room again while he conferred with Agatha.

None of them spoke. Sam felt drained.

He and Ann stood together before the arching windows as morning rolled across the dewy lawn outside. The rain had tapered off. Water still dribbled from the eaves of the gazebo just visible at the edge of the woods, a hundred feet away.

He should have been furious. This life—this perfect life—belonged to him. He'd been snatched away to help these people, given up a son for them, and all he'd received in return was a lifetime of foster homes and cubicles.

But he wasn't furious. He didn't have the energy to hate anymore.

All he could muster was a dull, aching longing. Longing to have Daniel back, and with Ann, be whole again. It wouldn't matter where they landed. They could live out of a hotel room until the day Sam died, and he would be the happiest man on Earth as long as he had them with him.

All three of them turned at the sound of the door. Denton looked a little pink. The remnants of an argument lingered on his lips and in the drag of his step as he planted a slip of paper in Sam's hands.

"Go to the address printed at the top of the page. Present it with your identification."

Sam turned the paper over in his hands.

The address was thirty miles away—CW Medical's private airstrip—followed by a flight plan for three that dead-ended in Africa.

On the back, in shaky, arthritic script, Agatha had written a single word:

Godspeed.

TWENTY FOUR

A GUST OF TURBULENCE shook the tiny Gulfstream jet. Lighting flashed outside the windows, followed a split-second later by a peal of thunder. It sounded close. Across the aisle, Crawford gripped the armrests of his seat. He loosened his tie. Sweat covered his forehead and his neck.

The deck bucked, dropped, and then leapt back up again so fast that Sam's head was thrown back into the seat behind him. He glanced over at Ann. Sprawled over the seat beside him, she had fallen asleep. Her head lolled against his shoulder. She looked more peaceful than he had seen her in years.

Ann had always been able to sleep through anything. It was an acquired skill. Too much shouting in the trailer when she was little, too many breaking bottles.

"Jesus. Oh, Jesus." Crawford squeezed his eyes shut as the plane banked sharply to the left.

Sam leaned across the aisle. "Don't fly much?"

"Hate these motherfuckers. Big jets, 747s, all right. Like sitting in a day spa for eight hours and then you're there. But these little—" An involuntary grunt welled up in his throat as the deck pitched again. "These little goddamn G5s—you might as well be coasting in a tube of tinfoil."

"You know … You didn't … you didn't have to come."

Crawford shot him a look. "Yes, I did."

"Not—don't take that the wrong … we're glad to have you with us. God, just to know there's one more person out there who actually—"

"I'm not doing this for you, okay?" He gulped and clenched his hands.

"Oh. I'm sorry, I … I just assumed … "

Crawford turned and squinted out the window. "How the fuck long can one storm last?"

The clouds flashed again. Another rumble of thunder. The plane dipped to the right, rolling up almost to its side. A cart somewhere up front slid across the aisle and crashed into the opposite wall.

No comforting spiel from the captain. No flight attendants, sent back to check on them. Agatha's all-access golden pass to Africa had gotten them off the ground and pointed in the right direction, but along the way, they'd been graced with the no-frills, barebones treatment. No cocktails, no peanuts, and a healthy dose of resentment from a crew dragged out of bed for nearly a full day in the air.

"Fuck," Crawford muttered under his breath.

"They might have some—a pill or something you can take."

"Don't believe in drugs."

Sam squinted at the Detective. For as much time as they had spent together the last couple of days, he now realized he knew very little about Crawford, personally.

"You wouldn't either, okay? If your wife took what the doctor ordered, followed the schedule, did what she was supposed to, and on the day … on the *day*, she … the baby came out … not breathing."

Sam caught his breath. "Crawford—Gerry … Christ, I'm sorry. All this—"

"No."

"All this—with the children and the … "

"What you're going through is worse. We never had a chance to … to bond with her. Get to know her. Hear her laugh and cry and start to learn words. She was just gone before any of that."

"So that's why … " Sam nodded toward the tilted deck, the rain streaming over the windows. "That's why—all of this? You and this case … because it seems like more than just professional interest."

Crawford smirked, bitter. "No badge, no gun. How professional can it be, right?"

The plane shook again. This time, Crawford didn't jerk quite as hard.

"You remember my nephew—the one I told you about?"

"Yeah."

"How we'd—he's always been like the son I never had. We'd play videogames, throw a football, do shit together on weekends. He'd come to the cop games, you know? Since his dad's one of ... since his dad *was* one of us ... Everyone said he could join the team when he was a bit older. You know, spot of nepotism, but hey, like anyone gave a shit ... "

"Sure."

"And barbecues, and hanging out, hitting movies ... " Crawford sat back and closed his eyes. "That was seven years ago. Last time he called me, he was nine or ten. Kid got his driver's license last year. Had to time it so he wasn't drunk or high, 'cause he knew, cop's son, they'd be watching a little closer. Bet it hurt, too—taking a day off."

"Oh ... "

"Hasn't been to school in a year-and-a-half. Still enrolled for whatever reason, but nobody sees him. His dad—Rich—tried to send him to military school, so he ran away from home. Guess when you become a teenager, it's not cool to have the police force as your family anymore. We're a real drag at parties."

"Gerry, I'm sorry ... "

"It was my fault. Stifled him. Never let him do anything you're supposed to do when you're that age. Turned him into a goody-two-shoes, and when he was old enough to figure that out, he started hating me for it. Rich and me. All of us. Now—with Rich dead ... I don't even know if the kid'll come to the funeral, but if he does, lord knows ... " Crawford looked across the aisle at him. "I need to show him that guys like the one who did this can't get away. He needs to know that. That we do something ... that *I* do something. Because if I fuck this up ... if he thinks this can just happen and the cops are gonna sit back and let it ... " He shook his head. "I don't think we'll ever get him back. I don't think we'll see him 'til he turns up somewhere in handcuffs, facing a life sentence. And that would kill me. I couldn't bear that."

Sam reached across the aisle to squeeze Crawford's shoulder. "Don't worry. Nobody's getting away with anything. Not anymore."

Crawford mustered a smile. "Good motto. I'll run that by the Captain, see if we can update some of our PR." He sat back and glanced out the window. "Well look at that. We're through the storm."

5

For a while, Sam was still too wound-up about everything to sleep. After a couple of hours, Ann snoring beside him, Crawford staring off into space, he finally managed to relax enough to close his eyes.

The plane shuddered.

When Sam craned his neck into the aisle, he could see something casting a long, narrow shadow from the window on the other side of the fuselage.

He recognized it in an instant.

Tearing free of his seatbelt, he dove across the aisle and pressed his face against the glass. Where was it? *Where was it?* Clouds curled in close to the hull to blot out the landscape below. The shadow remained, a spire of darkness against the fluffy white.

The dark tower.

And there it was again—smaller but clearer, reflected from the other side of the plane. He spun around and stumbled through the seats, but by the time he got to the opposite bank of windows, the fog had swallowed it again.

For an instant, it flashed over the flat-panel LCD that hung from the curving ceiling just before the cockpit. The screen switched back to the weather channel when Sam rounded on it.

Always there, always just behind him—never close enough to see.

"Sam." It was the copilot, a slim, brown-haired woman in her forties. The uniform hung loosely on her body, silver-gray hair cascading down over her shoulders and masking her face until she leaned over him. "Sam."

It was Grace. Grace Franklin, her sweet face creased with worry. "*Sam.*"

Sam woke up.

"Sam." Ann shook him. He looked at her in the seat beside him. "You were moaning."

He was drenched in sweat. He took a long pull from the water bottle in the seat pocket in front of him.

"I don't understand." She relaxed a little, now he was awake. "The dream—this tower, those drawings—the way the kids drew them, too. I get what Agatha and Clayton Wesley were doing. I still don't get this."

Sam shook his head. "Neither do I. I never have." He squinted past her at the window and the glaring white light of the clouds on the other side. "Maybe soon, though."

Ann drew in a deep breath and nodded. She followed his gaze outward toward the passing blue sky. Far below, the storm was still visible, a swirl of flickering grays. "You remember the first time we flew together?"

"Quebec. Just about froze to death."

A hint of a smile twitched at the corners of her mouth. "Just to say we'd been to another country."

"And the shitty motel. And the terrible television."

"But cheap food."

"Cheap *awful* food."

"And that asshole on the plane who kept saying Riley's diaper needed changing." Sam couldn't help but grin at the memory. "And you told him if he thought it was so bad, he could go change it himself."

"I wasn't the one who hit the policeman."

"He was a *mounty.*"

"Because that makes it so much better."

"He was being a prick. He thought that car was ours and you were already waiting in line for the food, and here I was, trying to get it through his thick skull that there was no way in hell I was going to sign the ticket when we didn't even bring a car to Canada ... " Sam trailed off, lost in the past.

He'd forgotten all about their trip to Quebec. One of a thousand memories he'd blocked off because they had included Riley. It was the most fun they'd had in their lives, a follow-up, makeshift honeymoon because neither of them had been able to afford something official when they got married at eighteen.

The second night of their stay, they had bundled Riley into a backpack and gone for a walk by a river near the motel. It was freezing, the banks covered in ice,. and the water was an appalling green-brown. There was a spot, though, maybe three miles from the parking lot, where all of the flaws had come together to form a fractured perfection. The gentle swirl of the water, the mist of their breath in the air, the stars in the sky, and the quiet burbling of their son.

Sam had looked at Ann, the moonlight shining in her eyes, and he had thought it was scary how much he loved her.

When he glanced across the seat at her now, he saw it again. That spark of the woman he'd married. The one girl who would talk to him in high school. The love of his life.

"Ann … "

"It was a good trip." She turned away, closing up.

"Ann, this is going to be over."

"We hope."

"Soon. And we're … we can be a family again."

For a long time, she didn't say anything at all. It was agony. Sam wanted to dive across the seat and throw his arms around her, to shake it into her head that it would be impossible to conceive of splitting up again.

"Perhaps," she said.

He clung to that word. That one word. Because it meant there was hope.

5

It was somewhere midway through the flight, suspended over the Atlantic Ocean, that it finally sank in with Sam what they were doing. Other than the Quebec trip, he had never been out of the United States.

The monumental scale of what lay ahead began to gape at him.

Ocean turned to beach and then to a rolling green carpet of jungle. Rivers cut through the trees, ribbons of reflected light. They were close now. Sam did not know how far it was, but no matter how much time he had left, he wasn't ready for this. He couldn't possibly be ready for this.

Twenty-three hours from home, and all he wanted to do at that moment was turn back.

"Oh, my God." Crawford was leaning across his row to stare out the window on his side of the plane. "Sam. Ann."

They struggled free of their seatbelts and scrambled across the aisle.

Mist encircled a range of mountains jutting through the forest. The sun-bathed peaks looked sharp, rugged, repelling the vegetation. They were so dramatic that Sam did not see where Crawford was looking until the plane banked toward it.

On the other side of the mountains lay what appeared at first glance to be a giant, gaping hole in the earth. It was so utterly black that it looked like an optical illusion. Nothing like this occurred naturally.

The airplane shifted and rolled away. Sam staggered forward, forehead bumping into the glass. "That's it," he breathed. He pressed a palm against the window, reaching, wanting to get closer. "That's Black Valley."

"Sam." Ann was standing in the aisle, squinting out the windows on the other side of the plane.

In the distance, on the horizon, he could just make out an uneven jumble of buildings that might have been Brazzaville—the capitol. It had to be at least a hundred miles away.

"Not that." Ann pulled him closer and motioned downward, directly beneath them.

The plane was descending fast as it circled back around toward a small village that rose out of the trees. Thick foliage bowed in around the edges of an airstrip, huts and cabins trailing off into the jungle.

Standing out against the miles of rugged natural beauty, a bright blue-and-white Hummer, the color of a preschool toy, sat parked just outside the fringe of the trees. A blotch that was the CW Medical logo was stenciled onto the side.

Sam gulped. "The itinerary said there'd be a car waiting for us."

"Yeah. But only one, right?" Ann pointed farther back, a few miles off from the village.

A small dirt road wove through the dense forest.

Shooting down it, fast enough to kick up twin trails of dust at their wakes, were two camouflaged military jeeps.

"Shit." Sam swallowed. "I think we're going to have company."

TWENTY FIVE

SAM FOUGHT HIS WAY to the front of the plane and pounded on the cockpit door. After a couple of seconds, the copilot stuck her head out. For an instant, it was Grace glaring at him. Then he blinked, and she was gone.

"We see them."

"Who are they?" Sam glanced past her to the captain, the instruments, the jungle streaming toward them through the front windows.

"Local militia. Take your seat please, sir."

"Why is there a—a militia coming to the airstrip?"

"I don't know. Did you make sure to schedule your flight two weeks in advance? Pay the proper authorities their dues? Clear the trip with Congo government?"

"Pay them their ... " Sam looked from her to the back of the pilot's head.

The copilot smiled icily. "Surely, sir, you were not under the impression you could simply waltz in here and expect a red-carpet reception."

Sam fought the urge to lash out at her. "What do we do?"

"*We* touch down, refuel, and go home. Standard procedure. *You*—you follow protocol." She glanced over her shoulder as the jet swung around and lined up for its descent to the airstrip. "Do everything they tell you. Cooperate in full. Or they'll shoot you."

"What will they want?"

She shrugged. "Ten thousand dollars? Twenty, maybe. You do have that, don't you? Otherwise, I'm afraid I haven't heard good things about the prisons in the area ... "

"I thought Agatha made all of the arrangements."

"Mrs. Pryce doesn't handle this part of the *arrangements*, sir. Mr. Wesley does. Perhaps you neglected to consult him about your visit." She looked him in the eye. "What a shame. Is there anything else we can help you with?"

The twin columns of kicked-up dust crisscrossed through the jungle. They had to be five miles away, maybe less. The airstrip now lay directly in front of the Gulfsream's nose.

"Just land," Sam told her.

"We're doing that."

"Do it faster."

The jet came down hard on the tarmac. Though the buildings surrounding it stood in leaning disrepair, the airstrip itself was immaculate. Clayton Wesley looking after his assets like a good businessman. And screwing the rest of the world in the process. Like a good businessman.

The Gulfstream's engines roared. Sam stayed glued to the widow, drumming his fingers on the seatback in front of him, watching the approaching dust clouds.

A small cluster of local villagers had gathered around the plane by the time the copilot released the door latch. Hot, humid air flooded in. Sam stepped outside into the merciless sun and almost gagged. Even when the forest came into view, even as they touched down, a part of him had still been living in some kind of closed-up, air-conditioned fantasy.

Suddenly, the mosquitoes, the sweat, the smell of diesel, the chirping of insects reverberating through the vegetation—

Suddenly, it was real.

Children stood in clusters beneath the sagging shacks, shielding their eyes against the sun. Mothers with babies peeked out through glassless windows.

Sam was sticky with sweat by the time he hopped down to the pavement. His clothes were rumpled, shirt clinging to his skin.

"Sir." A dark-skinned man in a collared shirt and shorts hurried over to him through the assembled crowd. He looked younger, fitter, wealthier than the others. "Welcome to the Republic of Congo, sir. My name is Ngouabi." He spoke with a heavy accent, but when he flashed Sam a smile, his teeth were white as pearls. "A car, it is waiting for you, sir."

Sam helped Ann off the plane and then they took off after the driver toward the bright blue Hummer. Ngouabi already had the door open by the time Crawford caught up with them. "You are familiar with this type of vehicle, sir?"

"Sure, yes." Sam squinted inside. Automatic transmission, GPS.

Ann hoisted herself up onto the side-mounted running boards and slid into the passenger seat while Crawford jogged around to the other side.

Sam turned back. At ground level, set against the sky, it was harder to see the dust clouds. He counted three dirt roads leading off from the village. "Ngouabi."

The driver had the rear hatch open. He was rifling through supplies. "These supplies, they are for emergencies. If you should—"

"Ngouabi, we don't have time. I need directions."

"Directions. Yes. Ah, yes. The central processing plant, it is marked on the radar—the global computer—the positioning system. Here, we have main offices, foreign relations, we have—"

"Black Valley. Is that the Black Valley?"

Ngouabi broke off, mouth open, mid-sentence.

A couple of the other villagers, crowding around the Hummer, stared and whispered to each other.

"Sam!" Ann nodded through the windshield.

At the other side of the airstrip, the first of the two army Landcruisers skidded out of the forest and barreled toward them. The airplane copilot ducked out to pull the door shut. The Gulfstream's engines were already spinning up.

Panic fluttered into Sam's chest.

The first Landcruiser was open in the back. Several men stood, shoulders braced against the roll bars, wind ruffling their hair. Holding machine guns.

"Please." Sam spun back to Ngouabi. "Which way? Which way to Black Valley?"

"You cannot go there. It is a place very bad."

"I know what it is."

"No one who goes there comes back. No one. It is the curse—"

"Which way?"

"The curse, they say. Life eternal, it was said, but it is a trap."

"Sam!" Crawford stared at the Hummer's engine and dropped it into gear.

The second Landcruiser hit the runway and picked up speed as its tires found traction on the concrete. The first was already halfway to them.

Sam grabbed Ngouabi by the shoulders. "Where's the Black Valley?"

It was a girl's voice that drew his attention. Standing between her parents, she was small and skinny, head shaved for the heat. She pointed and shouted something in Lingala that Sam could not understand. Her parents yanked her back as she started toward Sam, and stifled her mouth with their hands.

Sam looked where she had been pointing. A road jutted off from the airstrip, into the forest. "That way?"

Still struggling against her parents, the girl nodded.

"No! Sir, you must not!" Ngouabi grabbed at the door and then slapped his palms against the window as Sam heaved himself into the Hummer's back seat. "You must not! You will never come back!"

"Crawford—*Go!*"

Gravel spat from the Hummer's tires as Crawford floored it. They shot onto the runway and raced across, bounding toward the edge of the forest. Clawing at the back of Ann's seat, Sam heaved himself up and strapped on his seatbelt before twisting around to stare out the windows behind them.

The twin Landcruisers skidded sideways, splitting around the jet as it slowly rolled back toward the end of the airstrip.

Sam saw the men in the back of the first truck moving, taking up positions between the roll bars. "Crawford, look out, they're about to—"

Gunfire ripped across the runway. Bullets skipped over the pavement on either side of the Hummer, dotting the road with tiny flares of light.

Crawford zigzagged. The whole car leaned. Its center of gravity was high, and every time they steered one way or another, Sam braced himself against the door. It felt like they were going to flip over.

A sharp *crack* rang out from the rear windshield. Spidery fractures leapt across the glass, but it hadn't broken. Bullet-proof?

Evidently, Clayton Wesley had anticipated some trouble with the locals.

Ann let out a yelp.

Ahead of them, surging out of the woods, a detachment of half a dozen Congolese soldiers flooded over the mouth of the road. They were pulling a makeshift barricade after them, knotty wood from a fallen tree.

Sam heaved himself forward between the front seats. "Crawford!"

"I know!"

"You can't—"

"Shut up, Sam!" Crawford pushed the pedal to the metal.

The Hummer's engine roared.

At the last minute, the soldiers scattered, leaving the tree halfway across the opening. The car shuddered and then leapt up at a diagonal as it smashed through the wood. Chewed-up bark hammered the insides of the wheel wells, while the roof scraped through a thick snarl of branches and leaves.

The road dipped and then climbed sharply upward on the other side. As the Hummer dropped back into the dirt, the wheels spun and clamored for purchase amid the twigs and tiny rocks.

The airstrip dropped out of view. A moment later, the trees shook with a loud *crunch*, littering the roof of the Hummer with dead leaves and struggling insects.

"The—can you see the headlights?" Crawford fumbled with the dash.

As the forest pressed in around them, it blotted out the sun. The road narrowed, ferns, vines, and branches encroaching on the pathway until it became difficult to separate it from the slender gaps between the bushes.

Ann reached across, scanning the controls. She found the switch. Twin beams of light brought the air alive with swarms of mosquitoes, dirt, spores, fluttering leaves. There was movement everywhere.

Sam jerked as more light flooded in from behind. The Landcruiser.

It was maybe twenty feet back, and gaining on them. Nose protected by a heavy metal grille guard, it caromed off the tree trunks and punted rocks out of its path. The driver pressed forward, careless, determined.

Sam gulped. "Crawford—faster!"

"I'm trying!"

"They're catching up!"

"What the fuck do you want *me* to do about it?"

Sam swiveled back. His eyes fell on the equipment supply crate Ngouabi had left open when Sam had pulled him away, back at the airstrip. Wedged between a brick of flashlights, batteries, a First Aid kit, and a backup radio was a flare gun.

Unbuckling his seatbelt, Sam scrambled into the rear compartment and dug the gun out of the crate. He turned it over and hefted it in his hands. He'd never used one before in his life.

Crawford caught a glimpse of him in the rear-view mirror. "Sam, are you—what are you doing?"

"Taking care of that truck." He grabbed the inside latch of the rear windshield and twisted.

It sprang open. The noise of the jungle thundered in—snapping branches, spitting rocks and dirt, the roar of the two engines. The heat hit Sam's face in a wave. He braced his legs against the tailgate and aimed the flare gun at the smeared windshield of the Landcruiser, now just ten feet back.

The driver must have seen what he was doing.

Sam was just reaching for the trigger when a face and then the muzzle of a gun appeared out the passenger window.

"Shit! Get down!" Sam hit the floor as a barrage of bullets hammered the roof of the Hummer from behind.

"Jesus Christ! Jesus—" Ann doubled over, face against the dashboard. "Sam!"

Sam rolled to the tailgate, aimed at the Landcruiser, and fired.

A blinding red flare shot out of the gun, only to ricochet off of a low-hanging branch. It tumbled to the Landcruiser's hood and rolled off into the foliage.

Sam cursed. Frantic, hands shaking, he dug through the equipment crate until he found another flare.

The Landcruiser closed the gap. Lying flat across the rear compartment, Sam could hear the engine, the tires on the ground, the crunch of leaves flattened beneath them. It had to be only five or six feet away.

"Sam—the back! Close the back!" Crawford twisted around in his seat. In the moment of distraction, the wheel slipped from his hands, and the Hummer veered sharply to the right.

The car shook as the nose grazed a tree trunk. Metal ground against wood, shrieking and spitting sparks. The impact pitched Sam forward into the tailgate. He smacked his forehead and dropped the flare gun.

The Landcruiser slammed into them from behind.

Through the ungodly din, Sam heard a *click*. The machine gun. Ten seconds, and they would all be dead.

Sam threw himself at the flare gun. The Hummer bounced over another rock. The floor tilted. The butt of the gun edged away from him. Straining, stretching as far as he could, he finally got his fingers around it and grabbed it up. He forced himself into a sitting position, aimed, and pulled the trigger.

The flare exploded from the barrel. For an instant, everything seemed to freeze. Sam was suspended in a cloud of insects and grime, of spent bullets and splintered bark, of battered metal and thrashing branches—all of it bathed in red.

Then, the Landcruiser's windshield shattered. Sam didn't see where the flare hit, but a fraction of a second later, the truck spun out of control and smashed into a tree. The hood wrapped around the trunk, flinging the soldiers in the back out the open roof and into the forest.

The wreckage fell away in a hazy brown cloud as the Hummer continued up the hillside.

Sam sat back, reaching overhead to pull the rear window closed behind him. He was soaked in sweat, black with grime, and utterly, completely spent.

"Sam?" Ann undid her seatbelt and climbed over the center console. Her face appeared above the crest of the back seat. "Sam, are you ... Are you okay?"

Feebly, he managed a nod.

She took his hands and helped him over. They slid down the other side together. Crawford—face pale, knuckles white around the steering wheel—glanced at them in the rear-view mirror.

"That was stupid, Sam. You could've ... you should've been killed just then."

Sam gulped and squinted past him, out the windshield. "Where is this road taking us?"

5

As they crested the rise, the jungle suddenly fell away. They had been driving for almost twenty minutes. The airstrip and the village where they had landed was nothing more than a speck between cracks in the rear windshield.

Crawford braked. He brought them to a slow, grinding halt as the valley unfolded ahead. Slipping the Hummer into *Park*, he leaned forward until his face was almost touching the windshield. "My God," he said. "What is this place?"

TWENTY SIX

THE GPS MONITOR on the dashboard showed nothing but unbroken jungle ahead of them for miles on either side. At their backs, vibrant wildflowers, like fireworks, exploded from between the thick canopy of trees overhead and the huddled ferns and bushes on the forest floor. Birds flitted between the branches. Steam hovered about the tree trunks.

Ahead—

Blackness. A nightmare. The pages of Riley's sketchbook, brought to life.

The valley was not hidden in shadow. No mountain peak nor drifting cloud kept it from the sun. It was simply *black*. Utterly, horribly black. The leaves on the trees and the dirt on the ground—everything for as far as the eye could see looked as though it had been bathed in charcoal.

Lake Kitoto filled the valley floor like a stained oil slick.

At first glance, Sam saw none of it.

All he saw was the dark tower.

"It's real," he breathed. "God help me, it's real."

Several hundred feet tall, it bowed inward like an hourglass before falling to foundations that joined a cluster of other buildings hidden by the blighted forest on the other side of the valley.

Sam reached for the handle of his door. Crawford locked them all with the flip of a switch.

"Crawford—"

"Sam, it looks like the Black Plague out there. You have no idea what might be airborne. Opening that door could kill us all."

"But it's … I have to—I have to touch it." He couldn't explain it any better than that. There was something about the shape of the mountains, the color of the sky—something that tugged at his heart.

Ann twisted around in her seat to stare at him. "Sam are you sure you're—"

A loud *thump* shook the Hummer from the rear left corner. Ann broke off as the car shuddered forward a couple of inches. By the time Sam had spun around to look out the rear windshield, there was nothing. Only a swaying tree branch, animal tracks in the muddy road, a trail of broken twigs and flattened leaves.

"What was that?" Ann whispered.

"There's something out there." Crawford scoured the wilderness through his own window, nose touching the glass, eyes wide. "I think there's something out there."

Sam turned forward. "Drive."

The shapes of animals darted back and forth across the road as they descended. Whatever they were, they were moving too quickly for Sam to get much of a glimpse of them, but what he saw made him shiver. Gaunt, sinewy, they loped like hungry coyotes. Their fur was mangy and black as night. Eyes flickered through the broken vegetation. The whole forest was watching them.

Crows shook the upper tree branches, never quite taking flight, as if something held them down and kept them in this nightmare.

Sam gaped. Somehow, his sons had seen this. They had closed their eyes and seen this place, just like him.

He slid all the way to the left of the bench seat and pulled back the shade of the sun roof to see as much of it as he could. His eyes always drifted back to the dark tower.

Crawford flicked a glance at him in the rear-view mirror and saw where he was looking. "Nuclear cooling tower, I think."

Squinting at it now, he saw Crawford was right. It was distinctive in its tall, slender, bowing silhouette. His gaze trailed to the landscape rolling away from the road on all sides.

It was Ann who voiced the same thought as it crossed Sam's mind: "What happened here?"

Crawford stopped the Hummer at a fork in the road. He leaned forward, hunching over the wheel, and squinted down at a sign up ahead. There were two arrows, one pointing to the upward slope at the left, and the other, down to the right, toward the lake.

Time and calamity had left the lettering unreadable.

Sam was about to suggest the left fork when Ann pointed out her window. "There."

"There, what?" He scooted across the seat to her side of the car.

"I think I just saw something move down there."

5

The Hummer's tires slipped and slid, grasping for traction as the ground became soft and porous nearer to the lake. They rounded a corner in the road and Crawford slammed on the brakes.

A red-and-white metal blockade blocked their path. Reinforced girders shot deep into the ground behind it. It looked—permanent. Stenciled lettering covered the central crossbar:

No motor vehicles or electronic machinery beyond this point.

Another fifty feet down the road, the vegetation became too thick to see what lay any farther beyond. Something blocky and metal protruded through the treetops, maybe a half-mile away. It was impossible to make out more.

Crawford grimaced. "I could try to go around." He twisted the steering wheel.

Static flashed across the GPS display in the center console. The headlights flickered.

"Crawford." Sam shook his head. "Wait. Don't."

"We can't get out."

"There's a reason that sign is there."

"Maybe. Maybe not." Crawford edged the car up onto the sloping shoulder of the road and gave it a little more gas. The engine growled, sputtered, and then cut out altogether. Silence consumed the car. Crawford grabbed the key and twisted it in the ignition.

The Hummer gave an anemic cough. The interior lights came on, dimmer than before, and then flashed once and went out again.

Computer code scrolled across the screen in the center console, faster, page after page until it abruptly flicked to blackness.

Then—

Nothing.

Dead silence.

"I don't get it." Crawford pumped the accelerator. "This piece of shit is brand new. There's no way it just—just died ... "

"Crawford." Sam looked from the dead dashboard to the blockade and the blighted jungle beyond. "It's not the car."

The air was surprisingly cool, nothing like the stifling, humid heat back at the airstrip, but here, it tasted acrid, of smoke and warped metal and something even more awful. The ground was spongy beneath Sam's shoes when he stepped off the running board on the side of the car.

Ann and Crawford watched him from inside. Waiting, expectant.

He nudged the back door shut and checked his reflection in the window. No sores popping out on his face. No deep, internal pain, no burning in his lungs. He shrugged at them.

"No way to know what's out here without a doctor or something." He glanced at Ann. "You should stay here."

She opened her door. "Like hell."

"Crawford? If something happens to us, someone should stay back, be able to radio for ... "

Crawford stumbled out of the car. "If we're doing this, we're doing this."

Sam skirted up around the metal roadblock. The paint was chipped away, scratched, weathered. It appeared to have been there for decades.

"I don't think this is a good idea." Crawford glanced over his shoulder, up the valley. There was nothing but charcoal grays and blacks for as far as the eye could see.

"I know," Sam said. "But we don't have a choice."

Their feet crunched as they picked their way forward. Sam peered upward, through the dead tree branches. There was something strange about the forest—as though, rather than slowly succumbing to some natural disease that weeded out the vulnerable plants and animals, it had, one day, simply died all together in one terrible, monumental flash.

It remained as thick and dense as the jungle on the other side of the ridge. The only difference was that everything here was dead.

"Here … " Ann veered a few feet off the road, to the left, and craned her neck from the base of a tall concrete pillar.

Gray-brown vines wound circles around it. Twenty feet above, a metal arm arched out over the path. It was rusted nearly all the way through. A street lamp. The bulb itself hung from the end of the arm, but it had long ago shattered and been left to form the home for some insect that made a cottony nest in its shell.

Sam followed the tree line and picked out three others, equally overgrown, equally lifeless, as well as an old air raid horn planted on two tall wooden stilts.

The place looked like a World War II internment camp.

The moment they started walking again, the bushes rustled behind them.

Sam swiveled back. Crawford reached for his nightstick. The black brambles quivered. A couple of tree branches swung, as though from a gentle gust of wind.

But there was no wind.

Black Valley was the most airless place Sam had ever encountered. Here, it felt as though the entire world was holding its breath.

They waited nearly a minute. No other sound penetrated the silence. No insects chirped, no birds cawed. Everything stood frozen as wax. Ann shuddered.

It was the kind of stillness that could drive a person crazy.

Another twenty paces through the jungle and they came up against a tightly-woven mesh fence. The bushes and branches had grown through it, absorbing it, swallowing it whole. Sam brushed the vegetation from a decaying wooden sign planted in the dirt nearby.

Danger. Private.

They skirted along the length of the fence for a few dozen feet in both directions, but the forest was so thick that it made it difficult to fight their way around the underbrush. Somewhere, there had to be a gate.

Sam grunted as he stumbled into something sticking up through a snarl of tree roots. It rose to his waist, a rusted metal box with more writing stenciled into the front and a circular pattern of holes. A speaker.

It was a callbox, surrounded by nothing but untamed wilderness. Whatever road or path or entryway had once been there had long ago been swallowed by the valley. Finding it again would be hopeless.

"Give me a boost." Sam nudged Crawford and nodded toward the fence.

It was more difficult than he would have thought to scale it. The mesh was too fine to permit much in the way of hand- and toeholds, and it had been years since Sam had done anything more physical than shoot a few hoops with Daniel. The thought of that made him redouble his effort. He strained, sweating, and at last managed to grasp the top and heave himself up. For a delicate moment, he clung, perched, before he found a way to lift his foot over and drop to the ground on the other side.

He helped Ann down after him, and then both of them watched as Crawford followed on his own. His police training must have kept him in better shape. He was over in less than a minute.

Inside the compound, the trees were sparser. Crystallized grass crackled beneath their shoes. Once upon a time, it had probably been a pleasant meadow, crawling toward the verge of the lake. At the fringe of the forest, crouched between the trees, a metal structure loomed out of the rotting vegetation.

Concrete girders rose at angles, buttressing inward around the steel-and-cinderblock walls of a rotunda coated in soot, rust, and layer upon layer of grime. In style, it resembled the barracks buildings back at Ellis Ranch, though if anything, this place looked built to withstand even greater catastrophe.

Barred cages clung to each of the narrow windows, and heavy bolts pockmarked the doors. A cluster of antennas and satellite dishes rose into the sickly treetop canopy. Like everything else, they stood inert, lifeless.

"Sam ... " Ann had stopped to stoop beside a depression in the ground.

When he joined her, he saw it was more than that—a sinkhole, funneling to a black point, that stretched deep under the earth.

Footprints had eroded away the edges, and just beyond the outer-most set was a ring of stones very purposefully placed to encircle the trench.

It looked—religious. Ceremonial.

"And the trees, too." Ann pointed to the two tree trunks nearest them.

The bark was chewed up. It looked as though something had gnawed it away, leaving a pattern of tiny, ragged holes.

Several of the other trees bore the same markings.

Crawford squatted beside the two of them. He frowned. "What is this place?"

Sam shook his head. "You got me." He sheltered his eyes against the sun as he peered ahead, across the field.

Drawing up beside one of the poured stone pillars at the bunker, he turned back to survey the ground they had crossed. The dark tower rose up into the sky, on the horizon, but here, inside the com-pound of electric fences, the place looked almost peaceful. Idyllic.

They fanned out, taking stock. The complex consisted of two larger buildings and a string of half a dozen low, brick structures behind them. Nestled into the trees, overgrown and decrepit, they were blocky, rectangular—ugly. They resembled a highway motel that had been left to rot back into the soil.

Lights dangled from strings that wove from structure to struc-ture like an overhanging trellis. All of the bulbs were broken.

Five of the six buildings had been left derelict. Inside, metal cot frames held the tattered remains of mattresses, in varying stages of decay. Shriveled leaves and vines belched from the porcelain bath-room sinks.

Only one of the six doors was closed.

Sam tried the knob, and found it, to his surprise, unlocked. He eased it open and searched for a light switch, but even the one he found just around the corner did nothing when he flicked it.

The air smelled of kerosene. As his eyes adjusted, he picked out the curving glass bell of a lamp resting on a dresser. A stack of old books and papers stood beside the bed. Couched in pillow cushions was a plate that looked like it might have been used recently.

Life.

Someone lived here.

"Sam."

Sam ducked back out of the tiny apartment.

Crawford stood framed in the doorway of the larger bunker, blackness gaping around him. "You're gonna need to see this."

∽

Sam choked and covered his nose and mouth with his shirt collar as he stepped through the threshold. The air was thick with the smell of death—rotting flesh. Wet, burnt hair.

"Got a light?" he wheezed through the cloth.

Crawford slipped a flashlight from his pocket and gave a frustrated tap. "Nothing works here." It flickered and then went dark.

Filtered sun made it through grimy Plexiglas skylights to pool on a desk, a couple of chairs, a shattered glass coffee table, and a few picked-over baskets of books.

"What the hell is that smell?" Ann tramped in behind them.

Sam looked to Crawford.

"Brace yourself." Crawford led them to a door spilling off of the lobby at the opposite end.

Dread pooled in the pit of Sam's stomach as they approached.

Surely, it wasn't—it couldn't be—not like back at Ellis Ranch …

Ann took his hand. They drew to a halt as the room on the other side came into view. Sam heard Ann stifle a gasp.

It was a small, circular rotunda, a scientific laboratory with stations set up fanning out around the curving walls. Barstools, microscopes, and a stack of other equipment stood sloppily shoved aside in one corner. Blood covered the empty countertops. It splattered the walls, collected in puddles on the floors, hung from the ceiling in far-flung, caramelized droplets.

Flayed carcasses hung from the walls.

Sam swallowed back a jolt of bile that leapt to his throat. They weren't human. Matted black fur sat in piles on the floor, but the exposed muscle and bone were enough to make his stomach heave. They looked like the beasts Riley had drawn.

"They're fresh. Relatively." Crawford cupped his nose and mouth in his hand. His boots made sticky smacking noises as he slipped inside. "They haven't started rotting. And the blood … " He nudged the fur with the tip of a shoe. "Not all dry yet. Not by a long shot."

"Who would do this?" Ann backed against the wall, gaping. "Why? Why would anyone do this?"

"What are they?" Sam asked.

Crawford shrugged. "Not much of a hunter, myself. Look like dogs of some kind. Wolves, maybe? Through there ... " He nodded to a narrower door leading off the rotunda. "Used to be some kind of maintenance closet, by the look of it, but someone's turned it into a goddamn bone yard. Everything stripped clean. You ask me, they're being used for meat. For food."

Sam shivered.

Perhaps it was just the tint of the light through the ceiling, but the blood on the floor and the walls seemed to have an unsettling, grayish cloud in it. He squinted at the skull of the nearest creature. Its body had been flopped back across a lab station, head dangling, limp, from the edge.

There were too many ribs. The tail looked too long. The eyes seemed too far apart, and the jaws too large. There had been something wrong with the creature, even before it had been killed.

Two other small rotundas peeled away from the central lobby. One was filled with what appeared to be old scientific research. A rolling chalkboard stood before a wall covered in charts and maps of the valley. Reel-to-reel data tapes protruded on spindles from first-generation computers. Vacuum tubes, lights, switches—the lab looked like a NASA control room.

Something stood beneath a drop cloth at the center of the rotunda, and from the moment Sam walked in the door, he was riveted to it. Blocky, angular, it was roughly the size of a large fish tank or a work desk. The tarp was ratty, riddled with holes, but it was too dark to make out anything inside.

Sam made a full circuit around the outside of the room while Crawford explored the other rotunda and Ann looked for anything useful in the files at the lobby reception desk.

Sam wound up standing before the tarp. He nudged it with a foot. It seemed unlikely there was anything alive inside, though *life* was the precise impression it gave him. As though something were watching him from within. Beckoning.

Sam glanced back out through the doorway. Only Ann's legs were visible, crouching in front of the desk. A *clunk* sounded from the other side of the building. Crawford.

Drawing in a deep breath, Sam bent and pulled back the tarp. It furled to the floor with a soft rustle as he leapt away.

Standing against the door, he frowned and then slowly crept back in. He was being foolish. There was nothing underneath.

Or—almost nothing.

It was a glass case, walls crisscrossed with a mesh of reinforcing wire. It could have trapped a cheetah, but all it appeared to be protecting was a small pile of rocks. They were arranged in a cairn—slivered around the edges. Judging by the ragged sides, they appeared to have been chipped away from a larger deposit somewhere, though the faces left untampered-with were smooth as polished silver.

He wasn't aware how close he'd moved until his feet came up flush against the base of the container. His breath fogged the glass. He wiped the condensation away with an elbow, feverish, irritated.

Upset by the break in his line-of-sight with the rocks.

The black dust from outside had been kept there by the case, and when Sam wiped more of it from the surface, the cairn shone out at him, a striking blue-gray. It was captivating.

"Sam."

He jumped and whirled, blocking the container with his body.

Ann stood in the doorway. She looked poised, worried. "Sam, there are people. We've got company."

"Shit." He didn't want to go. He didn't want to leave this room. He lingered, the hand touching the fortified glass suddenly heavy as lead.

Ann was already darting back out, but she slowed when he didn't immediately follow. "Sam? What? What is it?"

"Nothing." He yanked the tarp back over the case before she could turn again. "Nothing. I'm coming. What people?"

There were two doors behind the lobby reception desk. One of them was still closed, obscured by a cluster of dusty oxygen tanks and wire-frame shelves. Flickering light spilled out of the second one, a trail of papers scattered over the floor where Ann had dropped them when she'd happened inside.

It was a small, windowless room. The walls were six inches thick, ceiling pointed in the center and held up by struts that looked as though they could lift an oil rig. Six old-fashioned television monitors sat in a bank against the far wall.

Five displayed only blackness. A grainy black-and-white image, laced with static, jumped in a circle from screen to screen, magenta and lime green around the edges, as though the TVs were being distorted by some kind of magnetic field.

"Security." Ann planted her hands on her hips. "Wait for it to come around. No idea why it's doing that."

Sam cocked his head, moving to follow the different camera angles as they traced their way in a clockwise arc. "I didn't think anything here was running," he mused aloud. His eyes fell to the workstation, bathed in an eerie, ghostly glow.

Pencils and exhausted ballpoints littered the controls, laced with the perforated edges of dot-matrix paper. There were a couple of dirty plates at the end of the desk, in front of a folding metal chair. Also, a coffee mug.

Something about it bothered Sam, but before he could put a finger on it, the screen in the bottom center came to life.

"There!" Ann bent forward.

Set against the latticework of lifeless branches, Sam could just pick out the roof of the bright blue-and-white Hummer parked beyond the barrier, up the road.

Ann leaned to touch the plate glass with her finger. "You see him?"

A split-second before the image winked away, Sam caught a blur of movement. The shape of a man. His breath caught in his throat. "Where's Crawford?"

"Not out there. He's in one of the other labs or something."

"Crawford!" Sam stayed at the bank of TVs. He waited for the image to come around again.

"Whoa, did you see that?" Ann was looking at one of the monitors stacked to the left. "Sam?"

"No—what? I was—" There was the Hummer again. The brambles and tree branches shook. There was already no sign of the man.

"That one." Ann patted the side of the screen. "Damn it, this takes so long."

Flash. Flash. Flash. The Hummer again. Flash. "Right there."

It appeared to be the field they had crossed on the way into the compound. The edges of the tree trunks at the corner of the frame were nibbled away, just like the one Ann had pointed out.

Now, an open-topped jeep was parked beneath them, driver's-side door hanging open.

Sam and Ann looked at each other. He was about to turn back, grab Crawford, and get the hell out of there, when the monitor at the bottom right corner of the three-by-two stack shimmered to life.

He froze in his tracks.

The image was a little blurrier than the others—something was on the outside of the bulging glass. Sam stepped forward, knelt, and wiped it away with his sleeve. It was steam.

From the coffee mug.

TWENTY SEVEN

SAM HEARD THE CLICK OF THE GUN at the doorway before he had a chance to look. Ann drew in a sharp breath.

The flickering black-and-white light from the TV deepened the shadows on the face of the woman at the door. There was something about her eyes that grabbed Sam. Something penetrating, elemental, hard-wired.

It was only when she took a step forward and moved her arms that Sam noticed she was cradling a hunting rifle.

Ann raised her hands, palms up, placating. Sam hastened to do the same. It hadn't occurred to him. He was still staring at the woman's face. As she advanced, drew nearer, he got a better look at her. She didn't appear much older than thirty, maybe thirty-five, but there was a certain haunted quality to her expression, the way she moved.

"Listen … " Sam took a step backward. The seat of his pants ran up against the security workstation. "Listen to me. We're only here for—"

The woman cut him off with what might have been a laugh. It sounded more like the bark of a wild dog. "I knew I heard voices. Knew it. Knew it this time. Knew they weren't coming from down there, either. I *knew* it."

Sam glanced at Ann.

She gulped. "Ma'am … " Ann squinted at the name woven into the tattered white lab coat the woman was wearing. It was old, worn, tears biting into the elbows, oil and grease stains up the stomach and chest. "Monica?"

Sam stared. Ann was right.

Monica – Research & Development
Lake Kitoto Complex

It couldn't be. If the baby in the picture was Sam, and Monica was indeed the woman to whom Grace had been writing, she would have to have been nearly seventy by now—early-sixties at the youngest.

Which meant one of two things. The woman standing before them had inherited the jacket from the real Monica, or the woman standing before them was somehow responsible for her death.

The barrel of her rifle dug into Sam's chest. "You're real. You are real. Aren't you?"

"I'm real ... Monica ... "

The woman didn't correct him. She smiled. Her teeth bore smudges and stains, yellowed in places and ragged in others. Her hair, too, a pretty chestnut brown, hung in mats around her head. Without the coat, she would have looked feral.

Suddenly, the grin dropped away. "You're not one of *them*, are you? Haven't seen you before. Might have heard you, though. Down there." She leaned in a little closer, letting the gun slip up to jab at Sam's chin so she could whisper: "Not many people I haven't heard down there. That's why people shouldn't go there. People will hear people, and not all people should be heard."

A bead of sweat trickled down Sam's temple. Beside him, he became conscious of Ann stealing a glance at the TV monitors. By the look on her face, whoever it was outside was getting closer.

A lone footstep echoed in from the lobby.

Monica—or whatever the woman's name was—jumped and screeched. Sam squeezed his eyes shut. He waited for the blast.

The gun barrel slipped off of him, and when he mustered the courage to look, all Sam could see was the back of Monica's head. She was skulking toward the door, low to the ground like a scared, hunted cat.

"They'll show you," she hissed over her shoulder. "That's our deal. They show people like you. Show them they shouldn't be here. Show them what happens to people who go where people shouldn't be. Unless you're one of them."

The tip of her rifle poked out the door, and in a flash, a hand grabbed it and yanked it from her arms. Monica cried out and dove after it. She collided with Crawford as he stepped into her path.

"Back off," he told her. "Back off and calm down."

"Crawford." Sam swiveled toward the TV screens. "Crawford, we have to get out of here."

"What?" He waved the butt of the gun at Monica. "Who's she? Why's she—"

"There are others. Coming for us."

A door banged somewhere outside. All of them fell silent. All except for Monica, who was muttering to herself stroking her arms as though caressing a phantom rifle. She jostled up beside Sam and squinted at his face.

"Stay there." Crawford started to wheel toward the lobby.

"No. You stay here, watch her." He sidestepped the reception desk and kicked a sheaf of crumpled papers out of the way to jog to the front doors. He had his hand on the knob when he thought to check out the slitted window just to the left.

Brushing aside a dusty blind, he leaned over and yelped. He was standing face-to-face with a man, hands cupped around the glass, squinting in from the other side.

Unshaven, short, graying hair. The soldier. The soldier who had come for Daniel at home and then in the hospital.

Sam stumbled back. He tried to catch the blind, but it slipped by just beyond his reach to clatter against the window.

The silhouette on the other side jerked away.

Then the knob turned.

Sam lunged, grabbed it, forced it back. The soldier shouted something from the other side and strained against him.

"Jesus!" Ann sprinted around the reception desk. "I'm coming! Hold it—try and—"

Sam threw his weight against the door as the soldier wrenched the knob and started to force it open. Ann dove, planted her feet against the door, and with their combined strength, they managed to get it shut for just long enough that Sam could turn the lock.

The soldier hammered on the metal panel from the other side. Through the narrow gaps of light in the blinds to the right and left, Sam saw movement, kicked-up dust, blurred, camouflaged fatigues.

"Shit!" He spun back, grabbing Ann by the arm to wrench her

alongside him as they ran for Crawford and the woman. "Where can we go? How do we get out of here?"

"No getting out." Monica sneered. "Everyone wants to get out, but there's no getting out. Not once you get here. Didn't the locals tell you?"

Sam grimaced, spinning, casting wildly about for options. "Crawford?"

"There are more guns in the other room. Looks like some kind of weapons cache, but I didn't see any doors."

Sam's eyes stopped on the second door, beside the security room. "What's in there?"

Monica's face paled when she saw where he was pointing. "No. We can't go in there."

"What is it?"

"It's nothing. It's just—dangerous chemicals. Not a way out."

With a straining effort, he hoisted one of the six-foot lead oxygen tanks and managed to drag it a couple of inches before his energy gave out. It was just enough to give the door a foot or two of clearance. Panting, sweating, he grabbed the latch wheel and spun.

"No!" Monica sprang and coiled her arm around his neck. She planted her feet on the waistline of his pants and scrambled up onto his shoulders.

Sam gurgled, letting go of the door to claw at her hands. Crawford and Ann set upon her, pulling, tearing, doing everything they could. Sam spun around and slammed her against the concrete wall. He felt the air shoot from her lungs. Coughing, she let go for just an instant.

Ann and Crawford leapt at the opportunity and managed to pry her off before she could make another grab at his throat.

The room spun around Sam. Colored dots crawled in at the edges of his vision.

"Maybe," he heard Ann saying, "if she cares that much, maybe it's a good idea to stay out. We don't know what's—"

A hollow *crack* rang out from the front doors. The lock was beginning to buckle. Whatever it was the soldier and his buddies were using against them, it was stronger than the screws that held the hinges together.

Sam gripped the wheel. "If it's dangerous," he rasped, "then maybe they won't think to look for us here."

The door came open with a grudging, grinding groan. Stairs descended into blackness on the opposite side.

"No ... " Monica flailed in Crawford's arms, but she sounded weaker. "No, it ... no ... "

Sam flicked the light switch just inside. Two dim bulbs flickered to life, hanging from a long wire that was strung down the length of the ceiling. The second dangled just over the door at the bottom, and beyond—an empty black void.

He rounded on Monica. "Down."

"No! Not me! Why me?"

"Because you know what we're going to find."

Another *crack* from up front. Tiny parts of the locking mechanism pattered to the floor. Monica flinched, but she didn't move.

"Crawford." Sam nodded to her.

Crawford jabbed her forward at gunpoint, slipping off the safety catch with his thumb. Slowly, reluctantly, Monica inched down the stairs. Sam wedged himself in after her and turned to help Ann through. Then, with a heave, he pulled the door shut behind them.

The latch sent a resounding echo down the concrete stairs.

It died in the doorway at the bottom.

Empty cobwebs covered the walls. Edging to one side to give Ann room, Sam stepped on something that came loose and clattered down the stairs. It rolled through the meager pool of light and slipped out of sight.

A candle—burnt almost to the puddle of melted wax it had left behind. There were more. Many more. Lining the stairwell on either side. Prayer candles.

Monica shivered and flattened herself against the wall at the bottom. "Don't make me go through," she whispered. "Please don't make me go through. It seduces me."

A *thump* came at the door above. Monica jumped and then threw a longing glance back the way they had come. "Please ... "

Even in the darkness on the other side, Sam had the impression of stepping into the mouth of somewhere unfathomably large. It was just a feeling. A particular feeling. Complete and total emptiness. Like standing in a cave that burrowed hollow an entire mountain.

Advancing, his shoes touched metal. Grating. A catwalk of some kind. He stopped when he ran into a handrail.

"Hold on; there's a light." Ann knelt and straightened with an old kerosene lantern. There was a mechanical switch on the side, connected to a flint. She pressed it, and with the spark, a tiny flame leapt out of the wick.

Flickering orange light touched their arms and then their chests and then their faces. The railing came into view, scored, paint chipped and peeling. Just to the right, it turned a corner and closed off the catwalk. A dead end.

It kept going in the other direction.

"What is this stuff?" Crawford wedged the rifle under his arm to brush dust from the shoulder of his jacket.

It glittered in the light—blue-gray. The same rocks from the case upstairs.

A shiver ran through Sam's body as he turned to stare into the inky void. Monica was watching him again. There was a strange look on her face. A look of clarity, certainty, as though, for a moment, the obsessive, neurotic twitching had left her mind sharp as a diamond.

"Do you like it?" she breathed. "You like it. Don't you?"

The catwalk sloped into another stairway. Down again. Deeper into the dark. Sam took the lamp from Ann and held it out over the rail. He thought he caught the faintest reflection from the opposite wall, maybe forty feet across, but there was still no hint of a floor.

"How deep?"

Monica didn't answer.

Sam shook her shoulder and held the light to her face. "How deep does it go?"

"No one knows."

"Bullshit."

She looked at him. "We tried to measure it, but our instruments kept breaking." The smile came back like a flame sputtering in the rain. "Some of the others say it goes to the heart of the Earth. All the way to the heart."

Sam scowled descended to the next platform. This one was wider, veering out over what felt very much like nothing at all.

Here, along the rail, the extra space had been used to accommodate a line of machines and crude scientific equipment. Tickertape lay coiled in a wire wastebasket where it had fed out of an old printer. Beside it, a flurry of old IBM punch cards, a ruler, a couple of spent pens.

Sam leaned across a switchboard covered in murky dials and knobs. Still nothing but blackness, below.

Footsteps passed by overhead. There were at least three different sets. They would be able to cover the entire facility in another five minutes.

Sam stooped to pick up the candle where it had rolled to a stop against one of the metal banisters. He dipped it inside the lamp, and after he had lit it, he leaned out over the edge and let go.

Crawford and Ann hustled up beside him and craned their necks to get a look.

The tiny sphere of light encountered, for a brief moment, the steep slope of another wall funneling downward. Then, nothing. It stayed lit for another ten seconds without encountering a single obstruction before it finally went dark.

Sam waited, listening.

The only sound from below was the whistle of a gentle breeze over stone.

Slowly, the three of them turned to Monica.

"Sometimes, I hear voices." She shrugged. "Vick said it was God. Said it was telling him what to do, and mind you, he's a scientist, not a Bible since he was old enough to say no. He said God told him he'd be safe if he stayed here forever. But then, he died in the flash." Monica crept to the rail. "Guess either Vick was wrong or God was. Right?"

"What flash?"

"The flash. *The* flash. The end of the world. You know. The Powers That Be sent us down here, slaving away for day after day, just on the off chance we could help them out. Those were the old days. Peaches. Some guy, maybe it was Vick, he brought peaches down here. Had them growing on a tree right outside, and everyone said that they shouldn't, they weren't supposed to be able to here. But then, there's a lot that happened here that was never supposed to. One day, though, like they say, it's all got to come to an end, I guess … If teacher knows too much, but the kids aren't learning anymore, what do you do with him? Put him out to pasture."

Sam stared at her. "Are you saying someone—someone tried to destroy this place?"

"Nope. That … " She rolled her eyes toward the ceiling, toward the ruins of the blighted valley. "That was a mistake. Human error. Summer solstice, some of the guys called it. Lit up the sky like the Northern Lights, and last I checked we weren't anywhere near the old North Pole. That was Donny's doing, because Donny's a pig-headed *asshole*, and he cracks under pressure. And that's a bad place to crack. Especially for someone who controls the weather. Wouldn't you say?"

"Donny ... Pryce? Donald Pryce? The Colonel?" Sam jumped when something hard and heavy smashed against the door at the top of the stairs.

The oxygen tanks? If the soldier set one of them off, positioned it just right, it could blow the door right off its hinges.

He wheeled back to the yawning pit and shuddered again, involuntarily. Its depth, the palpable emptiness, the vastness of the great unknown—

None of them scared him as much as the way it made him feel.

A part of him, buried so far down that it wasn't much more than a tiny voice in the back of his head, wanted to jump.

Ann took his hand and squeezed. "Sam. She's—this isn't getting us anywhere. She's crazy. We have to find another way out."

"Sam?" Monica shook her head and sneered to herself. "That's a funny name. I like it though. Reminds me ... " And then she looked at him. *Looked* at him.

Sam was about to ask her what the hell she was thinking when there was another thunderous blow from the top of the stairs. The door was buckling.

He took her by the arm and bent so that they were at eye-level. "Monica."

"No, it can't be ... "

"Monica ... or whatever your name is ... . Please. Please, we need your help. If there's any way out of here ... "

"You're not supposed to come here. You were never supposed to come back here. You weren't. What are you doing back here? You have to—no, let go!" She wrenched away as Sam tried to hold her still. "You have to *leave*. I'll fix your car. So it works. Adjust it, like it needs. Oh my God, you ... after *that*, after everything, why would you ever come here?"

She dodged him again, stumbling into the wastebasket. It tipped over and rolled through a gap in the handrail, vanishing into the infinite blackness. Monica shook her head, vigorous, obsessive, pacing in circles. "No, no, no, no, not after—no."

"Mon—"

She stopped short and grabbed Sam by the forearms. "You have to come with me. Right now. You have to come." Then she spun and darted into the dark, away from the gaping chasm. In less than a second, the shadows had swallowed her completely.

"Monica?"

Ann caught him as he started after her. "I don't trust her. How can you trust her?"

Another *thump*. Twisting metal.

Sam flinched and pulled Ann after him. "Because I have to. *We* have to."

In the light of the sputtering lantern, rusting old equipment rose up out of the shadows. At first, Sam could not make out what it was. Looming large, the size of a small car, the first piece sat with its nose against the wall. Dusty pipes dangled from its flanks, coiling away to drop between slats in the floor.

A rustle near the front drew Sam inward from the chasm. The machine funneled down to a point. It was threaded at the end, like a screw.

A drill. It was a massive drill.

Chunks of the cavern wall were missing where it had bored into the metallic blue stone. A few stray pebbles, ragged around the edges, lay scattered around the platform at its feet.

The noise came again—from inside the hole.

"Monica?" Sam dropped to his knees, and caught, in the corner of the orange glow, a hint of movement five or six feet into the drilled cavity.

No answer.

Ann again tried to stop him, but Sam walked a few paces past the equipment and found no other traces of Monica. He stooped, hunched his shoulders in, and stuck his head through the opening.

It smelled strange inside. The air was chalky and dry, but there was an oddly sweet tinge to the taste of it when Sam inhaled. He fumbled with the lamp and accidentally barked it against the lip of the cave. The kerosene sloshed back in the container, and for a moment, the darkness lapped back in, hungry, impatient.

When the light came back, Monica's face was six inches from his own.

Sam let out a yelp and staggered back. Monica caught the lantern before he'd dropped it.

"This way, this way."

Sam squinted past her. The tunnel—already no larger than a crawlspace—narrowed, sharp rocks jutting from the ceiling, the floor, and both walls. If it stretched much farther than ten or fifteen feet, there must have been more to it than Sam could see.

Ann squatted beside him. "No." Her voice was flat, stern, unequivocal.

Sam gulped and nodded in agreement. "We can't go in there, Monica."

"It will take you out. It likes you. You can get out. There is an opening. Up by the viewing circle. Where we go to appreciate its greatness. You can take this tunnel there. We have tried it. We all tried it."

Another squeal of metal bit through the air from upstairs.

Kneeling behind them, Crawford winced and raised the rifle from his chest. "Anything I should know about using this?"

Monica ignored him. She stretched out a hand. For a moment, Sam thought she was going to slap him, but instead, her fingers found his hair, and she tousled it, brushed it from his forehead. "You don't need that," she whispered. "You got away once. You can do it again. You are meant to do it again."

Sam squinted at her. There was something about her face, something that clicked in a part of his mind he hadn't, until that moment, even known was there. "Who are you?" He leaned closer as she withdrew into the cave. "What did you do with Monica? What do you know about me?"

"If you go now, you can still get away. You can be free of here. Free, once and for all."

"We don't want to leave," Ann said. "Not without our son."

Monica froze. Her body centered in the rough-edged passage, she had been preparing to stretch her hands to the walls at her sides and caress the smooth stone. She sat with her back to them. Her fingers trembled from the anticipation. "You have a son."

"Yes." Sam inched into the mouth of the passage. "Daniel. His name is Daniel."

"Sam, don't talk to her, we have to—"

"How old is he?" Monica still hadn't turned around.

"Thirteen. He's thirteen now."

"And they took him."

Ann stopped pulling at Sam's shirt. "How did you know that?"

Slowly, Monica pivoted around in the passage. Tears streaked from her eyes down the length of her cheeks to where they gathered on the tip of her chin. "Because that is what they do. They take. And they take. And they take and they take, and then when they don't find what they want ... then they kill."

Sam stared into her eyes, and it was at that moment that it clicked in his mind. Grace. She looked just like Grace. "M ... " Sam mumbled. "Monica?"

With a squealing, splintering *crash*, the door at the top of the stairwell exploded off its hinges. Sam heard it tumble down the concrete steps and slam to a halt on the catwalk over their heads.

In a fleeting instant, Monica sprang past them, lithe as a cat, and shoved Crawford into Ann. They tripped, stumbling into each other. Monica spun around and gave them another harsh blow that sent them pitching forward into the mouth of the cave.

"There's a fork ... "

Reeling, Crawford cocked the gun and started to sit up. "Get the fuck back or I swear I'll shoot."

"Listen to me." Monica crouched. The look was back, the fire in her eyes—lucidity. Determination. "I am trying to help you. There is a fork in the passage, fifty feet up. There is a pipe with an access plate. For the tower, to cool the tower with lake water, but it does not work anymore. The plate is controlled by a mechanical switch that I will throw. It will give you forty-five seconds to get through before the cycle begins. It is an—"

Clattering footsteps scuffled down the upper stairwell.

Crawford frowned at her. "What are you talking about?"

"It is an automatic cleaning routine, but there is no more of the chemical solution or the water left in the storage container. It will stay dry and it will complete in thirty minutes, and if you are to the other end in time, you can make it through the opposite access panel, and you will be inside the power plant."

Sam swallowed. "And that's where they have Daniel."

"Undoubtedly."

The footsteps crossed the catwalk, a babble of voices dying down as caution overtook the approaching team.

"Why are you telling us this?" Ann asked.

"Because … " Monica's eyes flicked to Sam. "I wouldn't let them have my son forty years ago. And I won't let them have my grandson now."

Then, with a monumental heave, she rolled the drill into place, blocking off the tunnel and shutting Sam, Ann, and Crawford inside.

TWENTY EIGHT

"SON OF A BITCH!" Cramped, barely able to move, Crawford braced his shoulders against the uneven ground and kicked at the head of the drill with everything he had. They were crammed so close together that Sam could feel every gasping breath the Detective took.

The drill rocked and then went still as Monica fastened some kind of harness to it from the other side.

Ann, squeezed between them, twisted toward Sam. "Sam, what did she ... what was she ... What did she mean?"

"She's crazy. She's out of her goddamn mind." Crawford kept struggling.

Sam stared at it. A shout arose from the other side, cut short abruptly—unnaturally. Scrambling footsteps dashed back and forth. The drill shook as something heavy crashed to the metal platform plank.

"Sam ... ?"

Sam felt numb. Could it be possible that the woman on the other side of that barrier—the woman facing off against a killer—was Sam's mother? She was young. Too young. It couldn't be true.

It couldn't.

Could it?

"Sam?"

"I don't know. I don't know." Sam scrambled back and twisted around until he was on his hands and knees. The jagged rocks on the floor of the tiny tunnel brushed his stomach as he started wriggling forward. "I don't know who she is," he grunted, "but if there's a chance this takes us to Daniel then we have to try."

The passage continued to narrow. Hard stone pressed in on him from all sides. He had been using the faint depressions and cavities as handholds, but the deeper he got, the less he could move his elbows without scraping against the walls.

"Sam ... " Crawford was panting, a couple of feet behind Ann. "Sam, this is stupid. We're gonna die in here. We walked right into a goddamn deathtrap. That woman out there, whoever she is—she's probably laughing her ass off. Sam?"

Sam focused only on the winding tunnel ahead, on making it over the next barrier, through the next squeeze.

The cave curled up and to the left, and as Sam tried to negotiate the turn, the pincer jaws of the floor and ceiling caught around his chest. His arms were pinned in front of him, legs dangling uselessly behind.

He shifted and thrashed his body, but he couldn't twist free.

Panic fluttered up in his chest. He was stuck.

Setting the kerosene lantern down in a small mesa on the sloping rise, he tried to find something he could use as a kickoff point with his feet.

"What's happening? Sam?"

"Can you push me?"

Ann grunted.

Sam squinted back down through the narrow fissures around his own shoulders and saw that Ann's arms were already caught behind her. She had been rocking, side to side, to keep moving. "Sam, don't tell me you're stuck."

The noise from outside, from the catwalks overlooking the crevasse, had faded to nothing. Perhaps Monica had overpowered the soldier and his men. Perhaps she hadn't. Or perhaps there was simply too much solid rock between them and her to hear anything at all.

The thought sent another jolt of frantic energy through Sam's heart. How far was it to the surface from here? How long would it be before anyone found their bodies?

It was Riley who sprang into his mind just then. Riley, the quiet one, who would rather have sat in his bedroom with a book through all the days of summer than spend a single night under the stars. Once, Sam had tried to teach him to climb a tree. Halfway up, Riley had gotten stuck, and he'd started crying. Sam had told him to hold on, to stay there while Sam climbed up after him. *"I'm coming,"* he'd said. *"But you have to hold on. You can't just let go. It's too late for that."*

"I'm coming," he thought again. *"I'm coming, Daniel."*

Elbows braced against a sharp stone, he squeezed his eyes shut and poured all of the energy he had left into his upper arms. Sweating, straining, dizzy and claustrophobic, he felt his body move an inch. Then another.

Jagged rock dug into his flesh. He felt warm stickiness pump out into his shirt, but then he was free.

The passage widened. Sam told Ann and Crawford to wait, and after he'd taken up the lamp again, he kicked away at the outcroppings that had caught him until there was enough room for them to make it through.

"Sam. We have to turn back." Ann was shivering, not from cold but from the same panic that had seized him.

Sam shook his head. "Not enough room to turn around, and we've come too far to back the whole way out."

"Sam—"

"We can't turn back now. It's too late for that." He squinted up the sloping tunnel. "Besides. We're there."

There was no way the drill had made it this far. Whether a crew had come in with pickaxes or the winding cave was some kind of natural air shaft, it spiraled on through the earth in a leftward curl. At the right, just as Monica had described, a plank of metal reflected back the dim flicker of the lantern.

Sam heaved himself up beside it and pressed his hand to the surface. Rough, uneven, it was half-eaten by rust. He pushed a little harder.

It didn't budge.

"Okay," he thought. *"Okay. Just give it a moment."*

He tipped the lantern toward his wristwatch. Somewhere along the way, the face had gotten scratched. Through it, the second hand ticked on. Five o'clock. Local time was six or seven hours later, but he could not quite remember when they had touched down or how long they had been here.

Five minutes passed.

Ann didn't say a word. Crawford, perched ten feet below on the upward curve, adjusted to a more sustainable position.

Another five minutes.

Slowly, the worry Sam had been staving off out of sheer will began to creep back in. What if Ann and Crawford were right? What if Monica was out of her mind? Or, worse, what if she had betrayed them?

He looked at Ann and she stared right back at him. What in hell were they doing?

"If I tuck my knees to my chest ... " Crawford's voice was ragged, hoarse from the dust and dehydration. "I might be able to turn myself around. I could guide you both, even if you couldn't do the same."

No. Sam blinked back the tears of frustration suddenly threatening to spill over. No. They could not have come this far, sacrificed this much, just to *give up*. For Daniel, for themselves, for everything that mattered.

Ann was still watching him. She reached out and pressed her sweaty palm into his. "We'll stay," she said, "a little longer."

Crawford grunted. "We're gonna die down here."

Then, with a grinding squeal, the metal panel moved.

The pipe on the other side was even smaller. It hugged Sam's shoulders like a straightjacket. There was no room for his arms in front of him, and when he breathed in, he felt the curved metal floor pushing back on his chest.

He had to keep the lamp in front of him, nudging it forward with his chin.

"Fuckin' ... *fuck.*" Crawford froze, halfway through the open mouth of the access panel. "There's no way—no way!"

"Crawford—"

"I can't breathe. This fuckin' place ... I can't—there's no way!"

The pipe was too small to see past his own body. He only knew where Ann was by the sound of her labored breathing and the occasional thump of her head against his shoes. They'd made it six or seven feet from Crawford's position, and it already felt like they had been trapped inside for an hour.

"Crawford, come on. You have to hurry."

"I can't."

Sam was suddenly aware of each passing moment, marked off by the pounding of his heart. "Crawford. It's going to close. Come *on!*"

Forty-five seconds, Monica had said. Forty-five seconds the panel would stay open, and they must have used at least thirty-five already.

Sam strained. The harder he tried to move, the more tightly the walls seemed to grip his body. "Ann, can you help him?"

"I can't move."

"Crawford!"

"Fuck!"

The sound of grinding metal filled the air.

"Fuck, it's—it's closing on me! *Holy fuck!*"

Sam was powerless. Powerless to help him. Crawford was going to die, ten feet away, and there was nothing he could do. "Gerry! We need you. None of us can do this without you." The grinding slowed. "Gerry?"

With an echoing *clunk*, the access panel slid shut. The air pressure in the pipe changed. The kerosene flame flickered. Sam held his breath.

"Gerry?"

A long pause. Heavy breathing. And then, small, weak:

"I'm here."

ა

The smell of the pipe made Sam's stomach churn. A mixture of mold, mildew, and bacterial rot, the occasional gust of air from somewhere behind them only made it stronger.

Every tiny curve put pressure on Sam's chest and back, but after a time, he began to develop a rhythm of movement that slowly but steadily conveyed him forward.

He was beginning to think they could do this, that they would actually make it. Then, with a sputtering *pop*, the lamp used up the last of the kerosene and flickered out. Blackness enveloped them in a heartbeat.

"Oh, Jesus. Oh, *Jesus.*"

Sam felt Crawford trying to thrash through the vibrations in the metal of the pipe.

"Gerry. Calm—Gerry, calm down. We're still here. Nothing's changed."

"Jesus, I can't—I can't see you anymore … "

"Stop." Ann sounded scared. "Wait a minute. Stop moving. Detective."

Crawford sucked in a shallow breath and froze.

The vibration in the curving walls continued.

"Sam … ?"

"I feel it."

"What is it?"

He gulped. "I don't know."

A loud, penetrating *chirp* shot through the pipe. Sam winced, jerking, trying, reflexively, to cover his ears.

"What the hell was—"

The sound came again.

Clenching his teeth, Sam squinted ahead, eyes straining. "There's something … there's a light."

"A light?" Crawford rasped.

"There's a—a red light. It's flashing."

Chirp.

"Maybe it means we're almost there." Crawford edged forward.

Ann sounded grimmer: "Maybe it means the cleaning cycle's almost over."

A gust of cooler air eddied up through the thin spaces around Sam's body. The odor was pungent, intensely concentrated. It smelled like dust and acrid soot and something organic. It smelled like the Black Valley.

It smelled like *outside.*

He heard Ann sniffing, making the connection at the same time.

The *chirp* came again. The intervals between them were decreasing.

It was an alarm.

"The lake." Ann shifted, head butting up again Sam's feet. "It's from the lake."

Monica had said the pipe was an old coolant channel for the nuclear generator. It drew on Lake Kitoto.

Now, it was starting up.

TWENTY NINE

THE PULSING LIGHT grew brighter as Sam thrashed his way forward. They rounded a bend in the pipe and the source came into view—a shielded red bulb cut into the curving wall right beside the claxon speaker. At this distance, the chirping was unbearable. Now, it was a shrill, almost-constant electronic shriek.

The air was moist, the metal trembling beneath Sam's stomach and sending ominous vibrations through his whole body. They weren't stopping to breathe anymore. Colored spots crept into the corners of his vision. He felt dizzy, arms and legs numb, rubbery. Beneath the thumping of his heartbeat and the buzzing in his ears, he thought he could hear a rumbling from somewhere scarily close by.

"The hatch! There's a hatch!" Sam redoubled his pace when he saw it, a rectangular gap in the side of the passage ahead that might as well have been a first-class ticket home.

His voice was lost beneath the alarm claxon, but the change of pace must have tipped Ann off. He felt her scrambling behind him, hair brushing against his ankles.

Five feet away. *Light*. Fresh air.

"Thank God," Sam thought.

And then the hatch began to close.

Heart pounding, blood pumping through his temples, Sam fought his way to the lip of the opening for all he was worth. He twisted his body around and thrust his shoulders through.

His arms came free at last. Bracing himself on either side of the hatch, he heaved himself out and planted his feet against the edge of the door. "Ann! Climb!"

She started wriggling through the opening. Sam couldn't hold it forever. His legs were going limp. He curled into a ball, bolstering them with his arms, his shoulders, with everything he had.

Ann made it outside and threw her weight against it. Together, they forced it back a couple of inches.

Crawford's face appeared, red, sweaty, gasping for air. "Holy ... holy—"

"Out! Get out!" Sam took Crawford's hand and pulled.

He was halfway out the opening when the water came. It surged up around his waist, thundering, gushing, forcing him forward.

Crawford yelped and gave one final, monumental push. The three of them tumbled to the metal, grated floor below as the hatch banged shut behind them and flooded with coursing lake water.

Sam fell back.

Ten seconds later—five, even—and they would have drowned.

It was nearly a minute before he could move. Finally, when he opened his eyes, it was not the yellow-orange of the evening sky that stared back down at him. A weathered metal bulkhead hung dotted with valves and curving pipes. The air was moist, stale, warm. Something deep inside the floor hummed.

They had made it.

They were inside the dark tower.

5

The support struts at the corners of the little room bore cracks that spider-webbed and multiplied into shattered concrete at the top. The ceiling bowed, steel crossbeams bent to the breaking point near the middle. Sam couldn't imagine what kind of weight they must have sustained.

As he stood, his clothes peeled away from the floor, wet, sticky, resistant. He was covered in avocado-colored slime that smelled like sea salt and rotten shellfish.

The only light came from below.

Peering downward through the grated floor, Sam could make out the dim shapes of gears, fan belts, machines slowly winding up after years of dereliction. Here and there, a wire-encased light bulb protruded from the soupy blackness, exposing in tiny orange pools more hardened struts and rivets.

Sam turned and bent to help Crawford to his feet. The Detective was shaking all over.

"Mother of Christ." Crawford glanced back at the pipe. It swayed gently in a series of bolted metal housings.

Ann squeezed his shoulder as she slipped past him.

At the far end of the room was a low, curving door, like a submarine hatch. Dangling wires, valves, and plumbing made the three of them duck as they picked their way toward it.

For a few seconds, they listened. Apart from the churning machinery, there was not a sound from the other side.

A pale glow bathed the corridor beyond. It was the only thing alive—a television screen, suspended from the ceiling by duct tape and a couple of bungee cords. Electrical wire dangled from its tail to swoop low over piles of ravaged, twisted steel.

When Sam's eyes had adjusted, he gaped.

The walls of the passage were bent outward. He'd thought at first glance that it was an architectural decision, but as the shape of the hallway came into view, he saw that they had not been built that way.

Pressure from above had forced them apart. The corridor came to an abrupt end not at a paneled bulkhead, but at a solid wall of wreckage. Twisted rebar protruded at jagged angles from smashed concrete, steel, and stone. Broken glass still littered the floor, mingling with the shattered plastic scraps of computer equipment and coating sealant.

Dust lay everywhere, thick as snow and gray as ash.

"This is just like what I found down at the bunker." Crawford was moving in the opposite direction, up the passage toward a makeshift wall of waist-high planks. He seemed a little steadier already.

The floor groaned beneath his feet. An echoing squeal reverberated away, far below. It sounded almost as deep as the underground pit.

The detective hoisted himself over the wall and nudged the butt of a cobbled-together gun emplacement—an assault rifle propped up on broken cinderblocks, muzzle jutting between chinks in the planks. More dust drifted into the air.

Bullet holes riddled the front of the barricade.

Sam frowned, approaching. It looked like someone had waged a war in here. The buckling walls were still pockmarked with the faintest shadows of chips and stains.

He was about to say something, but he stopped in his tracks at the sound of a voice. Ann and Crawford heard it too. They stiffened, everyone listening.

It was distant, tinny, metallic.

A flash of static flickered across the TV screen, followed, a moment later, by blocky, pixellated computer print:

System startup ... Please stand by ...

There was a buzz, and then a cracked fluorescent tube came to life somewhere beneath the piles of smashed wire and brick.

Sam glanced at Ann. "They're starting."

She nodded. "They know we're here."

"Watch your feet." Crawford guided them over the buckled barricade and the coils of barbed wire covering the floor on the other side. Four more TV screens were arrayed across the grating, propped up so that whoever had been manning the guns could watch them at the same time as they monitored the corridor.

Now, they all displayed the same message—*Please stand by ...*

On the other side of the wall, the corridor took a sharp turn before disappearing beneath more rubble dumped down from the next floor up. A pair of double-doors had split open on the right-hand side to reveal a fractured elevator shaft. The car rested three stories below, crushed to half its height from the final drop when its tow cables severed.

A ladder dangled from the opposite wall. Most of the screws were missing down one side, and as the vibration from below grew stronger, it swayed loosely back and forth.

There was no other apparent way up. Sam tried climbing into the wreckage on either side of the hallway, but it was too dense to make it more than six or seven feet off the floor. The holes in the ruptured ceiling were nowhere near large enough for him to fit through.

A narrow metal lip, maybe six inches wide, traced the perimeter of the elevator shaft. The lights both here and on the next floor up were broken. As Sam edged out, he missed a gap in the overhang and his foot slipped.

He flailed his arms and caught a chip in the wall that he used to pull himself back up, flush against it. His face left a sweaty smear when he finally worked up the courage to try again.

"Sam ... " Ann bit her tongue. "Be careful."

The closer he drew to the ladder, the less certain he became that it would hold. From three feet away, he could hear the screws creaking, metal housings grinding against each other.

He stole a glance over his shoulder and his palms went clammy. Forty-five feet didn't sound terribly far, but suspended over battered concrete and dented steel, it might as well have been a mile.

Vertigo seized him. Instinctively, he started to drop into a crouch, but there wasn't enough room on the lip to keep his balance. He felt his body tipping backward. Again, he grabbed at the wall, but this time, his fingernails found only flat, blank paneling.

At the last moment, desperate, panicking, he twisted around and caught the bottom rung of the ladder. It shrieked, shuddered, and dropped nearly a foot. Sam's stomach leapt to the back of his throat. Adrenaline pumped to every corner of his body. He squeezed his eyes shut and waited for the fall, but it never came.

The ladder was holding—

For now.

One rung at a time, as slowly and gently as he could, Sam began to climb. When he reached the next floor up, he stepped off onto the six-inch metal lip and waited as, one-by-one, Ann and Crawford followed.

The ladder thrashed each time any of them moved.

He had hoped that the next floor up might be more stable, but here, the elevator doors had been blown off their runners altogether. Through the gap, all he could see was a solid wall of more wreckage. A part of him wondered how there was any of the tower left, when so much of it seemed to have collapsed upon itself.

Finally, another floor-and-a-half up, Sam glimpsed an open hallway, light spilling out through the crack beneath the doors. He quickened his pace and scrambled to the top of the ladder. There, he flattened himself against the wall and waited, impatient, while Crawford came next. Ann was last, on the reasoning that if it could support both Sam and Crawford, it was fairly likely to withstand her lighter weight.

Crawford edged around to the opposite side of the shaft and fiddled with the doors as the same tinny voice crackled to life again. A public address system. Sam couldn't make out any words, but the voice, even distorted, bore a familiar cold, crisp edge.

Clayton Wesley.

Ann's fingers latched onto the metal lip. "Thank God," she hissed. "I was sure it was going to—"

The rung under her feet snapped in half. The jolt—sharp, jarring—wrenched four of the nearest studs loose from the wall. The ladder shook and then tore free.

Ann's legs swung out beneath her. Her knuckles went white, sweaty fingers sliding back, toward the edge of the narrow platform.

Sam doubled over and caught her by the wrist of her jacket as she was about to fall. The extra weight yanked him down.

For one gut-wrenching moment, he lost his balance. His feet slipped. Sam pitched forward.

Ann heaved her legs up onto the ledge and pulled Sam back a fraction of a second before he would have fallen.

Beneath them, buffeted by gravity and inertia, the ladder tore from the wall, spitting bolt after bolt as it peeled away and thundered down the shaft to land in a deafening crash on the roof of the elevator car.

Dust and grime rose, thick, into the air.

Coughing, Sam helped Ann the rest of the way onto the narrow ridge, and together, they edged to Crawford's side at the doors.

"Okay?" he whispered.

They nodded.

For almost a minute, the three of them waited. It was impossible that no one had heard them. As his breathing slowed, and there were still no footsteps from the other side, Sam pressed an eye to the crack between the elevator doors.

He could see nothing but a sliver of empty corridor.

Working together, the three of them forced the gap wider—a few inches at first, and then, when they still heard no signs of life, all the way to the frame. Cautiously, Sam advanced around the corner, into the passage.

The grating here was weakened, shored up with plywood struts and lengths of stolen pipe. At a glance, there seemed to be less damage, but when he looked closer, Sam saw that in fact, the entire floor had been gutted and put back together out of scarred planks and makeshift bits and pieces from across the rest of the facility. The walls were made of tarps, splintered wood, and even a few charred logs from the jungle outside. It was a shantytown cobbled together inside of a shell.

Sam was a few steps from the elevator, inching toward the next door down, when a voice from around the corner made him recoil and flatten himself against the wall.

He waited, listening.

It died out a moment later.

Sam held his breath.

Nothing.

Another step toward the gaping doorway. It hung open, fashioned out of a severed metal bar and a tattered shower curtain. Warm, orange sunlight streamed out beneath it.

"Sweep Thirteen, position and report?"

Sam froze again. It was a radio, the voice crackling through between bouts of static.

"Sweep Thirteen, what is your position?"

Silence.

Sam got to his knees and peeked around the threshold. Under the ragged edge of the shower curtain, he could just make out a larger room. Evening light painted the uneven floor in pinks and oranges, unnaturally bright and garish. Whatever it was in the air over Black Valley, it must have bent the rays of the sun across the color spectrum.

Monica had been right; it looked like the end of the world.

Stalls lined either side of the room, working their way toward the open window. Beneath more curtains, a forest of metal bed feet stood bolted to the floor. A dormitory.

"Sweep Thirteen, this is Command. Report back."

A faint breeze from outside ruffled the shower curtain. Nothing else moved.

Steeling himself, Sam rose and slipped inside, followed a moment later by Ann and Crawford. He stopped in the center of the room and turned in a slow circle. Eight cots surrounded him. Each was strewn with a small pile of photographs, weathered magazines, letters and envelopes.

He found the radio buried under the bed covers in the last stall on the end. It was a small handset, a walkie-talkie with a belt clip that must have fallen off by accident. Sam reached for it. He paused, hand on the snarled sheets and blankets.

The fabric was still warm.

"What the hell?" Crawford stood in the next stall over. He held up a curled poster dangling from a small chest of clothes and magazines.

It appeared to be the cover of a comic book. Cartooned, uniformed soldiers pressed knives to the throats of young women and children while the American flag burned at their backs. In a large, alarming font was the slogan:

Is this tomorrow? America Under Communism!

Ann squinted at the dateline across the top. "Catechetical Guild, 1947."

Of the other magazines and newspapers they unearthed, none was dated later than the fall of 1962.

Crawford shivered. "What, we just walk into a time warp?"

Before Sam could reply, footsteps clattered down the hallway.

The three of them dashed for the door, but it was too late to make it out unseen. Spinning back, Sam lunged into the first stall. He scrambled back and drew the curtain after Ann had come in behind him.

"Feet!" he hissed at her.

They hopped up onto the bed and tucked their legs to their chests. Three seconds later, Sam heard someone step through the shower curtain in the dormitory doorway. Footsteps crossed the room, fast, confident.

Moving toward the last stall.

The radio. Someone had come back for the radio that he had just slipped into his pocket.

Three stalls away, the intruder grunted. "Command, Sweep Thirteen. You sure it's not—"

He broke off as a squeal of feedback burst from Sam's pocket.

Sam wrestled the radio out and twisted the volume to *Zero*. He waited, not daring to breathe.

Silence. Another gust of stale wind.

Sam tried to crane his neck so he could see his wristwatch, but the face was too scratched to make out the time at this angle. He counted off fifteen seconds in his head. Twenty.

He started to lean to the edge of the bed. The bare springs creaked beneath him.

Suddenly, the cloth curtain exploded inward. Sam felt hands grabbing at his throat, fists swinging blindly at his face. He ducked and pulled Ann out of the way, spinning around to kick at his attacker.

The man had a gun out. Swatting at the cloth around his face, he popped off a shot that thudded into the clothing chest six inches from Sam's stomach.

"Don't move a—"

Before he could finish, Crawford flung himself at the man from behind. The two of them slammed into the floor beside the bed and tumbled over each other. Sam scooped up the handgun where the man had dropped it and expelled the spent cartridge with a *click*.

The fight came to an abrupt halt as the stranger rolled straight into the barrel of the gun. He swallowed, panting, and then, with a scowl, raised his hands in surrender. Like Monica, he appeared to be between thirty and thirty-five, but his eyes drooped from the same grizzled weariness, the same put-upon desperation of a man twice as old.

A weathered Army uniform was draped around his shoulders, the faintest remnants of a nametag pinned to his chest.

"You work here?" Sam jabbed the gun at him.

The man gave a terse nod.

"They have a boy. A thirteen-year-old boy. I want to know where he is."

A cruel smile spread across the soldier's face. He spat blood from his lip, where Crawford had hit him. "Sam Mackie. You're Sam Mackie, yeah? You're too late."

THIRTY

SAM FLEW UP THE STAIRS two at a time. He did not wait for
Crawford, who had stayed behind to tie and gag the soldier with
sheets from several of the other stalls. Some of the original structure
still remained on the next floor. The skeletons of walls, gap-toothed
and leaning, rose from a patchwork of metal planks and girders.

Larger holes were filled in with tarps or other pieces of rubble,
but as Sam edged around the corner of the curving stairwell, dappled
light pierced through a dozen tiny chinks and cracks.

Ann drew up behind him, panting.

Ahead, a long, narrow passage fed into a broader atrium, a hundred feet away. Five doorways opened into it from either side. Radio
chatter filled the air, whispering voices, static, a half-dozen conversations from everywhere and nowhere, all at once.

Sam rose to move off the last step. He froze as a figure in a white
lab coat jogged out of a door on the left. Long, black hair hung
around her shoulders, smooth, silky. Her hands worked to pin it in
a bun as she moved, eyes darting to her watch along the way.

It was Dr. Ko. Clayton Wesley's right hand, back at the abandoned building by the mall.

Anger flared up in Sam's chest.

The moment Ko had disappeared through a door on the right,
he burst from the mouth of the stairwell and took off running after
her. He was careful to land each footfall as gently as he could, staying

near the wall, trying to check for cameras in the tangled mass of pipes and wires on the ceiling.

"All personnel … "

Sam jumped and glued himself to a metal bulkhead.

It was a bullhorn, lashed to a coil of electrical wires, like the TV downstairs, with duct tape and splintered plywood.

" … be advised Sweep Thirteen is non-responsive."

Sam eased around the edge of another doorway and then drew back when he almost locked eyes with another man, inside. In the brief glimpse he had stolen, he'd picked out dirty white tile, stacked metal machinery and boxes of sharp instruments.

A radio beeped. More tinny voices.

From where he was standing, Sam could just make out the outline of the man's shoulders, reflected in a stainless steel plank.

He glanced back down the passage. Ann was right behind him. If anyone else came out, there was nowhere for them to hide.

Steeling himself, Sam darted past the doorway.

Another ten feet, and he had arrived at the room where Ko disappeared. She was not immediately visible around the corner, an entryway cordoned off with more tattered sheets and shower curtains.

Footsteps from the last door back propelled Sam inside. He pulled Ann after him, and they squeezed in, close together. Even though the air in Black Valley was cool, as though the warmth of the sun had been long ago leached away, Sam was sweating. He strained his ears for any sign of life from the other side of the curtain.

He was about to pull aside one corner when a voice reached his ears. Soft, melodic, it was singing.

He glanced at Ann. She cocked her head and frowned.

Shuffling forward, Sam held his breath and peeled back an inch of the curtain.

Through the narrow slit of light from the other side, he could see velvety black hair, a swaying white medical lab coat. He tugged the gap wider by a fraction of an inch. Ko stood reflected in a foggy mirror. Her eyes were closed. Twin candles burned on either side of the dresser in front of her, warming her face with a yellow-orange glow.

Her lips moved, ever so slightly while her fingers toyed with a necklace of black prayer beads.

Dread tugged at Sam's heart. The man downstairs had been right. They were too late. Whatever she had done to Daniel, it was over. He was gone, and now she was in here, grappling with her conscience.

In a sudden flare of rage, Sam tore back the curtain and lunged at her.

Ko's eyes snapped open. She started to swivel around, but Sam was already upon her. He smashed into her with the full weight of his body, sending her careening back against the mirror. The glass cracked. Her hands shot out sideways, reaching for something in the top drawer. In her haste, she upset one of the candles. It clattered to the floor, spitting sparks and hot wax.

Sam latched onto her wrist with an iron grip and clamped his other hand over her mouth.

"How could you?" Blood pounded in his temples. He forced her head back against the broken mirror. "How could you do it to him? How could you? He's just a little boy."

Ko, struggling for breath, stared back at him in panic and confusion.

Behind him, a radio crackled.

Ann crossed the room and bent to retrieve it from a folding table near the window at the end of the room.

"Sam."

"She did it." He squeezed harder on Ko's wrist. She cried out beneath his fingers and tried to shake her head. "She did it, Ann. She did it!"

"*Sam.*" Ann turned up the volume on the radio and planted it on top of the dresser beside him.

" … ready for you, Dr. Ko. Dr. Ko? Subject is ready. Where are you?" Static.

Sam looked from the little black speaker to Ko's terrified eyes. "Who's the subject? *Who's the subject?* Is it Danny? Is it my son?"

Trembling, rigid with fear, Dr. Ko managed to nod.

"You haven't started yet?"

A shake of the head.

Relief flooded through Sam's chest. He spun Ko around, meeting her eye in the fractured mirror. "You're going to answer them. You're going to tell them you're coming. And then you're going to help me get my son back. You make a sound, I swear to God, I will snap your neck. Nod if you understand."

The radio crackled again. "Dr. Ko, please respond."

Ko glanced at it, then back to Sam in the mirror. She nodded. The moment he removed his hand from her mouth, she gulped in the air. Sam picked up the radio and jabbed the *transmit* button with his thumb.

"Do it," he whispered.

"Dr. Ko ... " She cleared her throat, squeezed her eyes shut, opened them again. "Dr. Ko here. On my way—"

Sam released the radio and tossed it to Ann. "Good enough."

He spun her back around and glanced over the room. Two large bins stood beside the table, smudged white canvas over metal frameworks. One was draped with blue and green operating scrubs. Some had blood on them.

Sam shuddered and dragged Ko toward the other. It was filled halfway to the top with clean towels, folded uniforms, operating masks. "Ann." He bent, picked up a shirt and a mask, and tossed it to her.

She gave it a dubious once-over and then peeled off her filthy jacket.

"It will not work." Ko watched her.

"Shut up," Sam hissed.

"We have worked together for years. You do not think they know every person at this facility? And they are looking for you. They know what you look like."

"Swell." Sam shoved Ko over to Ann and quickly changed clothes himself. He drew in a deep breath and then stretched an operating mask over his mouth and nose. He checked his reflection in the broken mirror.

His hair was still a mess. Ann tossed him a cap.

Ko was right—it wasn't perfect. Anyone who looked for more than a couple of seconds would see the dirt caking his face, the empty ID badge sleeve clipped to his uniform. But a couple of seconds might be all he would need.

The radio came to life again as he was just helping Ann with a cap of her own.

"Dr. Ko, is there a problem?"

"No. I am on my way now."

Sam jabbed the soldier's gun into the base of her spine and shoved her toward the door. "Act natural," he hissed into her ear.

Two uniformed soldiers slowed when they saw Sam, Ann, and Ko emerge into the hallway. "Ko?" The one on the right, tall, lanky, looked Sam up and down.

Sam nodded at him and spun Ko away before she could tell him anything with her eyes. "Which way?" he whispered.

Ko started toward the door across the hall.

Sam pressed the gun deeper into her back. "You take us to the wrong place, you better be ready for some serious spinal surgery."

Momentary hesitation. Then Ko adjusted her course toward the wider atrium at the end of the hall.

"Hey. Hey, Doc, everything okay?"

Ko gave the soldier a nod over her shoulder that seemed to satisfy him, though Sam could not be entirely certain she hadn't made some other kind of signal at the same time.

They had just reached the end of the corridor when Sam glanced back and glimpsed Crawford in the shadows at the mouth of the stairwell. The soldiers were turning away, sniffing.

"You smell smoke?" The lanky one ducked into Ko's prep room.

The candle. Sam hadn't seen where it had landed. He was fairly sure it had gone out, but the wax on the floor, the cracked mirror—they would know something was wrong.

"Hey. Hey, check this out."

As soon as the second soldier slipped inside after the first, Sam tugged the operating mask from his face and met Crawford's eye. He jerked his head toward the atrium, and then he spun back and followed Ko through.

The passage opened out into a curving room. Thick, reinforced windows covered the entire far wall. The glass was coated, from the other side, with impenetrable black soot that rendered it completely opaque, but here and there, the structure had buckled.

Through a crack, Sam got a flash of the gaping, cavernous room on the other side. The tower. They were standing at the perimeter of the dark tower itself.

Old theater seats, cushions long ago stripped down to metal, sat facing the windows. Shadows covered the wall behind them, but as Sam moved past, he saw they were independent of his own. Nothing was casting them now. They had been burned into the metal itself.

Humming vibrations shook the floor and filled the air with a low, rhythmic buzz.

Ko drew up before another door at the opposite end of the room and waited for Sam to step around and open it.

Two guards flanked the entrance on the other side. They stiffened and stood to attention, pivoting when they saw Sam and Ann.

Sam barely noticed. His grip on Ko's shoulder slackened. He was staring at the cages.

Lining the walls of the short, squat room, they were stacked in blocks of six—eighteen, all told. They were fashioned out of bent, rusted metal bars, maybe four feet tall, and about as many deep. Like dog kennels. Steel water bowls littered the floor. The room smelled of old urine, sweat, discomfort. A single bare light bulb cast a dim glow from the doorway, leaving the farthest corners to vanish into shadow.

Even so, even in the darkness, Sam's eyes jumped instantly to the last cage, in the back. All of the others were vacant, doors hanging open.

It was the mop of brown hair, the curve of his shoulders, legs tucked up under his arms in a fetal position.

It was Daniel.

He looked so small, so helpless.

Sam swallowed back a choked sob.

Then a hand grabbed him by the elbow and spun him around. The guard on the left, gun already coming out of its holster. . " 'Scuse me, buddy. But who the fuck are you?"

In a flash, Ko leapt away from Sam, spinning to catch him in the shins with a sharp kick. She dodged as Ann tried to yank her back, parrying to swing a hard right-hook that sent Ann reeling.

Ko grabbed the radio out of her flailing hands. "General—Ko here. We got Mackie and the wife." She was already dashing for the cage as a voice came back through another burst of static:

"Understood."

Sam hit the floor hard. The air leapt from his lungs. Rolling over to hide the gun, he got to his knees before the guard slammed another foot into his back. He pitched forward, head smashing into the bars of another cage.

White bolts of pain shot through his temples. Firm hands grabbed him by the shoulders and spun him around.

Sam got a glimpse of the guard's face, sneering, winding up for another blow. He raised the gun and fired.

Warm droplets spattered over Sam's cheeks and then a heavy weight landed on his legs. The guard didn't move, blood belching from his mouth and the hole in his chest. He was dead.

Sam felt sick.

The second guard, wrestling with Ann, pivoted around to gape. Ann clubbed him over the back of the head and shoved him toward Sam. She scrambled to her feet and bolted after Ko.

The doctor already had the lock to Daniel's cage open. She cast it aside, clattering across the metal floor, and pulled the door open to lean in over the unconscious boy.

"Get away from him!" Ann lunged at Ko.

The second guard drew his gun in a flash. Sam, hands shaking, still reeling from the realization that he had just killed a man, took aim a second time, but he was too slow. He found himself eye-to-eye with the barrel of the other pistol.

The guard's finger jerked toward the trigger.

Sam caught the blur of movement a fraction of a second before Crawford threw himself between them. The weight of his body sent both guns spinning to the floor.

Momentarily taken by surprise, the guard stumbled back, and Sam laid into him with a volley of blows that made him double over and clutch his stomach.

"Danny!" Sam wheeled away as Crawford took over, pummeling the man to the ground.

Ko had Ann pinned to the floor, an arm planted across her throat. With her free hand, she was just slipping a hypodermic needle out of her lab coat pocket. Sam sprang and caught her wrist, swatting the syringe away and shoving her to the ground after it with a knee to the chest.

Ko grunted as she hit the metal planking hard. Her head flopped back and slammed against the bars of Daniel's cage.

"Kill her!" Ann snarled, voice still a rasp.

Sam shoved Ko back down as she started to sit up, planting his knees on her elbows, hands on her throat. He clenched his teeth so hard that his jaw hurt. Staring down into her face, he felt nothing but blind rage. "What were you going to do?" He tightened his grip. "What were you going to do to him?"

"His blood ... " Ko's eyes lolled back in her head, flitting in and out of unconsciousness.

"Why?"

"Blueprint ... reverse ... the radiation. Please ... not much time ... " She went limp.

Crawford hobbled toward them. The second guard was sprawled by the door, hands tied behind his back. "That's—is that him? In the cage?"

Sam and Ann flung open the barred door together. For a moment, they hesitated. Daniel remained still. If he was—

If they were too late—

"Danny." Sam bent, leaned inside, reached for his son's shoulders. "Danny. It's me ... it's us." His fingers brushed over Daniel's forehead. It was warm.

He was breathing.

Tears leapt to Sam's eyes. "Danny?"

Gentle but urgent, Sam dragged Daniel out and pulled the boy into his arms. He felt so light, so small, so young and defenseless. Ann fell forward and embraced them both as her whole body began to shake with silent sobs.

Then, rocking back and forth, the three of them together at last, the unthinkable happened:

Daniel woke up.

THIRTY ONE

"DAD?" Daniel squinted up at him, and then his bleary gaze found Ann. "Mom?"

Sam heard himself cry out, but it was as though he was seeing it all from somewhere far away. Feverishly, he brushed the hair from Daniel's face and looked his son in the eye. "Danny. Danny, oh my God! Danny. Are you—are you okay?"

"I'm ... " Daniel broke off into a yawn. "I'm tired." He squinted over Ann's shoulder, blinking. "Where are we?" He looked Crawford up and down. "Who's that?"

"Oh, Daniel. Daniel ... " Ann stroked his hair and hugged him tighter.

"Mom ... you're squishing me."

She smiled through her tears. "Sorry, baby. I'm sorry. I just ... we're just ... we're really glad to see you." She and Sam locked eyes. Pure happiness and joy radiated between them.

There was so much Sam wanted to say—so much Daniel deserved to hear—but every time he opened his mouth, he found all of his energy consumed in the effort not to burst out crying.

"What're you guys doing here?" Weakly, Daniel tried to stand. He squinted into the darkness, through the cage bars, toward the door. "Is this ... is this 'cause of the fight?"

"Fight?"

"At school." He rounded on Sam, worry suddenly etching his little face. "I'm sorry, Dad, I didn't mean to. It was just 'cause of

Ralphie, and I was all … tired an' in a bad mood an' the things they were saying, I just got—"

"I don't care about the fight, Danny." Sam smiled and hugged him again. Because he could. Because he was there and he was awake enough to hug back, and that alone was worth more to Sam than anything else in the world.

All at once, the rage was gone. The hatred, the fear, the desperation. He felt only euphoria. It was over. It was finally over. All they had to do now was get out of this wretched, awful place and never look back.

"Come on." Sam stood and helped Daniel up beside him. "Come on, guys. Let's go home."

A sharp *bang* echoed from the blinded observation room, just outside. All four of them jumped. Sam and Crawford locked eyes. The radio—the message Ko had sent to the "General," just before all hell broke loose.

Sam spun back, scanning the room. Between the blocks of cages at the opposite end, the walls bulged inward, away from the cooling tower. The dents and bulges created a buckled hole just large enough to fit through.

"Come on!" Sam yanked Daniel after him, Ann hot on their heels.

He dropped to a crouch and stuck his head into the ragged opening. A small tunnel snaked away through the rubble that filled the innards of the devastated power plant. It was impossible to see how far it went.

Drawing back, Sam turned to Daniel, but the boy was already shaking his head.

"Danny—"

"No."

"Danny, you have to do this."

Footsteps pounded toward the door. Crawford slammed it shut and threw the bolt a split-second before something slammed into it from outside.

"It's … look at it, Dad! It's gonna collapse."

"No, it's not."

"It is!"

"It's not. It can't. Danny." He took his son by the shoulders and turned him so that they were face-to-face. "You've got to be brave, buddy. You've been so, so brave already, and I'm so proud of you, you'll never know."

Daniel gulped. "Really?"

"Yes. Now, you've got to do this. Just this one more thing, and then we'll be home and everything's going to be better."

"You promise?"

Wham. Metal against metal. The door shook on its hinges. A dent appeared at shoulder-level. Whoever was on the other side must have been using rebar, a pipe, or something stronger.

Sam gritted his teeth. He refused to flinch. "I promise." He turned to Ann. "You go first, okay? Then Danny. I'll be right behind you."

"Sam—"

"Please. Just do it, okay?"

Ann sank to her knees beside him. "I love you, Sam."

He smiled. "I love you, too." He leaned forward and pecked her on the lips. It lasted less than a second, but it was all he had needed. When he withdrew, the panic and the doubt were gone. He was strong. Confident. Certain.

They could do this.

Ann drew in a deep breath, gave him one last, lingering look, and then pivoted around to climb into the narrow shaft. Daniel hesitated at the mouth, half-crouched.

Sam patted him on the back, reassuring but firm. "You can do it, Danny. You can do it."

Daniel bent, gave a little heave, and hoisted himself inside. Sam pushed him from behind. Two feet in, Daniel looked back over his shoulder. "C'mon, Dad."

Sam looked to Crawford. "Gerry—coming?"

Crawford stood by the front of the room, feet planted, shoulders braced, the second soldier's gun aimed straight out in front of him. He shook his head as the door rocked from another blow. "Go on ahead."

"Gerry—"

"It's him."

"It's … " Sam trailed off as he understood.

Crawford nodded. "*Him.* I saw. Before I closed the door. I saw the son-of-a-bitch."

The gray-haired soldier. The one who had killed Crawford's

brother-in-law. The one who, twice, had tried to kill Daniel. Sam, arms already inside the passage, faltered.

"Dad."

Crawford threw a glance in Sam's direction. "Go on, Sam. I got this."

"Dad!"

"I'm right behind you, Danny." Sam gave Daniel another push. "There's just something I have to do first."

"*Dad!*"

"Daniel. Trust me." He stared into Daniel's terrified eyes and he smiled. "After this, I'm never going to leave you again."

Rising, Sam drew his gun and wiped the barrel clean on the shirtsleeve of the blue scrubs he was still wearing. He took up a position at Crawford's side.

"Sam. Go with your family. I got this."

"You've had my back all along, Gerry. You have to know that I've got yours."

The latch shattered. The door burst.

Sam and Crawford opened fire.

Sparks exploded like fireworks from a metal panel suddenly spilling toward them. Their bullets ricocheted off the surface. Sam took a leap back as the plank rose and lunged.

The soldier had been ready, brandishing it like a shield.

Sam tried to dodge, but he'd been caught off-guard, channeling all of his energy into standing tall and strong, without a thought toward mobility. The plank glanced off his spine and heels as he tried to turn away. He pitched forward and managed to squirm out of the soldier's path as the grizzled old man hefted the shield and swung.

It connected with Crawford, who let off another shot before the soldier flung the metal plate aside and wrenched the gun from his hands.

Just as Sam was sitting up, a boot caught him in the chest. With a jerk, the soldier delivered a second kick to his chin that made his teeth snap together. Pain shot up through his jaw. Reeling, dizzy, Sam tumbled back and slammed against another one of the cages. The metal bars cracked against his vertebrae, and for an awful second, he couldn't feel anything but a dull, throbbing ache. His ears rang.

The room swam, and in the dim light, the hulking soldier was a blur, a shadow jumping, spinning, hitting faster than seemed possible.

He felled Crawford with fists to the detective's stomach and shoulders. Crawford wilted to his knees. The soldier shoved him onto his back and scooped Sam's pistol off the floor. Without a moment's pause, he cocked the gun and aimed at Crawford's heart.

"You like it here?" Sam's voice came out in a strained wheeze. The simple effort of talking was almost enough to make him pass out.

The black-eyed soldier looked at him, cold, uncaring, but for the first time, hesitant.

"Because you'll get sick, too. Then you won't be able to leave. But I wouldn't worry. They've got some real nice rooms downstairs. Shower curtains and everything."

The soldier snorted. "They've got a cure."

"Not anymore." Sam shook his head. "It just slipped through your fingers."

The soldier looked from Sam to the hole in the wall. Rattling steel echoed out from inside. Doubt flashed across his face for a solitary instant. It was all Crawford needed.

He sprang from the floor, propelling himself with all of the energy he had left.

The soldier saw him at the last moment, and pulled the trigger.

The bullet *thudded* into Crawford's chest in a sticky red explosion.

Sam lunged and buried his head in the soldier's stomach. A conjoined mass of three, they staggered back together, thrashing, clawing, battling for their lives.

"Left!" It was Crawford, voice choked with blood.

Sam heaved left as hard as he could. He had no idea where they were going. His head still spun and he couldn't get his bearings. He was operating on automatic, on pure, brute survival instincts.

He felt them collide with the window a fraction of a second before he heard the *crack*. It rippled through their three bodies. The soldier grunted. His back was to the wall, attention focused on the ragged hole, on Daniel.

The glass was already covered in a spider web of cracks and fractures. It shuddered, bowed, and then gave out.

Sam's stomach lurched. What had felt like a solid barrier suddenly shattered away behind him and left him tumbling over the window sill with the massive, bearish soldier on top. The full weight of the man's body crushed the air from his lungs and sent icy pain through his chest.

He couldn't breathe. His ears were ringing, and somewhere, in the vague, foggy distance, he was aware that he was about to die.

He rolled, arm over arm, tumbling through shards of broken glass, and then, suddenly, he was in freefall. The cavernous cooling tower rolled away all around him. The soldier clawed at his waist and let out a desperate yell. Then his fingers gave.

Sam watched him fall the four hundred feet to the cracked concrete foundation with an impassive distance, because nothing seemed real anymore. Perhaps he had fallen, too. Perhaps he was already dead, because he appeared to be floating over nothing.

"Sam." It was Crawford, but he sounded like someone else entirely. His voice was thick, straining, phlegmy. "Sam, help me out here … "

Numb, his whole body shaking, Sam slowly looked up to find Crawford leaning over him through the window sill. The Detective's face was beet-red and drenched in sweat.

It took Sam's fuzzy, addled mind a moment to connect the dots. Crawford was holding him. Over a four-hundred-foot drop.

His arms and legs felt like rubber as he tried to hoist them up over the lip of the sill. Crawford did his best to help. Sam hooked his arm over the top. Jagged glass slashed through his skin, and he slipped.

Crawford let out a straining growl through clenched teeth. Sam tried again. This time, he forced his mind off of the pain and concentrated only on saving his life. With a monumental heave, working together, he and Crawford lifted him back inside.

They tumbled to the floor together.

For several long seconds, neither of them moved.

When he could feel his arms and legs again, Sam sat up. Crawford had bled all over the place. His clothes stuck to him in dull red mats. His face was pale, clammy, sweating profusely. He looked sick.

"Gerry. Gerry, can you hear me?"

"Ain't fuckin' dead yet."

Sam smiled in spite of himself. "That's good. That's good news." He glanced to the hole in the wall. The hole through which the two people he cared about more than anything in the world had disappeared. "Do you think you can crawl?"

Crawford winced as he rolled up onto his side. "Dunno."

Sam hauled him to a half-stand and lugged him across the room, past the derelict cages, to the winding tunnel of rubble.

When he tried to crouch, Crawford doubled over and vomited. It was mostly blood.

His face was ashen when he straightened again. "I dunno, Sam ... "

"You can do this. You have to."

"Damn it, Sam, I've been shot."

Sam squeezed his shoulder. "I know. Going to make a great story for your nephew, isn't it?"

Crawford's lips flickered into a smile. "It would, wouldn't it?"

"No. It *will*." Sam hoisted him inside. Then he straightened and turned back toward the door.

"What the hell, Sam?" Crawford coughed, choking on his own blood. "What do you think you're doing?"

"Go, Gerry. Catch up with Ann and Danny. Tell them I'll be there soon. And tell them that when I come—nobody's going to be following me. Not now. Not ever again."

THIRTY TWO

SAM SHOOK KO AWAKE. He slapped her across the cheek when she moaned and tried to turn away. Her eyelids fluttered. She squinted up at him, and then, with recognition, came a scowl.

"Where is he?" Sam forced her up into a sitting position. "Where's Donald Pryce?"

Ko glanced at the door. "Mr. Mackie, this is not a good idea."

"You looking for your friend?" He heaved her to her feet and yanked her through the broken glass and splattered blood to the window. Holding her hands behind her back, he shoved her just far enough to see the body of the soldier, forty stories down.

Ko looked a little ill when he lugged her back in.

"Danny's gone. So is my wife. And you're not getting them back. You tell me where Pryce is, I'll let you go."

Her eyes darted from Sam to the window. "How long have you been here? You and your wife?"

"What does that—?"

"How many hours?"

Sam checked the scratched face of his watch. "Six, maybe, since we touched down. Why are you asking?"

"Then if you're smart, Mr. Mackie, you'll turn around and run after your wife right now. If you do not get her out of this valley in the next three hours, she will start seeing the first effects of the illness."

Sam stiffened. "You mean the pit. Those rocks—down there—"

"The pit ... " She arched an eyebrow, clearly surprised he knew about it. "Yes. The pit. That would certainly be a tough decision, wouldn't it? Let the wife die, or kill the son to save her? You would not be able to have both."

"Bullshit. Your plane left several days ago. If that were true, you'd be sick. You and Wesley, and all of the others."

Ko shook her head. "We go home to the CW compound, thirty miles from here, every night." She grabbed his wrist and squinted at the foggy hands of the watch. "Convoy rolls out in twenty minutes. But I doubt Mr. Wesley will be interested in providing your wife with any ... accommodations. Will he?"

Sam grimaced and backed her against the ragged edge of the window. He could see her face tense when the sharp glass touched her spine. "You want to make it onto that convoy? Start talking. Where is he?"

"Top floor."

Both of them turned.

The second soldier on the floor was half-sitting, hands and legs still bound, where Crawford had left him. Ko bit her lip, eyes flashing with rage, but he went on:

"Security code on the door is 21464." He grunted and lay back. "You were telling the truth, weren't you?"

"About what?" Sam edged toward the soldier.

"About only being able to save him. It sounds like the General. Stabbing his own son in the back and then leaving us here to die anyway."

Sam's hands fell away from Ko. He felt like he had just been dropped the remaining four hundred feet to the floor of the cooling tower. "Stabbing his *what?*"

ഗ

The whole way up, clutching the gun in his hands, Sam's head swam. Halfway to the top, the stairwell cut into the sloping hourglass tower and became a three-foot-wide catwalk with only a single handrail between him and the sickening drop to his right. He couldn't look down, but even with his eyes on the curved concrete, he felt like vomiting.

Part of it was the strain, extreme exhaustion, and part of it that he had not eaten since before the plane on the way down. Most of it was what the solider had told him.

The tiny apartment came into view as Sam ascended around the bulbous, blackened monolith of the tower. It was the only light, this high up—a two-room suite tacked on out of scrap metal and steal beams after everything else had been gutted clean. In spite of the way his heart was thumping in his chest, in spite of the shivering fatigue that gripped his whole body, Sam's skin broke into gooseflesh.

He could make out not even a silhouette in the glowing windows. That was somehow worse than a waiting army.

The catwalk widened into a grated platform—a porch before the shack at the top of the world. He paused, ten steps down, and turned back as a gust of wind swept off the lake and ruffled his sweaty hair.

The whole valley unfolded below, a black-and-white charcoal pit. The only color came from the sky, a deep, dark blue through which the stars were beginning to stick out. They shimmered, reflected on the tranquil surface of Lake Kitoto. A little way up the shore, clustered among the trees, he could just pick out a few antennas and satellite dishes. The compound. His mother.

As Sam began to turn back, he caught a glimpse of another pair of lights just cresting the lip of the valley, off to the west. They were red, winking in and out of view as they slipped behind broken branches and blighted tree trunks. A jeep. Ko and her convoy.

It dipped below the horizon, a moment later.

Then Sam mounted the last of the steps and drew up before the door. The windows were blinded by white butcher paper on the inside. The glow from within appeared soft, almost inviting.

As he was reaching for the rusted security keypad, Sam caught a glimpse of his face reflected back in the foggy glass. He looked weathered, haggard, half-dead. But in his eyes, he now saw something different. Different from that day, a lifetime ago, in the bathroom at the CW office when he had stared into his own soul and seen only grief and emptiness.

His body may have been battered, but his spirit was now more alive than ever before.

A pungent swirl of aromas hit him the moment he stepped through the door into *The General's* apartment. The light, bright in comparison to the fading glow outside, was still dim and uneven. There were two rooms visible from the entrance.

A pair of dusty sofas crowded the first, arranged around a small table. A bar crossed the wall to the left, ornate liquor bottles littering the surface. The floor and ceiling, built of scored steel no doubt lugged at great pain from somewhere far below, had been painted a vibrant green that lent the room the appearance of a verdant jungle.

Thirty or forty candles flickered from all corners, like fireflies in the night. Some of them were scented, adding a sickly perfume to air already heavy with cheesy musk and sweat and something even more repellant.

"Doctor … ?"

Sam froze at the sound of the voice. It was low, quietly ominous, threatening in its self-assured reservation.

Visible through the open doorway was something smooth and white, curving, polished. Porcelain.

Pipes ran the length of the opposite wall, coiled with wires that dangled to the floor and plugged into the back of rolling medical equipment.

Slowly, Sam advanced.

"That wouldn't be you, would it, Sammy?" He spoke with the faintest hint of a southern drawl.

Sam came to the doorway and stopped cold.

He swayed and reached to the frame on either side to steady himself.

All he could see was a leg. It was enough to bring bile bubbling to the back of his throat.

Bloated, hairless, and white as unbaked bread, it dangled over the edge of the porcelain bathtub like a dead slug. Yellow, uncut woodchip toenails curved away from the feet in barbed claws.

The leg shifted.

"It's you, isn't it, Sammy? Little Sammy. Little Sammy. Come inside. Come inside so I can see you."

Sam swallowed back the yell welling up from somewhere deep in him. There was no way around this. If he turned and ran now, he would never be able to look Daniel in the eye again.

One foot forward, then the other. He edged into the room.

It was difficult to see Donald Pryce, hidden behind the vast, mountainous porcine expanse that was the man's body.

To Sam, it took a conscious effort to recognize what lay before him as a human being.

It was not merely his size, not the folds of bleached flesh, the curling shelves of fat, the arms like stubs, hidden almost to the wrists beneath vast, cascading male breasts. It was not, either, the crisscrossing creases, the appallingly opaque brown water, the stench of a body unwashed for years.

It was the smoothness of the skin, the bald head, the cheeks like balloons, the eyes like tiny pinholes into an abyss so deep it might as well have reached to the center of the Earth.

It was that—and it was the face.

The face that was Sam's face, only stretched and distorted, couched in a bready bun of dangling flab. It looked pinched, compressed from all sides by his sheer girth and by something more— some cancerous malady outwardly invisible, save for the freakish slant it lent his features.

An olive-green Army jacket failed to reach around his shoulders. Medals, rank bars, and a nametag hung from the breast pocket. It could barely stretch across one arm.

Lt. Col. D. Pryce.

Pryce's beady, piggy eyes flicked in the jacket's direction. Sam doubted if he could see it over the hollow caverns and bulging summits of his cheeks and double-chins.

"My men issued me three field promotions." His smile made Sam want to scream. "I'm a General. I should be one of the most powerful men in the world. But you know that, I'd hope … ?"

Sam didn't reply. He was rooted to the spot by his own numb disgust and disbelief.

"Are you proud of me, Sammy?"

Proud?

"Are you? I would like that. If you were proud of me, I would enjoy that. It would give me pleasure, the likes of which I have not enjoyed in more years than you have seen." Pryce waited. His breathing was heavy, labored, wheezing, as though the mere effort of existing was enough to bring him to a sweat, even when he lay inert. "Sit down, Sammy." He nodded toward a small stool by the foot of the bathtub. "Sit down and talk to your Daddy."

Sam dropped onto the stool. He let his hands fall to his sides. The pistol slipped from his fingers to clatter to the floor. Pryce could not climb out and pick it up even if he had wanted to.

The General seemed to appreciate that. "I am not what you anticipated, I expect." He flicked a droplet of rancid water in Sam's direction. "Say something, son. You're makin' me nauseous, just sittin' and starin' like that."

Sam licked his lips. His voice felt like sandpaper on his throat. "You're my father?"

Pryce chuckled. His whole body shook in rippling waves. "I suppose she didn't put that in her little goodbye note when she sent you off to Grace. Didn't really end things on good terms, but I'd like to think she's the one who went off her rocker. Spent too much time alone with that goddamn pit."

"Monica. My mother, Monica."

"Prettiest damn scientist in the whole lot. I close my eyes, I still see her the way she was … and me, 'course. Me, the way I was, 'fore the meltdown."

"General … " It was more distant, less personal—safer—than *Mr. Pryce* or *Donald*. *Dad* would have been out of the question. He shuddered at the thought. "What … " Sam gulped. He tried to find words for all of the questions that needed asking. "What is this place? Why are you here? Why was Mom here?"

Pryce smirked. "Family history hour, eh? Well gather in, son, I'll tell you why the hell we're down here. Uncle Sam, Sammy. Uncle Sam and his fairy godmother, Johnny Kennedy."

"Kennedy?"

"Cast your mind back. History, I suppose it would be, for you. Bay of Pigs, 1961. Everything goes to shit. Big wakeup call for us and the boys in Washington. We got a gapin' Cuba-sized hole in our backyard fence. Everyone's scramblin', trying to figure out how we get 'em out. But a couple'a guys—they have this epiphany. There ain't a single fence so good that it's not gonna have some holes, and if we got 'em, so does Moscow."

Sam blinked, trying to make sense of it all. "Africa." He glanced to the muted window, the rolling landscape beyond.

"Give 'em a taste of their own medicine. That was the plan. But then they got scouts trolling the whole damn continent, and they start turning up these rumors about a place where people live forever. Cursed or somethin'. Sure, we were skeptical, but it was the Cold War. Us or Russia. We had to look."

"And when you looked—you found the pit."

Pryce closed his eyes. "The pit. And here we were. Everyone gettin' younger, gettin' healthier. Havin' a grand ol' time, but lonely as all hell. And Uncle Sam said we can't tell no one about this place, not even family. That's how your mother and I ... " He expelled a gust of stale breath from between his lips. "Well. I still feel bad for Aggie sometimes. But keepin' her out of here turned out to be better off, anyhow.

"You were the great experiment. First and only kid ever born down here. They kept waitin' for you to turn out to be some kind of Superman, but when you were just a plain ol' little boy, that's when they started cuttin' funding. Vietnam was takin' over. When Kennedy went down, that was it. Nail in our damn coffin. Recalled the whole team, but the first wave all died, soon as they got home. Not a word from LBJ for thirty-eight days.

"Then, Valentine's Day, 1964—platoon of Marines comes knocking on our door. With guns. Lotsa guns. We put up a good fight, we did, but when it became clear that they were just gonna keep on comin' 'til they'd wiped us off the face of the Earth, well ... I decided to give 'em what they wanted."

Sam sat back, reeling. "But this place ... all these people ... "

"A failure. Project Black Valley—deemed a failure. Never finished the weapon silos here, 'cause the research arm was a black fuckin' hole for cash that never produced a usable thing. Except you." Pryce opened his eyes. "Li'l Sammy. The apple of my eye." He grinned. "It was you that we all suffered for. You know that? The promise of you. The hope of you. Kennedy gave 'em Turkey, but he kept you a secret. They dismantled, they went home. We stayed here. Hopin' you'd be some kind of goddamn unkillable soldier." He snorted. "Well. They got the unkillable part right. 'Least, down here, it's pretty hard."

Sam swallowed. "What ... what are you talking about?"

"Do you know what it's like to live through a nuclear meltdown? Feel your flesh burned off your body? We tried to get away, but there ain't no safe distance down here. Not when they had this whole place turned into a shootin' gallery.

"Forty years, I've spent, waitin'. Waitin' to get out of here. Rebuilding, reconnecting, preparin'. Battling every cancer there is, and survivin' 'em all, because god damn it, that's just my luck down here." Pryce made a feeble effort to sit forward. Milky water sloshed over the lip of the tub to splatter to the floor. "I've turned on the light switch downstairs, Sammy. Now ... where's my bulb?"

It took Sam a moment to catch up with what Pryce was saying. Then he leapt to his feet so fast that the stool collapsed behind him. "You can't have him."

"I've earned him, damn it. I've earned a goddamn ticket outta here."

"No."

"You can have another son, Sammy. Hell, I'll even buy you one."

"You're not ... " Sam clenched his jaw, swallowed to keep the emotion down. "You are not ever going to see his face. Not ever. Not in your life."

All traces of the smile melted away into the flab hanging around Pryce's ghastly, chapped lips. "That's how it's gonna be, is it?"

"No. That's how it *is*. Right here, right now. This is the closest you're ever going to get to him."

"Well." A short, stubby arm reached beneath the opposite edge of the bathtub. "Then I guess, to be fair, the same's gonna have to be true for you."

Pryce flicked a switch with his thumb.

Far, far below, something very large and very important exploded.

It took nearly five seconds for the tremor to reach the apartment at the top of the cooling tower. Sam staggered. Turning away, he stumbled to the window, where he tore back the white butcher paper curtains and pressed his face to the glass.

Smoke curled from the bottom of the tower, six hundred feet below. "What have you done?" He rounded on Pryce. "What did you just do?"

"You know how hot a nuclear reactor gets, Sammy? You know how much effort it takes just to keep it cool enough for us to sit here and talk? What I did ... " He let the switch drop back to the floor. "Is decided to stop makin' that effort."

Sam stared. For ten seconds, he did not move.

Then, as the floor shook again, he picked up the pistol, shot his father four times, and turned to run for his life.

THIRTY-THREE

IT FELT LIKE A THUNDERING EARTHQUAKE. Every part of the building shook and swayed around him, the air alive with the groan of bending steel and the constant hammer of shattering glass and concrete. The place was tearing itself apart, and Sam was trapped in its belly.

If it was possible to experience the end of the world, Sam imagined it would have been something like this.

At somewhere around the middle of his descent, the P.A. system crackled to life. He thought it must have been his imagination, because between the shriek of metal on metal and the grinding roar of total chaos, he heard music drifting out of the tinny speakers.

It was the *Stars and Stripes Forever*. He couldn't hear the monologue blaring in the background, but here and there, he picked out a discernible world. *Russians. Moscow. Communists. Threat to our children.*

It was either an old automated recording, jarred loose by the imploding walls and severed wires, or Donald Pryce had somehow survived four point-blank bullet wounds to the face and come on the air to sing Sam to his grave.

Two floors from the ground, he realized he wasn't going to make it. It was something about the wave of heat at his back, the swaying tremble that shot through the structure and knocked him to his knees.

Fragmented tile rained around him. Shattered fluorescent bulbs, rebar and plumbing folded in half. It must have been just like this, the first time.

Fighting his way to his feet, Sam leapt over a yawning hole in the floor and made it to a window sill.

Thirty feet below, wheels slipping and sliding in the ashen dirt, was an old World War II Willys jeep. It was camouflaged, roofless, the back open to the air.

Sam's heart leapt in his chest.

Ann sat clutching the wheel, Daniel beside her, Crawford sprawled out in the bed.

Sam shouted down to them, but his voice must have been lost in the din. Bracing his elbow, he smashed away the rest of the already-cracked windowpane and mounted the sill.

The drop gaped back at him. It would probably break his legs. Possibly more. But he would live. He teetered on the edge, trying to brace himself.

Something behind him *cracked*. Sam looked over his shoulder.

Across the room, a large lead pipe climbed the wall. Two massive fissures scored its face, spitting high-pressure geysers of water. Sam recognized the shape and size of the pipe. He knew it intimately —inside and out.

The building shook.

The pipe creaked, groaned—and then burst.

Before Sam could make any decision at all, a ravenous tongue of lake water thundered through the window, to smash against his back. Just like that, he was flung outside, into the air.

It must have been only a matter of seconds before he landed, but to Sam, suspended over nothing, it felt like hours. He was suddenly aware of the whole valley around him, his family down below, and the lifetime of worry now at his back.

"Please," he thought. *"Please just let me survive this. Please."*

His leg caught the bed of the jeep and spun him around to hit the ground on his back. He lost feeling to everything beneath his right knee on impact. All other parts of his body hurt more than anything he had ever endured.

Gasping from the pain, Sam tried to sit up, but then there was water. Water everywhere, coursing, pulling, pounding—forcing its way up his nostrils, down his throat, into his lungs.

His body tumbled back, limp and helpless.

Just before he blacked out, he saw Ann's face as she twisted around in her seat. They locked eyes. And then—

Nothing.

5

Ann was screaming.

For some reason, Sam had it in his mind that she was going into labor. It was Riley. They were at the hospital, both of them eighteen, tapped out, already exhausted before it even all began.

His eyes fluttered open.

Water. There was still water. *Why was there—*

Another gushing flood peeled over the jeep's half-door and surged down across his lap.

"Dad?"

Sam's body was somewhere in the back, on the floor. His head lay in the seat beside Daniel. The boy looked down at him and squeezed his little hands into Sam's hair.

"Dad, are you awake?"

The jeep's tires spun, caught, and then jolted them forward. Sam managed to sit, but he was having trouble feeling his legs.

The car bounced through a pothole. The water rolled forward, and for an instant, he saw it—what was left of his right foot. Sam snapped his eyes shut and turned his head away. He couldn't worry about that. He shoved it into a compartment in his mind and bricked in the door until some other time.

Everything seemed to be happening too fast, too frantically. Wind thrashed in the dead, blackened treetops. Debris pattered down into the open back of the jeep. Flecks of mud spat across the windshield, over the sides, covering everyone's faces in brown speckles.

Sam stared at them. Something was wrong. Something was missing.

"Monica!" He swiveled around and grabbed Ann's leg. "Where's Monica? Where's my mother?"

Ann swatted him away to reach for the gearshift. "Daniel, hold onto your father!"

"I'm trying!"

"No … no, where's my mother? Ann? Where's Monica?"

"She went back, Sam. We saw her going in just before you came out."

"What?" Panic. Dread. He clamored for the gearshift. "We have to—"

"Sam, we can't!"

"We have to go back; we *have* to!"

"We tried to pick her up. She wouldn't come. Sam, she's trying to stop it. She's trying to save the others."

"No!"

"We need you, Sam. *We* need you."

He looked from her to Daniel, peering down at him, young face a twisted vortex of worry. He looked at Crawford, head lolling blearily in the back, blood somehow covering every inch of his skin.

"Oh, Jesus ... " Sam released the gear stick and let his body slump back down into the water.

Brittle branches snapped at all sides of the car. They were rocketing up the hillside, thundering toward the mountain summit, the edge of the great black blight. The jeep bucked back as Ann spun the wheel to bring them around a hairpin turn in the road.

For a moment—a fleeting blur of an instant—Sam got a view of the dark tower, the lake, the compound—

Of Black Valley.

"Mom," he breathed.

Then, everything lit up blue. It was as if the air itself had just caught fire.

A split-second later, the valley vanished behind the ridgeline.

Sam waited for the explosion, the cloud, the signs of certain death. There were none.

There was only stunning, breathtaking silence as every single one of the thousands upon thousands of living creatures inhabiting the jungle stopped croaking, cawing, chirping, and clicking, and brought the world to a standstill.

Sam held his breath.

Then, over the grinding growl of the jeep's engine and crunch of the tires on the uneven dirt road, he heard a frog croak. Then a cricket. Then another, and another, and just like that, the symphony of life was back.

Sam almost fell asleep the instant he dropped into the airplane seat. The only things that stopped him were his wife and his son—not wanting to be away from them for even a moment while he rested his eyes.

Daniel sat between him and Ann. The three of them huddled together, armrests lifted back to let them get closer. Hold each other. Be a family again for the first time in a very, very long while.

There was little in the way of medical supplies on the Gulfstream jet, but as soon as Ann had steered them onto the airstrip, the villagers called to the nearest hospital to send help for Crawford and for Sam's leg.

Once upon a time, he might have been annoyed by the delay—having to sit here, inert, waiting. Now, it felt like a gift. More time. More time with Ann and Daniel, and no other expectations than simply to exist and be together. The throbbing pain from his right hip down faded to the back of his mind. He was too serene, too happy to let it bother him.

The three of them were so tired that no one spoke, but they knew they didn't really need to. They were communicating more now in silence than they had over thirteen years of arguments and phone calls.

Sam tensed when he saw the Landcruiser bounce onto the airstrip.

"No," he thought. "Not this. Not now. Not after everything."

There was no point in running, nowhere to run to—no energy left to try.

The flight crew opened the bulkhead after a band of three Congolese soldiers had dismounted from the truck outside and come to pound on the hull. Two of them strode down the center aisle with First Aid kits. The third, their commander, waited until Sam's leg had been cleaned and wrapped in a temporary splint before he stepped forward.

"You are Americans?" His voice carried the same thick accent as Ngouabi's.

Sam, Ann, and Daniel nodded.

"You are on this plane by order of Clayton Wesley?"

Sam gulped. He remembered what the pilot had said on the way in. Wesley had a deal with the local government. He passed in and out of their borders by virtue of his pocketbook alone.

"No," Ann said flatly, before Sam could answer.

The commander's eyes narrowed. "You are, I think, just saying this."

"Why would we lie?" Sam asked. "What good would that do us?"

"We have recently registered nuclear activity at Lake Kitoto. Mister Wesley does not have permission to put the people of our country in such danger. Particularly not at a site of such spiritual significance. The Republic of Congo is holding him, his company, and his associates personally responsible. You are his associates. You will be taken into custody along with him."

"No." Sam sat forward and winced as hot pain coursed up his right shin. "No. We're not his associates."

"This is his plane, yes? You are traveling under the arrangements of the Mister Clayton Wesley?"

"No. Check our flight plan. Wesley's name is nowhere on it."

They had to wait for the pilot to request a copy by satellite fax.

The commander snatched it from him as soon as the printer was done, and scowled down at the page. "This is joke?"

Sam swallowed. "No. It's not a joke. I don't think."

"Then you tell me what this means."

Agatha's shaky handwriting: *Godspeed.*

"Turn it over." Ann pointed. "On the back."

The flight plan was signed by Agatha Pryce. Clayton Wesley's name appeared nowhere in the document.

Forty minutes later, the Gulfstream jet taxied to the end of the runway and then took off over the rolling jungle.

Black Valley was on the left-hand side of the plane, across the aisle from Sam.

He didn't bother getting up, not even for one last glimpse of the dark tower. He rested his chin on Daniel's sleeping head and stared into Ann's eyes. And it was just like they were eighteen again.

"Godspeed," he thought.

THIRTY FOUR

THE OFFICE WAS A MADHOUSE for the first month Sam was back. With Clayton Wesley under arrest on the other side of the world, the Board of Directors called an emergency meeting and voted him out within an hour. His shares fell to his nearest relative and investing partner: his sister, Agatha Wesley-Pryce.

She appointed Sam to the Board in her stead.

There had been no word from the Black Valley facility, and the governments of both the United States and the Republic of Congo were keeping the whole region officially shut down. The Department of Defense issued a statement blaming a recent nuclear incident in Congo on local guerilla warriors and terrorist extremists. There was no mention of the pit or the soldiers who had guarded it for the last four decades.

Sam was told that he could continue applying for permits to enter the country, but for the time-being, he could count on nothing.

One evening, he drove out to the North Satellite Library with a new Blue-Access card of his own. He stopped his car across the street, turned off the engine, and stared.

A few sooty bricks lay strewn across an empty lot. Construction signs proclaimed the site would soon be built into an upscale shopping mall.

Every afternoon at around four-thirty, before he left for the day, Sam took the stairs down to the IT department and sent a secure message to the computers at the compound on the banks of Lake Kitoto. One day, he knew he would hear his mother's voice again. For the time-being, he also knew she would want him to be there, at home, for his family.

On the morning of his first day in the new corner office, Sam ran into Bob Frankel on the way to the men's room.

Bob sneered. "S'pose you and Ramon's sister are probably pretty friendly these days, huh?"

Sam found a small research station Clayton Wesley had purchased in China seventeen years ago. He made Bob Frankel its new manager.

5

After Ann came back, things started to feel a little more normal again. They had a yard sale and finally dismantled Riley's old room. Crawford showed up to help. He was still on crutches, and he couldn't do much more than shout from the kitchen table and throw back beers, but he brought help.

His nephew was quiet and polite toward Sam.

"He's different around strangers than he is around me," Crawford grunted. "But he's getting better, I guess."

Sam came in at the end of the day, and for just a moment, frozen in the kitchen door, he saw Riley filling the gangly teen's silhouette on the couch beside Daniel. They were playing videogames and chatting as though they had known each other their whole lives.

Daniel looked over, and then Crawford's nephew did, too.

"What, Dad?"

"Nothing." Sam shook his head and dropped down behind them. "What were you guys thinking for dinner?"

5

Sun pierced the stained-glass windows and lit up the room in a fiery array of reds, greens, and blues. It was warm. Spring had come early, and the air conditioner at the funeral home hadn't been fixed yet.

Sam sat at the front, listening to eulogies by people he barely knew. When it was his turn, he talked for ten minutes. He cried a little. So did Ann. Daniel didn't say anything at all.

Outside, after they had buried the urn and shaken hands with everyone, Sam melted back as the crowd dispersed, and limped over to Daniel. His leg still ached every night, but it was getting a little bit better, day-by-day.

Daniel was sitting under a broad oak tree, watching from afar. Dappled sunlight swayed over his face.

"You don't hafta come over here if you wanna stay an' finish."

Sam didn't answer. He just plopped down in the dirt beside his son.

Daniel threw him a sidelong glance. "Mom'll be pissed." He nodded at mud splattered all over Sam's coattail.

"No, she won't."

Neither of them said anything for a while. The wind rustled the braches of the tree over their heads. Sam sat back and peered upward through the leaves. He looked from Daniel's somber face to the thinning crowd of black-clad people over by the gravesite.

"You ever want to learn to climb a tree?"

Daniel blinked and frowned. "Huh?"

"Like this one."

"Naw."

"C'mon."

"Naw, I don't want to."

Sam opened his mouth and then closed it. "Okay."

Silence. Daniel sighed. He glanced up at Sam, brow furrowed. "Riley liked to, didn't he?"

"What?"

"Riley liked climbing trees." Daniel was already starting to stand.

"No. Riley hated it. He almost broke both his legs the only time I ever tried to show him."

"Really?"

"Yeah. He told me he hated me, too, and then, after dinner that night, he threw five chocolate chip cookies at me when I asked if he wanted to try again."

Daniel laughed and relaxed again. For a minute or two, he sat back, smiling at the grass and looking faraway.

"What are you thinking about, Danny?"

"I wish I coulda known him, is all."

Sam sucked in a breath. "Yeah. He really wanted to meet you."

"He ... did?"

"When we came back from the hospital—Mom and I—and we told him he was going to have a little brother ... Riley hardly ever laughed. He was such a quiet kid. But that morning, when we told him about you, he bounced off the walls. It was the most excited I'd ever seen him in his whole life."

"Really?"

"Really. You're a lot like him, you know. But you don't ... I hope you know that you don't have to be. It wouldn't matter to me. Or Mom. Not a bit. He's gone, and he's not coming back, but we've got you now. And you're not going anywhere."

Daniel looked at him long and hard, and then he nodded. "I know."

"I mean it."

"Okay, Dad." He stood up and brushed the dirt from his pants. Sam got up, too. "Where are you going?"

Daniel was already a few paces ahead in the perfectly-manicured grass. "I'm going to say goodbye to him."

"Oh." Sam held back for a moment, but then he braced himself, and he followed his son. "I'll come with you."